NEW RELEASES

DALKEY ARCHIVE PRESS

CAROLE MASO

AVA

Now available in paperback is Carole Maso's acclaimed 1993 novel about Ava Klein, a professor of comparative literature and lover of life. As she lies dying, she recalls in lyrical detail the 39 years of her emotionally and intellectually rich life, as well as the horrors of her family's experiences during World War II. An ode to joy, a meditation on war, a celebration of life, *AVA* was unanimously praised upon its hardcover publication: "Poetic, rapturous," said the *New York Times Book Review.* "Like a piece of music, *AVA* uses repetition and thematic layering to create a shimmering, impressionistic portrait that eschews linear narrative in favor of the sensations aroused by resonant imagery."

"*AVA,* Carole Maso's third novel, is that rare event, a formal literary experiment that is also compelling as a work of fiction." —*San Francisco Chronicle*

"*AVA* reconfirms Maso's reputation as one of our most refined and daring novelists." —*Booklist*

274 pages
$12.95, paperback
ISBN 1-56478-074-0

NICHOLAS MOSLEY

Efforts at Truth

As a novelist, biographer, editor, and screenwriter, Nicholas Mosley has always been concerned with the central paradox of writing: if by definition fiction is untrue, and biography incomplete, is there a form that will enable a writer to get at the truth of a life? In *Efforts at Truth* Mosley scrutinizes his own life and work to explore the question, resulting in a fascinating autobiography.

"A novelist of rare philanthropic originality, Nicholas Mosley is also an autobiographer of exceptional candour. He seems to have made the efforts he avows, to reveal the truth about his life and work." —*Sunday Telegraph*

"Clever, anecdotal, suspenseful and funny." —*Sunday Independent*

"An exhilarating book. So intent is Mosley on himself learning from experience and reflection that he becomes an inspiring teacher." —*Observer*

"Always honest and intellectually provocative. An autobiography that unflinchingly bares both the heart and the soul." —*Kirkus*

DALKEY ARCHIVE PRESS

DALKEY ARCHIVE PRESS

MICHEL BUTOR

Portrait of the Artist as a Young Ape

Like James Joyce's and Dylan Thomas's similar titles, Butor's novel is part autobiography and part exploration of a writer's development. At the end of World War II a young man travels to a castle in Franconia housing the second largest private library in Germany. Days are spent steeping himself in the literature of alchemy—whose great theme was transformation—and nights are spent dreaming he is in a vampire tale out of Jules Verne, then a tale from *The Thousand and One Nights* in which a young man is transformed into an ape.

First published in 1967, Butor's "caprice" (as he subtitles it) may be one of the most captivating works about the growth of a writer's imagination. Translated by Dominic Di Bernardi.

128 pages
$10.95 paperback
ISBN 1-56478-089-9

SEVERO SARDUY

Cobra and *Maitreya*

The late Severo Sarduy was the most outrageous and baroque of the Latin American Boom writers of the sixties and seventies, and here bound back to back are his two finest creations. *Cobra* (1972) recounts the tale of a transvestite, star of the Lyrical Theater of Dolls, whose obsession is to transform his/her body. *Maitreya* (1978) continues the theme of transformation, this time in a humble cook who becomes a reincarnation of the Buddha. Transgressing genres and genders, reveling in literal and figurative transvestitism, these two novels are among the most daring achievements of postmodern Latin American fiction. Both are translated by Suzanne Jill Levine; introduction by James McCourt.

xviii + 273 pages
$13.95, paperback
ISBN 1-56478-076-7

"Severo Sarduy has everything . . . so brilliant, so funny, and so bewilderingly apt in his borrowings, his derivations, as well as in his inventions, his findings, he leaves one breathless, like a shot of rum."
—Richard Howard

"Sarduy is the master of wordscapes that dip, shake, and explode."
—Jerome Charyn, *New York Times Book Review*

DALKEY ARCHIVE PRESS

ELLEN FRIEDMAN & RICHARD MARTIN, eds.

Utterly Other Discourse: The Texts of Christine Brooke-Rose

The British novelist and critic Christine Brooke-Rose is increasingly being recognized as one of the most significant writers of the contemporary period. *Utterly Other Discourse* (a phrase from her 1984 novel *Amalgamemnon,* also available from Dalkey) provides a valuable introduction to her work; in fifteen essays—some previously published, some written for this occasion—scholars from America, England, and Europe examine her work from a variety of critical angles. Also included is the opening chapter from Brooke-Rose's forthcoming autobiographical novel, *Remake,* offering a rare look at the woman behind the texts.

232 pages
$29.95, hardcover
ISBN 1-56478-079-1

"If we are ever to experience in English the serious *practice* of narrative as the French have developed it . . . we shall have to attend to Christine Brooke-Rose." —Frank Kermode

"Miss Brooke-Rose is almost unique among our serious contemporary writers in attempting to enlarge the whole scope of the modern novel." —Francis King

JEROME CHARYN

The Tar Baby

Taking the form of a ribald parody of a literary quarterly, *The Tar Baby* is a brilliant, audacious novel populated by a variety of brawling academics and earthy townies. A commemorative issue honoring the late Anatole Waxman-Weissman, the novel/journal lampoons a number of academic fads and concerns as the various contributors expose their and their subject's many idiosyncrasies, while pursuing their own private agendas.

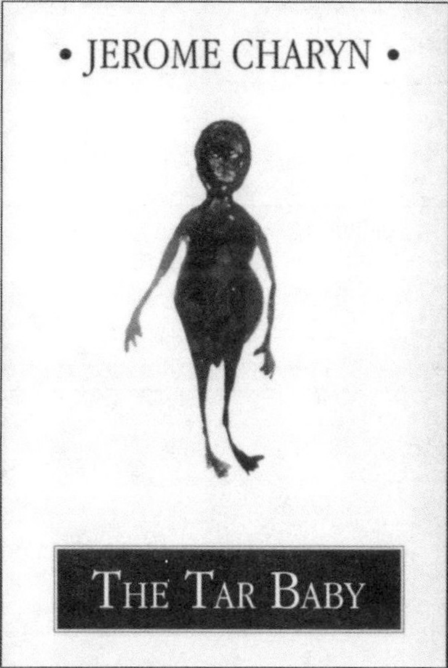

"Clever, witty, and different . . . Ribald, tongue-in-cheek, Nabokovian." —*Publishers Weekly*

"An object lesson in how visionary idealists become mired in mundaneness, and an ingeniously scatological and funny celebration of unsubduably dirty life forces."
—*Library Journal*

"An experiment in complex impressionistic and involutional form, striking and original in the extremes to which it juxtaposes comic stereotype and real suffering." —Albert J. Guerard

243 pages
$10.95, paperback
ISBN 1-56478-078-3

DALKEY ARCHIVE PRESS

Order Form

Individuals may deduct a 10% discount on orders of one book, or a 20% discount on orders of two books or more. The postage and handling fee for all orders is $3.00.

Date______________________

Title	Quantity	Price

Subtotal______________

Less Discount______________

Subtotal______________

Postage______________ $3.00

Total______________

☐ Check enclosed (payable to Dalkey Archive Press)

☐ Visa ☐ MasterCard

Acct no ____

Expiration date _____________________________

Name ____

Address ____

____

Send orders to:

Dalkey Archive Press, Campus Box 4241, Normal, IL 61790-4241

Phone: (309) 438-7555 FAX: (309) 438-7422

The
Review of
Contemporary
Fiction

Volume 15, no. 2
Summer 1995

ISSN: 0276-0045

Cover photos: Miriam Berkley (Elkin) and Renate von Mangoldt (Gray)

SUBSCRIPTIONS. Send orders to *Review of Contemporary Fiction,* Campus Box 4241, Normal, IL 61790-4241 USA. Phone: (309) 438-7555; fax: (309) 438-7422.

Single volume (three issues):
Individuals: $17.00; foreign, add $3.50;
Institutions: $24.00; foreign, add $3.50.

DISTRIBUTION. Bookstores should send orders to:

InBook, 140 Commerce St., East Haven, CT 06512 (national distributor).

Small Press Distribution, 1814 San Pablo Ave., Berkeley, CA 94702.

Indexed in *American Humanities Index, International Bibliography of Periodical Literature, International Bibliography of Book Reviews, MLA Bibliography,* and *Book Review Index.* Abstracted in *Abstracts of English Studies.*

The Review of Contemporary Fiction is also available in 16mm microfilm, 35mm microfilm, and 105mm microfiche from University Microfilms International, 300 North Zeeb Road, Ann Arbor, MI 48106-1346.

This issue is partially supported by grants from the Illinois Arts Council, a state agency, and the National Endowment for the Arts, a federal agency.

AN URGENT CALL TO ACTION

The National Endowment for the Arts (NEA), the National Endowment for the Humanities (NEH) and the Institute of Museum Services (IMS) are in danger of elimination by Congress. Besides the monumental effect such elimination would have on arts organizations, their employees, vendors and patrons across the United States, it would have a tremendous impact on the fate of culture in our society.

THE SITUATION IS ESPECIALLY DIRE FOR LITERATURE

The NEA's individual fellowships are likely to be first on the chopping block; their suspension will hurt writers disproportionately. Since 1990, 18 of the 22 recipients of National Book Awards, National Book Critics Circle Awards and Pulitzer Prizes in fiction and poetry have received Creative Writing Fellowships from the NEA, most of them early on in their careers long before they had received national recognition or commercial success.

The NEA also provides essential support to literary magazines and small presses. Presses such as Copper Canyon, Coffeehouse and Dalkey Archive have all received NEA support and, in the past three years, have all published National Book Award finalists, National Book Critics Circle Award finalists and winners of other major prizes. The NEA has also provided long-term support for Arte Publico Press, The Feminist Press, Graywolf Press, Milkweed Editions and many others. Literary magazines supported by the NEA include The American Poetry Review, The Americas Review, The Paris Review, The Threepenny Review and TriQuarterly.

The literary community needs to show Congress its support for a strong, uncensored NEA.

Here's what you can do:

❒ **Send telegrams to members of Congress:**
Call **1-900-370-9000**. An operator will tell you that the call costs $1.99 per minute and that you must be 18 or over. The operator will ask if you would allow the Emergency Committee to Save Culture and the Arts to send a mailgram in your name to your two Senators and one Representative. If you agree, leave your name, address and zip code which will be matched with the corresponding congressional district. Your home phone number will be billed. (Average length of calls is two to three minutes.)

❒ **Write op-eds or articles for local newspapers:**
Congressional representatives pay close attention to media coverage in their districts. If you need information on recent NEA grants awarded in your area, contact Anne Burt at LitNet.

❒ **Join LitNet:**
Send your name, address, phone and fax to: Anne Burt, LitNet Coordinator, at LitNet. We will add your name to our mailing list and phone/fax tree and keep you up to date as the NEA, NEH and IMS move through Congress.

The Literary Network

154 Christopher Street, Suite 3C, New York, New York 10014-2839
Phone (212) 741-9110 Fax (212) 741-9112

Steering Committee (in formation): Arte Publico Press, Associated Writing Programs, Council of Literary Magazines and Presses and Poets & Writers, Inc. *Sponsors* (in formation): Academy of American Poets, Coffee House Press, Curbstone Press, Dalkey Archive Press, Graywolf Press, Milkweed Editions, National Book Foundation, PEN American Center, Small Press Distribution, and Sun & Moon Press.

Contents

Stanley Elkin: An Introduction

Arthur M. Saltzman

LIKE HIS OWN Jim Boswell, that quintessential gate-crasher, Stanley Elkin turns up among a remarkable variety of exceptional company. Some critics have discovered him firmly planted within the Jewish-American tradition of Bellow, Malamud, Heller, and Roth. Other critics have detected him among contemporary social satirists and black humorists, listing him along with Vonnegut, Coover, and Friedman. Still another group emphasizes his place among our most self-conscious prose craftsmen, and they seat him at the same table as Gaddis, Gass, and Hawkes (while occasionally setting extra places for Barth and Pynchon). Undoubtedly, how a given literary critic categorizes a writer says more about that critic's predilections than it does about the writer's; nevertheless, the multifariousness of Stanley Elkin's reputation is striking, even apart from the automatic confusion associated with trying to define the character and scope of postmodern literature. That Elkin engages our appreciation on each of these levels and is granted these numerous affiliations by the critics testifies to the many different rewards he offers his readers. In short, he consistently displays the rare capacity for simultaneously pleasing and impressing his public.

It is my feeling that a study of Elkin's fiction most profitably begins with its most arresting feature: a richly metaphorical, relentlessly clever, unmistakably poetic narrative voice. Elkin enters our concerns through the ear. What are typically noted as his thematic trademarks—the preoccupation with selling and scheming, the presentation of the bizarre that has become the ordinary in American society today, the comedy that ranges from the philosophical to the pie in the face—evolve out of a fundamental interest in the primacy of voice. Elkin is equally at home in the tawdry environment of fast-feeding in *The Franchiser,* in the revised romantic realm of medieval Europe in *George Mills,* or in the confines of heaven and hell in *The Living End;* but each imaginative visit is chiefly an excuse to urge the word onward. In book after book Elkin reveals how ours is a world where the absurd is conventional and the surreal is real; to counter this, the play of language becomes his tonic for rousing us out of the stupor that comes from the customary.

From another perspective, Elkin's world is one that often consternates the aspiring self, for it reduces heroism to eccentricity and offers small chance for stature. Indeed, Elkin's heroes are second bananas, attendants to the mighty, born coat holders, observers from the wings. Their most satisfying achievements are verbal, and it is through language that they make their forays into the world. They are inveterate pitchmen: they espouse, expand, exemplify; they adopt attitudes and assess actions; they tell stories on themselves. Blame it on "something exponential in the blood"[1] that compels them to riff and rail against what they cannot defeat: their trapped span. Death has them measured. They audition in the gunsight: yeah, we're gonna shuffle, shuffle off this mortal coil.

Elkin himself anticipates the nature of his heroes when he advocates a brand of fiction the principal motive of which is to *sell language.* (We might think of Elkin's salesmen as vocalized vocations.) To the degree that one bends reality to his rhetoric, he fortifies being. The preoccupations of Boswell, Feldman, Gibson, Mills, and the rest recall Elkin's definition of writing as "a total bath in the self."[2] For the artist of the novels and for the artists in the novels, personal legitimacy directly results from verbal style. Unpacking themselves with arias, trying "to keep the feelings up, to make two dollars' worth of euphoria go the distance,"[3] Elkin protagonists are constituted, identified, and sustained by words. Sentences give the best of them.

We appear to be confirming Elkin's reservation for the elite party of stylistic jet-setters, for like them, Elkin locates heroism in the linguistic enterprise itself. Sacrificed in most instances are traditional notions of tightly structured plot, which are subordinated to the glamour of the wordy-gurdy energy of the narrative mind. "I sincerely believe," says the author, "that the sentence is its own excuse for being."[4] Most of Elkin's fiction is loosely episodic, as if to give the freest reign to the author's ingenuity on the levels of both occurrence and utterance. By Elkin's reckoning, form is rather intuitive: patterns are repeated from one episode to the next, so that connections between episodes are apparent without being overbearing or rigidly causal; a sort of "rhyming" between episodes substitutes for conventional linear plot development.[5] Sentence making is prior to structure.

Unsurprisingly, some critics are suspicious of what lurks beneath the sparkling surface of the prose, or they grow impatient with all the "preening" Elkin's language does. Others suggest that fiction so heavily encrusted with image and alliteration seems cold, distant, and unavailing. As for the characters, one reviewer feels them to be "separate from us, their gestures frozen . . . meant to be observed but not experienced, admired but not touched," and goes on to claim they are more like theses than people; a second reviewer is similarly dismayed by characters who are incarcerated in "deep wordy caverns of introspection. . . . Then the crunch comes. They discover that no one else is living there but them. The brilliant talker is the proprietor and sole inhabitant of his universe; and he might as well be adrift in outer space. His fatal proficiency in language has taken him clean out of the world of other people."[6]

These are by no means negligible objections, but we must understand that they derive from a prescriptive definition of the components of fiction that is largely irrelevant to Elkin and, for that matter, to a great many innovative and influential writers now writing. The virtues there may be in virtuosity depend upon just how accomplished a product we are discussing, and this criterion applies to the plastic arts as well as to literature.[7] Furthermore, even critics arriving from a staunchly realistic background can be contested on the grounds that Elkin's characters share an important distinction from the seedy solipsists with whom they are sometimes associated: however provisional or calculated their excursions into the world are—and given such a callous, inhospitable world, whose wouldn't be?—Elkin's characters thrive on contact. The fictions are nothing if not eventful; they are absolutely laden with incident. Moreover, the characters shape their words against the company of others. Who more than salesmen and joke tellers, who more than narrators, requires an audience? According to Thomas LeClair, this is the distinctive aspect of Elkin's style: "Because Elkin's purposes are the pressurized expansion of sense and the executed appeal to a felt audience—not the music of randomness or the song of solipsism—he mixes high and low elements, vernacular and literary, to achieve a charged communication."[8] From the hell-bound Ellerbee in *The Living End,* who locates one of his own murderers in order to "look for himself in Ladlehaus's glowing blisters," to God Himself, who in the same novel creates the universe as the ultimate example of Art for Art's Sake and then demolishes it all "Because I never found My audience,"[9] Elkin's characters conscientiously address the world. Whether they do so to upbraid it for its poverty or to implore it for better living conditions is finally less consequential than the fact of contact.

Were Dick Gibson to suspect that his radio broadcasts never pierced his glass booth, his very personality would begin to disintegrate in the manner of Beckett's spectral speakers. And as Feldman, in *A Bad Man,* asks from the abyss of solitary confinement, "How could he be Feldman if there was no one there that he could be Feldman to?"[10] If talk potentially fuels private obsession, it also promotes human community, an awareness of which, claims Morty Perlmutter, the Nobel Prize-winning anthropologist who first appears in *Boswell,* is what morality *is.* Unlike more astringent stylists and postmodern experimenters, who frequently subordinate or disregard such conventions, Elkin always returns to "the hard edge of personality,"[11] championing the policy of setting characters among other characters as being the foundation of fiction. Thus, in his study of "Irony in the Postmodern Age," Alan Wilde places Elkin not in the category of the reductive Surfictionists but rather in the category of those "generative ironists" who are motivated "to create tentatively and provisionally enclaves of value in the face of—but not in place of—a meaningless universe."[12] The Elkin novel is an invitation to life, not a rejection of it.

Of course, Elkin's heroes tend to abuse the privilege of being part of a society. Other people are eventually scheduled for incorporation by the appetitive self. Another contemporary novelist, Ronald Sukenick, in writing of the art of Wallace Stevens, provides an analysis that seems to elucidate Elkin's art as well: "When, through the imagination, the ego manages to reconcile reality with its own needs, the formerly insipid landscape is infused with the ego's emotion, and reality, since it now seems intensely relevant to the ego, suddenly seems more real."[13] Again, personal success is measured by how efficiently the hero manages to tailor reality to fit his own needs. Obstructed by other people, confounded by their eccentricities, the hero learns to take nourishment from his encounters with them. It is from this perspective that Boswell muses, "Really, it is remarkable how I continue to respect the very people I take advantage of."[14] It is also the perspective achieved by Dick Gibson, who learns that his ongoing effort to escape ordinariness and "live at the kindling point, oh God, *at the sound barrier*" leads to his becoming, as host of the Night Letters radio program, the elected *representative* of his perverse, desperate callers: " 'This is Dick Gibson,' he said, 'WMIA. The scrambled I Am's of Miami Beach.' "[15] Thus, Boswell, Dick Gibson, and the rest of Elkin's heroes do receive the world but according to personal agendas. We might say that, like Robert Frost, they have lovers' quarrels with the world, but they are always open to negotiation . . . to some extent. In book after book, from the vantage point of a complicit observer, Elkin gives "a kind of qualified yes" to the world.[16] So perhaps an accurate appraisal of the interrelationship between self and environment in Elkin's fiction sees it as a compromise: one seeks familiarity but familiarity on one's own terms and in keeping with one's own obsessions.

Few critics delay very long before noting the importance of obsession throughout Elkin's work. John Ditsky prefers the phrase "manic fortitude" —I might suggest "passion"—to enable us to recognize how the attitudes of Elkin's heroes are actually strategies for coping with and responding positively to the pressure of events, rather than excuses for cringing in isolation (a reaction to absurdity that is common enough in recent fiction).[17] However these attitudes are characterized, they at once provoke and grant authorial distance from what are termed in *The Dick Gibson Show* the "strange displacements of the ordinary" (222). This often-cited phrase implies that the impetus for storytelling is an appreciation of the unusual that is grounded in the usual; only a slight adjustment of vision is required to restore intrigue to our lives. As Elkin himself says in evaluating his unique viewpoint, "Not the idiosyncratic, not the strange, maybe not even the mysterious finally so much as the queer, protuberant salience of the obliquely sighted" engages him.[18]

Toward this end, Elkin courts the grand gesture. Prompting and prodding his characters, channeling them into outlandish experiences, he forces out their inherent rhetorical potential. All the while, of course, Elkin presides, directing and refining his art. In this way the progress of narrative relies upon the tension between overflowing intensity and extravagant behavior on the one hand—call it the ego's fire sale—and formal discipline on the other—between Boswell's "two kinds of intelligences, the obsessive and the perspectual" (*Boswell* 303). Consider Boswell, whose life more closely resembles the crazy antics of a 1930s screwball comedy than the devotions of his eighteenth-century namesake. He justifies his attraction to the bizarre as being an intuition of significance, "as though anything truly outlandish were a kind of signpost, an indication of a clumsy, cloudy truth." The reflection of the author is obvious: "I'm attracted to overstatement of all kinds—whether it's material overstatement, the overstatement of the neon signs on our Broadways, or spiritual overstatements, which others see as spiritual understatement. It seems to me that all these *things,* all this *crap,* is the true American graffiti, the perfect queer calligraphy of the American signature—what gives us meaning and makes us fun."[19]

Boswell and his successors in Elkin's fiction also imitate the author in being very deliberate about authoring their lives. They inherit Elkin's desire to fashion situations conducive to their egos' priorities; shambling knights of vocabulary, they list ever forward, coveting words like loot. Boswell keeps a journal in which he traces his accession to greatness; Dick Gibson makes demo tapes to preserve and promote himself; every Elkin hero is out to sanctify the self by securing his place in a difficult world, which is variously represented by uninspiring rooms in second-rate hotels, filthy wrestling arenas, cagelike condominiums, or the blasted landscape of hell. Each novel unearths "the beauty that sleeps in the vulgar."[20] Language at once confirms and confers that beauty. Consequently, art that "gives us meaning and makes us fun" is not frivolous; Elkin's art joins a rescue mission to save the world from settling for the mere, the ordinary, the absence of wonder.

For Elkin, then, plot may be described as the accumulation of experience toward the invigoration of voice. We also see the principle of accumulation at work in his narrative style. Most memorable are those passages that requalify and reformulate themselves, splicing in and adding onto themselves as though they were undergoing a prose version of nuclear fusion. Such a style might be called generative by virtue of its insistence on exploring and incorporating variations on the theme it introduces. While it is perilous to try to single out the best passages of the lot, this example from *A Bad Man* serves to illustrate the lush, cascading rhythms that have become Elkin's signature:

> He pushed the big revolving doors, feeling, as he always did, heavier, and waiting, as he shoved slowly on the door's metal rung to feel himself thicken with opulence, to become wider, gravid. The door spun him out onto the main floor, and he smelled at once the perfumes and face powders, the mascaras and polishes bright as sodas. By the high glass cases he knew himself some glamour mogul; by the lipstick cartridges like golden bullets a grand armorer, love's field marshal among those shiny warheads. Art, art, thought Feldman, impresario of deep disks of rich rouge, pastel as flesh, of fine-grained dusting powders like soft, fantastic sand, of big plush puffs and cunning brushes. He stood by lotions in bottles, by cylinders of deodorant in a female climate of balmy aromatics, in a scent of white gardens, think-

ing of dreamy debauches in palatial bathrooms, of comic blows, cutie-pie spankings with the big fluffy puffs. Here, where other men might have felt intimidated, Persian Feldman lingered, feeling the very *texture* of his wealth, his soft, sissy riches, the unctuous, creamy, dreamy dollars.

I am the master of all I purvey. (*Bad Man* 203-04)

The metaphors are as startling as ambushes: a holstered pistol is "some bent brute at a waterhole, the trigger like a visible genital"; enormous women display "immense bolsters of breast that piled and rolled on their chests like tide"; a dying child endures "malignant cells buttering his marrow with contamination . . . infections exploding inside his body like ordnance." Elkin delights in kicking at the custom-made beds in which language too often slumbers. Whether it be the contents of a department store in *A Bad Man,* the armorial trappings of a knight in *George Mills,* or the case histories of physical decay of the doomed children in *The Magic Kingdom,* everything occasions poetry. Elkin releases the vocabulary of a specific profession or circumstance, or he excuses his characters to brag, rant, plead, or promote, all to initiate provocative aural designs. Crowding the page with lexical flourishes, letting the play of sounds enchant sense, Elkin roots the reader to the verbal surface as a nearly self-sufficient concern. By inviting us to get carried away with him, Elkin seems to imply that the value of fiction is greatly available to those who attend to the texture of the text. Elkin loves alliteration and he trusts puns. Truth may just spring up in one of the surprising coincidences of language that are produced from playful associations of words. Donald Barthelme acknowledges this very point in regard to his own artistic method:

Take *mothball* and *vagina* and put them together and see if they mean anything together; maybe you're not happy with the combination and you throw that on the floor and pick up the next two and so on. There's a lot of basic research which hasn't been done because of the enormous resources of the language and the enormous number of resonances from the past which have precluded this way of investigating language.[21]

Barthelme hopes to disarm the codes and contents of contemporary society by mimicking the American talent for consumption; in his collages of dreck, he swallows down the world and supplants it with a verbal substitute that makes us see the world again. Elkin is also at war with inhibition. He loves catalogs, brand names, nouns that sprout from a thousand occupations. As we read, the tide grows and we pick up speed; adjectives and nouns collect, attach to one another, grow heavy, then tumble down the page. In the words of Alan Wilde we are witnessing another example of the postmodern writer's exchange of a scrupulously balanced "either-or" approach for the splendid, if at first unsettling, "both-and" approach to fictional form.[22] Just as the postmodern writer welcomes proliferation thematically, in the swelling, episodic adventures that constitute his novels, he does so stylistically, as evidenced by the contagion of lists and metaphors. Appetite rules: "It was incredible that anyone should ever get what he wanted, and I experienced, sharp as pain, deep as rage, a massive greed, a new knowledge that it was not enough, that nothing was ever enough, that we couldn't know what was enough or want what was enough. It wasn't even a question of deserts. Everybody deserved everything" (*Boswell* 386). Craving is hereby raised to an aesthetic creed.

"What do I do with my wonder, I wonder?" asks Alexander Main at the conclusion of "The Bailbondsman."[23] Elkin and his fictional stand-ins always answer the same way: reinfuse the ordinary with interest, overwhelm it with your own excesses. Returning the world to the word, Elkin reconstitutes mundane reality with the brashness of a street hawker, the inventiveness of a nightclub comic, and the insistent craft of a stonemason. With situations and characters as audacious as anything Dickens or DeVries dishes out, Elkin stumps for an art of abundance.

And he renews our perceptions with humor. Elkin understands that common sense and a sense of humor are the same thing moving at different speeds. Ironically, Elkin's reputation as a serious writer of fiction has had to overcome his talent for finding us funny, as though that were a specious accomplishment. On the contrary, as does the language in which it is conveyed, his humor unnumbs us as readers and makes palatable the philosophical considerations that underlie the fiction. In Elkin's hands comedy is a flexible, speculative mode; nothing is so dark or outrageous that comedy cannot contend with it. (What better denial of M.S., Elkin's longstanding affliction, than fiction that is so religiously antisclerotic?) Beached by disaster or disease, Elkin's heroes leave an outrageous, glittering spawn of associations. When Alexander Main announces, "I have no taste, only hunger" ("The Bailbondsman" 74), Elkin may be discreetly overruling the objections of critics whose preconceptions about the novel miss the point: he is less concerned with accommodating his vision to conventions of plot and character than with displaying the pleasures of breadth. The self must be stoked and fed; as a consequence, the self's "theatre of operations" is revitalized. Therefore, the self retains its integrity without cheating the world of its offerings; in fact, the world is newly minted by the lavish attentions of the artist. (*Everything* is a prominent word throughout Elkin's fiction, and that everything is sacred.) "How can you embrace anything but this world?" asks the author. "It's the only world we have."[24] Not rejection but integration: imagination encounters the world of and through language in every Elkin story, and the stores of both imagination and world increase.

NOTES

An earlier version of this piece appeared as "Ego and Appetite in Stanley Elkin's Fiction" in *Literary Review* 32.1 (1988): 111-18. Reprinted by permission of *Literary Review.*

[1]Stanley Elkin, "Pieces of Soap," *Pieces of Soap* (New York: Simon & Schuster, 1992), 180.

[2]Quoted in "Stanley Elkin on Fiction: An Interview," by Phyllis Bernt and Joseph Bernt, *Prairie Schooner* 50 (Spring 1976): 18.

[3]Stanley Elkin, introduction to *The Best American Short Stories 1980,* in *Pieces of Soap,* 204.

[4]Quoted in Bernt and Bernt, 16.

[5]Quoted in "An Interview with Stanley Elkin," by Jay Clayton, *Contemporary Literature* 24 (Spring 1983): 6.

[6]L. J. Davis, "Searches and Seizures," *Washington Post Book World,* 28 October 1973, 11; Jonathan Raban, "Taking Possession—New Fiction," *Encounter,* February 1975, 83.

[7]See William H. Gass, "The Concept of Character in Fiction," *Fiction and the Figures of Life* (Boston: Godine, 1971), 49; also Sharon Spencer, *Space, Time and Structure in the Modern Novel* (New York: New York Univ. Press, 1971), 161-70.

[8]Thomas LeClair, "The Obsessional Fiction of Stanley Elkin," *Contemporary Literature* 16 (Spring 1975): 156.

[9]Stanley Elkin, *The Living End* (New York: Dutton, 1979), 46, 148.

[10]Stanley Elkin, *A Bad Man* (New York: Random, 1967), 127; hereafter cited parenthetically.

[11]Quoted in "A Conversation with Stanley Elkin and William H. Gass," by Jeffrey L. Duncan, *Iowa Review* 7 (Winter 1976): 75.

[12]Alan Wilde, "Irony in the Postmodern Age: Toward a Map of Suspensiveness," *boundary 2* 9 (Fall 1980): 26.

[13]Ronald Sukenick, *Wallace Stevens: Musing the Obscure* (New York: New York Univ. Press, 1967), 14-15.

[14]Stanley Elkin, *Boswell: A Modern Comedy* (New York: Random, 1964), 128; hereafter cited parenthetically.

[15]Stanley Elkin, *The Dick Gibson Show* (New York: Random, 1971), 334; hereafter cited parenthetically.

[16]Quoted in Clayton, 5.

[17]John Ditsky, " 'Death Grotesque as Life': The Fiction of Stanley Elkin," *Hollins Critic* 19 (June 1982): 2.

[18]Stanley Elkin, "Representation and Performance," *Representation and Performance in Postmodern Fiction,* ed. Maurice Couturier (New York: Delta, 1982), 188.

[19]Quoted in "An Interview with Stanley Elkin," by Scott Sanders, *Contemporary Literature* 16 (Spring 1975): 131; 137-38.

[20]Quoted in Sanders, 139.

[21]Donald Barthelme, quoted in "A Symposium on Fiction," *Shenandoah* 27 (Winter 1976): 20-21.

[22]Alan Wilde, *Horizons of Assent: Modernism, Postmodernism, and the Ironic Imagination* (Baltimore: Johns Hopkins Univ. Press, 1981), 48.

[23]Stanley Elkin, "The Bailbondsman," in *Searches and Seizures* (Boston: Godine, 1973), 124; hereafter cited parenthetically.

[24]Quoted in Clayton, 3.

"A Hat Where There Never Was a Hat": Stanley Elkin's Fifteenth Interview

Peter J. Bailey

When I visited Stanley Elkin at his University City, Missouri, home in the fall of 1992, he was in the process of reading galleys for his then-forthcoming book, *Van Gogh's Room at Arles.* Elkin was capping off a very prolific decade with the novella collection, a remarkably productive decade for a writer who had resolved to stop writing novels after the publication of *George Mills* in 1982: he had published three novels—*The Magic Kingdom* (1985), *The Rabbi of Lud* (1987), and *The MacGuffin* (1991)—as well as a collection of essays, *Pieces of Soap* (1992). *Harper's Magazine* had just accepted his essay "Out of One's Tree: My Bout with Temporary Insanity," in which he describes the derangement he suffered as a consequence of doses of prednisone, an anti-inflammatory agent used in the treatment of multiple sclerosis. In that essay Elkin describes a bookcase in his upstairs hallway "high as a door and wide as a desk" which he calls the "Wall of Respect," its shelves containing "all the books I've ever written along with their British editions, and all the books I've written that have been translated, and all my paperbacks, and all the essays, introductions and prefaces I've done, and all the anthologies in which my work has appeared, and the magazines, anthologized or not, in which it *first* appeared, and the interviews I've given, and the articles, chapters and books about my work," and much more Elkiniana. What frightened and depressed him most during the two weeks in which he was out of his head, he explains in the essay, was the conviction that he hadn't written the books in that bookcase, that the anthologized stories were somebody else's work, and that all the reviews and critical analyses collected in its shelves dealt with some other writer. On the mid-October weekend when I interviewed him, Elkin sat a few feet from the "Wall of Respect," now moved into his study, answering questions about the oeuvre which, having been restored to him, could only be his.

PETER J. BAILEY: Your fiction seems to have become increasingly preoccupied with mysteries—particularly in the intrigue Druff stumbles on in *The MacGuffin*—but I take it from your essays that you've never been a fan of mystery novels? Why not?

STANLEY ELKIN: Because the mystery novel does only one thing or has only one place to go. I used to teach a course called the art of the novel—a course in genre novels. I'd teach a pornography novel, a kid's novel, a science fiction, a best-seller, and a "good" novel, and I always taught a detective novel. And it was astonishing to me how frequently in detective novels nothing happens but a kind of catechism between the detective and his suspects—it's nothing but questions. "Where were you on the night of?" "On that night I wasn't anywhere—I was out of it, I was out of town that night." You could turn to almost any page. Half the dialogue would be a question and half the dialogue would be an answer to the question. It's the seesaw rhythm that the genre falls into that finally is not very engaging.

Another thing about the detective novel is that it has no protagonist. The detective really has nothing at stake, except that he's looking to solve a puzzle, looking to solve a problem. It's like writing a novel about a mathematician, who's worrying about, you know, whatever mathematicians worry about, and you read the process of his solution to the problem. That makes a mathematician, but it does not make for a protagonist. Nothing happens to the guy. The detective is going to come out on top—you know that he's going to come out on top, you know that he's not going to die in the end. So he's in control, and it seems to me fiction is about people who are not in control. At any rate, you're right, *The MacGuffin* is a kind of mystery. But Druff isn't trying to solve anything. He is, and he ain't. He ain't in control.

PB: Do you agree with Druff that solutions are always less interesting than the mysteries?

SE: Oh yes. Oh yeah, that's always true. Think of any thriller movie. I mean they've really got you going, you're biting your nails, sitting on the edge of your popcorn, and then somebody comes crashing through the window with a gun and takes the knife away from the person who's going to kill the guy who's in trouble. You know, not god from the machine but the hero from the machine. That's the solution. One of the things about this movie that was so praised a couple of years ago—*The Silence of the Lambs* —*I* couldn't stand that movie, because they set the serial killer up as a brilliant, brilliant sociopath eater of women, eater of flesh. The FBI comes to him to find out what kind of guy would do such a thing to another human being. And he answers, "Ah, it just so happens he was my patient when I was a psychiatrist." This is some brilliant guy. And it's *always* like that.

The first shot, though, when she's walking down that corridor and you see him in that cage—that's stunning, that's really stunning. But once you finally get used to him in his cage . . . I mean, everybody's gotta be *somewhere*.

PB: The mysteries in your fiction (especially from *George Mills* forward) are, for the most part, deliberately limited, distinctly intricate human fabrications à la Alexander Main's creation of Crainpool. Is there a danger that in pursuing the humanly commensurable mystery of Crainpool's whereabouts, Main might too quickly disregard larger mysteries, more profound enigmas?

SE: I don't think he disregards larger mysteries. I think what happens is an anticlimax. It's exactly what I said about *Silence of the Lambs:* he attributes almost supernatural gifts of criminality to Oyp and Glyp, and they turn out to be common thugs and car thieves.

PB: Main turns Crainpool into a mystery he can solve.

SE: And frees him. He depends on Crainpool for the excitement of there being somebody who can get away from him. He *wants* a mystery he can't solve.

PB: One temptation critics often succumb to is finding a resonant line in a writer's fiction and designating it (and the work in which it appears) as a watershed, a turning point in his or her fiction, as the annunciation of a literary or philosophical change of direction. The line in "The Making of Ashenden" saying that the protagonist would "book passage to somewhere far, someplace wild, further and wilder than he has ever been before" would, then, be read as a declaration that your fiction would take a direction still more extravagant and extreme. Is this kind of interpretation pure critical fiction, or is there some validity in reading protagonists' fates as allegories of their creators' aesthetic directions?

SE: No, no. When Ashenden says that, he means it for Ashenden—it has nothing to do with my fiction, it has to do with Ashenden's life. I mean, how you gonna keep 'em down on the farm after they've been fucked by a bear?

PB: It seems to me that a number of your protagonists are betrayed by the achievement of that which they pursue: Dick Gibson by the audience to which he gives voice on the radio, Ben Flesh by the creation of a homogenized America that replicates his demyelinating nervous system. Does that strike you as a reasonable generalization?

SE: Yes, it seems to me that the fairies and the genies had it right when they said, "be careful what you wish for, cuz you're gonna get it." It's worked out in my life. I'm not gonna tell you what I wished for, but I got it. It always comes back, there's always a catch, and the catch kicks you in the teeth.

PB: In a previous interview you admitted feeling little sympathy with "literature of exhaustion" notions of the futility of language. Are you particularly conscious of your work as a corrective to ideas such as the erasure of the author?

SE: Well, I'm not in battle with the French, who do not sing to me, or of me, anyway, but I'm going over the galleys of a collection of novellas that is coming out in March, and I'm so pleased as I read this stuff aloud to my graduate student who's helping me correct the galleys that the language is as good as it's ever been. This is going to sound dopey, but I sometimes get emotional at how good I occasionally am. And I'm not just talking about the fireworks—I'm talking about getting Sam from one part of the room to the other part of the room. For me, language is still where it's at.

PB: A writer once told me that she thought it would be impossible for reviewers to overpraise any of her novels—that, given the work she'd put into them and the neglect into which they were likely to fall, no one could ever respond positively enough to suit her. Would you agree that reading reviews is necessarily a disappointing experience?

SE: Yes, yes I would. But I find that the good reviews are often just as dopey as the bad reviews. Except that often, when a reviewer catches something that I'm deliberately trying to do, that's sort of touching to me. So, in a way I don't agree with her. When the reviewer seems to have a kind of perfected pitch to the notes I'm sending out, I get all warm and fuzzy.

PB: Many of your novels tend to have very little in the way of specific news events, book titles, popular songs, or other such signals locating them in a specific time or place.

SE: I don't think that is true—as a matter of fact, it's something I have to watch out for. I remember when I was writing *The MacGuffin,* I had Bobbo Druff speculating about what he would do if he were President of the United States. Of course, the cold war was going on then, but it was the cold war as seen through the peaceable kingdom of glasnost and Gorbachev, and so in the original manuscript I had references to glasnost and *peristroika* until I decided that it would be better not to write something that would have to be footnoted a year and a half later.

PB: In one of your previous interviews you talked about not wanting to use details that would immediately be dated.

SE: Right—in *A Bad Man,* for example, I had Feldman rhapsodizing about the fact that he has a color television set. I was writing this in 1964 and '65, when color television was very, very rare, but now you see this guy rhapsodizing about his owning a color television and you think he's a madman. So it's best to stay away from that stuff.

As a matter of fact, in *The MacGuffin,* car phones were all new to me . . . I had been out to California, where everybody seemed to have one, and I was struck by the car phone, and I thought, this is something that will never catch on, so I gave Druff a car phone in the limo, but it was OK—I think I got away with it because of the way he *uses* the car phone.

PB: More than most writers, your work delves in nearly clinical detail into extremity, particularly disease. How do you respond to the oft-cited comment that your terribly deliberate anatomizations of illness in *The Franchiser, George Mills,* and *The Magic Kingdom* are your acts of revenge on the disease that has disabled you?

SE: No, it's not so—there's no way in the world I could ever take revenge on the disease that has disabled me. It just seems to me that disease, because it flirts with death, is a rather important subject to write about.

PB: You must have done a fair amount of research to create the seven afflicted children in *The Magic Kingdom.*

SE: Absolutely none. I have a friend here who's a pathologist—I asked him to give me the names of some childhood diseases, and he came up with maybe a dozen, and I called the Washington University reference library and asked them to send me some information about these diseases, and they were kind enough to Xerox some quite brief explanations of the diseases, their symptoms, the prognosis, blah blah blah, and that's the full extent of the research. I took the symptoms and ran with the symptoms was what I did.

PB: If you were to imagine an ideal response to one of your novels by an ordinary reader, what would it be?

SE: I think I'll go out and buy this for a friend.

PB: Is it fair to say that one of the questions you're usually balancing in writing your fiction is how much to let the plot machinery of the work extrude upon its surface? How much to refer explicitly to the MacGuffins functioning in the fate of the characters?

SE: Well, Dick Gibson has a sense of having a fate, and the Franchiser has a prognosis, which would be a kind of plot, wouldn't it? And Druff in *The MacGuffin*—it occurs to Druff that he has a MacGuffin, and therefore he goes out looking for his plot. It's a total accident—a coincidence—that he happens to really have one.

I was going to say that plots have become very interesting to me since I started working with the bubble machine. The word processor has facilitated not just the mechanics of one's writing but has actually facilitated plot, and I'll tell you why. You write on a word processor: you open the store in the morning, you do what you do, and then it occurs to you, gee, wasn't there some kind of reference to that earlier on? So you put the machine into the search mode, and you find what the reference was earlier, and you can begin to use these things as tools, or nails, in putting the plot together. The word processor facilitates the plot—I really mean that. When I wrote *The MacGuffin,* I was constantly looking back for general references to certain thematic key words, and that really tightens the nuts and bolts. Therefore, my plots have gotten better since I went to work with the word processor, which I did with *George Mills.*

The word processor enables one to concentrate exponentially; you have absolute command of the entire novel all at once. You can go back and reference and change and fix and . . . so in a way, all novels written on the bubble machine ought to be perfect novels.

PB: "Plot is people," you argue in the essay "Plot," "*But it is never other people.*"

SE: What I guess I meant is that plot is persons; it is never people. There's got to be that focus on one guy. It's the agenda of a single man or woman.

PB: And yet the novels many people consider your best—*George Mills* and *The Magic Kingdom*—encompass a number of points of view.

SE: Oh, I think *The Magic Kingdom* is clearly Eddy Bales's story. And *George Mills* is clearly George Mills's story—they're all the same George Mills, finally.

PB: All of the novels you've published have been dedicated to Joan Elkin, and yet you've never granted any of your protagonists the boon of a similarly loyal and valued wife. Is that an index of your notion of necessary differences between art and life?

SE: [laughs] No, it's not—it's because I love my wife. In *The MacGuffin,* Druff and his wife have a perfectly good marriage—he goes out on her for a night in a whole lifetime, but he comes back to her, too.

PB: In your interview with Tom LeClair some years ago, you insisted that your fiction—like Faulkner's, like Auden's poems—never changed anyone's life. Has your opinion on this changed at all?

SE: I don't really think that fiction changes lives . . . except it can maybe give you taste—I suppose taste can change your life.

PB: Somebody reads one of your novels, picks up certain rhythms, picks up certain kinds of ways of seeing things as being like other things—it's not a change of life, but . . .

SE: Yeah, but you're not going to go out and buy something.

PB: Maybe another Stanley Elkin novel.

SE: Probably not. I mean, I think I know most of my readers by name.

PB: In a *New York Times Magazine* article last year, you're quoted as saying, "I ride a pretty tight shotgun on myself, believe it or not, but when, in the course of human events, something occurs to me that gives a particular kick to a sentence, I'll probably let it pass." I think I could identify some of the kicks, but I wonder what, in your fiction of deliberāte excess, represents to you excessive excess, what kind of thing gets cut?

SE: The kind of thing that gets cut I don't remember because I cut it. In *The Rabbi of Lud,* when Goldkorn visits Rabbi Petch's place in Anchorage, and Rabbi Petch is terrified of weather—there's an awful lot of weather jokes in that section. I thought them funny, so I left them in, but I knew I could have done with a lot less of that. A lot of the stuff in *Rabbi of Lud* is just silly—I'll give you a much better example than the Petch thing. The stuff in Lud, New Jersey. There's a scene in which he makes a prayer in front of the *haverim*—this group of Jewish singers—and he's showing off for his daughter, Connie, insulting, defying God. That is just so outrageous, so unbelievable that I should have just—maybe I didn't catch myself. If I were to rewrite the book, I would catch myself. But there are things equally outrageous in *The Rabbi of Lud* that I let stand because they're quite wonderful, I think—the business of the twin Indians who grow apart, the guy with the flowers in his beard and the flowers finally fade—I mean I think that's wonderful, I get a kick out of just thinking about that. In the eulogy for Joan Cohen sermon Goldkorn goes on and on and on and on. That's cut by 33 percent and I should have cut another 33 percent. Hit 'em hard and get out.

PB: You obviously have mixed feelings about that novel.

SE: I still think the situation is an essentially good situation—how this guy destroys his daughter by insisting on being a rabbi in Lud. Another thing I love in that novel is the revenge scene which his daughter makes up, the business with the Virgin Mary—I remember having a lot of fun writing that. But I had no editor on that book, and I needed an editor on that book—I needed somebody to say "pull your horns in here, go slow, don't show off here." Though editors mostly leave me alone—except for Joe Fox, the editor I had at Random House, I've never had to answer to an editor—*Rabbi of Lud* was a book that could have used one, somebody to come in with a whip and a chair and say, "get back, get back."

PB: What role did Joe Fox play in your novels with Random House?

SE: Oh, he ran a tight ship—he questioned absolutely everything. And he would argue with me—and I would argue with him. But he was a wonderful editor; he was in fact the best editor I've ever had. I wrote five books with him, and he was really tough with me on *Boswell, A Bad Man, Criers and Kibitzers;* he was a little tough with *The Dick Gibson Show,* and not so tough with *Searches and Seizures,* because by the time I got to *Searches and Seizures,* I had become a good writer, I think.

PB: So *The Franchiser* was the first without him?

SE: Right. I was left alone with *The Franchiser* and with pretty much everything after that. But I've been blessed—I haven't had any dumb editors.

PB: Read any good novels lately?

SE: When I'm writing, I tend not to read, and I have been writing. The things that I read are things that people send me to blurb, and I can't get through those most of the time because they're no good. But Paul Auster's *New York Trilogy*—I liked that. Anita Brookner—oh, I think she's wonderful. She does things I couldn't possibly do—wouldn't know how to do. I love Bellow—I love his stuff.

PB: *More Die of Heartbreak?*

SE: I *loved More Die of Heartbreak;* matter of fact, *More Die of Heartbreak* was what gave me the idea for writing a political novel—*The MacGuffin.*

PB: Did you read *Rabbit at Rest?*

SE: Oh, yeah, I liked that a lot. I think it's not the best of the group; I think *Rabbit Is Rich* is the best of the group. I hated *Rabbit Redux.* When I went back to read *Rabbit, Run,* I wasn't as fond of it the second time around, but I wrote him a fan letter for *Rabbit Is Rich—it* was terrific.

PB: Has a critic or reviewer ever made comments on one book of yours that had an impact on the writing of your next book?

SE: No.

PB: You once traveled to a small college for a reading that has become the stuff of legend and an object lesson in how not to host a visiting writer. Care to recall it?

SE: Yeah. I was picked up at the airport by this guy in the English Department in Williamsport, the home of the Little League, but I didn't know how little this league was I was going to be playing in. For those times and those days, this was big money for me—I think it was five hundred dollars for three days' work, plus expenses. We got into the car, we start driving towards Lockhaven, and he doesn't say anything to me. Then finally he says, "We're not going to give you a party." I said, "What do you mean?" "A lot of people don't like parties," he says. I said, "Who? Who doesn't like parties?" Anyway, he wasn't going to give me one; he'd take me to the hotel room, he'd pick me up for the class and drop me off again, but I was on my own. I sort of didn't believe him—I didn't believe this was going to happen. So he left me at my hotel and told me he'd pick me up the next day at 10 A.M. This is one in the afternoon. There was a Merv Griffin festival on cable, so I watched that, and by the next morning I'm ready to see a human being, and the guy picked me up and took me to his class, and I did my thing. He brought me back to the hotel—he didn't invite me to dinner, nobody gave me dinner, I had dinner at the hotel, charged it to my room. On the third day he picked me up again and delivered me to the reading, which wasn't even in the auditorium—it was in the *lobby* to the auditorium. And people came—I mean, not a lot of people, there aren't a lot of people that go to Lockhaven State College—and I gave my reading. After the reading, I asked him, "Where's my check?"—because I was pretty pissed at this guy. He said, "That hasn't been made out yet." "Is it in the mail?" "No, I told you, it hasn't been made out yet." So he took me back to the hotel, and I asked at the desk, "Do you still do room service?" "Oh, yes sir, what would you like?" "I'm giving a little party in my room. I'd like sandwiches for about thirty people. I'd like a bottle of scotch, I'd like a bottle of this, a bottle of that, maybe some canapés—just send it up to the room and I'll sign for it." And they did—these fucking trays kept coming in. I had a sandwich, maybe I had a drink, and I flushed everything else down the toilet. Nobody's gonna give me a party, I'll give *them* a party. That's what happened to me at Lockhaven State College.

PB: You've been quoted as saying that you feel your books don't move some readers. Given the highly emotional content of much of your work, that seems strange.

SE: That was before *The Magic Kingdom*—I got mail from *The Magic Kingdom,* and a lot of readers—for me a lot—wrote saying they thought that book was moving. I answer all those letters—I hardly get writer's cramp—but I can't say my books don't move people anymore—not all of them.

PB: Do you think of your work as particularly intellectual?

SE: No—I don't think of myself as inaccessible at all. The language is high, and the sentences are long and convoluted, but they always come out right, and if you're willing to follow me through the dashes and the parentheticals . . . I don't think my work is inaccessible.

PB: There are some plot maneuvers you enjoy which—

SE: There is a certain kind of thing that I picked up from Faulkner, and that's the business of delayed revelation.

PB: In your introduction to a new edition of *Criers and Kibitzers,* you have some slighting things to say about "the shared communal linkages between the author and the compacts, struck bargains and done deals of a reasonable, recognizable morality" that underlie literary realism. How do you encourage students in your writing classes away from those easy bargains into the writing of a more expansive, linguistically sophisticated, imaginative fiction?

SE: I had a wonderful conference yesterday with a graduate student who told me, among other things, that writers write for emotional reasons, and I said No, writers do not write for emotional reasons—they write because they want to make something. I asked her if she knew the Stephen Sondheim musical with the number about making a hat—"a hat, a hat, I made a hat where there never was a hat." That's so moving to me I choke up when

I tell you about it, and I said *that's* what writing is about, that's what all art is about: you've made a hat where there never was a hat! That's why people write. I don't know if that answers your question, but that's how I try to engage students to get out of this one-on-one, tit-for-tat realism: make a thing that never was.

PB: "Because aesthetics is the only subject matter, because style is," your essay "The Rest of the Novel" contends. Isn't there a point, though, at which sentences begin coalescing into themes, ideas, into the magnetic fields of humanly conceived significance? I guess I'm asking, with David Dougherty, who's published a Twayne book on you, whether ideas aren't somewhat more prevalent in your work than you sometimes suggest they are.

SE: I don't think so, I don't think they are. I mean there are ideas in my work, yeah, but my work is not idea driven; it's event driven and language driven, and, I hope, driven by personality.

PB: "Story in its essence is nothing more than role being faithful to its nature, I said. The reasonable and recognizable being where it's at, I went on. Yes, and didn't Dorothy have those slippers with her all along? Aren't they just standard ordinary issue to anyone from under the rainbow? So that the furniture you use up in a fiction is only furniture you're furnished. Nothing up your sleeve unless you put it there in the first place?" Isn't this Dick Gibson's argument that there's no astrology, no black or white magic, no ESP or UFOs? That there's nothing but technique and the "strange displacements of the ordinary"? What about Ben Flesh's transcendent experience of getting a haircut? What about the dream the children on their dream holiday all dream?

SE: That's a leap—that's a stretch on your part, and on my part it's meant in a book called *The Magic Kingdom* as a magical instance. I mean, there are all kinds of magical things that happen in *The Magic Kingdom;* physics and natural law are in abeyance in that book. First of all, when they get there, there's a snowfall, but it only snows exactly on Disney World; across the street, there is no snow. The phrase that runs through *The Magic Kingdom* is "because everything has a reasonable explanation." There is no reasonable explanation. So *The Magic Kingdom* is one book, and another book is another book. I think that when Dick Gibson says all there are are the "strange displacements of the ordinary," he's talking about the people who appear on his show trying to steal his voice—Behr-Bleibtreau, whose way of doing it is to try to strangle him. Gibson at the end of this long night's journey into day is fed up with the hocus-pocus of self-proclaimed magi; it's the last time he has such a talk show. What I'm really saying, I guess, in that quote from "The Rest of the Novel" is that it's true that the only thing the writer works with is what the writer works with, is what the writer has allowed . . . he creates the parameters from the beginning of the novel. From the beginning of *The Magic Kingdom,* you know there's gonna be magic. You can't change the game plan in the middle.

PB: Would it be reasonable to say that Eddy Bale interests you less than other characters in *The Magic Kingdom* because there's nothing he wants to do in room 822?

SE: No—Eddy Bale probably interests me more than any of the characters in *The Magic Kingdom.* The kids are freaks. But Eddy Bale has sustained a real loss and suffered heavy casualties. He gets this mad idea that no other children must die. Of course they're gonna die. And he ends up with Mary Cottle in room 822 in the last chapter. What happens at the end suggests that every time you fuck, you create a monster.

PB: Is *The Magic Kingdom* finally critical of his project—of his dream holiday scheme?

SE: Oh boy. Oh boy. I got the idea for *The Magic Kingdom* when I was in England. On the television news there was this three-minute special interest piece about a bunch of British children who were being schlepped to Disney World in Florida—they all wanted to see Mickey Mouseville. You know, I was never going to write another novel after *George Mills*—I had decided I didn't want to write any more novels. And I was watching this thing, and I began to choke up, because I had never heard of terminally ill kids being taken. And they showed these kids: they were the lame, the halt, the blind, the failing—they were in terrible shape. And I thought, my God, how are these kids even gonna make it across the ocean, much less make it back? And I told Joan, I said I had an idea for a novel; it would be terrible to write such a novel, but it's a good idea for a novel. Now the challenge of *The Magic Kingdom* is to write the novel and not make it sentimental. And I don't think it is sentimental. I hate the idea of a Last Wish society and all that.

PB: One way of asking a question about the inevitabilities implicit in plotting might be this: In writing *The Magic Kingdom,* did you become aware first that one of the children would not survive the dream holiday, or that Rena Morgan would be the one who wouldn't?

SE: No, I knew that one of the kids was not going to survive; I didn't know who wouldn't. It was love—it was beauty killed the beast. It was love that killed the kid because cystic fibrosis is a lung disease, and she can't get past the orgasm. The punishment fits the crime.

PB: This is probably a question for critics to ponder more than for you to answer, but let me try it anyway: Is it possible for a man who once affirmed that the only psychological assertion he swears by is that "the SELF takes precedence" to write a book that, as your note on *The MacGuffin* designates it, is "a political novel"?

SE: Well, when you write a political novel—by that I meant politicians. With politicians, the self *does* take precedence, I assure you.

PB: Dick Gibson wants to live a life of cliché; Bobbo Druff experiences his MacGuffin as a principle of structure, as his life's latent architecture. Does *The MacGuffin* strike you as a novel which, in more somber tones, reprises some of the themes of *The Dick Gibson Show?*

SE: No. I think *The MacGuffin* is superior to *The Dick Gibson Show* because it's constructed so much more carefully—I had a bubble machine. I thought *The Dick Gibson Show* had a plot, but it wasn't as careful a plot as *The MacGuffin;* it was more the fireworks of episode.

PB: Good episodes.

SE: Right, but put 'em all together and I'm not sure they spell mother.

PB: You've often said that "fiction gives language an opportunity to happen." The book of essays you've recently published suggests that non-fiction provides something of the same opportunity. How, in your mind, do the opportunities differ?

SE: They don't. I never consciously planned to write a book of essays, but after I finished *The MacGuffin,* I wanted to get magazine assignments. *Harper's* gave me a wonderful assignment: cover the Academy Awards. And I got a series of other assignments, and it came to me that I had enough essays to do a book. I've noticed that all the recent essays tend to be autobiographical. There's one coming out in *Harper's* which is totally autobiographical—it's about my experience of temporary insanity. So I guess I talk about myself in essays. The essay is an opportunity for language to happen to *me.*

PB: At a time when the protagonists of novels are frequently dramatized as victims, your characters—I'm thinking specifically of Ben Flesh, Ellerbee, Eddy Bale and some of the children he brings to Disney World, and Bobbo Druff—refuse to take on the victim's mantle or strike conventional poses of victimization. Would you comment on that?

SE: No, but I would thank you for asking that question, because when I was first reviewed, again and again I was classified as an absurdist or a stand-up comedian or a this or a that, but most frequently the thing they had to say about my characters was that they were losers. I never regarded them as losers. The guy with the most energy was the winner. Was it Bellow or Roth who invented the term *victim literature?* I guess it was Bellow. And Bellow had repudiated victim literature after he wrote *Herzog.* He said there'd been too much victim literature. I don't see that his characters have essentially changed, but I don't regard Bellow's characters as victims either.

PB: David Dougherty suggests in his Twayne study that *The Franchiser* was originally conceived and the writing begun without any notion of Ben Flesh being afflicted with M.S. How did you originally conceive of that novel's progress?

SE: I got the idea for *The Franchiser* from an article in *Time* magazine about Kentucky Fried Chicken, and it occurred to me that a novel about a guy who has franchises would be a terrific novel to write. I was writing *The Franchiser* in 1974; my M.S. had been diagnosed in 1972, but it never occurred to me that Ben Flesh was going to have M.S. But then it seemed to me that the symptoms of the disease would be a nice metaphor for the energy crisis. I meant *The Franchiser* as my bicentennial novel—it did come out in 1976—and I wanted to make a statement about America and its loss of energy.

PB: Most reviewers and critics acknowledge the craftsmanship of your prose, but I do wonder if the imaginative range of your work is sufficiently recognized. The dodo scene in *The Dick Gibson Show,* the entire conception of *The Living End,* the Crusades section of *George Mills,* and the character interactions in *The Magic Kingdom* seem to me extraordinary deeds of literary contrivance. Do you agree that literary fabrication is an underappreciated strength of your work?

SE: You betcha. It's always seemed to me that the best kind of book is the open-ended book where anything can happen. I hate a book which has one premise, and the writer sticks to that premise so tightly that the writer has no room to breathe—the reader has no room to breathe.

PB: Is it fair to say that you write your novels to be reread, not just read?

SE: No, that's not fair to say. I don't even write them to be read—it certainly ain't happening.

PB: If there were a *Stanley Elkin's Greatest Hits II,* what would be in it?

SE: I regard everything from *Searches and Seizures* on, with the exception of *Rabbi of Lud,* as pretty good stuff. If *Rabbi of Lud* had had an editor, it would have been a good book.

PB: You've said that fiction says yes or no. Assuming that your fiction primarily says yes, I wonder which work you think says yes most emphatically and effectively?

SE: Actually, I think they all do, but probably *The MacGuffin.* Because Druff has his night on the town and deliberately drags himself home; he forgives Mikey, he accepts his life more than any other of my characters do, so I suppose it would be *The MacGuffin.* Also *The Franchiser.* The Franchiser, of course, says yes—he says "ah." But his yes is sort of muscling through, and it's kind of chemical—it's kind of a chemical yes. He's gonna feel rotten in the morning.

Words and Music

Stanley Elkin

IT STARTS WITH flawed genes or too many sweets, say, floss negligence, carelessness brushing, or grinding one's teeth, or following hunger into the heart of the bone, chewing along its fault lines, pecking and prying and gnawing and biting, puncturing, breaking through until I'm licking and slurping and sucking all the sweet central soups there like some Dracula of marrow. A few bad checkups here, a few more there, and before you know it's like pulling teeth. Well, it *is* pulling teeth. Or root canals like all teeth's brittle split ends. Canceling appointments, missing checkups till ultimately I'm gagging on appliances I don't even give my bite a *chance* to break in. Letting, I mean, my mouth go to hell altogether. Until—before you know it—literally, I have quite lost my whistle. Not just its trill and burr like a kind of yodel but the ability to even just pucker!

That's what happened to mine, anyway. Too much rough chewing took my whistle away. And my singing voice, too, that used to eschew any sense of time, propriety or place either, and once burst into something like song, my very own personal background music that followed me, under the breath at least, *everywhere*. Doing, for example, "Three Coins in the Fountain" the seven months we lived in Rome, or "Arrivederci Roma" the day we left it. And "My Kind of Town" in Chicago and "Autumn in New York" in New York even if it isn't.

Like that. The soul experiencing this sort of harmonic déjà vu all over the place, pumping mood like breath or blood, tunes a sort of running commentary on my life.

Is it too much to say, then, that songs, all songs, have something like nostalgia built into them even the first time you hear them, that they're as much about moments in time as stop-motion photography?

It's so hard to talk about art!

May I try on for size this proposition: that what happens in melody is its plot, that melody is to music what plot is to situation, and lyrics to time as theme is to fiction? Melody, that is, is the sequenced condition of things—as much at the generic center of a particular mode as broken, cheated hearts are in country music, or spit-in-your-eye feistiness in some sassy Broadway showstopper. Hey, look me over! Or try to conceive of a score for a movie Western that doesn't use the same sort of epic, archetypal chords as, oh, say, *The Magnificent Seven,* or of a musical code for suspense dissimilar to the sinister, accumulate paradiddles of *Jaws*. Yes, and it's almost impossible to imagine the busy, musical street business of the first few bars of "An American in Paris" imposed on a bucolic setting. A tune is a kind of vocabulary, the sweet agreeables of the heart and head, the head and blood.

You'd think a lyric would tell the story of a song, and often, of course, it does. Who could predict from just the melody of "John Henry" the outcome of the contest between John Henry and the machine, or from the tune of "Frankie and Johnny" which one, Frankie or Johnny, will be the one to bite the bullet? *I* can't even remember which one, Frankie or Johnny, is the dame!

But here's a better proof, I think. Why, except for its bridge perhaps, is all of a melody more immediately, and completely, available to the memory than its words? It's because, one, most music is logical, inevitable, and, two, because melody is essentially timeless, virtually impossible to mock, parody, pin to an era, or reduce to cliché. Dum di de dum dum, *dum dum!*

Lyrics, meanwhile, are positively driven by time and come to us—I had almost said come *down* to us; indeed, I *should* have said come down to us—with all the baggage and promise of incipient ruin like a date stamped on a milk carton, or the shelf life on the label of a prescription bottle.

Father, dear father, come home with me now!
The clock in the steeple strikes one;
You said you were coming right home from the shop,
As soon as your day's work was done.
Our fire's gone out, our house is all dark,
And mother's been watching since tea,
With poor brother Benny so sick in her arms,
And no one to help her but me.
Come home! come home! come home!
Please, father, dear father come home.

Father, dear father, come home with me now!
The clock in the steeple strikes two;
The night has grown colder, and Benny is worse,
But he has been calling for you . . .

Father, dear father, come home with me now!
The clock in the steeple strikes three;
The house is so lonely, the hours so long
For poor weeping mother and me,
Yes, we are alone, poor Benny is dead
And gone with the angels of light;
And these were the last words he said,
"I want to kiss Papa good-night."

I'm not a cruel man. The plight of the little girl in this sentimental song is heartbreaking. Wipe away the propaganda, all its abstinent, teetotaled vision, and we're still left with the *cri de coeur* of a lone little girl out of her element in some dark, blue-collar grogshop of the spirit. It ain't Heidelberg here, it ain't any comradely student princes off on a spree damned from here to eternity, baa baa baa. She's fallen among thieves and drunkards, sots and boozers, soaks and sponges. She's fallen among wife beaters and child abusers, deadbeats behind in the alimony. She's fallen, finally, among deaf, dead ears. But why assume it's a girl? Why the better to stack the deck, my dear, the better to stack a deck already stacked, enforcing and reinforcing it like some furious bucket brigade tossing sandbags at a flood. Because, given the circumstances of the lyric and the times, a girl is at least marginally more pathetic than a boy would be in such circumstances and, anyway, it's Benny who gets to die. And anyway, too, this is a song about innocence, all the more innocent, and thus discrepant, by dint of the unconditional love both the girl—"Father, *dear* father"—and the little dead-angel kid—"I want to kiss Papa good-night"—inside their thick, impenetrable innocence bestow on the son of a bitch.

Except none of it ever happened. The clock in the steeple never struck one, nor two either, so how could it ever have struck three? And anyway, are we expected to believe that the little girl delivers her bulletins hourly like 'round-the-clock all-news radio stations? Does she race home for an update after each failed plea? Does she even exist, or is she on loan from a nursery rhyme, some hickory-dickory-dock figment and avatar? "Poor Benny" is a nice touch, but he's all avatar too, as "poor weeping mother" is. All, all of them avatars, translated from fairy tale—dysfunctional as Hansel's and Gretel's damaged people.

But lyrics are about time, I said. They sink a song in it like flecks of carrot in a Jello mold—those angels of light, that clock in the steeple, the lack of central heating one may infer from that fire that went out. Time, they pin their characters to time like a calendar nailed to a wall. Though "Come Home, Father" couldn't be written today with a straight face it was never parody, never camp. Only time has worn away the earnestness of its lyrics and turned alcoholism if not into something funny, then into something picturesque, nostalgic as sepia tone. Now we've outdistanced the blunter sentimentalities but, working too close up, are probably still too unfocused to make out the sharper ones. Time *becomes* distance, and it isn't, I think, too unfeeling to suggest that one day, if they haven't already, AIDS ribbons will be as piously dated as yellow ribbons or that stumblebum dad in the saloon. With enough dough and enough luck even AIDS, with all its self-congratulatory death melodrama, will.

It's *so* hard to talk about art!

A march is not a love song, not even a love song to the flag. A ballad isn't a waltz. A waltz ain't the blues. Nor anthem, nor hymn, nor chantey, nor dirge. Not plainsong, not carol, not chant.

About art it's so hard to talk. One may only approach it ad hoc.

But *say* the love song. Since, since time, more people have been lovers than soldiers, more lovers than sailors, and more gone off in black tie or gowns to the ball than to funerals. More than all who've ever knelt in pews or rendered wassail, or stood to attention or lamented their luck in the 12-bar phrases and 3-line stanzas of the blues. So *say* the love song and let it stand for the rest.

Here's one by Hoagy Carmichael we get requests for every night. We like to think it goes something like this—

And now the purple dusk of twilight time
Steals across the meadows of my heart
High up in the sky the little stars tell I
Always reminding me that we're apart.
You wander down the lane and far away
Leaving me a song that will not die.
Love is now the star dust of yesterday
The music of the years gone by.
Sometimes I wonder why I spend the lonely night
Dreaming of a song?
The melody haunts my reverie
And I am once again with you,
When our love was new, and each kiss an inspiration,
But that was long ago;
Now my consolation is in the star dust of a song.
Beside a garden wall,
When stars are bright,
You are in my arms,
The nightingale tells its fairy tale
Of paradise, where roses grew.
Though I dream in vain,
In my heart it will remain:
My star dust melody,
The memory of love's refrain.

We apologize for our rendition, for our busted whistle and ruined mouth. We apologize for our broken breath and wasted voice. Written in 1929, "Star Dust" is perhaps the most popular American song ever, and though we make our obligatory manners over our poor performance, it's one of the points of this discussion that the *language* of "Star Dust," obsolete, archaic, quaint, olden, passé, fogy'd, old-fashioned, almost antique, is—as given its ulterior motives "Come Home, Father" never was—completely sincere.

Yet part of the pleasure one takes from the song today, most of its charm, comes from the sense of its being, well, pastoral, historical, built on a vocabulary of an ancien régime, and set back in some world, some unpolluted golden age whose like we'll not see again, Horatio.

Consider "the purple dusk of twilight time." Regard "the meadows of my heart." Look up, watch "High up in the sky the little stars." See her "wander down the lane." Hear the "music of years gone by." It "haunts my reverie."

This was, recall, "when . . . love was new and each kiss an inspiration." Such phrases, along with "consolation . . . in the star dust of a song. / Beside a garden wall, when stars are bright" and "The nightingale tells its fairy tale / Of paradise where roses grew" while "I dream in vain, / In my heart it will remain . . . The memory of love's refrain" speak to a love from the days when all love was Force 10 love.

I don't know about you, but I don't recall the purple dusk of twilight time, and there ain't any meadows in my heart. And what's more, the lanes she wandered in are all built up today, sunk into geology with the meadows, and developed, covered o'er with spiffy condominiums and malls. And just what *is* a reverie, anyway? Is it this like love trance? And though we're too far into history and I've never heard a nightingale tell its fairy tale of paradise where roses grew, I swear on my life I'd have loved to. Because it's of historical interest, and the pleasure I get from "Star Dust" is the same pleasure I receive from old grainy, black-and-white movies—not Our-Gang comedies but the *backgrounds* in Our-Gang comedies, not Chaplin but the *backgrounds* in Chaplin, the streetcars on the streetcar tracks and the boxy automobiles on the narrow roads, the skimpy telephone poles with their skinny wires, the storefronts and stone bank buildings and all the sweet, lovely, on-location, classic authenticity of the was.

Well, *pleasure*— What we're really speaking about, of course, isn't pleasure so much as affection, a few stops down from pleasure. Affection is, I think, always a little tainted by forbearance, one of the modest, milder virtues, saddled as it is with a faint whiff of condescension and all the noblesse oblige of an act of patronage. Mild curiosity and bland engagement are, I think, part of any stew in which affection is ingredient. Does that sound like true love? Not *true* love, it doesn't; and if I said "Star Dust" is a love song about Force 10 love, perhaps I should offer a disclaimer—that the notion of Force 10 love may not be all it's cracked up to be, or isn't all *I* cracked it up to be, and that the song's real thrust isn't love so much as bygone love, not yearning but yearning recollected in tranquility, *tranquility* recollected in tranquility—moony, spoony, souvenir love; love like a memento, lock-of-hair love, love revisited, as it is here, in a dark that grows from the purple dusk of twilight time.

And maybe what I'm really trying to say is that love isn't a fit subject for a good song. Or, if it's like the love pictured here, first love, past love, lost love, love left town on the last train out, for fiction either.

Yet the agrarian scenery in these tunes of the '20s and '30s and '40s is certainly interesting, as old postage stamps are interesting, as out-of-town newspapers are, foreign money. Purple mountains' majesty and seas shining from one coast to the next are all very well, I suppose, but we're down here in old time looking out—back—scanning, as Hoagy says in the song, "the music of the years gone by."

We're down by the old mill stream here, we're down by the riverside, we're down in the valley. We're way down upon the Swanee River. We're back home again in Indiana. We're away down South in de land ub cotton. We're Alabammy bound. We're home on the range. We're the farmer in the dell in the shade of the old apple tree in the good old summertime. We're swimmin' Moon River here. Sure, it's a field and stream vision. Listen to the mockingbird, though the nightingale sang in Berk'ley Square, too, don't forget.

Or maybe I'm wrong. I could be wrong. See? See how hard it is to talk about art? And though I think I'm still attached to the "as to" part of my argument (that lyrics nail a song to time), I'm a little nervous about that "is to" bit—that melody is to music what plot is to situation. Algebra was never my strong suit, anyway. No, my whistle was my strong suit. Until I lost it.

Is it too late to regroup, to retrofit my spilled logic to a different proposition altogether? May I say that it's all apples and oranges, apples and cactuses, apples and cuticles, apples and cowpies? May I say, that is, that melody is its own excuse for being and that lyrics aren't in it at all. That words aren't. And that if a march is not a love song and a ballad not a waltz or an anthem or a hymn or a dirge, why then neither are all of them put together a musical comedy, or an opera or oratorio either. In music, maybe words are beside the point, and a song is just so much more mixed media, and that pretty near all of them, by themselves, at least, are absurd. A lyric may be enhanced by a melody—almost always it is—but never the other way around. Indeed, because words—lyrics—are so time intensive, by necessity they almost always come with their own built-in obsolescence.

Which isn't to say that there aren't quite wonderful lyrics. There are. (Though less often, oh so much less often, given your Gershwins and Porters, Hammersteins, Sondheims, Berlins, Mercers, Brels, and Cahns, than you'd think.) Like everyone, I have a favorite song too, Ellington's "Sophisticated Lady," and the favorite part of my favorite song is the part that goes—

> Smoking, drinking,
> Never thinking
> 'bout tomorrow.
> Nonchalant.
> Diamonds shining,
> Dancing, dining
> With some man in a restaurant.
> Is that what you really want?

Hey, I'm old, but I ain't *that* old. Hotel tea dances in the Palm Court restaurants were before *my* time, too, but the sense of scene this song gives off is like a racial memory. That's its high point though. What follows, or precedes—I can't remember which—is a falling off, a retreat to the easier old fallback positions of almost Greek choric commentary and faintly scolding admonition—

They say sophisticated lady,
You know
You miss the dreams you dreamed long ago,
And when nobody is nigh
You cry.

It's that archaic word *nigh* that strips the song of the otherwise perfect strict immediacy of the past that the lyrics present and turns it into something, well, something picturesque, historical, yellow and dusty, something mediated mounted in a case in a museum. And why, incidentally, am I so certain that her binge—all that smoking and drinking and dancing and dining—takes place in the middle of the afternoon and not at night? There's not much in the lyric to suggest it, but it almost has to be afternoon because if it's a nightclub rather than a restaurant that would detract from the sophisticated lady's depravity, water her needs and obsessions. It would, that is, make her just another gay floozy in it for the laughs, a night on the town, not a sophisticated lady at all so much as a girlfriend, and maybe not even a girlfriend so much as someone along for the symmetry, a distaff double on a double date. It would, that is, disqualify "Sophisticated Lady" from achieving art because she will have been stripped of her character and turned into only one more innocuous, anonymous, lane-wandering, held-in-the-arms inspiration kisser, reduced to a mere subject for nightingale gossip beside the garden walls—a star dust creature of little more substance than Benny's sister, or father, or mother, or poor Benny himself.

Music has several advantages over fiction of course, its incredible, direct, point-to-point, nonstop trip to the heart being the chief of these. In music one claims an emotion simply by declaring it. "Allegro" is the musical instruction for "merry." "Allegretto" and "andante" decline tempo, and decline tempo like the emotional spectra of the blood, the composer's wish instantly father to the thought, winding and unwinding mood down to "malinchonico" by simple will. Everyone, if they've the math for it and understand the logic, can connect the synapses, and lay down a musical emotion as given and just plain *there* as a painting by the numbers.

Clearly, I'm special pleading, trying to make a case, but literature is harder than music. If only because it can go wrong so much more easily, or so much more recognizably, it's harder. It is. Clunkers in prose are easier to spot than clunkers in lyrics.

Take away, for example, the smoky melody from a beautiful song like "Body and Soul" and let stand the bad syntax of the following couplet:

My life a wreck you're making,
You know I'm yours for just the taking.

"As Time Goes By" is an American standard, a classic, but few wince, even those of us who aren't in love, when Dooley Wilson sits down at the piano and sings:

Woman needs man
And man must have his mate,
On that you can rely.
It's still the same old story,
A fight for love and glory,
A case of do or die . . .

A case of do or die? Of do or *die?* Man must have his mate? His *mate?* It really *is* a jungle out there. And Rick's gin mill is the same old saloon, give or take fifty years, where poor Benny's Papa hung out!

It's because melody hides language, as plot hides language. In life, of course, the life of men and the life of most fiction, there *is* no melody. There are only the props of personality, never a good measure of spirit because personality is merely an almost chemical reaction achieved when one player in an action rubs against another player in an action. But above personality, beyond it, overwhelming it, is character.

In good fiction, certainly in great fiction, character must be at once idiosyncratic—unique—and pertinent to the action—square peg per square peg a consistently logical bundle of being not shaped so much as *drawn out* by the situation in which a character may find itself—in both meanings, I mean, of the phrase.

But situation must never be outlandish, or, if it is, it must never be discovered in the act.

An example of an outlandish situation which is *invisibly* outlandish springs instantly to mind. The situation of Gregor Samsa, the young man who wakes up to discover he's changed into a bug and gradually accommodates to the idea that if he's to continue his existence he must do so not in fly-on-the-wall but bug-in-the-bed relation to other members in his family, doesn't seem in the least outrageous. Principally, I think, we accept Kafka's outlandish premise because it's stated up front. If we're told that the narrator of a story is a ghost, say, or as is the case in many of J. F. Powers's remarkable stories, a cat, we must be told so immediately. If we're given too many reasons, or any reasons at all, really, how it is that a ghost came to speak, or a cat to be Catholic, the fiction will very likely fail. We shall have been too caught up in the fiction's complicated mechanics, too ground down by its apparatus and machinery, ever to believe a word of it.

The other way Kafka gets away with his fable is more difficult to bring off and is the real art of the fiction. It's that accommodation the character makes, the many metamorphoses Samsa puts himself through—rather like those stages-of-death attitudes Kübler-Ross ticks off—from logical resistance to—there must be resistance, it must be logical—if not acceptance then something so like the end to a string of logical events that it is like acceptance.

A writer whose work I admire, Philip Roth, once published a novella so incredibly outlandish, so *very* visibly and preposterously outlandish as to be not only incredible but, in spite of its startling, astonishing premise, boring.

The novella is *The Breast,* the story of a professor metamorphosed into a single female breast—not overnight but piecemeal. Roth means, I suppose, to do homage to Kafka, but so clunky and willfully psychiatric are the story's techniques, so grim and determined to be humorous by means of its mannered, stately prose juxtaposed to its ludicrous subject matter, that the pressures of the tale result in a kind of twisted, busted torque. Plus Kepesh's reasons for turning into a tit are never quite good enough, anyway.

Because that, I think, the reasons a character does this rather than that, chooses that rather than this, is what plot is all about finally. Plot is reasons under the constant supervision of events. It's the marching orders situation gives will. It's character moving through time to all the strains and pressures of greater or—preferably—lesser traumas. It's the careful, gingerly side step of pressed, put-upon Self through all the snares and land mines of outside conditions. It is, to turn the tables on "Star Dust," tranquility recollected in emotion—the drive, I mean, for stasis, every human being's will toward some Ur-memory of contentment.

So literature is harder than music because all tunes may be arranged, and rearranged, their tempo and phrasing turned up or turned down to suit the styles and emotional instincts of their interpreters. Think, for example, of all the different renditions one has heard of "The Star-Spangled Banner." Think of Barbra Streisand's version of "Happy Days Are Here Again." In literature, however, unless it's performed on stage, there is no interpretation but the writer's. Books leave no wiggle room. What you see—or fail to see—is what there is. Literature is harder to do than music (and music is only the fall guy and straw man here) if for no other reason than that it has more to do and has to do it longer. A song gets in and gets out, but essays and stories and novels and plays have miles to go before they sleep.

The greatest difference between literature and other art forms though, its narrowest margin for error, is the fact that most all other forms are essentially generic. In painting there are landscapes and seascapes and cityscapes. There are portraits and abstracts and nudes. There is narrative painting and there are clowns. Washington crosses the Delaware and Indians fall off horses in battle.

In museums not only are all these paintings on display but they are on display *categorically,* arranged in some finite Dewey Decimal of the eye. What the artist saw, and when he saw it. If curators are, well, more knowledgeable than librarians, surely it's because they have so much less to know. And musicians the same. A musician can play everything, *anything.* All he has to know is how to read music. All he has to know is the score.

Hey, I'm kidding. I'm winging it, I'm making it up. Well, what would you do, what would *you* do when it's so hard to talk about art? To talk about art is hard. About art it's *so* hard to talk. Every generalization cancels every other generalization. Every rule has its loophole. It's *all* loophole. Because the truth is we've left too much out of the equation, and that, I think, is the rest of what I'm trying to say.

In 1961, Philip Roth wrote an essay in which he said that "the American writer in the middle of the twentieth century has his hands full in trying to understand, describe and then make *credible* much of American reality. . . . The actuality is continually outdoing our talents, and the culture tosses up figures almost daily that are the envy of any novelist."

I'll say!

And 1961 was the old days, maybe even, well, prehistoric, middle-of-the-twentieth-centurywise. There were no homeless in 1961, no AIDS, no Vietnam, no Watergate, no tapes; car phones didn't exist, heart bypass surgery, moon shots, frequent flyers. Spandex uninvented, health clubs, singles' bars.

Terrorism only in the talking stages and presidents safe on the streets.

There were no *blacks* in 1961. Hell, if Negroes had a problem, it was, raisin-in-the-sunwise, their own. Sure, and Persians made carpets. They stuck, I mean, to their knitting, and didn't go hitting on hostages. Who knew from Iran? Iraq? Somalia? Bosnia? No current events to speak of worth a damn at all, come to think.

Well, Khrushchev was going to bury us, and there was the A-bomb of course, and even a Soviet Union, but *that* was in another country and besides the wench is dead.

But that culture of Roth's that kept tossing up figures almost daily to scourge the novelist wasn't even a drug culture, hey, and, as I recall, Neil's girlfriend Brenda's mom found a pessary in Brenda's sock drawer in Roth's *Goodbye, Columbus* and *that* was a shot heard 'round the world, let me tell you.

You don't even know what a pessary *is,* do you?

So reality me no realities, and throw not up thy full hands in the face of thine efforts to understand, describe, and then make credible all talent's envied actualities. Because, if you want to know, there's bigger and better hobgoblins coming off the line every year, late, later, latest models—a built-in obsolescence worth half what the novelist gave for it the minute he drives it off the lot.

Three times a week a woman comes to my home to exercise me. By now, the ordinary sit-up and leg lift is beyond me, any only self-induced sweat, and the hobgobbled built-in obsolescence I spoke of is the body's. I am the hobgobble guy. *I* am. And when I tell you that thrice a week a lady I pay comes to my house to exercise me, the exercise she administers is so dubious no insurance company I know of will cover it, and I mean for you to understand that, generally, it is to exercise what macrobiotic diets or crystals in your pockets are to the treatment of cancer, say. She pulls on my limbs, she stretches my neck. I am choreographed through routines so passive that what is done to me is more like, oh, what's done to the Tin Woodsman by Dorothy with an oil can than anything responsibly called aerobic. So passive on my part, I mean, that, well, we actually chat. Not the *one* and *two* and *three* and *four,* or any of the standard grammar of the standard gym's difficult metrics called out like the barn dance, but the dazed laze of genuine gossip as a leg goes up or a foot gets rubbed—the principle, I'm told, is so my muscles won't atrophy, but I'm more like Claus von Bülow's wife's potched and pampered, luxurious comatosity than ever any toned-up gimp, behind the curve no-pain-no-gainwise as an arm gets raised or a calf gets squeezed. Chatting, gossiping, exchanging recipes, getting down, intimate as girlfriends, as guys in the *schvitzbad*.

And now Vikki was working with me on the bed. (In the six years she'd been coming to me, in the six slow, at once progressive and degenerative years of my disease, it's been necessary to take these exercises from the floor to the bed. I can get *off* the bed.) She's doing the one where, lifting my legs at the knees, working me like a wrestler, leaning on them with all her weight, she raises my ass to my ears, my knees to my chest, pins me. This is a position—I'm no engineer, I don't understand the principles of push and pull, of leverage and necessity, the laws of gasses and gravities—a position in which I find I am compelled to pass wind. I've always, I swear it, struggled against it, resisted, done all the internal, invisible isometrics and compulsories of decency, waged this armageddon of the personal, fighting off shame like The Guerrilla of Hygiene.

But, you know, after a while nothing human is alien to anyone. And we're chatting and I happen to mention that I won't be seeing her the following Monday, be going to New York, participate on this panel at the 92nd Street Y. "Oh," she says, "what's the topic?"

"Oh," I tell her, "Romance, Realism and 'Radical Disjunction': Has the American Present Moved beyond the Reach of American Fiction?" And I fart.

"Yeah," says Vikki, "like when wasn't it?"

Don't get me wrong, I'm for the good, I'm against the bad. There's too much suffering, there ain't enough justice. But it doesn't do a bit of good for me to say so because that's only standing up to be counted and it's pointless, finally, to study the good or try to keep up with the real when the novelist's red meat is now, was then, and ever will be, the words and music of his imagination.

Stanley Elkin: An Anecdote

William Gass

I FIRST MET Stanley Elkin when he was a graduate student at the University of Illinois. A magazine called *Accent,* on whose editorial board he served, had decided to devote an entire issue to the work of a heretofore unpublished writer named me. I taught at Purdue University, nearby, so it was simple enough to visit, to party, and I came away not unnaturally well disposed: to Stanley, many others, to streets, fire hydrants, to trees.

A year later—this was 1959—I came over to Urbana from Lafayette to put in a year as a visiting lecturer, dividing my time equally between philosophy, literature, and fiction writing—a split which proved worse than any pea's. The writers were wonderful (they usually are), but the English Department was full of scholars notable for notes they could write down but couldn't play; in the Philosophy Department perched a row of positivists so preserved in their opinions even the nits beneath their wings were stuffed; and the novel on which I had already labored a long time chose this moment to tell me my labors had been in vain. I found out that the streets flooded, that dogs visited the hydrants there as they did elsewhere, and that the trees were being cut down. I would rather relive that year than rejoin the navy, but that's about it. Stanley Elkin was certainly a welcome light in a dark time.

Of course, I liked the fact that Stanley seemed to approve of my work, and I was impressed by what he had just begun to publish. That was not all. I was impressed by his size, for Stanley was already larger than life. I was impressed by his youth, which I envied, for my habit in every enterprise was to put out my meager blooms only after the season was over, and all the vases had been put up. I was impressed by his wife, whom I coveted; by the raw unsauced way he devoured life; and possibly more than anything then, I was impressed by his stories, his anecdotal history of himself; not just by what those histories were or contained, although they rarely lacked interest in that regard; but by how he told them: how he entered into them, how Stanley, himself—always the subject—became objectified; became a character we all first heard, then felt we saw, emerge from our narrator's memory. Stanley also groused a lot. He wanted what he felt were his just desserts, his due, and to that end he kept accounts. Receipts, it seemed, regularly fell short. In addition, he constantly complained about his health, which was precarious; but those complaints were hard to believe, he seemed so robust.

Back then, in the first fuzz of our beginnings, what was hard *was* hard. It was hard to believe the way writing was difficult to do. Now, as life fills with irrelevance like a leaking boat, it is the easy, the simple, the trivial, that has become impossible. I think of our habits as organs outside us, as satellite cities or colonies overseas, by means of which we carry on an extended commerce; and as so often happens, the suburbs will swallow the city itself, the colonies rise in revolt; our habits no longer require an habitué, but think they can carry on by themselves. Stanley's—to me, imaginary—bad health set up shop, held fire and going out of business sales, only to reappear in another location with another name. I won't say that the dirty tricks life has played on him have made Stanley a better player of the game; but they have made him a better player of the game. Once his symptoms had surfaced like submarines—about that unmistakable reality, he grew grouseless; he grew brave.

There tend to be emblematic moments in a friendship, moments which more than mark it off but become almost its masonry. I had been able, that year in Urbana, to find quarters for only a half a year; so for the second semester my family had moved across town to a street whose elm trees were all coming down, where the noises of saws set your life on edge. However, we had a little housewarming and put on happiness like a paper hat. A few couples were to come for dinner. For the occasion every cloud in the sky burst. The rain did not come down in strings, it came down in horizontal planes. The streets in our neighborhood flooded; most of our guests refused to wade; the basement began to fill with water. I heaved washing and drying machines up onto blocks. The blocks were waiting in the basement like sandbags along a levee. Clearly this had happened before. Now I could see watermarks on the walls toward which this fresh flood rushed like a runner to the tape. The Elkins crossed the river, arriving with every pant and gown rolled up and nevertheless wet to the altogethers. We experienced the levity which local and still manageable disasters can generate. Every fifteen minutes I would throw open the door and look down the stairs where step after basement step was disappearing into the swill.

I then began to fear for the electrical system. Certain switches, I insisted, had to be unsnapped, fuses unscrewed, whichever it was. With the water nearer thigh than knee, and certainly over my rolled-up everythings, a flashlight held riflelike over my head, its beam pointing down like a toy sun, I began to wade around looking for the fuse box, of whose nature and location at this time I knew nothing. At my back I thought I heard the paddling of a waterbird. It was Stanley, almost as wet from head to toe as toe to head. "I thought if you were going to electrocute yourself down here," he said, "you ought to have some company."

Stanley lived, and still lives, in a state of quixotic excess. His weak heart hates the calm and simple center, and prefers to beat out at the edge of things. He sees—he has always seen—the path back in the way out to those edges; he knows the trials of the return; and this gives his understanding of events a shearing strength, a sense for the power in things that are coming apart which some of his readers regard as merely comic. That is: Elkin knows that a shoe put on is a shoe which will have to be removed, and he understands this not as a future foot will, but as the present one does. He renders the firstfootforward with the words which include the eventual two steps back. Yet, and this is the heroic part: the shoe goes on anyway; it fits; the forward step is taken.

Now Stanley is holding the flashlight, and I am taking teeth out of the mouth of this box. I haven't found the main switch. Do I want to pull the main switch? I don't know. Nor have I asked Stanley to go back upstairs and drip off in the kitchen. I try not to believe this is dangerous. I find the main switch looking like the shadow of a switch, not a switch. Stanley says: "I wish I had rolled up my shorts." So I don't pull the main switch. We'll dammit have dinner. It was rather a nice meal, too, I remember. Being alive, even all wet, put us in good spirits. We set a new watermark that night.

This is one of the few of Stanley's stories in which I am actually a participant. Normally I tell it, not as I have told it here, as Bill Gass would normally tell it; but as Stanley does, for his version is clearly superior. On the road, in Minneapolis or Atlanta, I often tell the story of the broken thumb at the drive-in, or of the time Stanley went to Hollywood to redo the computer's dialogue for that wretched movie, *The Demon Seed.* I enjoy the thought that Stanley will reach Dallas just after me, and people will say, as he begins his Herbie-Bogart-abroad stories, "oh, we've heard those." I have a million of his, and I'm quite a hit with a mouthful of beer.

Stanley, we joke, has the manuscript disease: M.S. From a trip abroad, I bring him back a cane, and then complain when he doesn't use it. Stanley no longer looms, as he did in the old days; instead he shambles to a chair or sofa, but in any room no one is larger or more alive. He lets us joke, not to save his spirits, but to save ours, which is generosity a degree beyond the generous.

But Elkin humor is always dark, people will say, so why shouldn't it sometimes be at his expense? And if I report that his new novel [*The Magic Kingdom*] is about seven terminally ill children, it will be hard to refute them. We have lately read of these vulgar benevolences: some stricken ten-year-old is flown to Florida; snatched out of the tropics and shown snow; put on the back of a horse and told to yell whoopee. How to reach through this disgusting exploitation, this seven-hankied sentimentality, to the pain? His work has always done so: his wit, his language, will find a way through these bogs of falsehood and fields of shit and give us back the tragedy.

I have often thought, the tables turned, how I would have called from the top of the cellar stairs toward the wet bottom of the Elkin basement: "Need some help, Stanley?" I would say, from my safe and sane position. "I'd join you but I'm wearing my new suit." "I'm hungry, so don't switch off the main."

These days, when we are all more than knee-deep in it, and someone is about to switch off the main, I find Stanley's novels more and more like his own wading figure. They say: "if you're going to go to hell in this stupid, senseless way, you might like some sane and generously human company."

Note: This essay originally appeared in *Washington University Magazine* (Spring 1984): 12-14. Reprinted by permission of *Washington University Magazine* and William Gass.

Photograph by Miriam Berkley

On Stanley Elkin

Jerome Charyn

WHEN I MET HIM, a great big rumbling bear of a man with eyeglasses that were like a luminous mask, the first thing he asked me was: "How much money did you make this year?" I was a pauper. I had nothing. It was the summer of '64. I was living on two hundred dollars a month, a permanent member of some mythic underclass that believed in the holiness of words. I ate chocolate pudding night and day, and my mouth was always coated with black. I left the closet where I lived in Washington Heights to visit Vermont and the Bread Loaf Writers' Conference . . . and I discovered that big bear. There was almost a Talmudic sense of recognition between us—we were rivals and friends in an instant, brothers out of some invisible barrio, filled with chaos and romance. We played Ping-Pong. We wrestled on the lawn. I couldn't beat the bear. He whirled me around and around like a battered top. We traded stories. He'd been born in the Bronx, like myself, or am I creating my own romance of Stanley's history? He talked about a cousin who became a gangster. Stanley abandoned the Bronx when he was five or six and moved to the Midwest. He was the first novelist I'd ever met who had a Ph.D. Dr. Elkin. I'd barely scraped my ass through college. The name of his first book was *Boswell.* He had the authenticity of an English don with the gruff manners of the street. He was the funniest man alive. He told stories with wonderful twisted jokes. He was always the essential victim of these jokes, the endless fall guy. Self-mockery was a kind of motor for Stanley: he lurched into long tales that always took advantage of himself.

He would develop M.S. in a couple of years. Perhaps there were already signs of the disease at Bread Loaf. He had no coordination in his Ping-Pong game. He would swing at the little white ball like a broken Babe Ruth. I hadn't read *Boswell.* But a year later I took my first plunge into Stanley's work, a story called "The Guest." It was about a misfit jazz musician, Bertie, who worms his way into an apartment in St. Louis. It had all of Stanley's beautiful banter but with absolute control. Bertie's a sad misanthrope whose only real address is a trumpet case. The story is both frightening and funny. It's about the danger point of isolation where the mind folds back in upon itself and plays all kinds of tricks. And Stanley himself seemed like the trumpet and the trumpeter, with a biting syncopation. I marveled at the story. Perhaps it touched my own sense of isolation, the longing for miraculous music that will soothe the angry bear inside all of us. "The

Hungry beating brutish one / In love with candy, anger, and sleep," as Delmore Schwartz once said.

And that's how my own brooding relationship with Stanley's language began. I still think of Bertie and the eye patch he wears. When he wakes up without his eye patch on, he panics. He opens his eyes and sees two heads. "At last, by covering all visible space, real or illusory, with all visible fingers, real or illusory—like one dragging a river—he recovered the patch and pulled it quickly over one of his heads."

And, like Bertie, I myself am a two-headed man.

Elkin before Elkin

Jerome Klinkowitz

NOT VERY MUCH HAPPENS in "A Sound of Distant Thunder," Stanley Elkin's first published story (*Epoch,* 1957) and collected with four other fugitive pieces in *Early Elkin* (Flint, MI: Bamberger Books, 1985). In it a store owner identified only as Feldman leaves his apartment, stops for coffee and a buttered roll at the deli where other merchants on the street start their day, then opens his shop for a virtually eventless morning and afternoon of just one potential customer and not a single sale. Feldman's in a quiet line, fine china, and can hope of moving fewer than a dozen sets per week at best, so even this apparent slowness is nothing extraordinary.

Like much fifties fiction, there's a minor action that the protagonist identifies as a subtle threat, one that serves to destroy everything by story's end. But for the bulk of Elkin's narrative almost nothing takes place—except a sales pitch summoned out of nowhere, delivered to the least likely of prospects, and accomplishing nothing at all beyond consuming time and energy like a black hole in the vast emptiness of this sadly quiet tale.

Yet what a sales pitch it is: a compelling argument that does less to move an unsalable piece of china than to define Feldman himself beyond the finest, most colorful description. From a world of ominous signs—a slow, hot season, little traffic, businesses closing or moving away, and presumably hostile blacks intimidating the remaining shopkeepers—Feldman's rapt promotion emerges as the story's sole element of action, its one moment of true life, as it were, in a world of entropy and death. For three full pages of the story's twenty-two, Feldman tries selling his customer something he doesn't want by telling him in massive, compulsive detail things he doesn't want to know. As readers, we know how hopeless it is—the guy wants Noritake, a "name," rather than any of the real china Feldman's shelves and tables display in such profusion. As a widely advertised and highly desirable brand, it is the one line a failing store would not have—appropriately so, for Feldman is a proud professional who sells fine china, not trends. Much more than a sales promotion, it is what Elkin in his introduction calls "the source for all the arias my characters often give themselves over to in my work" (xi). It is the operatic quality of self-definition, an argument for existence not by consequential action but in the very song of being that becomes in later canonical work the signal quality of Stanley Elkin's writing. This and *Early Elkin*'s other stories demonstrate something the author identifies as a key factor in all his fiction, "some up-from-nothing quality about life which says a good word for human possibility" (ix). All that nothing causing all that pain is achieved by Elkin's narrative descriptions; the redeeming achievement comes in his character's song.

The negativity of this story's world is all the more oppressive for the fact that Elkin's narrator generates much of it with his own vision, a vision that without the projective energy of spiel is a dim one indeed. Feldman makes more of the oppressively hot season than do others on the street and sees the street's declining business life as a dead end rather than as an avenue to better chances elsewhere. Mean in spirit, he cannot happily or easily accept a gift from a fellow merchant. Sent a potential customer by his brother downtown, he drives him away by condemning the man's own desires. When his brother confronts him with reality, he shouts him down and ruins a happy evening. Even when the story ends with violent action, it is one that's projected: not the firsthand experience of Feldman's store being looted and destroyed but his presumption of it.

That the presumption is a correct one simply confirms Feldman's projective powers. Like the aria he sings in promotion of his trade, his string of remarks directed to some black youths approaching his store creates something out of nothing—in this case, animosity. Bereft of customers, he nevertheless refuses to perceive their presence as anything but a threat, despite their stated intention of buying a special present for their mother. Another visit's inquiry about price proves contradictory. When the young men ask if the price would be lower if asked by a Jewish person, Feldman says no—and then just three pages later accedes to his brother's request that a business friend (not a Jew himself) be given a discount. Time payments are also denied, even though within the hour Feldman will note how most of his customers pick out what they want and then make the actual purchase a month later. That his projections are ridiculously askew becomes clear when he corrects his own observation that the area is turning African-American in demographic character: "the city was talking of building projects for them. In a year, maybe two, they would be off the street, and a lot of the Jews who had been frightened out of the neighborhood would come back" (18). Better then that Feldman live in his sales pitch, for here is animation beyond the self-fulfilling devastations of his own bleak prophecy.

Such is the function of an aria: as music modulates the voice into song, it evens out the rough edges and introduces lyric form into the otherwise amorphous nature of life—a life that without such sustaining power runs to catastrophes worse than formless. In "The Party," which first appeared in *Views* during 1958, dream serves as another way of generating an "up-from-nothing" view that speaks better than the day's events for human possibility. The protagonist is Feldman again, and he views this alternative to be "adultery" as he turns from his sleeping wife to steal his way into memories of childhood trips from Chicago to New York. Here the remove is double, for as Stanley Elkin notes of his own life in the introduction, the boy lives a much richer life on these trips east than he does at home, almost as if the bigger city and people there awake something secret within him. Singing this secret is the stuff of dreams, more arias to one's self that by story's end the protagonist is imparting to his own child at bedtime. In his dream life the characters speak a richer English, a music whose immigrant elision of the unimportant cuts out the "red tape" that binds too much of his life at home. As an adult, Feldman's motive to dream is a belief that happiness is deserved; because the more common aspects of life deny such happiness, they justify the adultery.

"Fifty Dollars," from *Southwest Review* (1959), also makes much of happiness and the curious ways one needs to get it. In the previous story Feldman had believed in happiness as a birthright; now, half a generation or so later, a woman named just Mary dreams of a disappointment with her father and regrets "the foolish assurances she had had to give her husband that she would always be happy" (62). His idea of happiness has been to move them into a tract development styled around a colonial motif to the point of corniness. When the development adds a shopping mall even more ridiculously tailored to a revolutionary war scheme, Mary blanches—not at its kitschy lack of taste but at her husband's ardent belief that these stores will fulfill her every need and answer for her ultimate happiness.

There's a sales pitch involved here, surely: the aria of residential blocks named after the original thirteen colonies and retail outlets following the same theme. There's even a promotion involved that figures in the story's center, as Mary unwittingly and unwillingly becomes the grocery market's five thousandth customer and wins a year's supply of bakery goods (she'd been seeking merely a loaf of bread) plus fifty dollars in cash to spend as she wishes—the assumption being that this marvelous center can supply anything she wants, making her perfectly happy.

As Mary shops for her prize, something special for her that her husband insists be beyond what they'd normally buy, she slowly learns the function of such music. Translating the fifty dollars into a material object will not only change it but will change her fate as well; it will make her the owner of a dress or piece of jewelry and not the winner of a fifty-dollar cash prize. Holding on to the money lets her maintain herself in the shopping center's world of impulses and signs, a place where stores are named after images rather than for the things they sell and where young salesmen have more than good looks, "looks which stood at a slight remove from handsomeness for being so jauntily dapper" (78). In such signs is the song of existence, as stylistically removed from the real world as Feldman's free-floating pitch in "A Sound of Distant Thunder" and his dreams of childhood visits in "The Party."

Placing these samples of genuinely early Elkin in perspective are more recent pieces—essays, really—that frame the collection. "The Graduate Seminar" closes things as something of a joke, one with an interesting history: from the introduction we've learned that in 1972, when editor Mark Mirsky requested something for his new magazine, *Fiction,* Elkin complied with a killed review from the *New York Times,* putting quotation marks around his critical comments on the work of Anthony Burgess and devising the silliness of a class trip as a framework for such professorial observations. A closing reference—"I'll find it in a moment, it was on the left-hand page. I have that sort of memory, I can always—yes, here it is" (104)—recalls a telling point in the volume's opening confession, "Where I Read What I Read," that he can remember the page, "what side, the left or the right, a particular passage appears on, even its generalized location, top, middle, bottom" (2). Why so? Because reading, as an act, involves the absorption of absolutely paid attention. And what does the writer offer in return for such attention? A willingness to create "the conditions in which language may occur" (103). It happens now and then in Burgess's work and much more often in Elkin's, such as in the bit of opening exposition when the graduate seminar undertakes its class trip to the Hall of Dinosaurs in the Carnegie Museum: "Pterodactyls, suspended from wires, floated in the deep green air of the place, skeletally beaked and frowning down on the ancient traffic like helicopter cops on the 5:30 news" (93).

"The Graduate Seminar," like so many graduate seminars, is a spiel, the professor showing off not just his knowledge but the ability to deliver it in a persuasive way. "Where I Read What I Read" is in similar fashion an account of how such spiels achieve their purpose—by captivating attention and removing the reader into language's own world, where things themselves are of less importance than signs at play. It answers the question of why write a story when the world is right there for the looking. The story transports us beyond that world even while sharpening our attention to it.

In 1982, at a conference in France hosted by the University of Nice, Elkin delivered less of a paper than a true spiel on two interrelated topics: his fictive art and the way he had to deal with the progressive debilitations of multiple sclerosis. The story he told was of getting an idea for a story; the occasion was a visit to the Metropolitan Museum of Art and struggling with its monumental stairs, his efforts with his walker making tiny children think that he was not "a cripple" but rather "the biggest toddler in the world." Such salesmanship for the pathos of his own physical condition made for an attention-getting, captivating spiel, just as convincing as his confession for enjoying such otherwise insipid occasions as academic conferences: "I love shoptalk." Shoptalk among the artists, spiels for the customers: these are the qualities of fictive language present in the earliest Elkin and evident in his most characteristic work since.

Stanley Elkin and "Everything": The Problem of Surfaces and Fullness in the Novels

Charles Molesworth

In at least three of his novels—*Boswell, The Living End,* and *The Dick Gibson Show*—Stanley Elkin does not become fully self-reflexive, and by ostensibly *not* writing about writing, he may be said to elude the category of *metafictionist.* Likewise, he has also been frequently quoted as rejecting the label of *black humorist.* Yet his work is avidly read and praised by many critics who champion those contemporary fiction writers who are often identified by either of these labels, or both. If Elkin is like, and yet unlike, Barthelme, Sukenick, and Federman, how can we best place him in the available spectrum of styles and postures? The improvisatory nature and feel of Elkin's work might cue us to accept all spectra in less structured ways, to hear the chorus as instead a babble, and take each writer and even each novel as it presents itself. While that is more or less what many general readers do, critics and academics often read novels, in one of their guises at least, as ways of problem solving. If a novel sets out to address a problem, whether of epistemology, sociology, psychology, or whatever, we have to have some prior knowledge of what the problem is and how it's developed historically. I propose to see the three novels I mentioned above as attempts to solve, fictionally, a set of problems, problems that have often been addressed by metafictionists and black humorists. Of course, if the novels are addressed under the guise of delight or entertainment, they may seem obvious, and any problem itself treated merely as a donnée for the tale's otherwise formless energies. Elkin's work can easily be read as sheer entertainment, and its apparent formlessness invites such a response. On the other hand, the novels can be more in the grip of the problems they address, with such apparent playfulness, than they are willing to acknowledge. My reading inclines to the latter probability.

Before spelling out this set of problems, let me say that I think Alan Wilde has the case essentially right when he defines Elkin's work by the term *midfiction.*[1] Midfiction, in Wilde's view, uses parable to enable the author to suspend his irony between the poles of mimetic realism and the free-play of metafiction's self-reflexivity. Parable "intends to render more fluid and existential our sense of the world's meaning and . . . our connection with it" (183). By using ambiguity, indirection, and open rather than closed forms, parables defy univocal interpretations or fixed contents, though they can exploit some or many of the features of traditional, mimetic realism. Elkin often employs the surface textures of realism, such as colloquial dialogue, standard exposition of spatial and temporal "scenes," consistent characterology, and so forth. Where he most clearly deviates from realistic canons is in his characters' implausible obsessions, the use of fairly frequent empirical impossibilities, and, rather than a constant welter of juxtaposition, an almost endless string of additional details or occurrences to the point of madcap exhaustiveness or an epistemological exhaustion. We're told a great deal about Boswell and Gibson, yet both characters are more reflectors of the experiences of others than they are deeply complex subjects in their own right. Also, and this contributes to the feeling of a parable (though it is not a characteristic singled out by Wilde), Elkin's language is frequently playful and spotted with puns and one-liners, but his style has a high percentage of sentences that are "merely" expository in a straightforward, prosaic way. The comparison many critics have made between Elkin and the patter of the stand-up comedian is apt, and I often expect Elkin to say, "Now seriously, folks," though if he did say this, we couldn't tell if he meant it straight or not.

Now, for the set of problems both faced by and embodied in the three novels: Can characters' actions be seen as governed by deterministic models of free will; can a story tell its whole secret by attending only to surfaces; and, finally, can a novel render justice, not to the complexity, but simply to the *expanse* of American life in the last half of the twentieth century? These admittedly general formulations will cover a great many writers' problems, obviously, but I suggest that Elkin is unique in the way his works interlock these three problems. Before looking at the novels, I would like to offer a somewhat fanciful reading of "The Making of Ashenden," from *Searches and Seizures.* Wilde is generally right in speaking of Elkin's non-self-reflexivity, but we might consider this novella as if it were a parable about fiction writing itself. Ashenden as novelist is engaged in a world of romance (romance as a literary genre, in the Fryean sense), for he conceives of an ideal, meets the ideal (Jane Löes Lipton), and yet has to pass through an ordeal before he can possess this transcendently meaningful "object." In looking to reclaim his innocence (the ordeal as he defines it), Ashenden might be understood to be driving farther and farther into the world of romance. His mythical parentage (earth, air, fire, and water) and the highly aestheticized landscape (like a compendium of European art) suggest he will pursue and persist in this quest, though clearly some of the details suggest Elkin is decreating the romance genre and its conventions as well. The encounter and copulation with the rutting she-bear that occurs in place of (or as an all-too-predictable obscene fulfillment of) this other-worldly quest is presented in very graphic, indeed mimetic terms, whereas the romance part of the novella is told in a sort of schematic plain style. The descriptions of the bear through a proliferation of metaphors (176) and the bear's vagina through personal testimony (180-81) reverse our ordinary expectations about what level of figurative language and tonal consistency are best suited for either realistic or metafictional writing. What Ashenden encounters (and verbally incarnates) in his quest is a raunchy, realistic world completely at odds with the generic elements of romance. Searching for an ideal, Ashenden is seized by the real. This, I would suggest, can be read allegorically as the fate of Elkin the novelist. The bear can be read satirically as a send-up of Faulkner's beast, Mailer's ethos in *Why Are We in Vietnam?,* Galway Kinnell's well-known poem, and other main embodiments of modernism's fixation on the primitive, and the cult of experience in American writing as well. Yet clearly Elkin's bear is a result of a fiction maker's love, a love of his own power (to shock, to convince, to defamiliarize) and a love of the recalcitrance of "reality."

Elkin graphically sends up the oldest story of all, changing it to read "Boy meets girl, boy loses girl, boy gets bear."

To put it bluntly, Ashenden the character is destined to find only art in his life—the archetypes of romance, the aestheticized landscapes of the estate, the conundrums of desire, and so forth. But in his art, that is, in his fantasy as he induces it in himself in the midst of the "unreal" landscape, he finds only reality—the mucus of rutting flesh, the bruises of desire's aftermath, failure and deception. The novella ends with a promising future: "seeing ahead, speculating about the generations that would follow his own, he thought, Air. Water, he thought. Fire, Earth, he thought . . . And *honey*" (188). Now Ashenden has a project, even a measure of immortality (rather than just a dream), and with it he affirms the elements of a world as well as the quintessence of sweetness. He has become part bear himself, a seeker of what is both raw and sweet, a symbol (and an object) that answers appetite. Elkin, allegorically, is affirming the power and hold of fantasy, romance, art itself, but he is also using art to affirm the surplus of reality, the uncontainable excess of the world that outstrips all our structures, both the rational and the imaginative. We're ready to laugh at the fictional bear, to enjoy the send-up of this all-too-accommodating and compromised symbol, but instead Elkin makes us believe in the very creatureliness of the bear, to see it as a manifestation of what Randall Jarrell called "the un-get-pastableness" of things.

We could turn my proposed self-reflexive reading of the novella another ninety (or 180) degrees and also use it to read Elkin's set of problems. Does Ashenden's romance-loving nature call forth the all-too-real bear as a fulfillment of his character? Or do the iron laws of literary determinism (Chekhov's gun that must be fired before the final curtain) dictate that anyone as starry-eyed as Ashenden must end by being sticky-fingered? Does Elkin deliberately undercut the bear's symbolic possibilities by obsessively insisting on the surface reality of the bear? Are the unreal landscapes of an English estate not really as truly full as they ought to be, unless they include a Russian bear who speaks in the International Phonetic Alphabet and is encountered against a background very like Hicks's "Peaceable Kingdom," that by-now clichéd masterpiece of American primitive painting? "There is no secret, of course; most of what happens to us is simple accident" (129), we're told in the first paragraph. "But surely something in the blood too, locked into good fortune's dominant genes like a blast ripening in a time bomb" (129), we're told two sentences later. The story says Ashenden's fate is a lark and an iron law, in other words, a magic parable. And the paragraph concludes with Elkin's version of radical individualism:

> Something my own, not passed on or handed down, something seized, wrested—my good character, hopefully, my taste perhaps. What's mine, what's mine? Say taste—the soul's harmless appetite. (129)

I suggest these words could easily and illuminatingly be taken as Elkin's own, an accurate description of the novelist's perplexed response to the question of proprietorship over his fictional universe. They could also be taken as the slogan of Elkin's prototypical character, the lonely standardized man of late industrial capitalism, fighting with and against the clichés of individuality, in a darkly fixed world illuminated only by his own changing desires.

Perhaps the "passed on or handed down" model most apt for Elkin's first novel, *Boswell,* is Flaubert's *Bouvard and Pécuchet.* With only one main character instead of the two clerks in the earlier novel, Elkin sets out to reveal a series of false or empty possibilities of meaning. Boswell's life is landmarked by a group of would-be heroes, a set of not-quite Dr. Johnsons who could supply Boswell's sycophancy with the focus it needs. From Penner the selfish ascetic, to Sandusky the broken-down strong man, to Messerman the rabbi with no congregation, to Lano the masochistic revolutionary general, Boswell learns how humdrum, how ordinary are the great and famous. Or rather, he doesn't quite learn this lesson in Flaubertian nullity until the end of the book. Then, having formed a club of Great Men, Boswell discovers "a new knowledge that it was not enough, that nothing was ever enough" (386) and ends by shouting "*Down with The Club!*" (387). Where Flaubert's clerks discovered only the endless pieties of the half-enlightened bourgeoisie, Boswell finds the insatiable desires of post-industrial man afloat in a world of means without ends. *Boswell* is a book obsessed with values, especially the value of learning how to live the good life, but it's also a book with no values to center its vision, and in this it most resembles its Flaubertian model.

The book's picaresque structure is ironically at odds with its obsessional characters and even its sense of character as destiny. "Oh, what a thing it is to be settled by our past—to be no better, finally, than our toilet training, than domestic arrangements we don't even understand at the time" (350). This lament against Freudian determinism can be read as a mockery of such explanatory schemes, but the novel offers it as at least as plausible as any other scheme. This particular passage occurs in a long sequence in which Boswell "practices" for death, trying through a series of madcap scenes to acclimate himself to the mortality he announces as inevitable (and inevitably repressed) in the very first paragraph of the book. (The themes of death's inevitability and the nature of greatness are never successfully mediated in the novel, in my opinion, and this more than anything gives the book its open form.)

The novel also uses its picaresque structure in an attempt to capture a fullness of material reality and incorporate its obsession with surfaces. One formulation of the concern with surfaces occurs as a parenthetical paragraph, but its offhandedness is, I would suggest, a clue to its very centrality in the novel. There are also similar reflections and formulations on the same theme scattered throughout the book, and the lack of inner reality in the novel is dialectically related to this theme. But here is the passage:

> (I have just thought of something. Perhaps cause and effect are somehow mixed up here. Perhaps we pick our leaders as we pick our actors—for their looks; perhaps the great are destined by nothing so much as their physical well-being; perhaps the world *is* all appearance. Is this the meaning of life? I may have stumbled onto something. I shall have to think about it.) (174)

If the world is to be known through appearances, then such principles of organization as subordination or hierarchy or classification must be revalued (and even discarded, perhaps). Furthermore, the emphasis on surface and appearance opens the door to inclusiveness, as principles of exclusion or selectivity become harder to justify. There is in *Boswell* a very brief interlude where the main character quite casually begins to photograph, at their request, a family in the park. Boswell imagines the family's domestic life as a "demolishment of empty space, an ethic of filled drawers, closets, rooms, houses, devoted as misers to some desperate notion of accumulation" (209). In photographing them, Boswell (and Elkin) sees them as perfectly normal; it's the narrative unimportance of the incident that makes the people so typical, so representative of the general object-world of the book. "Their substantial laughter, their little private gestures of affection seemed hollow but tremendously brave" (209). They are the irreplaceable but unimportant cogs in the wheels of the world's consumption, the lubricant for all the dominant market-oriented motives of modern production.

By demolishing empty space through the accumulation of objects, the people in Elkin's America seem to achieve their basic values, and this throws them into the maelstrom of inclusiveness, another source of the novelist's concern. Time after time we are given lists of things, occurrences, qualities, or even formulations of ideas or feelings, lists whose repetitiveness eventually feels like a desperate attempt to master the expanse or fullness of material life in America. I say expanse or fullness rather than plenitude, because this characteristic hardly seems a genuine cultural value or accomplishment, yet neither does it come into direct or explicit satirical focus. We might eventually feel Elkin attacks this acquisitiveness or materialism, but one could argue just as convincingly that he accepts it for what it is, a stable and inescapable aspect of life in post-industrial twentieth-century America. And it is not only things but people who fill and overfill our lives, as this following passage shows, when Boswell reflects on the people at his uncle's funeral:

> They were the supernumeraries with whom finally we spend more time than with those we dream of, as though the landscape of our lives has always to be filled with people, crowds, masses, populations, the tradesman who brings the bread, perhaps, the man who waits with us each day at the bus stop, those yeasty populations of the unknown, there by accident, to whom we talk and talk and talk. They are legion. How many words, I wonder, can have passed between us? How many gestures of affection or civility? (217)

These are the same people who become center stage actors near the end of *The Dick Gibson Show,* the Mailbaggers whose electronic community is both reified and displayed on Gibson's call-in radio program.

Indeed the climactic moment in *Boswell* occurs when the seeker realizes that it's not enough to "collect" great men or to conquer death, that the gathering of world leaders engaged in conversation finally isn't sufficient. What is really needed is a total fullness, a total incorporation of all reality, far beyond the select or elite (or artistic) refinement of reality as it might be filtered down to and through a single consciousness.

> It was no longer enough simply to live forever. It was no longer enough to be just one single man. I wanted to be everyone in this room and all the people in the crowds outside and all the people everywhere who had ever lived. What did it mean to be just Boswell, to have only Boswell's experience? (367)

The extreme and bizarre reality of Ashenden, preserved for following generations, is here imagined as the ordinary but all-inclusive experience of past generations. The art of selecting great men to teach us things has been replaced by the hunger to assume all of reality. The nineteenth-century myth of the great man has been replaced by the late twentieth-century myth of the universal common man.

Shortly after his marriage, Boswell is described by allusions to Hawthorne's "Wakefield" and Eliot's "Prufrock," both exemplars of the anti-heroic, men defeated by their own ordinariness and limited horizons. Though he is clearly in this tradition of the modern antihero, Boswell has little real angst, and very few demons, and his author's tone towards him is neither satirical nor acerbic nor even melancholic. There is irony, to be sure, in this antiheroicism, but only because we still expect some saving grace or transforming power to define the central character in the books we spend time reading. But for Elkin such an absence of heroism, or its ironic inversion, is merely par for the course in a world where the only measure of achievement is accumulation and the only test of reality is surfaces. Of course Elkin "knows" accumulation and surfaces can hardly ground any ethics that looks to be transcendent. But transcendence is not what obsessions are about. Knowing or desiring something obsessively is its own reward: "There are only two kinds of intelligences, the obsessive and the perspectual. All dirty old men come from the former and all happy men from the latter, but I wouldn't trade places. In this life frustration is the Promethean symbol of effort" (303). Notice, the Promethean *symbol* of effort, not the actual attainment of a Promethean status or essence, is what justifies the frustration endemic in all obsessive efforts.

There are many other passages in *Boswell* that deal with the set of problems I have formulated—determinism and free will, the persistence of surfaces and surface meanings, and the need to address and master the full expanse of the material world—and I will not take up more space listing them. I would like, however, to show briefly how these problems occur in *The Dick Gibson Show* and *The Living End* as well, and then conclude with some speculation on the nature of obsession and on Elkin's somewhat agonized relation to realism, two topics that are, I think, related to this triple thematic and to Elkin's mastery of his material.

Dick Gibson's struggle with what he calls his apprenticeship is an effort to master all the knowledge of radio, and through this all knowledge altogether. Even as he becomes "not just the voice of radio but radio itself," Gibson's fascination with voice is also a fascination with narrative, with the penchant for ordinary men and women to tell their stories obsessively. What Gibson discovers in and through these narratives is that people are surrounded by, drenched in, constituted out of the welter of clichés they have imbibed and recycled and appropriated since their first moments of consciousness: "his apprenticeship was truly finished, the last of all the bases in the myth had been rounded, his was a special life, even a great life—a life, that is, touched and changed by cliché, by corn and archetype and the oldest principles of drama" (105). The "oldest principles of drama" might well include those elements and characteristics that God requires in *The Living End* which are necessary for a simple, single reason: "*Because it makes a better story is why*" (144). The better stories are the ones that are built on corn, cliché, and archetypes, because they deal with the surfaces of things, they include all experience, and because they let us know all the stories are the same (and hence determined) while still deeply satisfying for each of us (desperate to believe in our individual freedoms). The entire part 2 of *The Dick Gibson Show* is an account of a panel discussion in which each panelist tells his or her story, complete with details, lists, repetitions, all the earmarks of obsessive talk. One of the panelists tells of a previous guest on the program, a memory expert named Arnold Menchman, the very redundancy of his surname serving as an emblem of his superficially duplicating, perfectly photographic memory. Another tells of his experiences as a druggist who enters into the destiny of his customers by observing the surface details of their lives ("do you know what I found out? . . . I found out *everything!*" [185]). As for the theme of free will, Gibson uses a number of aliases while working for a string of small radio stations, but finally calls himself Dick Gibson in an act of autonomous power, able to control his destiny while simultaneously, ironically, becoming a personality, the self-less moderator of other people's stories. (At novel's end he refuses all callers on WMIA, the "scrambled I Am's of Miami Beach" [334], unable to locate the enemy who "would have focused the great unfocused struggle of his life" [333]. No other, no self.) And at the beginning of his apprenticeship, Gibson loses his job with a Midwestern station because he deflates the audience's spirit and because the equipment fails; this is Elkin's way of supplying both a character-based reason and an empirical rationale, the freely willed and the mechanically determined.

Dick Gibson hears many stories throughout the book and most of them are marked by banality and cliché. It might be interesting to contrast this novel with Bakhtin's notion of the dialogic, in which the genre of the novel is defined as a compendium of voices whose forms are determined in significant ways by their expectations of being heard and responded to. To my ear, Elkin's characters' stories are not genuinely dialogic, resembling as they do the patter of the stand-up comedian. Or, to be more precise, their dialogic openness to response is very narrow, since they do little beyond pause over various puns and gag lines and are always rushing on to some usually pointless or predictable conclusion. Perhaps the most glaring example of this is the story (58-62) Miriam tells Gibson when they are residing together in Morristown, New Jersey. The long story concerns how she and her mother and sister conceal the disappearance of the family dog from their ailing father for fear the news would kill him. Eventually the father "discovers" the frozen corpse of the dog in a snow bank when he steps on it and breaks the animal's neck. Elkin's subzero shaggy dog story, this narrative does little to reveal Miriam's character or change Gibson's relationship with her. Its details are grotesque and amusing and full of "effects of the real" (to use Barthes's phrase), but its structure seems both too spontaneous and too willed to be aesthetically satisfying.

Perhaps the most revealing passage in the book concerns Gibson's view of his family and their character-playing shenanigans. (In fact, Dick Gibson's puzzlement at his father's meanings can be read as an allegory of the reader facing an Elkin novel.) This incessant role playing is frankly labeled a way of dealing with surfaces in order to avoid the inner feelings and states of mind that ordinarily are expected to be shared and tested among family members. The harsh truth behind the passage is how real it is despite its theatricalizing exaggerations. Notice, too, how the word *everything* occurs to convey the expanse of human situations and behavior, as if the family, like the novelist himself, felt compelled to include all their experience even if it has been transformed into a kind of indifference and superficiality:

They were zany, and Dick remembered why his family's characters oppressed him so. It wasn't simply that they worked so hard to show off. Rather it was that their divertissements were a delaying action that held him off. In a while they would drop their roles and behave normally. Their masquerades were reserved for homecomings like this one, or leavetakings, or their first visit to a patient in the hospital, say. It was their way of concealing feeling, thrusting it away from them until all the emotional elements in a situation had disappeared. In this way his family life was as sound, that is to say as even-keeled, as any. It was like living with lawyers, with cops who had seen everything. If he were to die right then and there, they would probably make his body a prop in a game, and the game would continue, the show go on until every last atom of their grief had been absorbed—until, that is, real grief would be ludicrous, coming so past its time. Oh, they were hard. He recalled the story Miriam had told about her father, how she'd had to shield him. Why, *his* family was like that and he hadn't even known it. Why couldn't folks take it? Why did they insist upon the quotidian? What was so bad about bad news? Surely the point of life was the possibility it always held out for the exceptional. The range of the strange, he thought. (75-76)

The strange and the ordinary truth merge into the theatrical, the stylization of communication acting as a way of deadening its import and the feelings that animate it.

In *The Living End* this same way of dealing with surfaces and including "everything" takes the form of all the clichés about Heaven and Hell being true: the pearly gates, the heavenly choir, the sulphurous stench, the sadistic multiplication of punishment and abasement. It is all as if Elkin wanted to see the afterlife as designed by some Popular Culture, Incorporated, a public relations triumph as everyone's hopes and fears are "perfectly" realized. God himself is both a free, spontaneous actor and a deterministic force, the "Microfiche God, Lord of the Punched Cards" who is nevertheless capable of being "mildly bemused as He had been briefly surprised" (102). God destroys "*everything*" (that final word of the book italicized in its manic inclusiveness), essentially because he has never found his audience. Without the theatrical "fix" of cheers, applause, and the adoration of fans, there's nothing left for God to do but deny the very expanse he is credited with creating. (One thinks of Woody Allen's one-liner from *Love and Death:* "God is an underachiever.") *Everything* becomes one of the book's key words, like *nothing* in *King Lear,* and *everything* means every thing that is conventional, even the conventional focus of consciousness, which is the individual self, both the source of, and a challenge to, such a totalizing notion.

But everything was true, even the conventional wisdom, perhaps especially the conventional wisdom—that which had made up Heaven like a shot in the dark and imagined into reality halos and Hell, gargoyles, gates of pearl, and the Pearls of Great Price, that had invented the horns of the demons and cleft their feet and conceived angels riding clouds like cowboys on horseback, their harps at their side like goofy guitars. Everything. Everything was. The self and what you did to protect it, learning the house odds, playing it safe—the honorable percentage baseball of existence. (45)

Notice how one set of clichés is explained in terms of other sets, as the theodicy is reduced to Hollywood Westerns and baseball lingo.

Athwart this conventionality are the zany turns and reversals that Elkin uses to make the story fresh. Joseph doesn't accept Jesus as the Messiah, Mary mothers another child, God accidentally kills someone in a moment of pique and Jesus has to redeem him. But such reversals are not articulated towards some coherent satirical aim, leaving aside the rather obvious point that the subject of the book is the received piety of totally empty forms of belief and worship. The novel, it seems to me, is best read as an allegory of the novelist's perplexity in the face of those insoluble problems I have mentioned. With the climactic line of the theodicy, "*Because it makes a better story is why,*" Elkin comes closest to announcing his poetics, closest to making the book self-reflexive, a story about the hunger for narrative interest. But the destructiveness of the deity might then be read allegorically as the fundamental smashing of the problems, an apocalyptic refusal to continue with either the interpretive manipulations of parable or the presumptive maintenance of meaning involved in realism.

A word or two about cliché. The consensus about cliché is that it is empty language, usage so dulled by its ready-at-handness that its semantic power has drained away. For Elkin, though, cliché is full of meaning. As he said in an interview, "To have affairs, to go to Europe, to live the dramatic clichés, all the stuff of which movies are made, would be the great life." The double-mindedness of a writer like Barthelme in the face of cliché is here made unequivocal. Elkin has an affection for the strange and spontaneous juxtaposition, but it's almost as if this affection feeds off the cliché, the way a figure feeds off its ground. Furthermore, with a phrase like "the dramatic clichés" we can hear in the adjective a strategy of recontainment. "Dramatic" often means startling, fresh; in this sense the phrase would be an oxymoron. Elkin's strategy is to foster the startling, the "strange displacements" not only against the background of the banal and stereotypical but *as* the banal and stereotypical. His belated sense of history and meaning leads him to prize clichés which start out as surprises and reversals of meaning but have themselves become familiar and predictable and hence narratively reassuring. What greater cliché is there than, "oh my God, I wish I could do something different with my life!"? Elkin's vision involves this switch in status and meaning between the spontaneous and the predictable, the fresh and the stereotyped; indeed, it isn't so much a switch as a looping, so that the two ordinarily opposing terms constantly change back into each other. Elkin's God, in *The Living End,* is like everybody's God and like no one else's, a God of surfaces and inclusion who ends by being both the source and the destroyer of everything.

Perhaps Elkin's most radical insight is his implicit equating of obsessiveness and cliché. Everyone in the books is obsessed with something, if only with telling his or her own story, so in a real sense to have an obsession is to be thoroughly predictable. With obsession, to borrow terms from Kenneth Burke, what we have is an inversion of the agent/agency ratio. What should be a means becomes an end, what should be a tool or object takes over the human agent and turns him or her into something like an appendage to a need or desire. Consider Angela, from *The Dick Gibson Show,* who is obsessed with the buzzer in her car's ignition switch that is designed to warn her she has forgotten to remove her key. The buzzing takes over Angela's whole personality, so that everything to do with the buzzing makes her both boring and interesting. Gibson tries to wean her from her dependence on the object, but she is beyond help.

> "Have it disconnected. You don't need it."
> "I need it. It's what—" The last word was lost.
> "What was that?"
> "I said it's what mourns. I need it. It's what says that everything isn't okay. It's my gadget for grief."
> "Get rid of it," Dick said.
> "Who would keen, who would cry?"

Without the material gadget, Angela would lose the center of her subjectivity; the gadget dehumanizes her and yet humanizes her at the same time. Of course, what the buzzer says, "everything isn't okay," is itself a cliché, one we could trace back to such high cultural sources as Virgil's "lachrymae rerum" or to popular phrases such as "Life sucks." Elkin doesn't apparently scorn Angela's shallowness, and even seems to see in her fixation a touching grace. The very oddness of her obsessional object both distinguishes her from and links her to all the other obsessive characters in the book, linked and yet stranded as they are by their communal identity as part of the Dick Gibson "Show." No one will ever be totally surprised by what they hear a caller say on these shows, nor will anyone ever be completely expressed by someone else's story. We all say, "I've heard that before," and "Wait till you hear *my* story."

To determine what level of realism Elkin's novels retain, or to ask *why* Elkin avoids operating in either a clearly realistic or metafictional or black humor style, is to ask very difficult questions. My brief answer would be something like this: Elkin is both baffled and stoic in the face of the expanse of material reality as well as the persistence and virtual inseparability of clichés and mythic patterns. This stoic bafflement leads him away from black humor or satire in the traditional sense, and also provides no ground for a transcendent spiritual or historical vision. As Thomas LeClair rightly points out, "Elkin's heroes . . . develop their obsessions from natural authorities, common needs, or the promises of a popular culture rather than from some social, psychological, or religious ideology" (147). Elkin's work might be read as the perfect fictional complement to the notion of our age as one marked by "the end of ideology"—but of course we now see how such a notion was itself sodden with ideological thought. In short, Elkin needs realism to anchor his stoicism, but he "violates" realistic canons because he is baffled by the very excessiveness of the banal in American life. No formal structure, no shapely closure can contain "everything," and the aestheticism implicit in formalist finesse or lyrical expressiveness will not answer to the overwhelming presence of surface meanings. Elkin's response is but one variation on what I would call the post-Joycean novel, that myriad attempt to redeem the commonplace without resort to patently transcendent means.

To give a longer answer to these questions would require more space than is available here. But I would suggest that Marshall Brown's superb article "The Logic of Realism: A Hegelian Approach" is a good place to begin. Of the three conceptions of reality—"the reality of universal types, the reality of individuation, and the reality of patterned regularity"—that Brown adduces as the bases for various theories of realism, Elkin grants credence to each but withholds assent from any. The reality of patterned regularity, relying on the predictability of "natural and causal forces," might seem the least important to Elkin. But as we've seen, the "originality" of his characters' obsessions only serves to make them part of the general pattern of behavior, since all people have some obsession. This dominant fact in Elkin's characterology folds back into the other two bases of realism, since we recognize in a person like Boswell or Gibson both the type of modern man and a fully detailed, finely "surfaced" individual.

What Brown's essay also allows us to see is how Hegel's triad of Contingency, Relative Necessity, and Absolute Necessity can illumine Elkin's project. Though many of his characters are known by their obsessions, and hence would seem defined by Absolute Necessity, people who are fully determined from within, not subject to definition by others—these characters nevertheless are often existing in a world of contingency, and thus reject any "form of grounding or causation" and refuse to be parts of a system. This is an elaborate way of saying that Elkin refuses to choose between free will and determinism as an exclusive or even dominant explanation of his characters' behavior. For Elkin, Absolute Necessity only springs from an unbreakable attachment to some reductive object or ineradicable fear that motivates the obsession. And conversely, his characters' apparent contingency, the madcap inventiveness of the plot, and the picaresque and open structure nevertheless reflect an inescapable sameness and limitation in people's lives and desires, bound as they are by "cliché, by corn, and archetype."

At the end of his essay Brown offers a quick historical sketch of "pre- and postrealistic styles," explaining that "loose but repetitive organization" is what marks postrealism, and we see how "Texture replaces shape as the unifying force." I have argued implicitly that Elkin's texture—the feel of his characters' obsessiveness, the lists, the madcap atmosphere, and so forth —clearly unifies his work more than any shapeliness of plot or clear teleological narrative development. But I also want to argue that Elkin's apparently loose and carefree texture, his prestidigitatious distance from severe meanings or "serious" characters, is not an escape from ideology and is not sheer entertainment. Elkin has views and he has problems. Like so many of his characters, Elkin lives in large part out of obsessions, locked in a pattern that is "justified" only by the judicious use of "taste—the soul's harmless appetite." But is it harmless because everyone shares it, or because it comes to nothing in the face of larger forces? The same two questions are what we should finally ask of any novelist's vision, as well as of his or her style.

NOTES

This essay originally appeared in *Delta* 20 (February 1985): 93-110. Reprinted by permission of *Delta.*

[1]See his "Strange Displacements of the Ordinary." Wilde also has a very sophisticated reading of *The Living End* in his book *Horizons of Assent.*

WORKS CITED

Brown, Marshall. "The Logic of Realism: A Hegelian Approach." *PMLA* 96 (1981): 224-41.

Elkin, Stanley. *Boswell: A Modern Comedy.* New York: Random House, 1964.

———. *The Dick Gibson Show.* New York: Random House, 1971.

———. *The Living End.* New York: Dutton, 1979.

———. "The Making of Ashenden." *Searches and Seizures.* New York: Random House, 1973. 129-88.

LeClair, Thomas. "The Obsessional Fiction of Stanley Elkin." *Contemporary Literature* 16.2 (Spring 1975): 146-62.

Wilde, Alan. " 'Strange Displacements of the Ordinary': Apple, Elkin, Barthelme and the Problem of the Excluded Middle." *boundary 2* 10 (1982): 177-99.

Final Things: More Letters to mzimmer%humanitas @hub.ucsb.edu

Alan Wilde

To: mzimmer%humanitas@hub.ucsb.edu
Subj: rumblings in the seminar

ANOTHER ESSAY TO WRITE. Up to more digital ramblings? I doubt this qualifies as Christmas cheer, but if you're agreeable, I'd like to sort out some preliminary notions and hunches before the holidays and then MLA blot everything else out.* Nothing as elaborate this time as "the novel in the nineties" or "fiction until the turn of the century." Just one writer instead of the whole spectrum of contemporary fiction; one novel, in fact. To be precise, three novellas in the form of a "triptych," as the dust jacket describes it. Though, come to think of it, the notion of the millennium as the boundary of my speculations is just as appropriate in this case, given the fact that the book is a world's-end theodicy—or rather an angry, no-holds-barred inversion of those traditional justifications that try to convince us all's well in the upper reaches of the universe. A parody of *The Divine Comedy,* among other things, that moves from hell to a purgatory of sorts to heaven, and in which, after an exorbitant explanation of His ways of handling humankind (entirely a matter of aesthetics, He announces: "It was all Art. *Because it makes a better story is why.*"), God "annihilate[s] . . . *everything.*"

The book, as you've gathered by now, is Elkin's *The Living End,* and what with God's borscht-belt, traveling-salesman, after-dinner routines and Elkin's own supercharged prose—the thrusting, jabbing language that both enables and rivals God's majesty—it's in every sense of the word a good show. Or so I thought until I taught it this semester and found myself challenged and broadsided from all corners of the room at once. Since the novel has always been surefire until now, it was an altogether strange and

*For an earlier installment of this correspondence, see "The Once and Future Novel: Letters to iwp1muri@ucsbuxa.bitnet," *ANQ* 5 (October 1992): 252-57. The change in E-mail address, noted here in the interests of verisimilitude, reflects a move from Bitnet to the Internet.

unexpected experience to find myself at loggerheads with the class. It went down like a glass of water, one student complained, pinpointing what he saw as its lack of narrative complexity. (Philadelphia water, said another, alluding to the book's scatological texture and Elkin's always unflinching acknowledgment of the body's infirmities and vulnerabilities.) Student #1 had a point, no question (so did #2, as a matter of fact): *The Living End* is a parable after all, and parables are, or pretend to be, relatively simple tales focused not on the complexities of narrative or character but on moral interpretation. True, Elkin's novel is arguably less ambiguous and oblique than the best of the parables we associate with the biblical Jesus. But not completely true. The book's plot—story, actually—resembles one character's description of his trip to heaven: "It was rather like a journey in films—a series of quick cuts, of montage"; and as in the works of so many other contemporary (and, yes, modernist) writers, montage speaks to the world's randomness and contingency. (It's also true, I suppose, that there's a fine line or two between the picaresque, the associative, and the inconsequent; and there's no doubt that, especially in "The Bottom Line," the work's second part, the narrative sags, as Elkin nods on his way from hell to heaven.)

I have to admit too that *The Living End* is less sinuous than "The Bailbondsman," my own favorite among Elkin's works, less outrageous than "The Making of Ashenden" (remember the bear?), the two novellas it asks to be compared with. It's what it shares with them, though, that matters: Elkin's bravura handling of language, which accounts not only for the book's creativity but for what I see as its equivocal ethical stance. But my students weren't happy about the language either. Not that they couldn't appreciate the freewheeling inventiveness or admire the promiscuous, metamorphic transformations of nouns into adjectives, adjectives and nouns into verbs, and so on. But the stylistic overload had all the appeal of a Christmas goose to a gaggle of New Age vegetarians, so the appreciation and the admiration were abstract, grudging: respect due to an old master while on an overly long, foot-killing visit to the museum. Which explains why I've waited until term's end to write to you about the book instead of facing up to it right after we finished batting it around in class. I was so taken aback by the response that I felt the need to ruminate a while.

It's been a strange, exciting, and perplexing semester, one in which I've felt as much my students' student as their teacher; and what I've been trying to puzzle out is what sorts of assumptions they bring to the reading of literature these days. It's certainly the case, as I told you before, that over the last several years I've found students less responsive to metafiction (and the profession as a whole, fortunately, seems to have taken a more worldly turn of late), so this semester I began with three works that are, let's say, divided in their aims: that flirt with rather than embrace the metafictional; that engage the referential as well as the reflexive (even if the notion of reference has less and less to do with any sort of simple mimesis); and that, in their taxonomic impurity, see language as something more than a self-enclosed echo chamber. (Mind you, I don't find anything metafictional about Elkin, but the centrality of language in his fiction in an age that views anything and everything, from cultural attitudes to the author to the self, as constituted in language made it plausible to include him with the others.) In any case, Auster's *City of Glass* generated a fair amount of excitement, if less than in the past. The students found it a bit too self-conscious, too *voulu.* The reservations that Auster generated ratcheted up several notches for Barthelme's *The Dead Father,* which struck them as much too ludic for their taste. (The sixties are over, and not even Camille Paglia is going to bring them back.) And then *The Living End* proved to be the final straw. What they minded was that aspect of the book that has always attracted readers, including me: the foregrounding of language, the fact that Elkin's words so deliberately and relentlessly call attention to themselves.

Hysteria threatened, believe me. It looked as if it was going to be downhill all the way to December. But when we moved on to Marilynne Robinson, Toni Morrison, Louise Erdrich, and Grace Paley, a great weight lifted off the class's collective chest. Oh, did it ever! Robinson carried off most of the honors—*Housekeeping* brought in a totally different literary weather front: oohs and ahs, excitement, awe, not to mention a good deal of defensiveness about my adverse criticisms of the book. Coming cheek by jowl with Elkin, she helped put into perspective the responses I'd gotten to *The Living End,* but in ways that I still find hard to accept. After all, has there ever been a more self-conscious, language-drunk book than *Housekeeping?* I remember with unseemly glee your remark that most people go into a demarol state when they read the book, and lord knows *Housekeep*ers brook no criticism. My class confirmed that in spades: for me, it was like stumbling, without the appropriately reverent attitude toward the master, into a coven of Joyceans. I also remember that Pauline Kael, when she reviewed the movie, remarked on the novel's bag-lady mentality. And I agree. When Ruthie and Sylvie cross the bridge, they move from myth to fairy tale, and suddenly everything that has haunted and preyed on Ruthie is unceremoniously shucked off. A remarkable book in many ways, certainly, and full of some wonderful writing, but also swarming with odd irresolutions and contradictions.

Anyhow, that's not the point. The question is why, as far as the class was concerned, Elkin played frosty moon to Robinson's dazzling sun. Part of the reason, I decided, is that my students are as hungry for complexity as any of the New Critics poststructuralism presumably put into permanent deep freeze. Another part, which may be corollary to the first, concerns their inchoate hunger for spatial form and characterological depth, neither of which Elkin provides. In other words, they're inclined to favor modernist experiments with narrative and character over postmodern attempts to abandon or pulverize them. But the most important part, which I can describe better than explain, has to do with an ideal of decorum (it sounds strange, I know, but no other word comes to mind), a Jamesian sense of what's fit. Robinson's bejeweled prose and overheated speculations are acceptable because they belong to Ruthie as the novel's narrator. *The Living End*'s language, on the other hand, suggests—or suggested to my class—Elkin's bull-in-a-china-shop's disregard for the canons of verisimilitude. Canons? Verisimilitude? Character? Form? Decorum? Has the wheel turned again? Are *différance* and dissemination following metafiction into the gray, subfusc corridors of literary history? Well, fourteen graduate students do not a movement make. Clearly, though, it's going to take some work to make the book feel as exciting and important to today's younger readers as it did to John Irving when he reviewed it for the *New York Times Book Review* in 1979. "A narrative marvel," he said; and the battering I took this term notwithstanding, I agree with that too. Enough for today.

logoff exit

To: mzimmer%humanitas@hub.ucsb.edu
Subj: rhetoric vs ethics

Can't tell you how happy I am that you like *The Living End.* I didn't need another arrow to the head—or heart. But you're right to ask what I mean by the novel's "equivocal ethical stance." That is, you're right that Elkin's overwhelming response to his distant, detached, modernist God is one of scathing fury. I agree completely. How could it be otherwise when the deity presents Himself as petty, vindictive, sadistic, legalistic, and egocentric: "a sucker," as He says of Himself, "for worship." And yet I'd argue that, as we read, something strange and unsettling happens. There we are, confidently following our moral compass, and suddenly the needle goes haywire. Don't you feel, as you read, a certain sympathy—maybe not sympathy, but admiration—for God? Well, maybe not admiration either, but a fascination with the Old Boy (something like what the characters in Barthelme's novel feel for The Dead Father) that translates into a pleasure we experience despite ourselves? After all, who among the book's characters is more energetic, imaginative, creative? And don't the novel's violent linguistic texture, its cascading inventiveness, its transgressive, projective deformations of syntax and diction inevitably ratify God's superabundant gusto? How, if we respond to the one, not to respond to the other? How to find God less extraordinary than the verbal medium that sustains Him and, despite what my class thought, gladdens us? But if that's true, it makes for problems—as it also does when we think about "The Bailbondsman" 's Alexander Main or the eccentric, eponymous protagonist of "Ashenden."

What I'm getting at is that, however genuine his indignation, Elkin can't help favoring the rhetoric of his characters over their acts—even if in the final analysis the rhetoric is *his.* And he knows it. Listen to these altogether remarkable comments from interviews with Jeffrey L. Duncan and Scott

Sanders: "Energy is what counts. . . . Whoever has the better rhetoric is the better man." "I'm attracted to the extreme. . . . I'm attracted to extremes of personality too. . . . I stand in awe of the *outré.* Those characters who are exaggerated seem, to me at least, more vital than the ordinary character, certainly more energetic. It's the energy which engines my work." And this too, about his characters again: "The fact that they may be outrageous or immoral doesn't mean that they're losers. It means that they are simply demonstrating the kind of extravagance—the kind of *heroic* extravagance, if you will—that makes them, in my view, winners." It's easy enough to agree that Elkin's work is an ongoing celebration of the extraordinary, the outré, the nonpareil, the immoderate, the excessive, the outrageous, the extreme (whoa: it's getting to me too!); but to get back to your point, what are we to think then when the totally sympathetic Ellerbee, sent to hell for reasons whose "pettiness signaled across the universe," contemplates "the real McCoy Son of a Bitch God Whose memory Ellerbee would treasure and eternally repudiate forever"?

If you're waiting for answers, they're not coming. I could retreat into the safety of New Critical "tension," and maybe that's the route to go eventually, but on the whole I don't think I'm prepared to do more than acknowledge this particular emblem of the way Elkin responds, with inconsistent consistency, to his world. So let's leave God in His heaven for now. There's another problem that's nagging at me, namely, how to reconcile Elkin's stylistic extravagance with the novel's repeated thematic confirmation of the ordinary. I think this one is more tractable, but since I'm working my ideas out as I go along, I'd better not count chickens just yet. What's undeniable is that virtually every character in the book thinks fondly and longingly of the ordinary at one point or the other—no modernist epiphanies or great moments here as they find themselves recherching *le temps perdu.* And it's just as clear that the ordinary is associated in the characters' minds with the heft, the unassuming solidity, of what they did while alive. So, unlike God, who, with his "thing for heights," is incapable of responding to "just ordinary earth," Jesus, as he says, "loved it there . . . I loved being alive," while the Virgin Mary is seen moments before the world's destruction "savoring the ordinary." There's something in Elkin—if only just something—that reminds me of the modest sense of sufficiency Max Apple developed in stories like "Eskimo Love," the ability to declare, as the narrator of that story does at its close: "It's enough." Or as one of the characters in *The Living End* puts it, "Life was its own gloss." Living over meaning: very Elkinesque. But it's Ellerbee again who most eloquently speaks Elkin's mind: "Let them have everything," he says with angry nostalgia from his whereabouts in hell. "Their pastels back and their blues and their greens, the recollection of gratified thirst, and the transient comfort of a sandwich and beer that had hit the spot, all the retrospective of good weather, a good night's sleep, a good joke, a good tune, a good time, the entire mosaic of small satisfactions that made up a life."

But the question's still hanging there: How does the ethic of small satisfactions sort with the extravagant rhetoric and everything it implies? What bridges the gap between the ordinary and the extraordinary? The clue, I've decided, lies in a passage that's always puzzled me. It's about Quiz, a minor character you may or may not remember. If you don't, he's the hypertense, malicious groundskeeper and janitor who uses a group of unwitting schoolchildren to stage elaborate games intended to convince the nearby-buried Jay Ladlehaus that what he hears (hears, but can't see, of course) are the sounds of a savage war between the Twin Cities. Anyhow, what's at issue is a description of Quiz's hypertension as "merely the obversion of his ensnarement by the real." And the point, I take it, is that, however inventive and resourceful Quiz proves to be in this and his other mean-spirited tauntings of Ladlehaus, he is finally a man without imagination. The *real,* then, far from being synonymous with the ordinary, is meant to suggest, not Ellerbee's transient comforts, but the life-defeating, the pedestrian, the commonplace. Which suggests, in turn, that the real, if it's to have value, needs to be mediated by imagination. Which leads to our further understanding that the novel's ideal is neither Quiz's nuts-and-bolts empiricism, with its distrust of the mysterious and the uncanny, nor God's severe, art-for-art's-sake aesthetic but the ordinary heightened, transfigured, made extraordinary. And that, of course, is precisely where language comes in and where, for now, I'm logging off. It's been a long day, and, like the abominable Quiz, I'm feeling "trade winded, testy."

logoff exit

To: mzimmer%humanitas@hub.ucsb.edu
Subj: the eschatological angel

Happy new year. Five days in New York have helped to make me feel less Quizzical, and the MLA provided an alternative explanation of why my students reacted as they did to Elkin. No doubt it's as risky to generalize on the basis of a handful of meetings as it was to draw conclusions from my seminar, but I can tone down what I decide to keep for the essay later on. Besides, friends who attended different meetings reported a not dissimilar sense of how things went. (Of course, birds of a feather, and so on.) In any case, everything crystallized for me in a forum called "Redrawing the Boundaries," where Marjorie Perloff gave a short extemporaneous talk on "interdisciplinarity," in which she argued that what we had at the moment in the profession was not too much of the interdisciplinary but too little. Critics, she said, had moved back to a pre-New Critical *thematic* approach to literature, and the fashionable boast of cross-pollinating literary texts with, say, economic, social, political, or sociological concerns usually meant that literature was being accorded the same treatment and the same ontological status as newspapers. All transparent content in other words, open for inspection by the unquestioning eye/I—but don't blame Marjorie for my glossing. Skip Gates, who complained about "the periphery determining the center" (the center being literature), said much the same; and between them they managed to suggest the once familiar, now radical notion that there's something literary about literature. Good news, isn't it, to be told for the first time in years that taking account of the formal properties of novels and poems doesn't automatically tar the critic as a reactionary prig or, worse, bigot.

Yes, very cheering, I thought, to watch the worm turning, even doing a little dance. But what, I hear you asking from the other side of the continent, has all of this to do with Elkin and the perplexities I expressed about my students' reactions to him? Well, it goes back to something I talked about a few letters ago. Elkin, along with most so-called postmodern writers, provides none of the solace of Eliot's mythical method. Far from offering "a way of controlling, of ordering, of giving a shape and a significance to the immense panorama of futility and anarchy which is contemporary history" (to resurrect that sounding manifesto of another age), Elkin aims to *reveal* chaos. So no structural consolations, no Woolfian line down the center, no heterocosms that raise us above the fractured world. And if you add to that the absence of psychological depth and complexity (long gone the consolations of James Mason in *The Seventh Veil,* where, thanks to Freud and Rachmaninoff, the tortured intricacies and hidden secrets of the self ultimately resolve themselves into great chordal unities), all the impact of the novel *as literature* depends upon our response to style, to texture, to language—to language as the bottom-line aesthetic principle of *The Living End.* All of which is to wonder, along with Marjorie, whether our primary task as teachers and critics these days isn't to teach students not only the pleasure of the literary text but (with a bit less attention to the intransitiveness of *jouissance*) their responsibilities—their active role in making sense of novels and poems.

I think I've veered off course by at least ninety degrees. That's what five days in NY and more coffee than I ordinarily drink in half a year will do. Sorry about that, and apologies for delaying my thanks. That was way beyond the call of friendship to start rereading the book, even if you've only made it to p. 23 so far. Sharing a Swiss-cheese memory, I understand the compulsion to raid the literary lost-and-found in search of what's slipped out of sight—or mind. But I'm more pleased than guilty, to tell the truth, since you've provided me with a nice way of finally getting the linguistic ball out of the air and through the hoop. I agree that in those opening pages the style is uncharacteristically simple, just as the narrative is unusually lean and rapid. But that's strategy, all very deliberate and calculated. It's on p. 24 that things suddenly become Elkinesque, as Ellerbee, listening to an angel discourse on "thanatopography," accepts the fact that he's in heaven, not dreaming all this. What convinces him is the mushrooming of his vocabulary in ways that allow him first to understand and then to give a name to the "eschatological angel" who is his companion. But the sea change in his vocabulary matters less than its purpose, which Ellerbee is now himself able to identify. "Why do we do that?" the angel of death asks him; and Ellerbee's answer is: "To heighten perception." That's it, the mother lode, the moral center of Elkin's work—and one way of coming to understand where he belongs, or doesn't belong, in the spectrum of contemporary fiction. Because language makes the ordinary extraordinary, his fiction transcends the limits and categories of realism; and because expanding consciousness is by any reckoning a moral enterprise, Elkin's work sheers off from metafiction as well.

I'm going to have to insist on this, underline it, make it central. There's a fascinating moment, a little later in hell, when Ellerbee accidentally backs into Ladlehaus, his murderer's accomplice, who by all rights ought to be unrecognizable to him after all these years. The narrator's comment is: "It was Ellerbee's vocabulary which had recognized him . . . just as it was Ladlehaus's vocabulary which had recognized Ellerbee"—an elegant formulation of the fact that we grasp the world through and thanks to language. But there's more to it: if Elkin's linguistic aim is not to enclose (Eliot's shaping and ordering) but to open out, to create, it's also true that language is the instrument not only of creation but of *self*-creation. What I'm getting at is that the centrality of language for Elkin translates on Ellerbee's less literary level into the affirmation and confirmation of the self. Do you remember Ellerbee's small-satisfactions speech, which I quoted in another letter? It's preceded by this: "He abandoned hope, and with it memory, pity, pride, his projects, the sense he had of injustice—for a while driving off, along with his sense of identity, even his broken recollection of glory." In other words, identity is both valued and assumed, along with memory, pity, pride, and the rest. Now, it's also true that Elkin's view of the self is more existential than essentialist; that his interest in his characters has less to do with what they are than with what they make of themselves; and that the acts that define them are primarily acts of language. But that doesn't change the fact that what centers the book—maybe all of Elkin's fiction—is the need for the self's survival as it interacts with others and the world.

Another taxonomic grace note or two here: if Elkin's structural and characterological strategies set him apart from his modernist predecessors, his focus on the self separates him just as surely from what usually passes for postmodern and poststructuralist belief. The fact is (not that it matters a whole lot), he's hard to *place*. Rereading *The Horse's Mouth* the other day (Cary's hard to place too, come to think of it), I was struck by the resemblances between Elkin and Gulley Jimson but also by the differences. At the risk of conflating real writers and fictional characters in the manner of our last VP, I'd say that Elkin suggests Gulley without the sentiment(ality), without the devotion to solid forms, depth, color, and, most of all, without Gulley's underlying belief in unity: the metaphysical assurance that comes "straight from the stable." Nor are things any neater *within* the contemporary fold. For me, that is, Elkin's another of those who inhabit a literary and moral middle ground between the extremes of God and Quiz, to turn them into emblems (I hope not parodies) of the intransigently, amorally aesthetic and the narrowly, minimally defined realistic. So what to do? My temptation in light of all this is simply to ascribe to him a severely modified humanism—a belief in the capacities but also in the limits of the individual—and to see Elkin himself as the last of that battered tribe: a latter-day, less hopeful Gulley, cultivating his capacity for anger and outrage, showing himself more Orc than Los.

But it's probably best to skip these imperfect comparisons and sad honorifics; and no one wants to hear about the last this or that anyhow, least of all if this manhandling of categories leads slyly to the usual critical sounds and gestures of closure. On the other hand, how exactly do you avoid the swell and swagger of heightened prose when your ears ring with Elkin's rhythms and coinings? How do you avoid the temptation of rising to the rhetorical occasions that he creates, especially when the subject is final things: death, doomsday, heaven, hell, and, as the book ends, the world's destruction? In that perspective the choice, it seems to me, is either rhetoric or silence, which is precisely what makes so splendid the energy, the overload, the zest of Elkin's language; the headlong rush of words, images, catalogs that defies considerations of both form and verisimilitude; the vast imagination of suggestion and implication—all of which justifies the rhetoric in the face of the silence to come, makes it necessary, gives it (as it also gives Cary's novel) its existential meaning. As for me, wisest not to try to compete. Better the computer version of a dying fall . . .

logoff exit

Nemeses and MacGuffins: Paranoia as Focal Metaphor in Stanley Elkin, Joseph Heller, and Thomas Pynchon

D. C. Dougherty

SINCE THE 1960s many influential American writers have constructed important narratives around characters who are explicitly or implicitly paranoid. Critics associate Thomas Pynchon's work with this concept almost as often as with entropy, but several other novelists, especially Stanley Elkin and Joseph Heller, feature characters who are clinically paranoid. The purpose of such "paranoid fictions" is not, however, to represent aberrant psychological states but to explore the metaphoric implications of the condition. For these writers paranoia is an especially effective metaphor for their characters' sense of powerlessness and for the consequent notion that in an apparently random universe one way individual human beings can assert their own meaning or significance is to identify a nemesis, thereby justifying the assumptions that one's life seems to be a "plot" and that whatever happens is the result of a definable cause.

Traditional definitions of paranoia describe a type of mental illness characterized by delusions of persecution. Patients, fantasizing that someone or something is out to get them, believe their misfortunes, real or imagined, result from these fictional adversaries. In the general community paranoia and its symptoms provoke negative associations because the condition is delusional, because paranoid personalities project their problematic self-esteem (whether social, economic, intellectual, or erotic) onto the world around them, and because patients in advanced stages of the condition sometimes view their lives as "plots" in which something or someone manipulates events to frustrate their expectations, hopes, or aspirations. This fantasy of victimization is expressed aphoristically by Pynchon's fourth "Proverb for Paranoids": "*You* hide, they seek."[1] The writers considered here are more interested, however, in the *signification* than in the *pathology* of paranoia. They examine its implications politically (Heller), epistemologically (Pynchon), and psychologically (Elkin).

Of the three, Heller comes closest to a traditional, clinical application of the concept. His masterwork, *Catch-22,* revolves around the notion of victimization by an authoritarian "they," a military bureaucracy that willingly sacrifices individuals in its quest for power. His bleak study of the corporate wasteland, *Something Happened,* is similarly organized around the belief held by success seekers that their every move is watched, analyzed, and evaluated by another "they," corporate decision makers whose favor employees must cultivate.

The very concept of "Catch-22," which significantly adds a compound word rich in paranoid connotations to our collective vocabulary, is so very frightening because it is, in its sinister way, quite reasonable:

> There was only one catch and that was Catch-22, which specified that a concern for one's own safety in the face of dangers that were real and immediate was the process of a rational mind. . . . Orr would be crazy to fly more missions. . . . [B]ut if he didn't want to he was sane and had to. Yossarian was moved very deeply by the *absolute simplicity* of this clause of Catch-22 and . . . its *spinning reasonableness.* There was an *elliptical precision* about its perfect pairs of parts that was graceful and shocking.[2]

This concept and its consequences destroy the lives of human beings who come under its control. By attempting strategies of defiance, as Yossarian does throughout most of the novel, one actually courts being persecuted. On his hit list Cathcart writes "*Yossarian!!!(?)!*" (215) and another colonel calls him "that other dirty son of a bitch we don't like" (79).

It appears, then, that characters in *Catch-22* aren't paranoid at all if their dread of persecution isn't delusional. Still, Yossarian's principal discovery, the one that empowers his eventual decision substantively rather than symbolically to defy the military bureaucracy, establishes Heller's version of paranoia as a metaphor: "Catch-22 *did not exist,* he was positive of that, but it made no difference. What did matter was that everyone *thought it existed,* and that was much worse, for there was *no object or text* to ridicule or refute, to accuse, criticize, attack, amend, hate, revile, spit at, rip to shreds, trample upon, or burn up" (418; emphasis added). Catch-22 gets its power from its being an illusion, something its victims cannot challenge directly—the ultimate Catch-22. Heller's theme is that a bureaucracy can exist as a victimizing institution only because its victims consent to its existence, and their consent is a type of paranoia, a belief that "they" really can conspire to direct our activities.[3]

Generally credited with pioneering the use of paranoia as a literary symbol, Pynchon uses the word frequently and playfully—six "Proverbs for Paranoids" appear in *Gravity's Rainbow* and a rock group emulating the Beatles calls itself "The Paranoids" in *The Crying of Lot 49,* where several minor characters exhibit classic symptoms of delusional paranoia. Pynchon, however, is more ominously obscure than Heller in defining the nemesis. His characters contend epistemologically with the possible existence of an unidentified, perhaps unidentifiable, "them"[4] instead of bureaucratic underachievers.

In *The Crying of Lot 49* Oedipa Maas, trying to execute her ex-lover's will, stumbles onto a chain of implication that suggests the organized existence of a counterculture called Trystero. As contradictory evidence accumulates about this Trystero, Oedipa begins to hope that she is paranoid, that this is all a delusion. Pynchon does not reveal whether she is, so we cannot therefore rule out this option any more than she can. The network of clues throughout the novel, however, suggests that there is a Trystero, but its nature is unknown and its purposes are inscrutable. This is Pynchon's point. Neither Oedipa nor the reader can know what to make of these phenomena, and all the evidence she accumulates continues to work against certainty.

The extraordinarily high frequency of coincidence in Pynchon's fiction suggests that his characters' lives do reduce to "plots." As Oedipa and Lieutenant Slothrop in *Gravity's Rainbow* gather evidence that might lead toward a synthesis, more and contradictory evidence turns up to undermine or contradict any reasonable conclusion. His characters therefore resort to paranoia, or just to hoping they are paranoid, as a means of explaining their lives rationally. In his epistemological approach to the metaphor, then, Pynchon treats paranoia as a "desperate rationality" or an insistence that, if events themselves will not make sense, one can impose logic and consistency on them by transforming their randomness into the consequence of the will of some nemesis.

Although connections between Stanley Elkin and mainstream postmodern writers like Heller and Pynchon have not been extensively discussed in critical journals, Elkin deploys the paranoia metaphor frequently and in a comparable way. Whereas Pynchon treats it epistemologically, in that his characters resort to paranoia to explain inconsistencies and coincidences in the external world, Elkin invests subtle psychological meaning in the metaphor, in that his characters often develop paranoid pathologies to assure themselves that they have individual worth or a "destiny." As Elkin said in an interview, most of us who progress psychologically beyond the child's playground stage don't really believe we have enemies.[5] On the other hand, for children, and for adults who remain childlike, identity and ego can be reinforced if a person can define his importance by establishing that someone or some group considers him or her significant enough to identify as an enemy.

Therefore, paranoia operates as a signifying motif in Elkin's work and as a complement to Pynchon's and Heller's uses of this key postmodernist metaphor. His characters, usually obsessive types who throw themselves into a vocation or a role to assert their identity, often become convinced that they are persecuted, that someone has singled them out for victimization. This delusion gives them a sense of importance, an illusion and conviction that their lives matter. This theme is especially central to *Boswell: A Modern Comedy, The Dick Gibson Show,* and *The MacGuffin.*

James Boswell, modeled loosely on Dr. Johnson's biographer, cultivates celebrities' attention to give his life significance. This is itself an implicitly paranoid fixation, for James is unable to locate an intrinsic worth in his existence, so his "campaigns" to make celebrities take notice of him give him an opportunity to validate his self-worth by forcing influential people to pay attention to him.

An early episode suggests the outlines of Elkin's version of paranoia as metaphor. Boswell's professional wrestling career ends when he fills in as adversary for one John Sallow. Rumor has it that Sallow once killed a man in the ring, and James's paranoid imagination eventually invests Sallow with the attributes of his alias, "The Grim Reaper." He enters the contest, which he has contracted to lose, believing this is the ultimate mythic confrontation: "Come on, Sallow, old enemy, Boswell the Big goes against the Angel of Death to save the world. . . . I would save it anyway, anonymously, nom de plumely. In St. Louis I would whip death's old ass."[6] Boswell has elevated this fixed wrestling match into an archetypal confrontation in which he takes on humanity's archenemy to save the world, a classic savior complex associated with certain paranoid delusions. He has absurdly transformed a professional wrestler into the personification of humanity's common enemy to give his work and life cosmic significance.

Elkin both expands and intensifies his version of paranoia as metaphor in *The Dick Gibson Show,* a novel about a radio announcer who, like Boswell, has many professional identities but no authentic private self. Although he uses several occupational aliases, Dick's birth name is never disclosed: "When Dick Gibson was a little boy he was not Dick Gibson."[7] His identity is formed by his professional affiliation with radio.

Any media personality must cultivate the public's interest, but Elkin's hero wants, really psychologically needs, to achieve individual validation as a public persona. Fame and greatness in the entertainment industry are, however, transitory. This instability results in Gibson's fundamentally paranoid effort to establish his self-worth by identifying a "nemesis." He summarizes his disappointed aspirations this way to a one-night stand: "That I would even have *enemies.* . . . Is there a *nemesis* in the house? . . . [T]hat I'd have *enemies* like Dorothy had the Witch of the West. . . . That I'd have this goal, you see, but that I'd be *thwarted* at every turn. . . . But that I'd always bounce back" (270; emphasis added). At this point in his career, when he has successfully established himself as a pre-Larry King call-in show host, Dick confesses disappointment that his life is *not* a plot, that he has not made enemies who, by identifying him as worthy of their hostility, would validate or warrant his importance.

For Gibson, and to a lesser degree for the heroes of *Boswell,* "The Bailbondsman," and *The Rabbi of Lud,* paranoia is an illusory means of measuring and rationalizing one's self-worth in direct proportion to the importance one can compel others to attach to his or her life. Because he identifies himself with an industry that rewards one's ability to create a good impression in others' minds, Gibson views his worth primarily in the notice he can make his public, especially his employers, take of him. Professional concerns give way to paranoia when Gibson decides that, if he cannot force others to accept him as a great man, he will cultivate their enmity. When that notice is not forthcoming, he actually invents their enmity.

This pattern organizes three of the novel's key episodes. Early in his career Gibson, calling himself Marshall Maine, broadcasts at a Nebraska station owned by the Credenza family. He initially tries to win the family's approval, often fudging professional standards to curry favor with these brokers of power and respectability. He searches the wire services for human interest stories they'll like, occasionally making these up when the wire services don't provide them, and selects music to flatter their tastes. These efforts add up to his adopting a flunky's role to cultivate powerful patrons, much as Boswell does.

His subsequent efforts illustrate Elkin's characteristic variation on the paranoia metaphor. When their approval doesn't come, he attempts more drastic measures to get their attention. He adopts tones they won't approve while reporting the news and plays records they probably won't like. When this also fails to provoke a response, he makes up gossip about family members, leaving the microphone open so that his slanders will travel over the airwaves. If he cannot persuade them to accept him, Dick intends to make them acknowledge his importance by chastising him. At first he hopes to "*force a confrontation,* convinced that only through a *showdown* could he ever hope to *negotiate his brotherhood* with the Credenzas" (34; emphasis added). His hope that a confrontation (leading to negotiation) will result in reconciliation (establishing parity) ends when the brothers visit and threaten him, and he absurdly expects them to electrocute him. His violent death would vindicate his importance; he would matter enough that an influential nemesis would choose to destroy him.

This is, however, a self-aggrandizing fantasy; the "nemesis" has become so utterly indifferent to him that family members have stopped listening to the station. Yet recounting the event from the perspective of many years later, Gibson claims exclusive blame for putting the station out of business. His paranoia, which in this case compensates for a frustrated desire to make others grant his life significance by elevating him to the status of an enemy, leads to a complicating delusion that magnifies the importance of his actions by perpetuating the illusion that he has had a definitive impact on his environment.

Gibson's paranoia becomes even more crucial in the novel's most enigmatic episode, the broadcast of a panel show from Hartford several years after the Nebraska adventure. This episode mixes realism and fantasy to such a degree that it is finally impossible to ascertain exactly where realistic narrative ends and paranoid projection begins.[8] Literally, the guests on Gibson's show include four community members who appear frequently to promote their special interests and a guest, Dr. Edmond Behr-Bleibtreau, who is reported to specialize in "mind over matter" and to use his "knowledge of psychology in unusual, if unspecified, ways" (137). But the panelists behave unexpectedly. Instead of a discussion, they engage in long monologues, each confessing a shameful secret from his or her past, then lapsing into catatonic silence. Unable either to control or to account for the content (usually vulgar and self-incriminating) or tone (confessional monologue) of his ordinarily predictable panelists, Dick struggles to discover a rational explanation for their conduct.

In this episode Elkin's handling of paranoia is closer to Pynchon's epistemological approach than it has been in previous novels, in that he too explores paranoia as a metaphor for the impulse to impose rationality on an irrational situation. Trying to make sense of this inexplicable breach of radio decorum, Gibson seizes upon Behr-Bleibtreau as the cause of his guests' revelations, therefore as his show's "enemy." As the situation becomes progressively lunatic, Gibson becomes firmly convinced that his panelists become catatonic because Behr-Bleibtreau literally steals their voices. This interpretation evolves into delusional paranoia when he suspects that Behr-Bleibtreau intends to steal Dick's voice and that the shrink actually summons a demon, Sordino, to assist him. This is self-aggrandizing as well as delusional; in Dick's fantasy Behr-Bleibtreau must try to take Dick's voice because, after all, Dick's the star of this show and to steal everyone else's voice without taking his would be to deny his importance. Moreover, the projection enables him to defeat not only Behr-Bleibtreau but the forces of darkness as well (as Boswell hoped to "whip death's old ass") while protecting his symbolic self, his voice.

Years later, a successful Gibson is frustrated that his life has not come to the denouement of its "plot" because still no adequate nemesis has yet appeared. When his amiable talk show, the "Night Letters," makes a sudden shift toward a morbid and confessional mode, Dick looks once more to paranoia to explain the random, unexpected turn toward solipsism and the sudden emphasis on human misery. Recalling the Hartford show, he again suspects that some "enemy" is responsible for this challenge to his ideal, evolved format. He believes that callers may be Dr. Behr-Bleibtreau disguising his voice or that the psychiatrist may be influencing certain callers to telephone the show. At a picnic the station throws for the show's regular listeners, Dick absurdly expects Behr-Bleibtreau to try to assassinate him (as he expected the Credenzas to kill him in Nebraska). He enacts a clichéd hero's pose by standing on a pitcher's mound at the park in which the picnic is held and giving the assassin an easy target.

Is this a suicidal, fatalistic gesture, or is it a logical extension of Dick's brand of paranoia? It is suicidal insofar as Dick genuinely believes in his private myth of Behr-Bleibtreau as the enemy who by opposing him gives his life signification. But the gesture is also a logical consequence of Dick's paranoia. He believes so thoroughly in his destiny as a great man that he is willing to court death, if necessary fantasizing the assailant who will slay him, to energize his life as a meaningful plot. If he's worth assassinating (a fate of important people—ordinary folks are murdered), his life must mean something.

Recently with *The MacGuffin* Elkin has revitalized this motif, characters who seek to discover rational explanations for potentially random events. Robert Druff's creating the MacGuffin is a direct result of his paranoia, which Elkin explicitly and magnificently defines as "all the compounding interest on disappointment, the wear and tear of ambition."[9] No longer young, Druff has, like Jerry Goldkorn in *The Rabbi of Lud,* settled for less than a fully engaged life. With a history of health problems that would make any physician's accountant rejoice, he fears that he may not last another decade and regrets that he has not done all he might have with his life. He has been neither a scrupulously honest nor a successfully crooked politician! His chauffeur tells him, "you could have been a contender" (16), and this cliché haunts him throughout the two days that make up the novel.

This revelation that he could have been a contender sets Druff wondering what his life might have been. He realizes that because of his "bland ambition" (254—a pun on the title of a book by Watergate conspirator John Dean, who certainly knew something about paranoia), he may have settled for second-best in his career and his life. The MacGuffin, a concept derived from the coincidental circumstances energizing most Hitchcock films, is a way to get his life reorganized, to set it into motion as a new and vital plot. If someone considers Druff significant enough to spy on him, as he suspects his chauffeurs of doing, or especially to conspire against him, then he must matter. And just as his amorous career seems to have ended, a buyer named Meg Glorio (!) shows up at a hangout for politicos, then puts the Commissioner back into commission. Can such events be serendipity? Especially when nothing in Meg's apartment seems to be her own; when it's full of Oriental rugs, the very things the late Su'ad, around whose possible murder the novel turns, smuggled; and when a gentleman caller turns out to be a banker who just hours ago offered Druff a bribe to look the other way on the Su'ad business. Can anyone blame Druff for wondering if there isn't more coincidence to this than a body can stand?

A MacGuffin for the filmmaker is a plot instrument, something that sets events into motion. For Elkin it is first a metaphor for an existential condition and eventually an imagined presence willed into quasi-existence by Robert Druff. Even its attributes seem contradictory. At one moment, the MacGuffin is a guardian angel (229), at another a wolf "howling at the door" (253). When he cannot locate his MacGuffin, Druff invokes it; but later, when he locks it outside, he feels "cozy" without it.

The MacGuffin is much more than a device to get Elkin's plot into motion. Druff, hoping to grasp at some meaning in the twilight of his political career, such as it has been, needs his MacGuffin to energize his life, to give it meaning. He even realizes as the novel ends that he and his MacGuffin are codependent and that MacGuffin's role is to give order and symmetry to his random experience: "If MacGuffin was the *principle of structure* to Druff, of *pattern* and shading, and all the latent *architecture* of the old man's life, what was Druff to MacGuffin? Why, raw material" (283; emphasis added).

Elkin has been intrigued by paranoia as a literary and cultural metaphor since the 1960s, but his focus has been on the psychological and compensatory implications of the metaphor, whereas Heller has been concerned with politics and Pynchon with epistemology. With Heller, Pynchon, and possibly Don DeLillo and Philip Roth, Elkin articulates a uniquely postmodernist hypothesis that paranoia is, for novelists of the final decades of our century, a powerful and effective metaphor for the lost aspirations and missed opportunities of people in search of rational meaning in their lives.

NOTES

[1]Thomas Pynchon, *Gravity's Rainbow* (New York: Viking, 1973), 262.

[2]Joseph Heller, *Catch-22* (1961; New York: Dell, 1979), 47 (emphasis added); hereafter cited parenthetically.

[3]Perhaps this is Heller's main theme, but its external manifestations change. In *Something Happened* employees invest power in a corporate bureaucracy that exerts authority because of their fear and subservience. In *Good as Gold* similar bureaucratic power is distributed among the family, the federal government, and the university system. Even the history of art and culture could be called conspiratorial in *God Knows* (1984; David's God is a paranoid's delight) and *Picture This* (1988).

[4]Although this is the subject of many studies of Pynchon, two approaches challenging mine should be noted. Scott Sanders, "Pynchon's Paranoid History," in *Mindful Pleasures: Essays on Thomas Pynchon,* ed. George Levine and David Leverenz (Boston: Little, Brown, 1976), 139-59, drawing on Richard Hofstadter's "paranoid theory" of American culture, contends that "paranoia is a secular form of the Puritan consciousness" (144) with its emphasis on power, authority, and a punitive other. By contrast John Johnson, "Toward the Schizo-Text: Paranoia as Semiotic Regime in Thomas Pynchon's *The Crying of Lot 49,*" in *New Essays on "The Crying of Lot 49,"* ed. Patrick O'Donnell (New York: Cambridge Univ. Press, 1991), 47-78, drawing on semiotic theory, argues that both Oedipa and the reader are trapped in a despotic semiotic regime characterized by indeterminacy or unknowability.

[5]The conversation occurred in February 1989; relevant portions appear in my "A Conversation with Stanley Elkin," *Literary Review* 34.2 (Winter 1991): 175-95.

[6]*Boswell: A Modern Comedy* (New York: Random House, 1964), 99; hereafter cited parenthetically. In an interview Elkin called this episode "phony allegory" and "a parody of Boswell's obsession with death." See Doris Bargen, "Appendix: An Interview," *The Fiction of Stanley Elkin* (Frankfurt: Lang, 1980), 233. Significantly, Elkin's first treatment of paranoia as metaphor antedates any novel associated explicitly with the concept except *Catch-22.*

[7]*The Dick Gibson Show* (New York: Random House, 1971), 3; hereafter cited parenthetically. Valuable analysis, although not directed at the paranoia motif, appears in Peter J. Bailey, *Reading Stanley Elkin* (Urbana: Univ. of Illinois Press, 1985), 53-98; and Bargen, especially pp 152-62.

[8]This, of course, implicates the reader in the paranoid crisis of determining what is real and what isn't—Pynchon doesn't have exclusive claim on the "implicating-

the-reader-as-paranoid" motif. The episode is discussed more fully in my *Elkin,* chapter 4, where it's compared with the "nighttown" or "Circe" episode of Joyce's *Ulysses.* Although Elkin's verbal techniques are often compared with Joyce's (an association he emphatically minimizes), so far as I know no other attempt to demonstrate extended literary influence exists.

[9]*The MacGuffin* (New York: Simon & Schuster, 1991), 19; hereafter cited parenthetically. While he was writing the novel, Elkin told me Druff "finds it fascinating to have a MacGuffin, something to energize him, to organize his life as a plot" ("Conversation with Elkin," 187; see also pp. 187-88 for his comments on Hitchcock's influence).

The Escape from the Curse of History in Stanley Elkin's George Mills

Peter G. Christensen

STANLEY ELKIN CONSIDERS *George Mills* his greatest achievement. He once taught a course in which students read both *George Mills* and *Bleak House.* At the end of the semester they had "smarter" things to say about their teacher's magnum opus than about Dickens's masterpiece.[1] I would like to know what they said, since scholarly critics are in such disagreement, particularly about the meaning of the sermon at the end of the novel. The last George Mills declares that there has been an enchantment rather than a curse on the family over the past thousand years. He also denies that he has been saved and declares that he has experienced no grace. Consequently, we are forced to reconsider all the previous action and revise our estimation of the novel. What is the reality status of the curse that disappears at the end, indeed, which never had any power at all? Was it real or just a psychological illusion? After all, Elkin, who believes in the "myth of progress," also stated that *George Mills* "is about a man who has been stuck for a thousand years in a myth."[2] Is the curse a myth?

Mills confesses in the key passage of his sermon:

> "I was kidding you," he said. "I ain't saved. I spent my life like there was a hole in my pocket, and the meaning of life is to live long enough to find something out or to do something well. It ain't just to put up with it.
>
> "I'll tell you something else," he said. "It wasn't a curse," he said, into his text now, "it was a spell, an enchantment, a thousand years of Sleeping Beauty, a thousand years of living on the dole.
>
> "Hell, I ain't saved," he said, oddly cheered. "Being tired isn't saved, sucking up isn't grace."[3]

The narrator goes on to tell us that "he stood there, in what grace he had, relieved of history as an amnesiac" (508). This conclusion seems peculiar since we would anticipate finding the word *spell* here, not *history.* The question arises, does Elkin see belief in the curse as an enchantment, that is, a type of self-fulfilling prophecy, or is history itself the enchantment we must refuse to accept?

There is a concrete element to the curse: history itself is the curse we need to reject. In other words, the thousand-year sleep does not come from believing in something imaginary. After indicating that this theme has been only partially pointed out in the previous criticism, I will show how comments made by Elkin during interviews offer the key to this interpretation. After reading the final scene, I will move back through some important passages from the other sections of the novel, indicating how Elkin enjoins us not to invest our emotions in trying to reach historical understanding or in hoping for historical progress.

The best reading of the novel is found in David C. Dougherty's 1991 book on Elkin, for he realizes the importance of renunciation in the sermon scene. He gives his estimate of the last Mills:

> He has ended the curse. His efforts to end it for himself fail, but his own grace is the knowledge that the Mills life is not exclusive to Millses and that one individual can make a difference by refusing to contribute to history. . . .
>
> *George Mills* is Elkin's meditation on how history can entrap individuals but not without their consent. . . . Even [Mills's] limited victory over the curse is what he does not do (procreate) rather than what he does (ameliorate).

For Dougherty, Elkin "argues that human freedom, while limited by circumstance, has as much to do with what we make of our lives as destiny or fate."[4] The triumph of the last Mills stems from his refusing to have children. However, this insight is somewhat obscured by Dougherty's belief that the curse is more concerned with class oppression in history than with the unimportance of history itself.

Peter J. Bailey's reading suggests that rather than an epiphany about renunciation, we have a confession of the need for belief in the unproven or unprovable. Bailey says that Mills knows that the possibility that he has a sister who ends the curse is a small one and that the hero is just putting his hope on a long shot.

> The idea of a sister is padding, then—it is a deliberately assumed form of protection against reality's splinters, against the mind-poisoning possibility that the doom has not been cancelled, that the fate will be lifted. Mills's embracing of this illusion unites him with the members of the congregation he is addressing, who place their faith, as he does, in some *deus ex machina* that will intervene to lift them out of the lower-middle class.[5]

This view appears to proceed from the assumption that the curse is real, and given the unknowableness of the world, a person who places faith in religious things unseen is making a reasonable choice. Bailey is right in showing that the curse is not canceled by the appearance of a woman looking like Mills's sister, but I would say that the grace she represents is connected not only with religion but also with the utility of historical amnesia.

In his 1985 article on *George Mills* Maurice Couturier argues that the last scene indicates the novel's message of social solidarity. George Mills finally says something for his own sake rather than for the sake of somebody higher on the social ladder, as his ancestors did. Mills is "an ectoplasm who starts to speak, to communicate, who finally experiences the joy of cooperation."[6] I would suggest that this new-found social solidarity comes not from shaking off oppression but from living on a level of existence withdrawn from the lure to become like your oppressors.

Thus we have proposals that Elkin is promoting the need for renunciation, spiritual faith, or human solidarity. We are looking at the same elephant from three sides. Let us turn to the interview material to see if Elkin reveals some clues to his overall intentions. Elkin has claimed that he is "not a 'thinker,' "[7] thus we have no formal exposition of the philosophy behind the novel. When David C. Dougherty asked Elkin if Mills's feeling saved has anything to do with his refusal to propagate the family line, Elkin responded by casting doubt on the validity of Dougherty's thesis:

> That's incidental. The only way to break the curse is not to have any more male children. One way to get outside history. [He] gives a sermon. . . . All he has to tell these people is that the meaning of life is to know something, or to live long enough to do something well. He means that. And he doesn't know *anything.* He doesn't understand what those symbols on a package of cigarettes, the universal product code, mean. And he doesn't do anything well. Yet, there's a kind of leap of, not faith, but of brotherhood, at the end of the book. (185)

According to Elkin, Mills developed the belief that he had grace just as a way to "turn off" his wife when she was "coming on to him." This is no more than a conning; it is "instantaneous bogus." However, he then begins to feel that there is a "kind of grace never to expect anything" (Dougherty 184). We must pick up the subtext here and realize that renunciation of having children is only a part of the larger refusal of expecting anything from the march of history.

Although the ending of the novel may appear to some readers to suggest that the curse was unreal, that is, psychological only, such a view leads to a complete misinterpretation of the novel. The reality of the curse is suggested in the interviews. Elkin told Richard B. Sale that the reader must "accept the premise that somehow all the Millses are superintelligent but yet never get anywhere because of several reasons, one being the curse." Elkin recognizes the problem: If the Millses are so smart, why do they not escape from the lower classes? He states: "So sometimes it gets the novel in trouble to have the characters superintelligent when they have no credentials for their superintelligence. I hope I'm covered by the curse, and since these people just waft, like things in aspic, into their own history, I hope I'm covered by that, too."[8] It would seem that something about the curse must be tangible; otherwise it would make little sense to think of the unsuccessful Mills men as superintelligent. We should accept Elkin's words to Jay Clayton in a similar vein. In this interview Elkin stressed the idea that each Mills son is "totally different" from his father; "they each try to break the pattern, and they all fail." They are "furious at the preceding generation of Millses that got them into this."[9] The sense of struggle enforces the idea that these are not men who suffer primarily because they mistakenly take a family legend to be a real curse.

In a discussion with Marc Chénetier, Elkin apparently endorses the idea that the curse is a type of political oppression. Chénetier asked Elkin to compare whatever interest he had in history to his obvious lack of interest in politics: "[*George Mills*] is a manufactured history, something I invent, and to the extent that *George Mills* is political—and I don't think it is particularly political—it's merely a matter of *us . . . them.* I guess that's the essence of all political thought. *Them* oppresses *us. Them* oppresses Mills and his people."[10] Here there is no suggestion that the Millses are complicit with their own failure to achieve. It would be a mistake to think that the message of the novel is about "us against them" in the world rather than the limitations of politics itself. The model of political repression runs on simple binaries which offer nothing as rich as the activities of daily life.

Later in the interview with Chénetier, Elkin indirectly offers a way to understand how to escape politics, oppression, and the curse:

> . . . I think that regularity and the dependable, the good, the true and the beautiful, I think that the ordinary and the quotidian are the only things that count in life. Glamour is attractive but it can kill you. It can kill you faster than cigarettes. What can't kill you is routine, what can't do you harm is keeping your nose clean, what can't ever hurt you is doing whatever people tell you to do, minding your own business, minding the story, minding the conventional wisdom and only in your head giving in to the imagination. (29)

When Chénetier asked if there is a part of routine that "can dull to death," Elkin responded, "Yes, I suppose there is" (29), but Chénetier did not follow this line of inquiry, as Elkin obviously wanted to defend routine. Considering that the Millses got stuck in a routine, except for numbers I and XLIII, and that the latest protagonist is trying to escape from their legacy or example, this defense of the quotidian seems puzzling, perhaps even contrary to Mills's injunction in his sermon that we ought not "just to put up with it" (508). In effect, however, we should not put up with what the upper classes dish out. We should develop our own routines that leave them out entirely so that we are not exposed to the lure of historical progress.

In order to give credence to Elkin's view of his own work in the interviews, we must offer a new interpretation of the curse, grace, and history in the last scene. The curse on the Millses is their belief that any true liberation comes from engagement in historical forces that have the surface appeal of affording a potentially better life. History is the curse because it cannot deliver what it promises; only a life of pure interiority as awareness of what is lasting and separable from specific historical manifestations can ultimately offer grace to the individual in this world. In this view faith in messianic Marxism, relevant here because it might appeal to people like the Mills men, would be the most blatantly stupid example of subscribing to a historical curse.

The curse which is exposed as a fraud in the last scene is not a curse of the rich on the poor but rather the "spell" that makes us think that our human needs can be fulfilled in historical progress, evolutionary or revolutionary. And indeed, although the general standard of living has been rising in the Western world since the First Crusade, we have seen that the "thousand years of living on the dole" (508) does not represent a refusal to take action toward a better life but the ill-advised willingness to accept the little bits of hope that ultimately get worn down in your fingers without a trace.

Consequently, the refusal to have children becomes a reasonable philosophical position for those Millses who have contemplated it as a means of escaping from the curse. We should remember Elkin in an interview noted that Mills created the idea that he was saved when he refused to have sex with his wife. This refusal of potential generation is linked with grace, the grace to deny parental illusions. Parents are always hoping for a better world for their children, but such hopes are misguided, denying the realization that we must transform the world around us by an active advance to pure interiority. Refusing to procreate means much more than symbolically calling an end to history; it is the honest recognition that we have no reason to hope that historical change will ameliorate life.

Thus when Mills speaks in his sermon that "being saved" is not just putting up with things, we are being told not to wait for external improvements in our circumstances but rather to tend our own gardens. Contrary to the reader's first suspicion, grace is not what one receives when the curse is over. We do not "find" grace because that would require some postulated external force to lift the veil of historical thinking. No, grace itself is the lifter of the curse/spell of historical thinking. Grace comes for Mills from making the leap of faith that he has a sister with a Florida accent from the surely inconclusive and probably preposterous premise that the existence of such a woman without an accent guarantees the existence of one with an accent. We are not dealing with a hunch that may reveal the truth in the absence of documented evidence, as is the case with Quentin and Shreve in *Absalom, Absalom!* but with a lie which is better than truth because it is judged on the basis of its consequences, not its correspondence to reality. Thus Mills can rewrite his story of the Depression years of his family and stand "in what grace he had, relieved of history as an amnesiac" (508). The ending reminds us somewhat of the last scene of Jean Anouilh's *Traveler without Luggage* where amnesia provides Gaston, the hero, with the opportunity to reject his former self and create a new (albeit literally "false") family.

Such an adversarial attitude toward history is not surprising from a novelist who told Doris Bargen that, despite exceptions such as Richard Henry Dana's *Two Years before the Mast,* "literature doesn't really change the world." According to Elkin, "It's too bad, but unfortunately, the writer is—at least the fiction writer—a relatively impotent fellow. Let him stick to his last. And his last is the realm of the imagination, the realm of style, the realm of trying to amuse people, not improve them."[11] The writer should stick to the only world that he has control of—the world of words—and avoid trying to influence history for the better. The writer's situation parallels that of Mills, who can gain control of his world by closing his eyes to historical events as much as possible and concentrating on the wisdom of living by means of the proper focusing of thoughts.

Elkin allows himself to rewrite the history of the Depression, granting Mills's mother a child whom for historical circumstances she could not afford and whose prenatal health was jeopardized by lack of money for nourishing food. We had previously been relieved of the eras of Godfrey of Bouillon and Mahmud II by Elkin's nonsatirical, philosophical trashing of history. Some readers may think that Elkin is satirizing the First Crusade by showing unheroic actions behind the scenes—a knight and less-than-squire who end up in the Polish salt mines. However, Elkin maintains that he is not a satirist.[12] Instead, his concern is much deeper: to give us a First Crusade in which traditional historical causality has been removed. The "fuzzy spiritual politics of Christianity" do not survive beyond the single phrase that dismisses them, and what we have instead to provoke the journey of Guillalume and Mills is not religious feeling or political opportunism but just a bored nobleman's desire to work a "great joke on Godfrey [of Bouillon] and his envoy" (Elkin 2). Elkin writes: "(This all by oral tradition of course, the hand-me-down history of a millennium of Mills raconteurs, impossible to check, particularly the motives of the lord, his pop. But what else could it be? . . . What George thought now was that Mills must have had it from Guillalume himself" (2-3). History itself is the joke, a sicker kind than the one worked by Guillalume's father. At least the familial joke is part of the eternal world of parents humiliating their children—something we can see through and a behavior we can try to avoid.

The desire to find meaning in history is also exposed to ridicule in Elkin's treatment of the Auspicious Incident, the name given to the massacre of the Janissaries under the order of Mahmud II in June 1826 as part of his Westernization policy. In *George Mills* this event is rewritten not only to throw out the accepted historical motivation but to replace it with the personal. The bloody event is treated as the outcome of a series of blunders involving the apolitical and uncomprehending Mills:

> So they were feeling pretty good, Mills and Bufesqueu. Splendid, in fact. Two reluctant recruits who not only had conquered a major world capital but in the act of conquering it had turned round and conquered by way of ricochet the very force in whose name they had done it. And if five thousand men had died in the Sultan's surprise bombardment—if, indeed, a week after the event, perhaps a couple of hundred of their former comrades were still smoldering—it was nothing either of the condemned men cared to take on his conscience. (405)

In this version of the Auspicious Incident the Sultan is angered by the overturned soup kettles of the Janissaries, and rumors are spread about an incendiary. One might argue that the ahistorical emotion of rage stands in for political motivation here, but in this universe the historical motivation is just a veil behind which the nonideological truth of the event as a personal, stupid rage lies.

Once we understand the importance of escaping the curse of historical thinking, we can see the arrangement of the five sections of the novel as steps on the way to that realization. In 1097 (part 1) the Millses are cursed never to understand what is going on behind the scenes. In Florida in the 1930s (part 2) we have a glimmer of a better world where the ego does not exist, and the striving for material improvement is subjected to scrutiny. Our desire for this egoless world is strengthened when we learn the dying Judith's mantra in the 1970s (part 3). The role of Mills in the slaughter of the Janissaries in 1826 shows that action (ego) will provide no escape (part 4). Finally, the sermon in 1980/the present affords us the final revelation to let go of history.

The idea of history as veil is specifically introduced in the first extended mention of the curse:

> So he knew his life and, dimly, the lives of his progeny, knew that all men are the founders of their lines, was reconciled, however uneasily, to what seemed to him his excellent educated guess about his fate— to be first among little guys, little men: God's blue collar worker. To serve, to travel for others; to see much of the world without in the least knowing what stood behind whatever had been left outside, up front, there for all his furlough'd, shore-leav'd fellows—the waterfront bars and strange hoosegows and chief points of interest, all its—the world's—Tours Eiffel and Empire State Buildings, all its Chinatowns and interesting cathedrals. (12)

The reader might first think that "what stood behind" was the historical cause for the phenomena he sees, especially as we are told that the Mills men never "learn the language or the customs" (13). The Millses are "history's not even peeping Toms" (13). On reflection, we realize that they are cursed not to have the insight to recognize history as the Emperor's new clothes. They just follow in the tracks of those who claim to know where history is leading, thus ending up "in the trenches and foxholes of French or Indo-Chinese or Korean earth itself, or cooped up in Japanese and German and Holy Roman Empire and Hanseatic prison camps" (12-13). Without the historical ideologies masking barbarism, we might better understand the world than the Mills men do.

The "tapestry condition" takes an insidious hold over the first George Mills because it gives undue representation to external historical oppression and blocks us from interior freedom. The problem is not that some people are aristocrats and some people stable boys but that we are tricked into thinking that equalizing the class structure will make us better people. Once Mills starts to act like a proletarian awaking from oppression, Elkin tells us that human problems are not solved by this kind of revolt:

> Humiliated, his life proscribed and red-lined from the beginning, and angry now, heavily caused as an underdeveloped nation or a leftist history of legitimate beef, no longer soft-soaped by life, and suddenly frightened too, frightened beyond immediate threat, frightened to the bone, scared right down to hope itself.
>
> He knew he had to escape. Not because he thought things would be different elsewhere—he knew they wouldn't—but because he needed comfort and even his own old turf would do. (Nor did he care about Guillalume now, whose people had perpetrated the tapestry against him.) (29)

Plucky George Mills survives because he reacts on a bodily level of escaping death, not because he thinks that there is less external oppression somewhere else. We are asked to take the situation across history: even if we are citizens of the underdeveloped nation exploited by capitalism and imperialism, we must put our oppressor out of mind as someone in control rather than stick to a revolutionary course that only reminds us at all points that the imperialist still determines what we think.

Later, in the Polish salt mine Mills is able to resist oppression not by revolting but by concentrating on the most animal activities:

> Law proscribed his life like those, to him, mysterious rules of curteisie—the knight's complex code, the squire's. One had almost to be a very musician of citizenship. It was safest to sleep (though one could not oversleep), safest to take one's meals silently in the mess, safest to crap (though one's bowels were subject to salt inspections), to pee (encouraged as an evidence that one was not pilfering salt), safest finally to be about the merely physical business of one's person. (33)

Lost in the Poles' web of customs, strange rules, and taboos, Mills's way out can only be through the universal and the egoless, the common functions common to people despite the inherited weight of historical traditions.

Unfortunately, the first George Mills does not have the religious devotion to reinforce his turning from the world of historical events. When he escapes, he puts together a sermon that only parodies the idea of reverence. He exhorts the Cossacks who threaten his life, "He [God] wants you to eat nuts and boil your grasses for soup" (40). Then Mills travels around Eastern Europe, performing a "mumbo-jumbo of condimental transubstantiation" (42) with his salt tricks. Ultimately he gets to go home because he has escaped history with Guillalume thanks to the "wrong turn" near the Rhine, whereas those who actually entered history, Guillalume's brothers, not surprisingly, are all killed.

In the second section of the novel it is Wickland's long conversation with twelve-year-old George about the family curse that provides the key thematic material about history. Wickland speculates on Mills's mother's attempt to escape the curse of her husband's family and talks about the married couple's hope of having a daughter. Wickland talks about George as a "myth victim" in a way that suggests at first that the curse is really just a fantasy on the part of the Mills men that there is a curse. Wickland makes specific comparisons between young George's father and Oedipus:

"That's why, squeamish as he was, he hid out in basements and cheerfully shouldered other people's garbage—to subdue allure and retract hope. He was a victim of myth and handled himself as other myth victims have, finding his solutions in amateur and immediate expediency, rarely reading between the lines, which is where fate always has its way with you. Told, say, that he would murder his father and marry his mother, he would quit Corinth; or that no man born of woman could harm him, he would confidently chum even his enemies." (173)

The use of *myth* in this conversation is ambiguous, and it reminds us of Elkin's own use of it in his conversation with Joyce Renwick.[13] Does *myth* here take on the meaning of nonlogical thought and mystification, or are we supposed to believe that there was a supernatural curse beyond Mills Sr.'s control?

Wickland eventually indicates that for him *myth* means false belief. He says that George's father believed that bad luck would kill Nancy. When George intervenes, apparently to suggest that this idea makes no sense, Wickland responds, "It does if you believe you're a myth victim. If you believe a thousand years have been up to nothing but shaping the fate of a single man. Expediency. Flee Corinth, kill a man, fall in love, marry. Tell yourself that your hands are tied" (174). Once George's father is unambiguously presented as this kind of unenlightened "myth victim," he no longer can be considered analogous to Oedipus, who, after all, in Sophocles' play was *not* the victim of a delusion but the victim of a real curse on his family.

The internal contradictions in Wickland's story indicate that he cannot be considered a reliable explicator of the working of the curse. Even so, we have some indication that he does not believe that one can escape the curse by ending belief in a bad fate. Wickland states that George's father comes to believe that maybe there will be an exemption for him. In other words, he hopes that he can escape the curse by not "believing" it to have efficacy in certain moments. However, we learn that this idea of the possibility of exceptions is also a dead end:

"He still believed in his fate, you see, still saw himself in the myth victim's delicious position, squeezed dry of force to change his life, with, at the same time, his eye on all the eleventh-hour opportunities that could change it for him. Almost, as it were, on fate's side, confident he'd broken the code, taking the position that destiny has its fine print, oracle its double entendre, that whatever happens to people is a trick—God's fast one." (175)

So George's father hopes that he will have a girl to be named Nancy, but it turns out that George himself is born instead. Belief ultimately did not make any difference.

We are only presented with a glimmer of the truth that the curse is connected to believing in history rather than to believing in doom when Wickland begins to tell about Mrs. Mills's desire to abandon her husband:

> "Quite simply, she was bored. Fed up. She was the myth victim's victim and, now she had heard the whole story and was actually a part of it, wanted nothing more to do with a man who saw everything that happened to him as a decree, a doom, whose every action, no, *activity,* whose every activity was part of some ritual of resignation, who believed, and performed *because* he believed, that history was looking. Or not history, autobiography, diary, home movies, and scrapbook and finally album—all self-absorbed church rolls and records, deeds and registers." (176-77)

The truth is not completely accessible here, for it is hard to tell if the phrase *or not history* means family history. Yet the cumulative weight of the years suggests the uselessness of any historical view, even a familial one: "He was not even serving God, only some image of his own abasement, his soul gone groveling beneath the thousand top-heavy lean years of his second-fiddle fate" (177).

In short, Wickland seems to have some blurry vision of the truth. Similarly, when he speaks of Cassadaga, the community that thrives on spiritualists, as the place where "ego did not exist," he does not understand that this egoless state can lead to religious devotion. Instead, the ego only "merged with bereavement" in a town where "grief was the single industry" (176). The desire of the community is for communication with the dear departed rather than perfection in devotion.

Religious devotion is presented as a more viable alternative than belief in history. Mills, who claimed before he meets Judith Glazer that he does not believe in God (65), is brought to place more faith in the practice of Christianity at the end of the novel than he had before, even though we do not think of him exactly as a Christian. In part 3 we are pointed to this ending by the death of Mr. Mead, who a few minutes before he expires, thinks of saying, "There is almost certainly no God." He "would tell George Mills not to bother about his salvation if he could" (209). Nevertheless, after his passing a few moments later, the narrator tells us, "He is already dead when God comes to collect him" (211).

When they arrive in Mexico (later in part 3), Mills tells Judith his family history, as yet unenlightened to the fact that their journey casts doubt on the meaning that he finds in the curse. They are trying to find a cure for her cancer in a more "backward country" than the United States. This irony escapes Mills when he narrates to her the family story: "he told her about the first George Mills, he described Cassadaga for her and the Mills who had intrigued with courts and empires, filling her in on how the family had bogged down in history, how it remained untouched by the waves of rising expectations that had signaled the rest of Western civilization out of its listlessness" (248). Judith, as victim of the modern mental asylum, and as an inoperable pancreatic cancer patient, does not share in this myth of progress, and her meanness and pettiness indicate her rage at knowing that the "march of civilization" has not kept her life from being a nightmare. Subjection to her unadorned physical suffering helps to draw Mills's eye away from historical ameliorism.

After her death we learn that Judith's mantra was *Mahesvaram* (328), which means "great God" and is used as a name for Śiva. According to John A. Grimes in his *Concise Dictionary of Indian Philosophy,* it is the fifth of six states of consciousness one experiences after knowing the world as unreal in Vīra Śaivism. He enumerates them thus: "one shares the bliss of *Śiva* (*aikya*); one sees God (*linga*) in oneself and everywhere (*śarana*); renunciation of the ego (*prānlinga*); offering all objects of enjoyment to God (*prasādi*); firm belief in the existence of God (*maheśvara*); and performing rituals and possessing devotion (*bhakta*)."[14] Although it would be a mistake to claim that Elkin is advocating a turn to Vīra Śaivism specifically, we can see that the rejection of history is easy to correlate with the idea of knowing the world as unreal. Thus it would seem that Hindu liberation into a state where space and time are abolished and the eternal mode of existence is achieved should hold major attractions for Elkin.

Nor should we insist that Elkin presents here a sympathy for Hindu religion in general but rather for the third of three general trends in Hinduism outlined by Mariasusai Dhavamony in his study of devotion in Śaivism. He characterizes three routes for fellowship with the eternal:

(*a*) the self-glorification of a yogi trying to realize the eternal and spiritual essence of his individual self in all solitude by means of rigorous asceticism, training, and mental exercise; (*b*) the self-illumination of a non-dualist who attempts to behold "the non-two-ness" of all that exists in identity with his ultimate self, realized as the universal, eternal, and unique Being by means of what he calls higher wisdom; and (*c*) the self-surrender of a God-lover in the loving devotion to a personal God, who tries to achieve union with God in a spirit of love and dedication.[15]

The route of self-surrender in loving devotion is the closest of the three to Christian experience, and there is some risk of using Western concepts here in a way that disguises the Hindu character.

We find in Constantinople (part 4) that the Mills men have not yet rejected the High Church pretensions of their ancestors that stand in the way of devotion. The George Mills of the 1820s liked to go to Anglican churches to see society. He says:

But I've been in even fewer chapels than churches, for if vicars and services make me uncomfortable, ministers and everything low church embarrass me. I'm not religious or even much of a believer so much as this snob of God. If there *is* a God He's an aristocrat. He'd have gone to the best schools and He'd speak in low tones this absolutely correct accent. He'd sound like the vicar and never shout or even raise His voice like all those others with their full lungs and loud, harsh words prole as low company. (367)

When we reach the end of the novel we see at the Virginia Avenue Baptist Church that the lower classes have a devotional enthusiasm that leads to concentration on God and eternal matters. Thus the desire to know God is maintained as a far better option than the desire to know the history of the world.

In section 4 we also see that there is no way that the Millses can escape from the curse through taking concerted action which affects history. Even heroic deeds that lead to a historical event such as the Auspicious Incident, the murder of the Janissaries, ultimately fail:

> [Bufesqueu] meant their two-man invasion of Constantinople, the pair of them taking the city by storm. Mills smiled. They *were* grand. No Mills since the first George Mills had been grander, and even if his own had only been a sidekick's grandeur—briefly he wondered if it were enough to lift the curse—a crony henchman's auxiliary one, Bufesqueu couldn't have done it by himself. It had been his name, the living legend's, that had been passed in the street. George was satisfied. They had taken Constantinople together. (404)

In addition, "They had done more, and this was something else he couldn't get over"; "The Janissaries no longer existed" (404). Thus a Mills finally makes his way onto the pages of history, only to find that the curse cannot be broken by his becoming a historical personage.

In part 5 George does learn something from Judith's turn to religion, for when he explains the curse another time, he describes it in terms prompted by his Mexican experiences: "Then he tried to tell them who he was, how there had been a George Mills since the time of the First Crusade. He told them about the curse they lived under, the thousand years of blue collar blood. He told about the Millses' odd orphanhood, their queer deprivation of relation" (505). Now the family tragedy is part of their separation from others, a situation symbolically rectified by the church service. When Mills mentions the family's "long, strange allegiance to class," he knows that the "God panic" can be seen in his eyes (505). Thus we are not surprised by the lifting of the curse when he actually delivers the sermon and is relieved of history. The small and personal aspects of life are affirmed, rather as Elkin defends them at the end of his essay on Arthur Schnitzler in *Pieces of Soap*.[16] Since Elkin claims to believe strongly in individualism,[17] then he must believe that we gain access to this individualism in the private sphere. Surely, Elkin's message will not be one that will please his politically engaged readers. On the other hand, it can only consolidate his reputation among postmodern hermeneutes of suspicion.

Elkin seems to be attacking the idea of meaning in history because since the time of Hegel, philosophers have tended to find either the hero or the masses as carrying meaning with them. Clearly the Millses are not heroes, and for them to subscribe to a Hegelian view of progress in history means to emphasize their own meaninglessness. On the other hand, the triumph of the masses seems to be the aspect of Marxism with the least plausibility today, and it is no bad reflection on Elkin that he does not believe in it.

What remains curious is Elkin's self-professed belief in the myth of progress: people by and large have more than they used to have.[18] In a sense this is true in the novel, as we move across history from stableboy to sheetfolder to furniture repossessor. For Elkin, however, material welfare allows the opportunity for the practice of philanthropy, literature, and self-reflection. Nevertheless, it should not be considered an end in itself, and we should not look for fulfillment in historical change.

NOTES

[1]David C. Dougherty, "A Conversation with Stanley Elkin," *Literary Review* 34.2 (Winter 1991): 183; hereafter cited parenthetically.

[2]Phyllis Bernt and Joseph Bernt, "Stanley Elkin on Fiction: An Interview," *Prairie Schooner* 50.1 (Spring 1976): 22; Joyce Renwick, "Stanley Elkin: An Interview," *Mid-American Review* 5 (1985): 63.

[3]Stanley Elkin, *George Mills* (New York: E. P. Dutton, 1982), 508; hereafter cited parenthetically.

[4]David C. Dougherty, *Stanley Elkin* (Boston: Twayne, 1991), 39, 37.

[5]Peter J. Bailey, *Reading Stanley Elkin* (Urbana: Univ. of Illinois Press, 1985), 211.

[6]Maurice Couturier, "Elkin's *George Mills,* or How to Make an Ectoplasm Schmooze," *Delta* 20 (1985): 89.

[7]Thomas LeClair, "Stanley Elkin: The Art of Fiction LXI," *Paris Review* 17 (1976): 60.

[8]Richard B. Sale, "An Interview with Stanley Elkin in Saint Louis," *Studies in the Novel* 16 (1984): 325.

[9]Jay Clayton, "An Interview with Stanley Elkin," *Contemporary Literature* 24 (1983): 10.

[10]Marc Chénetier, "An Interview with Stanley Elkin," *Delta* 20 (1985): 17; hereafter cited parenthetically.

[11]Doris Bargen, *The Fiction of Stanley Elkin* (Frankfurt: Lang, 1980), 240.

[12]Scott R. Sanders, "An Interview with Stanley Elkin," *Contemporary Literature* 16 (1974): 131-45.

[13]Renwick, 63.

[14]John A. Grimes, *A Concise Dictionary of Indian Philosophy: Sanskrit Terms Defined in English* (Albany: State Univ. of New York Press, 1989), 340.

[15]Mariasusai Dhavamony, *Love of God According to Śaiva Siddhānta: A Study in the Mysticism and Theology of Saivism* (Oxford: Clarendon Press, 1971), preface, n.p.

[16]Stanley Elkin, "Foreword to *Arthur Schnitzler, Plays and Stories,*" *Pieces of Soap* (New York: Simon and Schuster, 1992), 214.

[17]Jeffrey Duncan, "A Conversation with Stanley Elkin and William H. Gass," *Iowa Review* 7 (1975): 55-56.

[18]Bernt and Bernt, "Stanley Elkin on Fiction," 16.

Of Red Herrings and Loose Ends: Reading "Politics" in Elkin's The MacGuffin

Patrick O'Donnell

> "Listen, life is either mostly adventure or it's mostly psychology. If you have enough of one then you don't need a lot of the other."
>
> —His MacGuffin to Bobbo Druff

LIKE JOHN MARCHER, that paragon of the midlife crisis who, in Henry James's "The Beast in the Jungle," waits all of his life for something to happen to him, only to find in the end that it has (and therefore never did), Bobbo Druff of Elkin's *The MacGuffin* perceives his fate to be that of a man to whom nothing will happen. Bobbo has "settled for City Commissioner of Streets in a relatively out-of-the-way, not much more than middle-sized city with no major league baseball franchise. A kind of Indianapolis. A sort of Memphis, Tennessee. City Commissioner of Streets a thousand years in a sort of Memphis."[1] At the end of two days and a night in which he imagines or discovers that, indeed, something is happening to him and that he may be at the center of a political cabal involving his son, his son's dead girlfriend, his new mistress, his chauffeurs, the mayor, and everyone from his local pharmacist to a stranger who gives him a lift while hitchhiking, Bobbo is in the paradoxical position of thinking he may be nearing the end of his life's journey simply because events have conspired to turn nothing into something, to turn "psychology" (his inner voices and demons) into "adventure" (a routing of experience into narrative, that which can be seen, heard, and told). On the other hand, he might be making all of it up, inventing the adventurous, conspiratorial self as a defense against boredom and what he perceives to be his imminent death.

As Bobbo puts it to himself in the novel's final pages:

> If nothing happened to you you had to fall back on your character, spinning your life out of whole cloth, disaffiliate from the world. What he had had for an enemy had been merely his own body, his diseases, how they'd make him look in his suits. He wished now he had gone further in politics, drawn opponents from out of the woodwork, campaigners who might have gotten the goods on him, or even just slung a

little mud. He'd been lazy with his life. Some stinginess of energy had stalled his heart, disengaged him and woken MacGuffins. (271)

Bobbo's dilemma in this moment is that he is nearing the end of a day he thought might be his last but which turns out to be a day like any other, yielding truths that he should have known all along, concealing the meaning of the "whole cloth" of his life but offering tantalizing clues and numerous red herrings about that hermeneutic content. His problem is that he has gained partial knowledge of—as he puts it elsewhere—life's sheer ongoingness: "Life goes on. Life goes on even in the chase scenes. Life goes on even as Grant and Stewart and Kelly and Bergman run for their lives. They would have Kleenex in their pocket, lipstick in their purse. In the climates calling for them they would have Chap Stick, sun block, insect repellent. They would have diarrhea equipment. . . . A glorious drudgery, life goes on. It goes on and goes on" (147). An endless, metonymical process, "life" for the Commissioner of Streets leads nowhere in particular, yet each bypass and dead end promises a potential direction, a means if not an end. This paradox is at the crux of *The MacGuffin,* and of Elkin's fiction at large, which can be construed as an ironic attempt to generate narrative order out of the engagement with life's chaos (despite Bobbo's protests to the contrary about "disaffiliation")—ironic, because this construal is always accompanied by the sense of its own fictionality, as if "life" were nothing more than the recognition that we make up plots and stories in order to nourish the lie that there is some necessary "shape" and telos to individual and social existence.

To see the subject of *The MacGuffin* in this way is to reflect upon what has always been a complaint about Elkin's fiction—that it lacks plot and cohesion. Almost in the form of a redress to this criticism, *The MacGuffin* is plotted with a vengeance, and the activity of plotting, or being plotted against, constitutes its structure in a mockery of both paranoia and Pynchonian "preterition," the other side of paranoia, sheer chance, pure coincidence mythologized as "fate." Titled after the device attributed to Hitchcock—the switched suitcases that plunge an innocent, random traveler into an international conspiracy; the mistaken name or face that confers upon the naïf "too much" knowledge—Elkin's novel coins "the MacGuffin" as a metaphor with multiple (seemingly endless) meanings for a man who would seek to convert contingency and the quotidian into mystery. During the forty hours in which we follow Druff's mental and physical wanderings, the Commissioner of Streets evolves from a bored but mindlessly content political hack into the detective/victim/hero of his own story as he unearths what he sees as a plot involving smuggling, money laundering, and murder in the formerly dull streets of his city. Given the nature of his position—the man who controls the traffic—his role seems apt: hypnotized by the mediocrity of the city bureaucracy, a good "civil servant," sleepwalking his way through life (Bobbo carries on most of the important conversations in his life while sleeping), he awakens at the seemingly accidental death of his son's Muslim girlfriend (she is killed by a hit-and-run driver while legally crossing the street at a traffic light near the university) and finds that there are routes, connections, and traffic flow he has never before noticed. He takes on, or is possessed by, a MacGuffin, which manifests itself, variously, as an object (like the Oriental rugs that keep cropping up in places as dispersed as his mistress's apartment, the mayor's car, and a synagogue), a far-fetched coincidence (a wrong number, a name in the obituary column), or a homunculus with whom Druff conducts full-scale conversations about evolving plots and false leads. In essence, he "falls back on character" as he begins to see his life as a story; he develops a sense of an ending even though everything tells him that the traffic will continue to flow long after the Commissioner is gone; he manufactures an "adventure"—a mock odyssey—complete with an adultery, the traversal of a labyrinth, heroic confrontations with the enemy, a reunion with his lost son, and a return to his wife's bed that brings a kind of mythic order to his shapeless existence.

Elkin's conflation in *The MacGuffin* of the manufacturing of adventure and the making of identity has parodic resonance when we consider that the novel itself is a generic adventuring through *The Odyssey,* the "political" novel, detective fiction, Hitchcock movies, romance. Elkin's novels have often involved protagonists whose vocations within specific generic circumstances serve as vast, radiating metaphors for the pursuit of order and identity amid worldly disarrangements and entropies: the titular character of *The Dick Gibson Show* extends himself as a signal on a frequency that—through sheer repetition—converts noise into message; Ben Flesh, of *The Franchiser,* seeks in his wanderings across the interstates of America to consolidate both a personality and a financial empire; Eddy Bale, in *The Magic Kingdom,* conducts a tour of dying children through the hallucinatory but disciplined realm of Disney World. Elkin's familiar theme—"in the face of death, peregrinate"—makes its appearance in *The MacGuffin* but with specific elaborations upon the *political* nature of the formation of nomadic identity in confrontation with mortality and the heterogeneity of that formation, its circumnavigationality, its purely circumstantial makeup. These are conveyed, I will suggest, by the peculiar and spectacular Elkinian "mix" of generic hybrid and metaphoric excess or overdetermination that do battle in *The MacGuffin,* certainly on the level of plot but also in terms of rhetorical and hermeneutic conflict, metonymy and metaphor fighting it out, serendipity and conspiracy having their day, legibility and paranoia happening upon each other in a dark alley.[2]

Certainly one of the genres that *The MacGuffin* plays upon is that of the detective novel or crime thriller, more specifically, the *noir* thrillers that first became popular in the thirties and forties and that helped to give rise to the cinematic genre of *film noir.* Though Alfred Hitchcock is not generally considered a *noir* director, certainly such films as *Spellbound* (1945),

Strangers on a Train (1951), and *Psycho* (1960), as well as color films such as *Rear Window* (1954) and *Vertigo* (1958), both borrow from and contribute to the genre more typically represented by Billy Wilder's *Double Indemnity* (1944), Jacques Tourneur's *Out of the Past* (1947), Rudolph Mate's *D.O.A.* (1949), or Carol Reed's *The Third Man* (1949). The classic *film noir* works on both visual and thematic levels: high-contrast lighting, sharp angles, a sense of impending doom, and a display of "basic instincts" combine to provide a representation of a world out of joint and a protagonist usually on the verge of extinction who is forced to confront his or her own guilt-ridden past along with its culmination in crime or victimization. To this blending of technique, mood, and moralism Hitchcock brings (not uniquely) what might be called the epistemological issue, especially in his characterizations of men or women plucked out of everyday circumstances and plunged suddenly, through a series of fateful accidents, into the heart of a mystery and circumstances over which they have no control. The main function of such characters is to assimilate, sort through, and interpret the increasingly rapid influx of information that comes to them in the form of "clues" about their circumstances: where they are; who they are; how they got here; how they will get out. Here, "the MacGuffin" makes his entrance as an agency that, metaphorically, curves one line of parallel trajectories just enough so that the lines intersect, giving rise to the case of mistaken identities and mysteries to be solved by vacationing merchants or hapless college students cum detectives.

Elkin gestures toward his employment of the Hitchcockian schema not only in the title but throughout the novel, particularly in one of his conversations with his MacGuffin, who has been promoted from plot device to something like a possession demon:

> Hey, goes MacGuffin, I've been there and gone. Are you psycho, or what? You fair give me vertigo. Until you've walked thirty-nine steps in my macmoccasins, kiddo, don't you be comin' up in my face like you be some man who know too much.
>
> Why?
>
> Cause it give me the frenzy.
>
> It do, do it, Mr. Bones?
>
> Without a shadow of a doubt, Rebecca.
>
> Well, I'll be spellbound, Druff went on.
>
> You will, will you? goes MacGuffin.
>
> Didn't I say so?
>
> Yeah, you said so all right, but between you, me and the lamppost *I* say you're for the birds!
>
> Oh yeah? Oh yeah? A bunch of rugs mysteriously shows up on a bunch of floors and the lady just vanishes? (260)

Like the typical Hitchcock protagonist, Druff wakes up one day to find himself (reflexively, after all, in a novel titled *The MacGuffin*) in the middle of a Hitchcock movie, scrambling for the knowledge that will either confirm the fact that there is a conspiracy abroad or provide convincing evidence of his own paranoia. Yet, unlike Hitchcock's naïfs, Druff is already a man who knows too much: he is a seasoned politico, an experienced ward heeler, a participant in backroom decisions and petty municipal graft (though, in his own mind, he has his standards—he makes deals that allow him to conduct his business as Commissioner of Streets more easily but never, he argues, for personal profit). Indeed, it is precisely his political savvy as Commissioner of Streets that causes him—without any evidence at all, just the inconsistent voice of his mocking MacGuffin—to suspect that the accidental death of an innocent pedestrian is part of some larger scheme involving rug smuggling in his fair city. In the Hitchcock thriller the man who comes to know too much is forced against his will to move out of a narcissistic personal realm into the world of crime and politics and to recognize that the line that separates the two is illusory, a point often made in Hitchcock by the paralleling of the immersion into conspiracy with a voyage into the "unconscious" past. In many ways Jimmy Stewart is the archetypal Hitchcock protagonist precisely because his bumbling, low-effect, slightly amnesiac personality is seemingly so at odds with the complex, repressive, yet streetwise precincts of politics, double crosses, and criminal conspiracies that, ever surprised, he is compelled to traverse. Druff, on the other hand, should know better, for he is a man who not only has politics constantly on his mind (he does, after all, have a MacGuffin) but might also enthusiastically support the notion that *everything* is political, from the phenomenology of the streets to his early efforts to get his future wife, Rose, into bed: "They were seated on the edge of the cot now. He tried to draw her down, to get her to lie beside him, but she resisted. . . .(Of *course* political. Political certainly. Bargaining actual territory, dividing physical spoils, making these Yalta arrangements, so that it was somehow agreed without one word passing between them that he could do this but not that, that but not this") (73-74). This suggests that in some ways Elkin reverses the Hitchcockian scenario I have sketched: rather than moving from the "personal" to the "political" and discovering that they are one in his forty hours, during which time he is compelled to recollect his marriage, his relation to his son Mikey, his political career, Druff discovers that the "political" is "personal." He finds that city streets, which he had always thought of in terms of routes and connections, maps and contracts, are full of people on their way to individual destinations that he had never before considered; he is struck by the revelation that the political order is a fragile construct that may effect personal catastrophe but that may also crumble under the weight of historical accident; he sees his paranoia given over to indeterminacy.

Such knowledge is disturbing to Druff, who really does want to live his life as a protagonist in a Hitchcock movie, where the MacGuffin is a constant that guarantees "the spirit of narrative" (189), where "like a guy in a detective story" he can serve as "the truth mechanic" (199) and "give in to his fiction" (203). In short, a kind of novelist-politician, Druff wants civic (i.e., narrative) order in a world given over to disorder; for him, "politics" is a hermeneutic activity that allows one to see the hidden connections between things, and a good politician engaging in realpolitik not only knows about those connections that are "really" there but draws power from them. Having discovered an Islamic carpet in, supposedly, a rabbi's bathroom, Druff argues to himself:

> I appreciate the powers of paranoia. They are surely considerable. But before you go rushing off to find a shrink, consider, I'm a politician. Trained in the random, in the chance remark and glancing blows of everybody's mouth news, in on all the late returns and other counties heard from, in absentee ballots and the planetary swing vote, in the graciousness of concession speeches lived through twice, once on the phone from my hotel, then in the ballroom. Trained, when it comes down, in the thick skin of the professional politician, his water-off-a-duck's-back bathing habits and almost Christian bygones-be-bygones vision. So, sure, I'd have spies. Of course I'll have enemies. An odds-on favorite, for God's sake, a hell of a bunch more likely to have a MacGuffin of my own than that there'd ever be, now I see its tight weave and, to judge by the Chinese water torture it'd probably have to put up with in here, the colorfast qualities of its terrific, mysterious dyes, its rich fringe and intricate design and peculiar shape, what is almost surely a Muslim prayer rug right in the rabbi's crapper! (177-78)

Druff's self-defense is reasoned in a peculiar manner: he is *not* paranoid (making up connections and seeing coincidences where none exist) because he has stumbled upon the "clue" of the rug ("almost surely a Muslim prayer rug") in the labyrinth of a temple that Druff himself admits is possibly not a temple at all. What allows him to see the clue is the paradox of his politicality, his "training in the random," which suggests that politics is, precisely, the disciplining of the random, the organizing of uncertainty. The reasons for Druff's apocalyptic state of mind during the forty hours in which he is possessed by the MacGuffin are both "personal" and "political." Being a politician, he should have noticed the conspiracy he has walked into long before now, for it is the role of the "good" politician (and novelist) not to star in the Hitchcock movie but to direct it; thus he regards his naïveté as a failure of his political prowess and a sign of impending death, for Druff is nothing if not a politician. But there is also the possibility that the conspiracy—unnoticed until it is too late and now out of control—signifies for Druff a political failure in a larger sense, that is, the failure of "politics" as such to bring order to the universe, to mobilize the random, to strategize the indeterminate. To draw out this point, it is important to regard *The MacGuffin* as a political novel.

As I have suggested, Elkin frames *The MacGuffin* as a narrative hybrid: it engages in the tropes and strategies of the detective novel as formulated by Chandler and Hammett; it parodies the devices of *film noir* as redefined by Hitchcock; it contains elements of romance, farce, confession, and adventure; it is, being a novel by Stanley Elkin, comic throughout. *The MacGuffin* not only parodically "quotes" Hitchcock and the *noir* genre (especially *D.O.A.*, which contains a protagonist who is *certain* he has only forty hours to live) but a number of other films and film genres, perhaps most notably *The Grapes of Wrath* in a conversation between Druff and one of his drivers ("You're up against me. Look for me on the monuments, I'll be waiting for you. Look for me along the ledges. Down by the railroad tracks where the freight trains live. . . . Expect me in the cages of the tigers and the bear pits at the zoo. I'll be right there behind you on the newspaper that lines the bottom of the bird cage. We're into melodrama here, turf, putsch and the Higher Bullshit" [130]). The generic nomadism, the parodic and comic effects of *The MacGuffin* work both to divert us from and to point us toward how intensely "political" this novel about a small-time politician in a middle-sized American city really is. To return to the "clue" that Druff finds in the "temple," he is startled by an incongruity ("a Muslim prayer rug right in the rabbi's crapper") that underlies what remains, for many, the major political crisis of the second half of the twentieth century. The Arab-Israeli conflict haunts *The MacGuffin* and stands behind Druff's low-comic dilemmas. It appears in his cogitations (is it possible that Jews killed Su'ad, his son's girlfriend and a Shiite Muslim?) and his anxieties (if she is smuggling rugs into his city, where is the money going? is she a terrorist raising funds?). It stands behind his conclusion—the "solution" to the mystery—that bankers who have loaned her money under the table so that she could illegally import the rugs to finance pro-Arab causes are responsible for her death: "Thinking, she was financed by . . . merely hardened *bankers* who, when she couldn't pay back her loans . . . then, though I can't prove this either, struck her down in what wasn't quite yet even her prime, because, well, just because, because downtown had become too tame" (277-78). The Arab-Israeli conflict has come home to roost, as it were, in Druff's city. Its presence, as he infers it, gives a sinister turn to his sense that "everything is political," for now we are not talking just about courtship or rug smuggling but the crisis that I would argue in Elkin's view, left unresolved, spells Armageddon.

The peculiarly comic apocalyptic tone of *The MacGuffin* can be accounted for by this last somber point. For Druff, there is the continuous sense that he is living in the end time. True, he concludes that "life goes on and on"; he survives his "last" forty hours and comes home to sleep, the mystery unresolved but the detective at rest, finally shed of his MacGuffin. But the "loose end" of Su'ad's death—her corpse—still remains. Throughout his odyssey Druff continuously projects the possibility of his own personal extinction, and though he may attempt to convert red herrings into "facts" in a paranoid drama ultimately "resolved" by his son's revelations (Su'ad, apparently, actually has been smuggling carpets) and an apparent acceptance of the ongoingness of existence in the face of personal tragedy, Elkin does not so easily let his protagonist, or the reader, off the hook. For what is left unaccounted for in *The MacGuffin*—what remains untouched by Druff's detective work—is the political machinery ("the bankers") responsible for Su'ad's death, which has been shown to be at work as much in Druff's city with its small-time bureaucracies and backroom deals as it is in Washington or Tel Aviv or Riyadh. Druff's growing awareness that "everything is political" comes home with a vengeance and, along with it, an exhausted sense that there is nothing to be done about the pervasive powers that have caused Su'ad's demise and certainly that there is no "political" solution to the mystery of her death nor to the larger regional conflict that lies behind it. On the one hand, Elkin's comic characterizations of the figures implicated in the conspiracy he uncovers work to undermine the severity of the threat: How could one possibly take seriously the Keystone Cops routine of Hamilton Edgar, a university lawyer, and Dan and Jerry, two bankers, as they guide Druff through the maze of the "temple" to the suspicious rabbi's study, where they propose ways to handle Su'ad's death so that both the city and the university can bear little fiscal responsibility for it? Alternatively, it is precisely the slapstick shenanigans of the various participants in the conspiracy that lend to *The MacGuffin* the bleak sense that the larger sequence of historical events referenced by the murder of Su'ad and its aftermath is equally a clown show, the Three Stooges at Yalta, the Marx Brothers sitting at the table between the PLO and the Israeli prime minister. Such revelations and contradictions destroy any notion of "politics" providing a solution to serious political problems or (Druff's shattered hope) standing as a bulwark against chance and chaos. If anything, Druff's journey discloses the fact that everything, from individual careers to political conspiracies, operates according to some principle of randomness that subverts the rage for order. Druff is implicitly forced to confront the idea that anything can happen, and that what happens does not necessarily have a logical reason for occurring; just the opposite: things often happen by accident, and accidents often conspire to eventuate in "history." Here, "politics" is but the illusion of control over events gone out of control, the mirage of rationality in the face of the utterly irrational: ethnic hatred, greed, the desire for power—all deployed under the sign of "politics."

Stanley Elkin has always been fascinated by power of all kinds: how it works, how it flows, how it is gained and lost. In *The MacGuffin* he writes a novel in which there does not appear to be much real power of any kind: these small-time politicians, these local bankers, lawyers, bureaucrats and their petty antics—what kind of real power could they have? Yet Elkin's strategy in the novel, which is to generate parodic comparisons and connections between the politics of everyday life and "politics" on the global scale, compels us to reflect on the thousands of daily political acts that constitute contemporary reality. Power, in this sense, is everywhere, the engine of every human exchange, the very medium of our communications and discourses, all our trades and deals—and it is under no one's control. That Druff, the individual agent, may wander the streets, his route ruled by coincidence, hailed by strangers and collaborating in plots about which he has only partial knowledge, is both a source of comedy in *The MacGuffin* and a cause for anxiety about entropy leading to that death toward which all of Elkin's protagonists (and, inferentially, the planet itself) seem driven. This is to recognize the anti-utopian nature of Elkin's comedy, perhaps most riotously conveyed in the "hell" of *The Living End.* For Elkin, "politics"—defined in *The MacGuffin* as the mechanism that imposes upon randomness an illusory order or, in more sinister terms, as the black market process by which "politicians" make hay out of complex and deep-seated cultural differences—cannot redeem history. Nor will the fact of mortality —that last and most certain accident—be unseated by all of our clumsy, flimflam attempts to attain dominion over it.

NOTES

[1]Stanley Elkin, *The MacGuffin* (New York: Simon and Schuster, 1991), 254; hereafter cited parenthetically.

[2]Readers may have noticed that the cadences of my commentary are pale imitations of some of those found in Elkin's fiction: in part, this is deliberate; but in writing on Elkin (as on Faulkner), the commentator finds it nearly impossible not to be infected or contaminated by these seductive and invasive prose rhythms.

A Stanley Elkin Checklist

Arthur M. Saltzman

Novels

Boswell: A Modern Comedy. New York: Random, 1964; New York: Berkley, 1967; New York: Warner, 1980.

A Bad Man. New York: Random, 1967; New York: Warner, 1980; New York: Dutton, 1984.

The Dick Gibson Show. New York: Random, 1971; New York: Weidenfeld and Nicolson, 1971; New York: Pocket, 1971; New York: Warner, 1980; New York: Dutton, 1983.

The Franchiser. New York: Farrar, Straus and Giroux, 1976; Boston: Godine, 1980.

The Living End. New York: Dutton, 1979; New York: Warner, 1980.

George Mills. New York: Dutton, 1982; New York: Thunder's Mouth, 1991.

The Magic Kingdom. New York: Dutton, 1985; New York: Thunder's Mouth, 1991.

The Rabbi of Lud. New York: Scribner's, 1987.

The MacGuffin. New York: Linden/Simon and Schuster, 1991; New York: Penguin, 1992.

Novellas and Fiction Collections

Criers and Kibitzers, Kibitzers and Criers. New York: Random, 1966; New York: New American Library, 1973; New York: Warner, 1980; New York: Thunder's Mouth, 1990.

Searches and Seizures ("The Bailbondsman," "The Making of Ashenden," "The Condominium"). New York: Random, 1973; New York: Pocket, 1973; London: Gollancz, 1974 (retitled *Eligible Men*); Penguin, 1977 (retitled *Alex and the Gypsy*); Boston: Godine, 1978.

Stanley Elkin's Greatest Hits. New York: Dutton, 1980.

Early Elkin ("A Sound of Distant Thunder," "The Party," "Fifty Dollars," "The Graduate Seminar"). Flint, MI: Bamberger, 1985.

Van Gogh's Room at Arles ("Her Sense of Timing," "Town Crier Exclusive, Confessions of a Princess Manqué: 'How Royals Found Me

"Unsuitable" to Marry Their Larry,' " "Van Gogh's Room at Arles"). New York: Hyperion, 1993.

Uncollected Short Fiction

"The Dying." *Illini Writers* 4.1 (1950): 10-18.
"Alone Is Hurt Too." *Illini Writers* 4.3 (1951): 11-19.
"The Bottom Line." *Antaeus* 28 (Spring 1978): 7-30.
"The State of the Art." *TriQuarterly* 44 (1979): 230-59.
The First George Mills. Dallas: Pressworks, 1980. (Limited edition of Part I of *George Mills,* illustrated by Jane E. Hughes.)
"Corporate Life." *Chicago* 34 (March 1985): 157-59.

Screenplay

The Six-Year-Old Man. Flint, MI: Bamberger, 1987.

Nonfiction

Pieces of Soap. New York: Simon and Schuster, 1992.

Uncollected Nonfiction

"Miss Taylor and Family: An Outside View." *Esquire,* November 1964: 43+.
"The World on $5 a Day." *Harper's,* July 1972, 41-46.
"Inside Jean-Louis Trintigant." *Oui,* January 1973, 84+.
"Representation and Performance." *Representation and Performance in Postmodern Fiction.* Ed. Maurice Couturier. Montpelier: Delta, 1983. 181-91.
"Joe McElroy Introduction." *Review of Contemporary Fiction* 10.1 (Spring 1990): 7-8.
"On Jerry Charyn." *Review of Contemporary Fiction* 12.2 (Summer 1992): 124.
"Out of One's Tree: My Bout with Temporary Insanity." *Harper's,* January 1993, 69-77.

Alasdair Gray: An Introduction, of Sorts

Mark Axelrod

In an age of specialization, in which one does not write fiction but "genre fiction," in which commercial success or disaster is the standard by which literary artists are supposed to rise or fall, can there be room for a diversifier of texts, for someone who undermines the notions of realism and reality, for someone who undermines the notion of linearity of plot and homogenization of form? Very little. At least in North America. Gratefully, Scotland has not been appropriated by the United States publishing moguls and (fortunately for Scotland) Margaret Thatcher did not "privatize" the novel, and so Alasdair Gray survives behind the gray and gelid gates of Glasgow.

But how can he do it? How can he withstand the onslaught of the mercurial demons of the publishing industry, the banality of some critics, and the festered words of some reviewers? He simply ignores them and writes on. What seems to be Gray's trademark, if not his logo, is the diversity of his texts not just in content but in context as well. From *Lanark* (1981) to *Poor Things* (1992) we get a sense of Gray's creative mobility, an attitude that eschews conventionality, eschews the commonplace, and doubtlessly eschews the word *eschews.* Gray's innovation in the novel (postmodern or otherwise) is his manner of banishing the so-called real to the wasteland of the mundane. He tends to that on multiple levels: textual, graphic, orthographic, typographic. His approach to the novel is not restricted by the conventions of the genre, since the rules are not necessarily broken but rearranged. In his essay "Alasdair Gray and the Postmodern" Randall Stevenson believes Gray functions within a postmodern tradition, and he stresses the work's uniqueness as "postmodern artifact" and its political significance to Scotland.

The novel is not dead for Gray nor has it ever been a dying genre (except possibly in the United States where it's always been dying) for someone who perpetuates the novel tradition of making the novel novel. What has contributed to the novel's professed demise has been a kind of approbation of the past and, in a kind of Forsterian eulogy, a yearning for those thrilling stories of yesterday told in the thrilling manner of yesterday. When one engages Gray (and one surely does engage Gray), he or she is often compelled either to comply with his station or move on. The fact he employs any and all means to shape his textual universe should not be looked at pejoratively, as something akin to a literary misdemeanor, but as something affirmative.

To that end one can either like what Gray does or dislike him for doing it, but the work itself tends to stand beyond the critical judgment of whether or not it is real, whether or not it obeys Forster's rules or James's or Scott's or Balzac's, and whether or not it tends to pluralize the bandying of those scurrilous organs called words. We are blessed with a surfeit of Grayish testimonies to art and to a mixture of madness. For those unfamiliar with Gray (and there are a bevy of beatific readers who are) these essays allow an insight into the man and his work which is both edifying and entertaining.

One might wonder where, with *Lanark* as a point of departure, Gray would or could go. In stylistic terms, however, it was just the beginning of a series of texts that played with form; the playfulness is not merely an exercise to frustrate the notions of realistic fiction but a kind of political temper that advances an ideology that encompasses much if not all of Gray's work. In *Lanark* we are struck with a polymethodic examination of a politics of language and a circumvention of expectation. A decade in the making, *Lanark* brings the characters of Lanark and Duncan Thaw (the former's alter ego) into the cataclysmic confrontation of discovering one's purpose in a society (or is it a civilization?) that is bent on following the dictates of entropy and dissipation. The form of the novel mirrors that movement toward dissipation, structured as it is with book 3 beginning with chapter 1 followed by the prologue followed by book 1 followed by book 2 followed by book 4 and an epilogue, a movement that calls into question all sorts of notions about linearity.

What appears to be the normal for many becomes the abnormal for Gray. Gray's work comments on the relativity of what is normal/realistic in political, institutional, and sexual terms. As George Donaldson and Alison Lee write in their essay, Gray abuses literary conventions and genres, questioning literary conventions and mixing realism with fantasy in combinations that strike the reader as perfidious. Long live perfidy. The notion of this coalescence of fantasy and reality especially in relation to satire is the focus of much of Gray's work in which the coalescence of these worlds, found in novels such as *Lanark, 1982 Janine,* and *Kelvin Walker* (about a hero who challenges the authority of what's normal in a way that Gray does in text), is seen on a global, mass-market scale. In *1982 Janine* (1984) our hero Jock McLeish, suffering the throes of middle age and the grogishness of Scottish whiskey, suffering from divorce and celibacy, engages in long monologues with himself and eventually with God, which lead him to an attempted suicide and catharsis. But amid all of McLeish's angst there's the inducement of Janine who is part of his sexual fantasies, which include domination and bondage as yet other escapes from the rigors of dissipation.

Like Janine, *Something Leather* (1990) deals with notions of sexuality. Though the plot revolves around June, a divorcée who is seduced by two women who run a rather intriguing kind of leather shop, we find Gray using sexuality to address concerns about class and privilege, where sexuality is politicized in much the same way that language is politicized. The politics of language is at the core of "Alasdair Gray: The Voice of His Prose," where Philip Hobsbaum traces the texture of Gray's prose as part of a tradition stretching from Defoe to Borges; he uses the Russian formalist notion of *ostranenie* (making strange) or relating similarities in things that are seemingly dissimilar in works like *Lanark* and *1982 Janine.*

In *Unlikely Stories, Mostly* (1983) we get the most unlikely of stories: from a man who splits himself in half to an epistolary presentation by a court poet of Marco Polo, each of the stories depicts its own allegorical persuasion and its own political perspective. From "The End of the Axletree," about the absurdity of nuclear proliferation, to "The Great Bear Cult," we get the absurd presentations of absurd events, like a Scottish version of Kafka.

Poor Things continues the Grayan tradition of absconding with the preconceived notions of truth and reality and asserting the author's right to dictate the architectonics of his own work at the levels of composition and textual layout. Gray constantly calls attention to his material and the means by which it is produced; thus the formulation of the visual plays as much a part in the evolution of the novel as the text itself. From the narrative portraits to the visual portraits, Gray incorporates elements of postmodern fiction in delightfully eccentric ways. *Poor Things* not only extends Gray's narrative range but expands the possibilities of what can be done with the visual in terms of the novel.

It would appear that with *Poor Things* Gray has closed the circle of *Lanark.* In a letter he writes, "I have recently started a science-fiction novel which I hope will leave me with NO NEED TO WRITE MORE FICTION." This decision is the proverbial double-edged sword: a science-fiction novel by Gray begs the possibilities of the visual and opens wider the door to new horizons of the novel; but a last novel by Gray saddens the reader/writer who always looks to the birth of a new novel as a reaffirmation of the possibility of the new and of the ending of *Lanark:*

I HAVE GROWN UP. MY MAPS ARE OUT OF DATE.
THE LAND LIES OVER ME NOW.
I CANNOT MOVE. IT IS TIME TO GO.

But like Beckett's reprise, "I can't go on, I'll go on," Gray has gone on with his latest novel, *A History Maker.* It would seem that the infection is pervasive and should continue to be so. Long live infection.

An Epistolary Interview, Mostly with Alasdair Gray

Mark Axelrod

MARK AXELROD: You are most widely known for the richly imaginative and what Robert Crawford called "labyrinthine" novel *Lanark: A Life in Four Books,* a novel that is as stunning in its narrative as it is bizarre in character and setting. For those who have read the book but were a wee bit confused by the setting in book 3, was it meant to be an apocalyptic vision of Glasgow or of a general gloomy setting?

ALASDAIR GRAY: I meant to write an exciting story about the world I was in, of which Glasgow was the biggest and nearest part. The gloomy and apocalyptic elements came easily to me because when four years old, I had sat with my mother and father and heard Neville Chamberlain, the prime minister, announce that Britain was at war with Germany. From then on, for five years, street lighting was not used in Britain and when the siren was heard we all stopped what we did and went to air-raid shelters, sometimes getting up in the middle of the night to do it, sometimes stopping our lessons in the classroom. I enjoyed the excitement. Then one day we went to school—my sister and I, with our mother—and buses came to the school and took us out to bits of Scotland I would otherwise not have known. We were *evacuated,* first to a farm in Perthshire, then to a flat above a tailor's shop in a small mining town. Then my father (who had been a private, then a quartermaster sergeant in the 1914-1918 war and had worked a box-making machine in a factory between the wars) got work as a manager of a hostel for munition workers created by the government in the Yorkshire market town of Weatherby. In the course of these flittings I sometimes had nightmares and bad asthma attacks, though my mother ensured I was safe, and the British government, by introducing strict food rationing, ensured that the generation of working-class children who grew up during the war were healthier than those of any preceding generation. As Kurt Vonnegut puts it—Imagine that! So my tendency to think the world catastrophic or apocalyptic came from the experience of it. But I did not think it a hopeless place, and the world of *Lanark* was meant to excite and interest, not depress. Our world is apocalyptic, don't you think? The places Lanark and Thaw inhabit are more orderly and human than many parts of modern Britain, U.S.A., Iran, and Chile.

MA: The notion of a "Life in Four Books" presupposes a linear progress, yet *Lanark* is not constructed in a traditionally linear way, moving as it does from book 3 to prologue to book 1 to interlude to book 2 to book 4 and an epilogue. How do you harmonize the artificially constructed life of the novel with the "real lives" of Lanark and Thaw?

AG: I felt no need to harmonize them. I yoked the bits together and expected the reader's interest to flow over all, as my imagination had done.

MA: Both Joseph Campbell and Mircea Eliade speak of quests as a kind of "enlightened return" unlike Nietzsche's "eternal return" which is divorced from any kind of spiritual enlightenment. A number of novels of character, *The Stranger, The Sorrows of Young Werther, Hunger,* have elements of this quest motif. Lanark too seems bent on a quest. Did you have such a notion in mind when you wrote the novel and if so what was Lanark's quest?

AG: The quest was to find more love and sunlight. He gets them on the last two pages.

MA: There are parts of *Lanark* that are reminiscent of Andrei Biely's *St. Petersburg* and John Barth's *Giles Goat-Boy.* In *St. Petersburg* it is the property of the city and its colors; in *Goat-Boy* it's the bizarrely realistic (I refrain from using the term *magically realistic*) handling of institutional bureaucracies. Not that either text directly influenced your approach to *Lanark,* but what were some of the texts that did and why?

AG: The first book was probably Shaw's *Adventures of the Black Girl in Search of God,* for my father once told me he read to me when I was very small, and I kept asking him, "Will the next God be the real one, Daddy?" I read Ibsen's *Peer Gynt,* when an adolescent, in Archer's translation. (My dad had become a Fabian socialist through his First World War experiences, so we had all Shaw's plays and his "Quintessence of Ibsenism," which probably put Dad onto Ibsen.) *Peer Gynt* is the quest of nineteenth-century man in search of his soul or true self—it takes him through scenery as wild, yet oddly familiar, as Bunyan's *Pilgrim's Progress,* which I could not enjoy because I did not want to be a born-again Christian. Then there was Melville's *Moby-Dick* with its combination of great idioms: natural history, factory ship, oil industry, Shakespearean monologue, Yankee wisecracks, Wordsworthian meditation. Then Kafka and Kafka and Kafka.

I remember a children's prose version of the *Odyssey* read when nine or ten. The idea of a voyage from one magic island to another gripped really hard. Of course the quest here was to get home again, but the journey interested me more than hope of arrival. There was also the Quest for the Golden Fleece in Kingsley's *The Heroes,* the adventures of Jason and Theseus, the quest of Gawain in a child's Mort D'Arture version—also Sinbad, whose adventures are all voyages in search of wealth by trade or good luck. Then I read Amos Tutuola's *The Palm Wine Drinkard,* a quest into the African bush to bring a tapster back from the world of the dead, where the scenery and episodic nature of the story were very like those of Shaw's *Adventures of the Black Girl in Search of God.* And these stories exalted because they let me into a life of important, surprising, dangerous adventures, while leaving me perfectly safe. But at the end, Kafka was the most useful, because his heroes were all dull strivers, heroic only in their persistence in a world like mine. The city where the bank official Joseph K struggles for acquittal from a nameless crime could easily have been Glasgow—the slums with law courts in their attics, the artist's tenement studio, the foggy, nearly empty cathedral struck me as Glaswegian. So did the land surveyor's struggle to get his *position,* his work in the town confirmed by the officialdom of the adjacent castle. But the quest of the young boy in *Amerika*—I forget his name—struck me hard, though I noticed it was based on *Oliver Twist.* The description of how he at last joins the Nature Circus of Arizona—the new deal which can employ all the homeless of America and Europe—was proof that even Kafka could write a good ending out of a world like mine—that human government was redeemable.

MA: That approach to institutional dogma and criteria, whether academic or nonacademic, seems to have been a part of your work as far back as the short story "The Wise Mouse," written when you were in secondary school. Is this kind of obstreperousness a genetic perturbation of Alasdair Gray? If so, why?

AG: My approach to institutional dogma and criteria—let's call it, my approach to institutions—reflects their approach to me. Nations, cities, schools, marketing companies, hospitals, police forces have been made by people for the good of people. I cannot live without them, don't want or expect to. But when we see them working to increase dirt, poverty, pain, and death, then they have obviously gone wrong. Is it mere obstreperousness to show them wrong? The genetic perturbation you refer to is a sense of justice. Everyone suffers for it, so it is an ingredient in all fiction except the most blandly escapist.

MA: One cannot overlook the dual dimension of Duncan Thaw as an artist and a litterateur, a combination that is clearly expressed in your own work. Was there ever a preference for the word over the image or vice versa?

AG: Never. I preferred Disney films to all others as a child and their words and sounds and images were simultaneous. The first books I read had pictures in them.

MA: Your illustrations are visually unique and doubtlessly Gray. Where do they fit into the texts? In other words, do you think of them with the text, as a prelude, as an afterthought?

AG: As an afterthought. My illustrations are not essential to the text but intended to make it more enjoyable. With my paintings, the image is first, of course.

MA: I read somewhere that you declare you have no religion, yet a character like Duncan struggles with the Judeo-Christian perplexities of God. How do you reconcile that in your writing?

AG: I don't reconcile it. I present it by (sometimes) describing a Thaw, a Lanark, a Jock McLeish haunted by an idea of God, which I am sure haunts many modern people without congregations who, doubting the eternity of mere selfish chaos, feel the possibility of eternal goodness.

MA: You spent a number of years, formative years, as a playwright and screenwriter before you began writing fiction. How did that training help you in your fiction? And did you ever think that you or anyone else could have scripted a novel like *Lanark?*

AG: You're mistaken there. I started writing fiction—silly little stories—when quite small and started the Thaw part of *Lanark* when eighteen, not realizing the job would take twenty-five years. Meanwhile, I lived by art teaching, scene painting, portrait painting, then, by a piece of good luck, playwriting. The discipline of writing the novel helped the plays as much as vice versa, since both used a lot of dialogue. I have made a film script of *Lanark,* though I never expected to. Other writers could make different filmscripts of it, if they were paid enough.

MA: There are, of course, dramatic stylistic shifts between Lanark's story and Thaw's story. The prose not only shifts in density and complexity but in tone as well. Was it difficult for you to make those adjustments in prose style and was there a particular style you preferred?

AG: No. I was unconscious of any adjustments except the rewriting needed to make sentences sound easy on the ear. When the ear had no trouble with them I assumed they were as good as I could make them. In one place where I wanted a piece of description too exotically colorful for my own powers I stole a passage from Edgar Allan Poe, but the only conscious struggle to get the proper style was in the Art School summer holiday 1953 when I started trying to write *Lanark.* After two months I managed the first chapter of book 1; I had at last found a voice like a calm, mature adult. From then on I could always achieve that voice in writing, when I worked at it. My speaking voice is normally gushing and childish.

MA: Many of Unthank's inhabitants suffer from the despair not only of the gray skies of its bleak setting but from diseases that are as horrific in name as in substance, diseases like Dragonhide. What was the significance of these creative maladies?

AG: I suppose they were, or are, metaphors for bad mental states, like the tortures in Dante's *Inferno.*

MA: In terms of reality the Lanark part and the Thaw part correspond to a semiautobiographical narrative and a surrealistic narrative which is highly politicized. There's almost a bicameral nature to the novel, which some have said doesn't coalesce. What unifies these seemingly disparate parts of the novel?

AG: The only thing that *can* unify it is the readers' enjoyment. But if you like I'll give a breakdown of the parts which shows why I feel they amount to one life.

Book 3: A life from twenty-one to thirty years. Our man shifts from Bohemian underemployment into the professional middle classes, meeting girl, losing her, wooing her, finally bedding her, and being moved chiefly by a wish for a clearer, more sunlit, and loving life.

Oracle's Prologue: A life from middle age through senility to death—nothingness—then birth into an infancy whose sensual richness ends at the age of five years.

Book 1: A life from five to eighteen years of a working-class Glasgow Scot, a very insecure lad indeed.

Book 2: Eighteen to twenty-one years. He tries to become a great artist but lacks the resources. Collapses, dies.

Book 4: Thirty to seventy years. Our man still struggles toward the sunlight of a better life, having and losing his family on the way, unexpectedly winning acclaim and power which turn out to be shams, but waiting at last for death in the place he knows best under a sky full of discovered sunlight. He has also discovered he was always loved: that his lack of it was nothing but his own mistake. I know that the infancy of the Oracle does not quite describe the first five years of Thaw's life, nor does the senility and death of the Oracle follow the old age of Lanark, nor does the young manhood of Lanark follow smoothly from the adolescence of Thaw, though the Oracle claims one is the other's reincarnation. But my continuity of discontinuous people springs from a socialist democratic faith in all of us incarnating the eternal imagination—differently. Forget the discontinuities, enjoy the range!

MA: Many American readers might be unaware of the relationship of your work to the tradition of Scottish fiction. Where do you see yourself in the evolution of Scottish letters? What Scottish writers do you admire?

AG: I see myself as another Scottish writer nurtured by the postwar welfare state. I admire Douglas, Henryson, Lyndsay, Burns, Scott, Hogg, Galt, Carlyle, Hume, Adam Smith, Brown (*House with Green Shutters*), Stevenson, McDiarmid, McCaig, Leonard, Kelman.

MA: Let's talk a little about the Scottish fiction scene. Is there anything like a Scottish literary community here? Certainly there are those who are Edinburgeans and Glaswegians, but do the two ever come together or is there more that separates them than just a train ride?

AG: Glasgow and Edinburgh and Highland and Island writers come together at readings. Scotland, for all its internal social and geological diversity, is so small that the writers soon hear of each other, and the Scottish Studies departments of our universities and our small literary magazines keep Scots who want new writing informed of it. Edinburgh publishers—not London ones—were first to publish the poems of Liz Lochhead, the fiction of James Kelman, Agnes Owens, and me, who are all from the Scots middle west. Sorry! I've remembered that Kelman's first book of stories was published in the U.S. by Puckerbough Press through the good offices of Mary Anne Hughes. But Scottish writers no longer group themselves in mutually antagonistic clans. This does not mean we are a community. Does any nation contain a single literary community outside the literature department of a university? Does the U.S.? Does England?

MA: As a follow-up to that, you've done a lot of work in broadcast media: film, television, radio. What do you think the status of the Scottish media is at this point?

AG: Between 1960 and 1978, I had about fifteen plays broadcast by English and Scottish radio and TV stations. I felt then the Scottish media were feeble imitations of the English and (in the case of the BBC certainly) mainly controlled from London. Our news coverage is still feeble, cowardly, noninvestigative to the worst abuses of government, business, and law. But we now have one or two comedy series that only Scotland could produce—good ones.

MA: You've been lumped in the group of postmodern novelists. I've always had a problem with who is and who isn't a postmodern writer especially in light of such prepostmodern writers as Sterne, de Maistre, Diderot, Machado de Assis, etc. It's been said that your novels have "a modish, often naive urge simply to flirt with fashionable styles, or to flaunt a new, post-postmodern pretentiousness." What's your opinion of that?

AG: Like you, I have never found a definition of postmodernism that gives me a distinct idea of it. If the main characteristic is an author who describes himself as a character in his work, then Dante, Chaucer, Langland, and Wordsworth are as postmodern as James Joyce, who is merely modern. The opinion you quote does not say whether the critic who uttered it enjoys my fiction, though the verbs *flirt* and *flaunt,* the adjectives *modish* and *naive* culminating in the thunderous *postmodern pretentiousness* sound disapproving. But they also suggest I am the prose equivalent of new nursery wallpaper, which at best contradicts the notion that I'm gloomily apocalyptic.

MA: You obviously take typographic liberties in your work as well. What motivates you to use such graphic devices and how do people react to them? One would think they might bristle at such an intrusion into the text.

AG: I use a variety of typefaces where this makes the story clearer. Thus in *Poor Things* the letters of Bella and Wedderburn are printed in italic, a type based on handwriting rather than Roman chiseling. In *1982 Janine*—an interior monologue novel—the speaker has a nervous breakdown conveyed by three columns of different typefaces on the same pages, each a stream of thought or feelings at war with the rest. I do not know how else I could have done it. Since a lot of people buy these books I think they give more pleasure than pain.

MA: In *1982 Janine* there is a decided shift in the narrator. The characters in *Janine* are extremely different from those in *Lanark.* Was there a particular reason for doing that?

AG: I wanted *1982 Janine* to be about someone whom people accept as utterly ordinary. Thaw and Lanark struggled against their surroundings: Jock McLeish never did. Like Walter Mitty, he asserts himself only in fantasy. Of course, nobody is ordinary inside themselves, and if *1982 Janine* is any good it shows this. But the difference from *Lanark* came from a wish to show what lay under at least one ordinary surface, hence the very different person he is and people he knows.

MA: In *Unlikely Stories, Mostly* two specific tales, "Prometheus" and "Five Letters from an Eastern Empire," deal with a character who writes poetry. But Alasdair Gray doesn't write much poetry anymore. Why not? And have you ever been taken with doing anything in the manner of concrete poetry? It would seem your gifts with pen and ink would result in some highly imaginative works.

AG: The emotion that moved me to verse was always the loss of someone I loved. I have lost nobody dear to me since the eighties, so the only verses since then (apart from comic ones) have been the report on a flight to Berlin. I have also written a couple of verse plays which no director is interested in. Maybe one day an inspiration or commission will move me to verse again. I cannot foresee it. As far as doing concrete poetry? No—though I enjoy it as done by Edwin Morgan and in your *Neville Chamberlain's Chimera.* It seems that I cannot *start out* to be visually playful. I have to start any work I do—painting or writing—in a conservative way which uses an already well-known form. Only when safe with it does the possibility of fracturing it somewhere and grafting in something unexpected (to give new height or depth) occur. Of course, in *Chimera* you play with the formality of a hockey score card, concert ticket, or—my favorite, I think—the map of the Great Lakes destroyed by our sorry obligations to our stockholders. But making these needs the superimposition of one complete idea on another, I can't build that way. Not on a page. Or not yet!

MA: What was the genesis for *Kelvin Walker?* What were the political reasons for writing it?

AG: *Kelvin Walker* was first written as a television play in 1965 but had more than one origin. The first was a scene I imagined in 1959 or 1960 in which a dour dependable Scot of the technician type (like Jock McLeish) is bullied into sharing his home with—and by—a Bohemian artist with a very attractive girlfriend. The plot was to be the seduction of the girl by the apparently quieter, more ordinary man after a violent quarrel between her and the man she mainly loved. But all I got written was a fragment of the scene where this happened, because I could imagine no interesting social setting. Around the same time I was accosted—twice in a café, once in a hospital waiting room—by strangers who said, "Excuse me, but would you mind if I engaged you in conversation?" and went on to tell something weighing heavily on their minds at the time. Their stories were different but began with the same formal Scottish inquiry. Then I read a literary magazine containing a scene from J. P. Donleavy's *Fairy Tales of New York:* one in which a young man whose only talent is verbal adroitness talks himself into a high position in a New York corporation. And then in 1964 I got a telegram from a friend in the London BBC, telling me to phone him, reversing the charges. I had no telephone then, was living on the social security dole with my wife and our one-year-old son, working at painting except when too depressed to paint, when I would work on *Lanark.* I phoned the friend, Bob Kitts, who had become a TV documentary director on an arts program called *Monitor.* He had persuaded his boss (Huw Weldon) to let him make a forty-five-minute film about an almost wholly unknown poet and painter—me. He arranged for me to leave the Sauchiehall Street labor exchange (where I had to sign in punctually once a week), go by taxi to Glasgow airport, collect my tickets at the B.E.A. desk, fly to London, and be met by a glossy Daimler, which drove me at once to the headquarters of BBC television, when Britain had only one TV channel, and that was it. So from being a state-supported pauper, I became *simultaneously* a Scot on the Make in London who felt himself on the verge of Wealth and Fame. I did not get them: but I suddenly imagined Kelvin Walker with his Nietzsche-inspired conviction that invincible self-confidence, a clear head, and a sharp tongue could get him onto the social ladder a few rungs from the top. Bob's television film did not get me the mural commissions I hoped for but paid me enough money to live by doing what I wanted for twelve months or more, and in that period I wrote the television version of *The Fall of Kelvin Walker,* which was broadcast by London BBC in 1968 (though bought two years earlier) and published as a novel in 1985: when a Scottish BBC TV producer invited me to lunch and explained that he thought it would make a splendid television play. As to my political reasons for writing it—I had none at all. The politics of any story I tell are the politics of the country where I live. The prime minister and newspaper owner in *Kelvin Walker* were as necessary to it as King Arthur and Merlin to a medieval romance. I was told later that many on the BBC thought Kelvin Walker was based on David Frost, but I had never seen Frost. I did not own a TV set in those days.

MA: You wrote to me in a letter that your recent novel *Poor Things* would be popular with both academics and nonacademics. That statement brings the notion of audience into question. From your previous works it would appear that appealing to a specific audience in the way a commercial novelist would appeal to a specific audience is lacking. But how do you approach this notion of audience, whether that be a Scottish audience or an international audience?

AG: I do not need to *approach the notion of audience,* since I write a language which, if purged of repetition, pompous cliché, and needlessly long words, makes sense to most people. If an American reader finds my Scottish references and idioms more confusing than the Wessex ones of Hardy and the Irish ones of Joyce, it is because I am an inferior writer, not because I write with a narrower audience in mind. But since university teachers lecture on my books and students write dissertations on them, I have grown conscious of my academic audiences and afraid of seeming their property. *Something Leather* was perhaps my most successful effort to break with them. But I still meet decent, intelligent folk who say they feel they *ought* to buy a book of mine but fear it will be too clever for them.

That is what comes of being praised or condemned as a postmodernist. It is as bad as being praised or condemned as an exponent of Marxist dialectic. I told you *Poor Things* would please academics and nonuniversity folk because I enjoyed writing it so much I was sure many would like reading it. It contained no original devices at all. The editor's introduction of long lost narrative was in *The Master of Ballantrae.* That book, as well as *The Moonstone* and *Frankenstein,* is told by a narrator who quotes long narratives by other people, many of them letters. But why explain where I got the tried and true ideas for constructing the *Poor Things* automobile? I want the reader to enjoy driving it.

MA: The introduction to *Poor Things* is in the best tradition of the seemingly disenfranchised author from Voltaire to Cortázar. Yet you have total control of your material literally from cover to cover: text, illustrations, criticism, even the blurbs are yours. Perhaps no other author has had such complete production control as you have. In working with publishers, has that kind of control been easy to obtain?

AG: Yes. My first book, *Lanark,* was published by Canongate, a small Edinburgh publishing house who gladly allowed me to design it. They would have had to pay someone else to do it had they not. The publishers (not me!) received a Scottish Arts Council design award for the best designed book of 1981. *Unlikely Stories, Mostly,* more copiously illustrated, won another design award, and had my own spoof review printed on the cover, which the Penguin paperback version was careful to copy. British publishers know it is financially sensible to make my books look the way I want them to because many readers and critics like them that way. George MacBeth thought *Something Leather* an unsuccessful novel but said it *looked* beautiful. Of course, my control of design and cover does not extend to paperback and foreign editions. The American Random House edition of *Something Leather* shed my illustrated initial capitals from the chapter headings, took the golden wasps from the binding, put a dark dark dark jacket in place of my heraldic bright challenging one, and sold badly. But maybe the story is to blame. I never overestimate the value of the package.

MA: On whom did you base your illustrations in *Poor Things?* Jean Martin Charcot appears to look a lot like Montesquieu. Were there models for these?

AG: Charcot was indeed based on Boldini's portrait of Montesquieu. The portrait of McCandless was taken from Paul Currie, of Baxter from Bernard MacLaverty, of Bella from Moray McCalhine. The first two are friends, the third a friend and wife. I drew them because their faces fit the characters and I like having faces of friends in my books—though I gave Bernard a more miserable expression than I have seen, to make him conform to Baxter—also wilder hair. The faces of de la Pole Blessington and Blaydon Hattersley were inventions.

MA: So where will Alasdair Gray go from here? In an interview with Kathy Acker when you were a mere child of fifty-one you said, "I'm pretty sure that I'm not going to write any more fictional works," and suddenly we have *Poor Things.* You obviously have more ideas to work on, so what can we expect in the future?

AG: I've finished *The Anthology of Prefaces* started five years ago. I hope Iain Browne, film producer, gets the financing to make the *Lanark* film and that Sandy Johnston directs it. I'm starting another big mural in a Dunferm-line museum soon. That's all.

The Anthology of Prefaces

Alasdair Gray

General Preface

"EVERY PREFACE," SAYS William Smellie at the start of his preface to *The Philosophy of Natural History* published in Edinburgh in 1790, "Every preface, besides occasional and explanatory remarks, should contain not only the general design of the work, but the motives and circumstances which led the author to write on that particular subject. If this plan had been universally observed, prefaces would have exhibited a short, but curious and useful history both of literature and authors."

This plan, of course, was never universally observed but it has been widely observed. Few great writers have not placed before one of their books a verbal doorstep to help readers leave the ground they usually walk on, and allow them a glimpse of the interior. Prefaces are advertisements and challenges. They usually indicate the kind of attention the book requires, the kind of return it is meant to give. It has been possible for at least two centuries for anyone who enjoys a good library to collate, at very little mental expense, the best part of this history of English Literature by those who created it. If I am the first to turn Smellie's suggestion into a book it is because former critics have been blind to a useful task which would not stretch their brains. To wheedle a big advance from my publisher I take English to be the language of more nations than England, more islands than Britain, more continents than Europe. I also take Literature to be any book worth reading, so include prefaces to works of religion, law, science, philosophy, history, travel, biography and Johnson's dictionary. Prefaces to poems, plays and stories outnumber these. Imaginers like Shakespeare, Burns and Mark Twain wrote for all sorts of people, not for a specially educated part of them, so their fictions make better sense to most of us than the treatises of Isaac Newton, whose discoveries are now more easily learned from modern books by lesser authors. Yet I include Newton's advertisement to his *Treatise on Opticks,* as a pithy specimen of scientific prose.

By preface I mean any beginning entitled preface, prologue, introduction, introductory, apology, design, advertisement or explanatory, and some beginnings which are not labelled, but prepare the reader for what follows without being essential to it: like the first thirty-six lines of Barbour's

Bruce, the first two verses of *Gawain and the Green Knight.* I also include some dedicatory epistles which avoid sycophancy by making a political statement (see Coverdale to Henry the Eighth) or giving a specimen of the author's style (see Sterne to William Pitt). I had meant to exclude pseudonymous prefaces, but this would eliminate Defoe, whose prefaces to his fictions are all lies. So I include the pseudonymous. In very few places I break the rule of giving one preface per author, and after prefaces to the Bible give the first three verses of Genesis for comparison. The prefaces are ranged chronologically to display sometimes gradual, sometimes quick changes in English over the centuries. Before printing came or became common they are placed in the supposed order of writing. Most authors' preambles have been magnificently crisp. Milton's preface to the second edition of *Paradise Lost* is four sentences, so is the Notice and Explanatory to *Huckleberry Finn.* I seldom use a long preface to a less important work when an author has put a brief one before his best. This makes it possible to print, without cutting, good prefaces which are essays and manifestos. I list four pleasures I hope you will find in this book, with the nastiest first.

1. Seeing Great Writers in a Huff

Prefaces to first editions usually try to forestall criticism, those to later editions frequently counterblast it. An author's best defence is to explain why he wrote, but some resort to unfair tactics. The conservative monk who wrote *The Cloud of Unknowing,* the sturdy corrupt journalist who wrote *Moll Flanders* were very different men, but their preambles indicate that their books will be abused or misunderstood by the vicious. The commonest defensive tactic is the lofty intimation, the second commonest is its counterpart, the poor mouth. Both are symptoms of intelligences uneasily exalted or depressed by their social standing—a frequent British disease. In his preface to *Utopia* (not included here) Sir Thomas More loftily intimated that he writes for the discerning few, not the multitude. He had good reason to say so. *Utopia* was written to introduce King Henry VIII and the literate part of his nobility to some old-fangled notions of tolerance, social welfare and equality under law. It was written in Latin, circulated in manuscript, and not printed till after his death. Yet his example is followed by several great writers who want to be enjoyed by as many readers as possible. Listen to Wordsworth: "Those who have been accustomed to the gaudiness and inane phraseology of many modern writers, if they persist in reading this book to its conclusion, will no doubt, frequently have to struggle with feelings of strangeness and awkwardness." He certainly enjoyed constructing that sentence but our amusement is partly at his expense. The Americans are better at critic-deflecting irony because they treat their readers as equals. See Twain's Notice again and the last sentence of Hemingway's introduction to *A Moveable Feast.* I give no examples here of the poor mouth defence but refer the reader to Goldsmith, Burns, and Charlotte

Brontë's preface to her sister Emily's *Wuthering Heights.* (This last, by the way, with Engels's preface to the English translation of Marx's *Communist Manifesto,* is an exception to the rule of having every preface by the book's author.)

2. The Biographical Snippet

Some prefaces blend declarations of faith with a personal experience, so we discover Shelley writing and sunbathing on a platform of green turf high among the ruins of the baths of Caracalla, and Shaw conversing gallantly with a London prostitute, and Synge with an ear to a chink in the floor, eavesdropping on the kitchen maids in the room below. These feed our love of gossip.

3. The Pleasure of the Essay

Preface essays vary as greatly as authors. *The Lady of the Lake* explains a historical stage which should interest more than the Scots. Lawrence's preface to his translation of *Cavalleria Rusticana* is a fine essay on modern fiction. An essayist's remarks, of course, only please when they confirm our settled opinions. As a Scottish socialist who thinks a federation of British republics a necessary step toward the creation of humane democracy I am delighted by Shelley's statement in 1820 that, "If England were divided into forty republics, each equal in population and extent to Athens, under institutions not more perfect than those of Athens . . . each would produce philosophers and poets equal to those who (if we except Shakespeare) have never been surpassed"; also by Mandeville's remark a century earlier that small, peaceful, self-supporting states are the best homes of happiness. Those who find such statements comic, unconvincing or irrelevant will find plenty of remarks to support their own prejudices.

4. The Pleasure of History

Great literature is the most important part of history. We forget this because we are inclined to see great works as worlds of their own rather than phases of the world we live in. No wonder! At first sight the differences in style between Chaucer, Shakespeare, Dickens and today's newspaper are so great that it is easier to read them as descriptions of wholly separate worlds, instead of the same world at different times and places. It is almost impossible to imagine a passage of history in any solidity and fluidity for more than a few years. But we may get some experience of a civilization over several centuries from extracts which let us see, on adjacent pages, language changing from decade to decade in words of authors who usually know they are changing it. The taste, rhythm and meaning of a statement is the taste, rhythm and meaning of life when it was uttered. So for comparison I include five versions of the start of the Bible most Christians use, one by an Anglo-Saxon, the rest in Chaucerian, Tudor, Stuart and modern translations.

But I want the book to be popular, and know most of us were taught just one way to spell the words we use, that other spellings are wrong or unreadable. To many an original page of Chaucer or Shakespeare therefore seems a gloomy exam they need extra teaching to pass, when the knack of understanding it can be picked up in an afternoon by anyone who thinks of it as an interesting puzzle, a pleasant word game. *Storyss to rede are delitabill, Supposs that thai be nocht bot fabill* invites us into a great region of our language and history, and with a little thought is as easy to follow as the speech of Nigger Jim in *Huckleberry Finn.* But it takes time to see that, so in this anthology early verse prologues are printed facing modern translations. I have translated with three aims: to explain obsolete words; to preserve the original rhythm; to leave untouched what makes sense as it stands so that readers (glancing across at the original) see how little the translation is needed. But I have spoiled the flavour of prose before A.D. 1500 by modernising some prose without giving the original, and elsewhere have turned *v* into *u, u* into *v, i* into *j, j* into *i, f* into *s* where this will make sentences look less strange without misleading the pronunciation. The Anglo-Saxon alphabet had two letters we do not now use: one for the soft noise which starts *thud* and ends *bath,* one for the lightly buzzing noise which starts *the* and ends *breathe* and *wreathe.* I have replaced both by *th.* Other shady practices are listed in an apology at the end of the book.

To stop the whole collection looming up in a single daunting heap I have cut it into periods and put a historical essay before each. I sometimes quote other writers without inverted commas. If you find parts unusually fine or pompous you may be appreciating Edward Gibbon or Thomas Babington Macaulay: but I also quote from other work of my own. I acknowledge my sources as completely as possible at the end, only remarking here that Philip Hobsbaum's study of English literature, *Tradition and Experiment,* along with Green's *History of the English Speaking People,* helped to inform my views of the whole.

Since nobody reads a book like this from start to finish I advise you to tackle it like a reviewer, going first to the author and period you like best, then fishing for tasty things in other places. I hope you find them.

Everything Leading to the First English

MR. MACQUEDY (producing a large scroll): "In the infancy of society—"
THE REV. DR. FOLLIOTT: Pray, Mr. Macquedy, how is it that all gentlemen of your nation begin everything they write with the "infancy of society"?

—Thomas Love Peacock, *Crotchet Castle*

ABILITY TO IMAGINE AND SHARE NEW THINGS IS UNIQUELY HUMAN AND DISPLAYED IN CONVERSATION, WHICH IS NOT.

Babies embarrass masterful men, who find it queer that once they too could only wail, suck and excrete. When one year old we totter through a bewildering world on unsteady legs while small birds of the same age have already flown, mated, built nests and begun feeding their own children. What unique ability in the following years enables us to handle the world in so many surprising ways? Some say nothing but the strength and intelligence to grab what we want, even from our own kind, and do it in gangs. We would have nothing worth grabbing if that was the whole truth. Our unique ability is to imagine and make something new we can share with others. Conversation, not theft, most explains us. It supplies and shapes the whole matter of our thought, yet we think little of it because all vocal creatures use it. Birds start singing before dawn to stir each other into briskness for the day ahead, then keep up a quieter texture of noise till sunset, announcing their position and territory with calls which also tell when they are congregating toward food or dispersing from a danger. Cats meowl in chorus to declare their separate identities, sexual readiness and united cattishness. For the same reasons our ancestors the tree-rodents must have scolded and chattered a lot.

THE EMANCIPATION OF OUR FACES BY OUR HANDS. ALLOWS THE PLAY OF MUCH MORE UTTERANCE AND EXPRESSION.

Though bigger than squirrels they were as alert, inquisitive, and varied in their diet, eating nuts, snails, berries, eggs, carrion, fruit and lice. Conscious choice (*dare I eat a peach? Shall I part my hair behind?*) began with this variety of edibles and increased when we came to scramble on the ground. Like pigs we grubbed up roots, like foxes grabbed fresh meat, but we grubbed and grabbed with forepaws, not snouts and teeth. Our faces were free to play with a range of utterances and expressions which should still be one of our great freedoms. Some scientists think the big human brain developed through ape people discovering more and more things to do with their hands while using these to do more and more things. Our ability to remember and choose between a large number of actions at last wiped from our nerves all but one inbred skill other beasts use, replacing the rest by a wholly new one.

INSTINCTS REDUCED BY ABILITY TO CHOOSE FROM MANY ACTIONS.

The surviving instinct is imitation; the new one is making shareable signs for things. Both appear in children learning to talk. They get words by imitating their elders, while inventing names of their own for their favourite objects. The inventions are usually ignored, and even if not the children stop using them because imitated words are more useful, but this private gibberish shows intelligence, not folly. At the same age children without dolls take a handy object and treat it as they want to be treated or as they wish to treat others. They make it a sign of life and hold communion with it. By shaping sounds and handling objects, by attaching memories and hopes to them we learn to converse with ourselves and others. Conversing with ourself is thinking. Conversation with others enlarges that.

IMITATION, INVENTION. THROUGH PLAY WE LEARN TO TALK AND THINK.

About 6000 centuries ago folk like us began moving through the world, each generation surviving by habits learned from elders but habits which could change in a lifetime if the surroundings changed. From a genesis in Africa our tribes moved to Asia, peopling the Chinese plains so densely that most big migrations after that pushed west and south, though ten thousand years before Christ some Asian families crossed the Bering strait into America and began peopling it from the northeast. "Men can get used to anything. What scoundrels they are!" said Dostoyevsky, recalling life in a Russian prison camp. In a half million years our tiny tribes went everywhere, sometimes fighting each other for fruitful territories but usually adapting to a world they could not change much. It passed through three ice ages. Where food was abundant our average height became six feet or more. Usually we were more dwarfish because we kept exhausting food supplies or becoming too many for them. Our skins grew pale in the cloudy north, black in the equatorial south and in east Asia lost a fold of eyelid, but our racial differences were slight because everywhere we strove to keep the same pattern of brain and skeleton by changing our minds, tools, clothes and houses. We changed them through conversation, invention and imitation, being all the time

The words are in Crime and Punishment, *and refer to how fast folk adapt to mental and bodily abuse. The power of adapting by which we survived ice ages can destroy us under bad governments, when resistance from underlings should cause adaptations on top.*

VERSATILE BRAINS WORK TO KEEP BODIES SIMILAR.

goaded by questions no human brain can avoid.

How did I get here?

What must I do to live?

Where in the world am I going?

These are the first questions children brood upon when they start thinking. Answering them created the vocabulary, art, science and faith of early as well as modern people.

The science of tribal folk could be used as wrongly as our own. Some cleared ground for planting by setting fire to it. This made the soil less fertile, so their descendants had to change habits or territory. But they did not knowingly poison the earth as we do.

Early answers have been deduced by seeing how the earliest known stories of the pastoral Egyptians and Greeks agree with those of tribes still living in prehistoric ways. Most folk who live directly from the earth believe all they see and feel is alive and holy, and all earthly creatures were originally born by earth through a sexual wedding with the sky. They believe death will return them to a timeless state already occupied by ancestors who converse with them through traditions, memories and dreams. They do not think themselves more important to the world than the flocks or kangaroos they depend on or the crocodiles they dread. Their customs and taboos are intended to revive the beasts and ground that feed them. Most tribes have a priest-doctor to ease pains and illness with traditional prayers and remedies, who recites the stories of the tribal ancestors, and is sometime inspired by a crisis to say what they would have done. Many bushmen and esquimaux are so widely scattered that they do without governments. Closer knit tribes are co-ordinated through assemblies of family heads, one of whom judges disputes between them and speaks for them in dealings with other tribes. A younger member of the leader's family sometimes inherits the job, but if incompetent gets replaced by someone the assembly prefers.

PRAISE OF THE FIRST MAKERS.

Fewer folk got born before the first city was built than were born in the first sixty years of the twentieth century. They discovered all the main skills we now live by, the skills which make our science possible. The cleverest modern invention is a self-firing bullet which carried three men to the moon and back, burning most of itself up on the way. Imagined beside the first efficient axe, canoe or plough it seems astonishingly useless. Yet we can feel why most in the nineteenth century who first glimpsed how long people had lived on earth had a low opinion of the first human tribes, believing they were practically speechless or had nothing very good to say because they lived without writing. City dwellers also want simple answers to the question, "How did I get here?" and who can start trying to imagine over half a million years of human life—at least 240,000 nameless generations—without weariness and despair? It is a surer reminder of death and the end of fame than a tour of all France's military graveyards. So we call the first ninety-nine percent of human history *prehistory*—a hardly readable preface to a tale which starts a few centuries before Moses and Homer, takes in all the great human names and leads straight to you and me.

The creation of settlements peacefully, and by platonic methods.

Settled farming began. In fertile places folk grew so productive and thick on the ground that they supported market places where craftsmen dealt in woven goods, pottery and metal utensils. I like to imagine these places expanding through peaceful trade into the earliest cities. Plato thought the first city-states were made by armed hunters on horseback invading valleys of farming people and building central strongholds from which to plunder them. Both things happened.

THE FIRST BANKS, ARMIES, KINGS AND SLAVES: INHERITED POWER OF A FEW, INHERITED POWERLESSNESS OF MANY.

Between six and four thousand years ago twenty cities of at least 10,000 people were built in Asia and northeast Africa, each for a while the capital of a nation formed and destroyed and reformed by combinations of trade and conquest. They were as different from each other as modern Peking, Delhi, Rome, New York, etc., but had some things in common. Each stood on a plain beside a great river, among fertile farms productive of grain. At harvest time the city revenue officers, who were priests aided by soldiers or vice versa, gathered much of the grain inside the city walls where it became the wealth of the state: the food of folk who did not live by producing what was essential to life but by managing those who did. A big grain store had the power of a modern bank; those who owned it had time to consider problems of survival from a leisurely distance. A sack of grain could nourish a family for a fortnight, so might be used to buy both goods and labour, and buy them cheap in years of famine. Beside a priesthood, army and craftsmen each city had a class of slaves originally created through warfare; but later people—even the original producers of the grain—sometimes sold themselves into slavery to avoid starvation. And each city had a king, originally the commander of a conquering army. Such armies only work with a supreme commander, and when successful can put him in charge of everything. Since underlings grow uncontrollable in states where the bosses openly fight each other for power, the officers of state supported a single boss who in peacetime inherited the job from his dad. This stabilized ruling classes but ensured that a good king was a lucky accident, or that anyone could do the job. It was too shameful an arrangement to be openly admitted. Kings were advertised as deputies and descendants of a great god in the sky—the sun itself—and most of them believed it.

Even Napoleon and Hitler did not believe they had been given power by greedy folk profiting by their cunning and indecency. They thought they were guided by a star or supernatural intuition.

When social grabbing and shoving dominate architecture it builds Norman castles, Victorian prisons and cotton mills, modern tower blocks, car parks and shopping centres: structures designed to take in as much as possible at a few guarded entrances and elsewhere show nothing but forbidding surfaces. Most cities have looked better than that. Borges describes how one appeared to a barbarian it attracted.

He sees something he has never seen, or has not seen . . . in such plenitude. He sees the day and cypresses and marble. He sees a whole that is complex and yet without disorder; he sees a city, an organism composed of statues, temples, gardens, dwellings, stairways, urns, capitals, of regular and open spaces. None of these artifacts impresses him (I know) as beautiful; they move him as we might be moved today by a complex machine of whose purpose we are ignorant but in whose design we intuit an immortal intelligence.

From The Barbarian and the City by Jorge Luis Borges.

The intelligence which makes a city attractive is knowledge and craftsmanship working for the good of the majority; in the variety of convenient goods and luxuries which are suggested, made and shared when many sorts of people talk together. But knowledge dies if not widely shared. Some cities had libraries of law tables, religious and medical treatises, historical and astronomical records, maps, poems, stories and tax registers: all destroyed when the small class who used them was defeated by conquerors of a different tongue. The Aryans who destroyed the earliest Indian cities and their writings did without writing for a thousand years. All the writings of ancient Babylon, Crete, Carthage and Etruria have vanished except a few undecipherable inscriptions. Many Egyptian and Assyrian texts

THE LITERATURE MADE BY VERY FEW FOR VERY FEW DOES NOT LAST.

survived but for fifteen centuries nobody could read them. Only China was so densely peopled and efficiently organized that every conqueror before the Euro-American invasion of 1839 had to govern it by learning the ways, language and the writing of the conquered.

But the learning in the shattered libraries was not wholly lost. Every alphabet the world uses was adapted from the scripts of Sumeria, Assyria and Egypt by nomads and seafarers who traded with them. These mobile people needed letters for contracts and bills. They also wrote large agreements which are the best human laws, with some undiscussable dictates which are the worst. Then they wrote down the best songs and accounts of the heroes who made their nations, and so many loved these books that buildings were not needed to preserve them, the national epics were so continually copied and recited. Ancestors of literate folk started talking to them through books. Imaginative descendants talked back. The book of Isaiah was put beside Moses, the plays of Aristophanes beside Homer, so later readers heard their ancestors talking to each other. Different national literatures began conversing. Oriental Buddhism happened when some Indian texts reached scholars in China, inspiring them with hunger for more. Barriers of desert and perplexingly different script stopped Indian and Chinese books informing European readers, but the thought of half of the world has been shaped by intercourse *between,* intercourse *with* the books of three Mediterranean nations.

How written learning was saved by mobile folk and spread to many.

Inclusive literature widens conversations through time and space.

The earliest and most influential books belonged to the nation which commanded the least territory and sometimes none. They have lasted over 3000 years because they were the shared intellectual homeland of people who sometimes had no other. The Jews were wandering herdsmen who became guest workers in Egypt, first in a privileged state, then, as their numbers increased, in an oppressed one. They got so used to settled life in Egypt that when their slavery grew unbearable they escaped to the desert intending to make a homeland in Canaan, but a generation passed before they were strong enough for invasion and conquest. In the years between escaping political oppression and founding their state by more of it they put in writing a queer and powerful idea: the world and its creatures were not originally born from acts of love but acts of

The culture of the Jews.

Literature released from territory and made impervious to conquest.

will expressed through language. One eternally single masterful man-god imagined light, sky, sea, sun, moon, dry land, the plants and creatures, then made them in that order by naming them. This took five days. On the sixth he made a man out of earth to be owner of the earth, and made him of a mature age because nobody can manage a big property when young and babies embarrass masterful men. From one of the earth man's spare ribs god made him a wife, to reproduce copies of him by the animal method. But Adam lost his great property by obeying the wife instead of the god who made him. He and his descendants became miserable toilers and wanderers to the time they escaped from Egypt, when the one god offered the Jews a special contract: if they would follow and have faith in nothing but his words he would give them a secure homeland.

THE JEWISH VISION OF A LOST HOMELAND, LOST PEACE IN THE PAST.

This creation story insults women and defies every commonsense fact but one: where people and nations constantly jostle each other for territory nobody feels secure, and many think life is a crisis between a once happier state and a future they hope will be happier for their children at least. Moses told a horde of fleeing gypsies that they were potential landlords, that the world had been made for them by an imagination and will like their own, and could be repossessed. In a century the Israelites made the contract he had drawn up with god on Ben Sinai come true. They were inspired to grab a land of milk, vines and cities from the Philistines, a race of sea-raiders who had grabbed it a century or two earlier. Many folk wanted that land. In the eight centuries before Jesus the Jews were conquered by the empires of Assyria, Babylon, Persia, Greece and Rome, disasters which they read as punishment for ignoring god's word or as tests of their faith in it. Later the Eden-to-Canaan story became the first gospel of the Christians and Mohammedans because it explained their feeling that life was a crisis too. It could also be twisted to justify almost any war. Arabs, Crusaders, Spaniards, British, Americans and Israelis have soothed their consciences with it while killing and robbing weaker people. But the Hebrew bible is not a safe prop for heads of state unless they have popular support. God in these books is not symbolized as a man in a strong position. The Jews thought it blasphemy to symbolize him at all. God is the creating mind known

THE JEWISH VISION OF A PEACEFUL HOMELAND IN THE FUTURE.

Many scholars now think the Old Testament was edited into its well-known form 2 or 3 centuries before Christ, when the rabbis cut out all evidence that their ancestors who invaded Canaan had as many gods as the Egyptians and Philistines. If so, Moses is as mythical as Romulus and King Arthur. This will not worry those who find most truth is declared in what people most lovingly make—in our fictions, homes and religions. William Blake wrote that the one god of the Jews is the poetic imagination, and rightly, because all other gods have been shaped by it.

by the truth of words spoken through the mouth of anyone: a preacher denouncing those who cheat the poor of their property and try to bribe god with religious services, a survivor lamenting among the ruins of a city, an outcast crying in the wilderness. The Hebrew gospels contain good songs, stories and sermons which don't mention god at all. Many kinds of education can be got from it.

The culture of the Greeks.

There is a different account of Mediterranean life in the poems of Homer, which tell how a lot of small piratical Greek states and islands combined to attack the city of Troy, and the adventures of one pirate on his way home. The Greeks were descended from Eurasian invaders who learned from Egyptian, Jewish and Carthaginian traders. Their ships and manners resembled those of the Vikings, their communities were not much more than a chieftain's palace with some adjacent farmsteads and a harbour, yet Homer's poems have almost universal human sympathy. The besieged Trojans are presented as more noble than the invading Greeks, nor is the Greek victory a success story. All leaders in that war are shown as eventually losing life, dignity and decency by it, while periodically discussing with a sort of baffled wonder the insufficient reasons for fighting like this in the first place. They talk like intelligent soldiers in any war. Yet along with the wasteful fights, strategies and excursions Homer describes the work by which life is maintained: how cattle are slaughtered and cooked, how a household launders its sheets, the design of a woman's woolwork basket and the pruning of a hedge. When a hero and his men get trapped in a cave by a one-eyed giant, half the story is how the monster keeps his flock of sheep, makes cheese of their milk and loves a favourite ram. Homer's view of life is tragic. He has no hope that human history will ever make up for the unjust things people do to each other, but mingled in the tragedy he shows the eternal gods who are the cause of it and comic relief from it. The Greek gods are manlike and womanlike too. They are the undying forms of love, wisdom, belligerence, art, craft and government which inspire us to greatness yet turn us against each other.

An example of Homeric realism: Achilles, the best Greek fighter, suggests that the Greeks go home because their general is unjust and their war futile. Thersites, an ugly soldier of lower rank, loudly agrees. He is beaten for his impertinence, the higher officers unite again and the war continues.

By the fifth century before Christ there were many literate Greek states and colonies round the Mediterranean and some developed conversation to an astonish-

When the people of Greek states grew too many for the food supply the government sent ships of young volunteers to a harbour on an uninhabited coast and helped them build a town there to trade with inland natives. Since most of these new states were made without warfare by free people they had many forms: hence many Greek debates about the best political constitutions.

ing extent. In Athens every man who was not a slave or immigrant was expected to attend parliament and openly discuss matters which in other cities led to riots and bloodshed. Should Athens go to war or make peace? Should workmen be compensated for injury by their employer or by the state? Could local millionaires justify their huge incomes? Was the price of food too high? Decisions on these matters were reached by a majority vote and the defeated minority accepted the decisions as law until they could get them reversed. In the city square public lectures and discussions were a common source of entertainment. Is the best system of government monarchy, aristocracy or democracy? What makes a man a good citizen? Is the sun a white-hot ball of iron larger than the Greek mainland or a whirlpool of fiery particles which coalesce on the horizon with the dawn? Is the universe made by chance operating on a chaos of elements with eternity to play about in, or did an eternal mind form it from the start? And how do the other people answer these questions? For though the Athenians thought themselves special they knew that the customs which made them special had been picked up from other people or recently invented.

The Athenian rich owned slaves, but some Athenian democrats said human beings were naturally free, so slavery was evil and should be abolished. Plato and Aristotle disagreed.

This Athenian freedom of thought, speech and action was financed by a naval fund. Other Greek states paid Athens to protect them from the vast empire of Persia in the east, and if they refused to pay the Athenian navy attacked them. Over the bodies of men killed in that warfare an Athenian statesman announced that Athens was setting the world such great examples of democratic tolerance, social welfare and civic achievement that the neighbours should gladly pay for these; but they didn't. The Athenians left great writing: among it the history of how their empire was destroyed by the wars to maintain it.

The culture of the Romans.

Historians love the Roman empire because it left clear accounts of those it vanquished and the vanquished left very few. The Roman

Only the Romans ruled for centuries over many other lands. Rome began as a small republic of belligerent farmers. Theirs was not a democracy on the Athenian plan. The plebeians were represented in the senate by just enough elected speakers to give the state unity in a crisis. Rich families managed the government and officered the army, writing their laws and reports in clear, curt, pithy Latin. Using Latin they conquered and taxed every civilization round the Mediterranean and many tribal nations beyond, but Romans who wanted ideas along with big estates stocked their libraries with Greek writing. For centuries Greek poetry, history and philosophy were as beyond the scope of a Latin author as the Greek art of making bronze statues was beyond the Roman craftsmen. As the republic ended in conspiracies and civil war some Romans feared their achievement and language was also ending. The best account of Mediterranean civilization was still Homer's. If Rome ended without getting into a great book then the best thing its empire had done was preserve and propagate the work of the Greeks.

Tacitus put the truest account of how the empire grew into the mouth of a Pictish chief: They make a desert and call it peace. *Tribes who resisted invasion were taught by massacre not to do it again. The fittest survivors were then forced to labour on roads and mine work or sent abroad as slaves. The remainder were taxed to uphold the local Roman garrison and send tribute through it to the capital. Later empires also used these methods, saw themselves as heirs of Rome and called it civilization: a word which means city life, but is now a badge by which rich nations compliment themselves and each other.*

Twenty-seven years before Christ Augustus Caesar became first Roman emperor with the help of Maecenas, the richest and cleverest Roman banker. After defeating all his rivals in the civil war Augustus (I quote the Oxford Classical Dictionary) "assured freedom of trade and wealth to the upper classes," and, "gave peace, as long as it was consistent with the interests of the empire and the myth of his glory." He and Maecenas knew a Latin poet who cared for human culture and had proved it by writing fine poems about the cultivation of land, doing for Italy what the Greek poets Hesiod and Theocritus had done: making verse about peaceful farming and everyday faith. Encouraged and funded by the most powerful men in the new empire Virgil, who hated war, wrote a Roman epic to rival Homer and justify the Roman conquests.

A TRIUMPH FOR STATE PATRONAGE.

He had no crude love of earthly power, and like all deep thinkers on human history was more disturbed by the sufferings of the defeated than dazzled by splendid winners. He did not describe the empire growing from a small thatched republican town to a marble-surfaced, world-bullying capital. His story describes the struggles of a Trojan refugee, Aeneas, who escapes from Troy while the Greeks loot and burn it. Aeneas leads his son and a few survivors round several Mediterranean shores, suffering hardship and abandoning the woman he loves before reaching Italy and fighting to found the state which will become Rome. Homer's heroes (Achilles and Ulysses) are moved by a greed for fame, wealth and luxuries. Virgil's Aeneas is a modest, careful, steady man guided like Moses by one idea: to get a home for his people. During his struggle the gods encourage him with a vision of the future when his

Ulysses is also moved by a wish to get home, but moves so slowly that on the way he lives for 8 years with a goddess on an island.

greatest descendant, Augustus Caesar, will make a peaceful home for all mankind by becoming the first emperor to rule Europe, Asia and Africa. Virgil fell ill before completing this epic and died after ordering his secretaries to burn it. He has been called a perfectionist who did not want to be remembered by something incomplete. The obvious reason is his loss of faith in government by conquest, loss of faith in Caesarism. Augustus Caesar preserved and published the *Aeneid.* It has been used to excuse him and his kind ever since. Kaisers and Czars adopted his family name. Dutch, English, French and German kings have been sculptured in the armour his statues wear. Most autocrats prefer imitation to creation.

A vision of universal Roman peace made through warfare is rejected by the poet who describes it, promoted by the emperor who ordered it.

In his novel *The Confidence-Man* Herman Melville says few books contain a truly original character and no book can contain more than one. A truly original character (says Melville) makes the readers see themselves in a wholly new way, and he mentions Hamlet and Milton's Lucifer. He had Jesus of Nazareth in mind but was too cunning to say so. All we know of Jesus is four short books written in a Jewish dialect of Greek over fifty years after his crucifixion. They describe him as the living body of the god who made the universe and say he loved and loves people equally, even his enemies. They say he will give eternal life and happiness to all who believe in him, and prove it by loving each other and forgiving who hurt them. This message is either total rubbish or tells the whole truth about how we should live with each other. Hardly anyone has the strength to wholly accept or reject it, and those who explain why they partly reject and partly accept it end by describing themselves. The portrait is never flattering.

A truly original character gives a loving recipe for peace which none who hear are able to wholly grasp or reject.

I am introducing elements of English literature, so having mentioned the Christian gospels I need only mention a story added to them by the fathers of the Christian church: the story of the devil. They got it from an old Hebrew tradition which the rabbis who edited the Hebrew scriptures had mostly edited out. This says God was *not* alone before he made the world but lived in the heaven of an earlier creation with lesser gods, his servants. One of these rebelled, was cast out with his followers, and became the devil. God then made people to serve him instead, but first made the world as a ground where he could test their loyalty. The test was

Christ's followers bring in the Devil.

the rebel god, allowed by the strongest god to roam the world goading people into rebellion too.

No advantage of race, wealth or cleverness was needed to become Christian and the earliest commentors on Christianity say it was widespread among slaves and women: those whose lives the empire spectacularly cheapened. Roman justice, Roman triumphs and Roman circuses had turned organized cruelty and the murder of the helpless into civic duties, common conveniences and popular entertainments. Like the law in all countries Roman law was mainly devised to protect the property of those who had a lot and allow the owners to do what they liked with it. Roman law defined slaves and infants as property. How the Romans used slaves and prisoners of war in the Colosseum is well known. In the streets outside, inconvenient babies, mostly girls, were left in urns in public places to die or be picked up by those with a use for one. Rich people did this with their own surplus children: why not with the children of their slaves? It was sometimes cheaper to buy or inherit a working adult than pay to rear one from infancy. It is no wonder that the verbal kingdom of Christ speedily grew more popular than the earthly empire of Rome: that when the empire weakened through outside attack and internal revolt, the Caesars allied themselves with the heads of the Christian church. When Christianity was made the official religion of the empire many Christians attacked the temples and synagogues of their neighbours and fought each other over the nature of the man who told them to love their enemies. If Gibbon is right in thinking this alliance destroyed that empire we should still all thank god for it.

The Roman Institutes of Justinian *is the first book read by law students in mainland Europe and Scotland. Its primary purpose is to preserve the property of wealth-inheritors (Patricians) from the wage earners (Plebeians).*

THE CAESARS PROLONG THEIR EMPIRE BY ALLIANCE WITH THE BISHOPS OF THE CHRISTIAN KINGDOM TO COME.

In the fourth century of the Christian era Saint Jerome translated the Jewish and Christian Greek gospels into Latin, putting the Bible beside Virgil's *Aeneid* as the greatest classic of Latin literature. Monks and scholars copied and preserved them till the invention of printing, for though very different they inspired a similar hope. The Bible promised a future heaven, perhaps even a heaven on earth, for those who joined that pilgrimage to the New Jerusalem which started when Moses led god's children out of Egypt. Virgil suggested that centuries of earthly warfare would one day end in a well-governed, peaceful kingdom for

THE JEWISH-GREEK-ROMAN-CHRISTIAN SYNTHESIS.

everyone. At the present time (Britain 1989) the idea that world history or any people's history can move toward a better state for all is widely advertised as socialist or utopian, but certainly impractical and out of date. Most prosperous people believe no better state is possible for anyone. This too will pass.

In its republican youth the Roman empire depended on local farmers who worked their own land. The Caesarian empire was ruled almost exclusively by money-lending slave-owners who were defended by armies increasingly recruited from foreigners. That the armies chose the Caesar was the only vestige of democracy, and they chose men who paid them as much as possible. The taxes maintaining them were increasingly levied on the poor. Small farmers became slaves on the great estates, craftsmen left the towns and became itinerant because they could not pay these taxes. The exploiters of the system kept it going by various shifts, but population declined and fields went out of cultivation. A dietician has suggested the imperial rulers lost their grip because they ate food seethed in lead vessels, which damaged the brain. Some emperors were certainly lunatics, but no class of rulers has yet turned a cruel, disaster-bound system which profits them into a decent, safer one which does not.

Thomas Carlyle points out that most history describes not how life was lived, but how it was interrupted by invasion, warfare, plague, famine, riot and other diseases. Yet all this time, *he says,* fields were sown and reaped; the builder built; the writer wrote. *Between 400 and 1400 A.D. the best farming, finest building, ablest writing in Europe was maintained by the monasteries: small self-supporting states in which nobody was a property owner, and which gave most members and many visitors the benefits of a well-run commonwealth: schools for the young, hospitals for the sick, a bed for strangers, a livelihood in return for useful, peaceful work. The vow of celibacy ensured that the communal property was not split into parcels for children to inherit. The good of their children is the strongest case people have for supporting and benefiting from injustice.*

About 400 A.D. the Chinese empire had expanded beyond the wall built to protect it, displacing fierce nomads who suddenly invaded Europe from the east. The Roman empire had always been under threat from German tribes in the northern forests and these too now helped to break it up. Caesar Constantine had already shifted the capital from Rome to Byzantium, which became the centre of the biggest and richest region to survive the crack-up. Rome dwindled to a collection of vast half-empty buildings housing a Christian bishop. Elsewhere in Europe a few towns became separate communes ruled by Roman law but fed by traders who mainly bartered: otherwise such towns' government was the protection of local war lords who taxed by plundering. Folk cannot be plundered continually unless allowed time to recover. From this social chaos grew feudal Europe: a collection of states whose fields, cottages and strongholds were not owned by the users but rented from a landlord who was ultimately a king. Rent was paid in produce or labour or war service, not money. Even in the towns money was only used as a means of exchange, so for nearly a millennium Christians thought money-lending for profit was an unnatural vice.

That millennium was once called The Dark Ages, as if a foggy valley separated the sunny heights of pagan Rome from the bright slopes of Renaissance Italy; but these ages seemed as bright as ours to most who dwelled in them, and there is continuous information about every province Rome lost (except Britain) because Christian priests remained active where the legions perished or retreated. The strength of literate thought, or of god's word, or of both, is shown in how fast the belligerent invaders got christened. Chieftains who had worshipped Thor and Woden in the German forests conquered Paris and Toledo, Arles and Ravenna, yet their children became kings who adored the relics of martyrs, discussed the Holy Trinity with archbishops and gave monastic lands to abbots. The new military rulers did not know how to read, write or talk easily in the language of the natives. In the Christian church they met an organization so strong and popular that two centuries before it had christianized the previous military rulers, supported them and survived them. The church had bishops and priests in every town and most settlements. Their monasteries were now almost the only homes of ancient learning. The few kings who tried ruling in spite of the church were soon replaced by better Christians everywhere, except Britain.

German, Vandal and Gothic invaders speedily adopt God's written word.

In Virgil's first pastoral poem a small farmer robbed of his land by the government laments that he and those like him must now disperse:

The state of Britain.

To Scythia, bone-dry Africa,
the chalky spate of the Oxus,
Even to Britain,
that place cut off at the very world's end.

Britain is now the home of nearly fifty-six million people (56,000,000), over nine-tenths of them in dense urban clusters. Of the remaining land nearly half is very fertile and supports mixtures of arable and cattle farming. The rest is mountain, hill, moorland and downs where very few folk live because it is used for sheep farms, military projects, cheap forestry and the sports of the wealthy. When Julius Caesar invaded Britain it housed about six-tenths of a million (600,000), and they

BRITAIN A THINLY PEOPLED WILDERNESS, MAINLY FOREST AND MOORLAND.

dwelt mainly in the high valleys, the bays and islands round the coast, on the moorlands and downs where the great stone monuments and earthworks stand. The land now occupied by our cities and agriculture was mostly swampy forest, for fertile soil near slow wide rivers can only be cultivated when the banks are made firm and the ground is drained. There was farming here, but in clearings. The legions subdued Britain up to Pictland, though their hold on Wales and the north was slight and they did not touch Ireland. They built towns supported by villa farming and linked by roads which pierced the deciduous jungle. General Constantine was opposing the Picts in 306 A.D. when his father died and the troops proclaimed him Caesar. It was he who, without being christened, made Christianity the official Roman religion, then moved the imperial capital east. Two and a half centuries later a historian and diplomat in Constantinople wrote a book saying an area of Britain is under so thick a layer of snakes that none can stand there, some air so poisonous none can breathe it. He says many think Britain a home of the dead, that boatmen on the French coast ferry ghosts by night across the narrow channel to the British shore. Like the planet Mars in the early twentieth century Britain had become a place of which anything could be imagined. The English were there.

ROMAN CULTURE IN BRITAIN.

THE SCIENCE-FICTION OF PROCOPIUS.

The press of populations westward which drove tribes of fighters down into Italy, France and Spain had pushed other German tribes across the sea in ships. Their skill in woodcraft is proved by their ships, in metalwork by their weapons. In the Romanized Britain of the south and east they found woodlands like those they had left but without enough natives to support them as a ruling class. At home the Anglo-Saxon tribes only elected a king for the duration of a war. The wars establishing their settlements in Britain never ended because they were soon fighting or preparing to fight each other. Many little quarrelsome kingdoms were founded, six with the names and territories of modern English counties. Their wars created slaves as well as kings. The remaining Britons were forced out among the Celtic nations of the westward coast, which was now called Wales. Rivers, homesteads and boundaries, even days of the week were renamed in German and with names of northern gods who replaced Christ.

GERMAN INVASIONS—HERE COME THE ENGLISH.

ANGLO-SAXON CULTURE.

In a 600 A.D. code of Anglo-Saxon law, the fines for injuring a man's English slave are much greater than for injuring his Welsh slave (See Ine's Code*). In time of famine poor Englishmen sometimes became slaves of the wealthy in return for food.*

What we now call the North Sea became a German sea with German tribes and kingdoms on its coasts from Norway down to France in the west, from Kent up to Edinburgh in the east. But the Germans in mainland Europe were being informed by the language and faith of those they conquered. In the lands lost by Roman Britain the British, Roman and Christian thought vanished as completely as the art of building with stone and brick.

CELTIC CULTURE.

But though the North Sea had become a German Mediterranean the Irish Sea was still a Celtic one, the kingdoms of Ireland on its west coast, the islands and peninsula of the Scots to the north, Strathclyde and Cumbria and Wales to the east, Cornwall on the south. These had been governed by alliances of tribal chieftains and a hereditary class of poetic lawmakers who sang of the chieftains' prowess and judged their disputes. Without pressure of conquest the chieftains were now adopting Christianity, several of them becoming missionaries and priests. Monasteries were founded where monks copied Jerome's Bible and other Latin classics while writing their own chronicles and poems in Gaelic as well as Latin. For two or three centuries before the Viking invasions knocked everything about, this Celtic Mediterranean was a safe place for scholarship. The cathedral island of Iona became its spiritual capital. Two seas and stormy new pagan kingdoms separated this Celtic church from the Roman one, which for a while had little time for peaceful scholarship. Mohammedan raiders were taking Africa and Spain away from Christianity; in north Europe the priesthood were helping the fierce gothick monarchies against Attila; the Roman and Byzantine bishops were quarrelling about the nature of the Holy Trinity. As a result of these upheavals Irish-Scottish scholars had a high reputation around the Latin-Greek Mediterranean. Irish Celts founded monasteries in Burgundy and Switzerland. This Christian scholarship on the far side of a pagan wilderness encouraged the view of Britain as a dank dangerous forested place lit by supernatural gleams. The English settlers there had this view of life in general, when they came to write it down. Reader, after another four paragraphs and a prayer you will reach the start of this book.

LITERATURE AND THE CELTIC CHURCH.

Before 900 A.D. the Irish were also called Scots. North of Clyde-Forth most Scots were called Picts, and in Strathclyde and Galloway, Welsh. Pelagius was the best known Irish scholar. Because corrupt priests blamed the original sin of Adam for their crimes, he urged more faith in human reason, saying, "If we ought, we can." He was a poorer theologian and psychologist than St. Augustine, and condemned as a heretic, though Italian bishops supported him at first.

In the seventh century Northumbria became the big-

THE CULTURE OF NORTHUMBRIA: A CELTIC-ENGLISH SYNTHESIS.

gest and most stable English kingdom, holding back Picts north of the Forth, Mercians south of the Humber, and driving the Welsh of Cumbria further into the west: yet it was christianized by monks from Iona in what seems less than fifty years. At Jarrow, Wearmouth and the Holy Isle of Lindisfarne they and their pupils made gospel books in a style the *Encyclopaedia Britannica* calls Hiberno–Saxon, which means Irish–English. The initials of words were surrounded or filled with richly interwoven Celtic scrolls and spirals, skilfully inlaid with gold and the jewelled colours the Anglo-Saxons used in their finest metal ornaments. Remember a piece of music, or a building, or machine, or anything which gave you delight along with astonishment that people could make it. Pages of the book of Kells and the Lindisfarne gospel are as good as that. Until the ninth century such books, with church ornaments of metal and ivory, were Britain's only notable export—the continental clergy wanted them. And at Whitby in a monastery with a Gaelic name (Streaneshalch) the new Christian learning stirred two very different people into making the first English literature.

Saint Augustine, sent by Pope Gregory, landed around this time in Kent and founded Canterbury. For half a century the southern Roman Church and the Celtic northern one were divided by the pagan alliance of Mercia. At Hilda's abbey the priests of Iona and Canterbury met to decide which should have priority. Hilda was for Iona. The Northumbrian king voted for Canterbury, which prevailed.

Hilda's uncle was a pagan Northumbrian king, a successful warlord who gave his name (Edwin) to his northern capital (Edinburgh). He got baptized five years before he died and Hilda, then thirteen, was baptized with him. She became a nun, an abbess and a saint, after ruling the double monastery for nuns and monks at Whitby. While working there she learned that a local herdsman thought he was a poet, though he had not composed anything. An angel in a dream had ordered him to sing about "the beginning of things," but he was too ignorant to start. Hilda tested the man's talent by getting priests to tell him the Christian creation story and to write down what he made of it. His verses were good. He never learned to write but was enrolled in the monastery where he dictated more poems.

ABBESS-PRINCESS + SHEPHERD-POET = FIRST ENGLISH LITERATURE.

The snobbish idea that poetry is writing has cut it off from music, so most good poetry is not now popular in Britain and the U.S.A.

Any talent which gives a good new thing to others is a miracle, but commentators have thought it extra miraculous that England's first known poet was an illiterate herdsman. They forgot three things.

ONE

POETRY IS SPEECH.

Poetry is a kind of speech, not a kind of writing. For

over half a million years poets learned to make it by hearing it sung or recited, then by repeating it with the changes and additions they preferred. In a very few places, three or four thousand years ago, writing approached poetry as a humble secretary, able to record an especially good poem so that later folk could not change or lose it. The vulgar notion that a poet must be a writer arrived when a lot of wealthy literate folk decided nothing good could be made without the help of their expensive educations, except by a miracle. In Hilda's day even emperors could not write. Nobody expected it of a poet.

TWO

A POET'S TRAINING.

After hearing and repeating poems until the rhythms and the vocabularies are in their nerves, poets need long uninterrupted spells of talking to themselves. Herding once allowed this. From Theocritus in ancient Greece to James Hogg twenty centuries later, the link between herding and poetry was so famous a literary cliché that even writers forgot it had been a fact.

THREE

A UNIQUE PATRON.

The miracle was a clever strong ruler using her learning and advantages to free a poet in the slave class. Most patrons who want poetry seek it where Augustus and Mycaenas searched—in a social class close to their own. With more like Hilda literature would not now contain such huge silences and absences about the lives of most people. She really was a saint.

So now English literature can start. A monk who got learning from the Irish Scots is taking dictation from a herdsman singing to him in a Northumbrian dialect of Anglo-Saxon. He sings a Jewish creation story transmitted to him through at least three other languages by a Graeco-Roman-Celtic Christian church. Since the verse forms and vocabularies in his nerves were learned from pagan German warrior chants, his Genesis poem is colder, fiercer and more spooky than the version most of us know: the version authorised by a Tudor head of state nearly a thousand years later. This is also because he prefaces his Genesis with the story of how god's chief angel became the devil. The monk

In his History of the Church in England *Bede says the poet herdsman had listened hard to singers and wanted to be one.*

writing this uses an alphabet close to our own, a Roman adaptation of a Greek adaptation of a Semitic adaptation of an Egyptian adaptation of signs used first beside the Euphrates river in the city of Sumer, later called Babylon, five thousand years before Christ.

The Anglo-Saxon alphabet had two letters we do not now use: one for the soft noise which starts *thud* and ends *bath,* one for the lightly buzzing noise which starts *the* and ends *breathe* and *wreathe.* I apologise for replacing both by *th.* This compromise will not stop you getting some taste of the language the poet and the monk used, if you murmur aloud Christ's best known prayer in Anglo-Saxon. The better known Tudor English version will help understanding. Note that in 650 the *c* is always hard, and a final *e* is pronounced, so *rice* sounds like *ricki.*

CHRIST'S PRAYER: c 650

FAEDER ure,
Thu the eart heafonum,
Si thin nama gehalgod.
Tobecume thin rice.
Gewurthe thin willa on eorthan
swa swa on heofonum.
rne gedaeghwamlican
hlaf syle us to daeg
And forgyf us ure gyltas
swa swa we forgyfath
ure glytendum
And ne gelaed thu us on costnunge,
Ac alys us of yfele.
Sothlice.

CHRIST'S PRAYER: c 1550

Our father.
Whyche art in heaven,
Halowed be thy name.
Thy Kyngdome come.
Thy wyll be doen in yearth,
as it is in heaven.
Geve us this daye
our dayly breade.
And forgeve us our trespaces,
as wee forgeve them
that trespasse agaynst us.
And leade us not into temptacion.
But deliver us from evill.
Amen.

All these old English words contain sounds of words we still use in similar ways, apart from *rice* (realm, or *reich* in German) and *sothlice* (truthlike or truly). *Gewurthe* means worth be given: the unwieldy *gedaeghwamlican* has daily inside: *hlaf* means loaf: *gyltas,* guilt: *gyltendum,* guilty-doers-to: *costnunge,* a bad or costly choice: *alys,* release. If spoken in northern accents Christ's prayer in Anglo-Saxon sounds oddly familiar. Some Scottish and Northumbrian folk still say "oor faither" and "thoo art."

Read on, please.

Time Travel

Alasdair Gray

I DISCOVERED AN ODD THING about my left foot when about to pull on a sock this morning. In the groove between the second and third toe, reckoning from the big toe, is a small grey pellet of chewing-gum. I do not chew gum, or know or remember meeting anyone who does. I sometimes patter about this room in my dressing-gown and bare feet, but I never go out of it, and nobody comes here nowadays except the one who cares for me, who is Zoë I believe. And hope. Zoë would never play such a sly wee disturbing trick as putting a sticky sweet between the toes of a sleeping man. Her tricks were all bonny and lavish. I once came home to find that a friend had given her back money we had lent him, money we had stopped expecting to get back, though we needed it for food and rent. Zoë had spent half of it on food all right—we had food enough to last a fortnight. She had spent the rest on flowers. The bedroom floor was covered with vases, jugs, bowls, pans, basins, kettles so full of irises, lilacs and carnations that the bed seemed afloat in a small Loch Lomond of blue, purple and crimson petals. The scent nearly knocked me out. I had to be angry. I saw the loving goodness in that gesture, but had I encouraged lavishness we would have ended up homeless. She knew it, too. Once when I chose to be lavish she grew thoughtful, worried, then angry. She wanted me to be careful and mean so that she could be lavish, which does not explain how this chewing-gum arrived between my toes.

I do not believe in miracles. I believe the human mind can solve, rationally, any problem it recognizes and closely attends to. I decided not to finish dressing before I solved this one, though I usually earn my pocket-money and the right to stay here by working on the problem of time travel. I dropped the left sock on the floor (Zoë would pick it up) and from a sitting posture on the edge of the bed moved to a prone one on top of the quilt, which I must remember to call *a doovay.* If I do not learn to use the new words people keep inventing I will one day find I am talking a dead language. I decided to tackle the problem of the chewing-gum by a strategy combining Algebra, Euclidean Geometry and Baconian Induction; but feeling slightly cold in my semmit and single sock I first crept under the doovay and wrapped it round me because a snug body allows a clear mind.

GIVEN: M – Me who sometimes patter barefoot round this room. P – Pellet of gum stuck to the foot of M. UG – Unknown Gumchewer who is the source and prime mover of P. R – Room that M never leaves and UG never enters. W – World containing M, P. UG, R and other items and events.

REQUIRED: To find the likeliest event or events which could move P from the mouth of UG to the foot of M while preserving these conditions:–

1. M and UG remain ignorant of each other.

2. M is ignorant of P before finding P between his toes.

3. UG is ignorant of P's movement after it leaves him, but not while it leaves him. (Chewed gum only leaves a mouth by being swallowed or spat or removed by fingers and flicked into air or removed by fingers and attached to other item: all of which are conscious acts though soon forgotten.)

CONSTRUCTION! – Yes, I was now ready and able to set out the problem in geometrical space-time. I needed no pencil, paper, ruler or compasses. The decay of my organs and senses stops me doing or showing much to other people but strengthens my ability to see things inside. When completely dead to the world I expect to see it all perfectly. Without even closing my eyes I now visualize this:

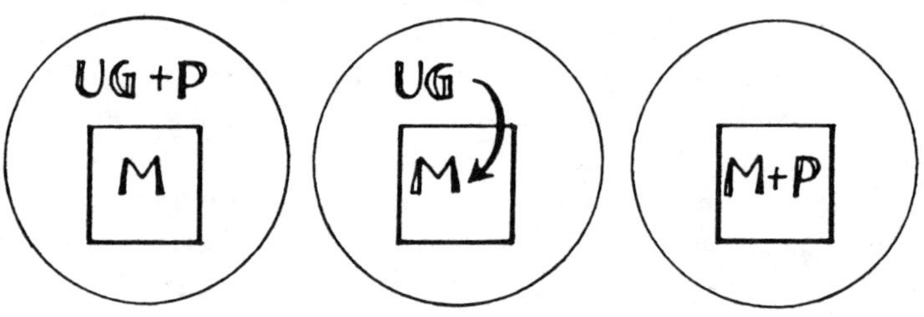

The circles represent the world, the squares my room, the curved arrow the movement of the pellet into the room. Could I picture a single, simple event able to fire P for Pellet from the world outside onto the dark green mottled linoleum of this floor, from which the pressure and warmth of my foot later detached it? I pictured one easily.

Outside my window is an ash tree which looks insanely active, even when standing still. Three tall trunks diverge upward from the same root, and a few boughs or long branches fork from these in elegant curves, but most of them grow straight for a yard or more then, as if turning a corner, bend abruptly up or down or sideways, then undulate, zigzag, spiral, turn steep U-bends or suddenly explode outward into a lot of smaller branches, themselves as knotted and twisted as the tentacles of an arthritic squid. On the day I discovered the chewing-gum all these trunks, boughs, branches with their twigs and leaves were swaying, writhing, lashing about and reminding me they were rooted in a space of grass too smooth to be called a field, too rough to be called a lawn. I seemed to remember an asphalt path between the tree and window, but nearer the window than the tree. I easily imagined a stout sturdy man wearing boiler-suit, Wellington boots and cloth cap who strides along that path chewing a piece of gum which gets so flavourless that he fixes it to the ball of his thumb near the tip, bends his strong middle finger until the top edge of the nail touches the crease in the joint of his thumb then, using the thumb as a lock he builds up muscular pressure in the finger until, seeing an open window just ahead he mischievously aims his hand, unlocked his thumb and (without pausing in his stride) flicks slings catapults the pellet through onto the floor of the room, remaining as ignorant of me as I of him, at that moment. But the window is never open, so I must now seek a more complex though equally elegant solution to this problem.

Is? Now seek? This problem? I seem to be conducting my investigation in the present tense, though I certainly began it in the past. Time travel is unending. And I am sorry that the continually shut nature of the window has made that stout man improbable. For a moment I thought him a friend. I used to ask the one who cares for me (not Zoë, the other one) to open this window on sunny days, but he or she always said, "Sorry Dad no can do. It's against the rules. Why do you think we paid for air-conditioning?" I don't know why we paid for air-conditioning. I hate it. I learned to hate it in the 1980s when I was famous. I must have been, because people kept asking me how it felt to be famous. I always said, "Fine thank you, the perquisites are useful." The only perquisite I can now recall is flying from airport to airport all over North America, and sleeping in hotels, and appearing on platforms in conference centres. The airports, hotels and conference centres were very similar buildings with the same kind of furniture and windows which could not be opened because of the air-conditioning. The air on the aeroplanes was fresher, though I could not open windows in those either. The only openable windows I saw in America belonged to cars speeding from one building to another, and would have poisoned me with exhaust fumes had I opened them. So I am used to breathing stale air, but it has damaged my memory. I do not know why people thought me famous, and asked me all over America, and why I went. It must have been a lie. When I was small, and passionately wanted to tell my mother something, and suddenly found I could not remember what it was, she always said, "It must have been a lie."

Wait a minute! I remember something said by a man who was introducing me to a big audience in Toronto or San Francisco or Quebec or Chicago or Montreal or Pittsburgh or Vancouver: *the most humane, far-sighted and lucid thinker the 20th century has known,* he called me. Yes yes. I travelled all over North America because I enjoyed the introductory speeches. This casts no light on the problem of the chewing-gum. I now know that UG could not flick or spit P for Pellet into this room. I am sure UG did not swallow it. Even if such a pellet could keep its colour, adhesiveness and integrity through a digestive tract, bowel gut and sphincter, its position after that would make its entry into my room improbable, whether UG defecated into a public sewage system or crapped behind a hedge. The following construction shows the likeliest chain of events. X represents a commonplace item in the world outside my room and later within it, having been brought from there to here by . . . but the item itself will indicate who brought it, so *visualize!*

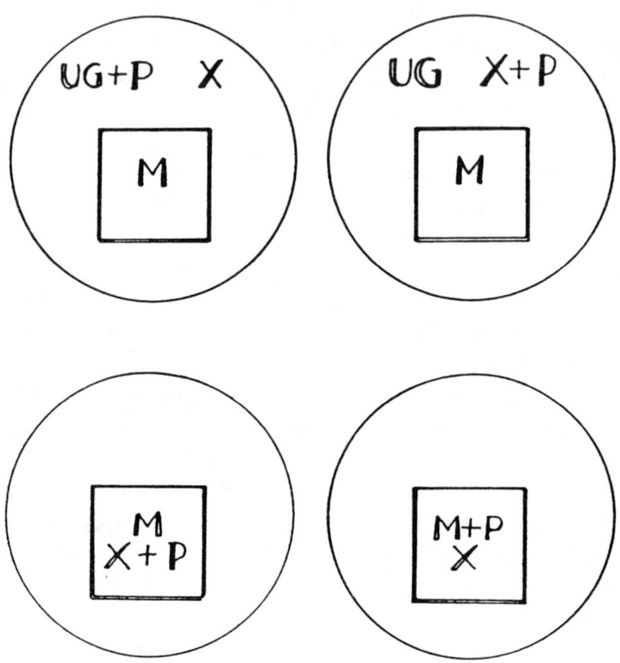

In this construction UG gets rid of P by casually sticking it onto X, which is carried into this room by Zoë, or by one of the other people who look after me, or by a visitor. But nobody has visited me for years so the fame did not last.

The problem had now been carried as near to a solution as this method allowed. I love the deductive method. No wonder its union of Greek geometry and Islamic algebra has seduced nearly every Continental thinker from Descartes to Lévi-Strauss. However, to identify X I needed the inductive method, the practical British approach devised by the two Bacons and William of Occam. I was making a list of everything in the room I could have trodden on when my attention was distracted by the queer behaviour of a chair I had known for years. It stands between my bed and the window, but nearer the window than my bed. I must describe how it usually appears before telling how it acted on the day I found the pellet.

It is a low, light arm-chair with a wooden frame, made not long after the Second World War when money was more evenly spread, materials were in short supply, extravagant use of them was thought wasteful and ugly. Yet this chair does not look cheap. The elegantly tapered curves of the legs, the modestly widening, welcoming curve of the arms owe something to Japan and Scandinavia as well as aeroplane design. The seat and back are not thickly upholstered but so well supported that they feel perfectly comfortable. All the furniture Zoë owned looks and feels good. There was once another chair exactly like this one, and a sofa matching them. If people wanted a standard arm-chair I would honestly propose this one, as James Watt proposed a healthy workhorse without defects as the standard by which the power of artificial engines is measured to this day. Or does that last sentence show I am living in the past? Have engineers stopped measuring the strength of engines in horse-power? Are horses as extinct as whales? Is the Watt no longer a unit of electrical force? Watt was an 18th-century machinist from Greenock who invented the coal-fired water vapour engine. Has Rudolf Diesel's compression fired oil vapour engine supplanted Watt's terminology as well as his machines? Don't panic. I suspect this is a word problem, a quilt-doovay problem, not destruction-of-Scottish-achievement-by-German-achievement problem. Unless I describe the usual colour of the chair the oddity of its conduct a week ago cannot be described.

The parts of the woodwork designed to be seen have been polished, stained and varnished to a medium chocolate colour that almost hides the grain. The upholstery is covered by a russet red fabric I found annoyingly bright before it faded. When in bed I view the chair in profile, like the chair Whistler's mother sits on, and see a tall narrow hole in the fabric of the back of the side, a hole through which at least twenty-four inches of pale unpolished unvarnished timber appear like a bone seen through an open wound. This hole has not been worn or torn open but shredded, as by a cat's claws—threads and shreds of fabric dangle down from the edges all round it. In the years when I rummaged in cupboards I found other evidence of a cat: a plastic feeding dish with FLUFFY printed on the sloping sides, and behind containers of Marmite Yeast Extract and Granny's Tomato Soup a tin of Whiskas Supermeat, Chicken and Rabbit Variety. Most sinister of all, behind the long-lost matching sofa I once saw a cardboard box more than two feet square with an arched hole like a door cut into one side, and crayoned over the sides and top a pattern suggesting brickwork, with the words CAT-PALACE, MOG-A-DEN and FLUFFY HOUSE. This writing was not in Zoë's hand. It suggested that before she helped me up from the pavement and brought me home here she loved another human being as well as a cat, somebody who enjoyed fishing. There was a wicker creel under the bed, an angling rod in the wardrobe, waders in the lobby press. I said nothing about these articles and one day I came home and they had gone. I said nothing, because out of sight is out of mind if I want it to be, nor did I mind Fluffy ripping at the chair. Cats invented themselves by clawing their way up and down tree trunks and scratching soil or grass over their excrement. Forbidding cats to scratch is like forbidding humans to cut their nails and hair. Also, the chair was not responding to Fluffy in the year I found the pellet. It was brightening and darkening. The dim russet fabric glowed and flickered, then leapt into dazzling vividness like when new, but with a moving pattern of leaves dancing over it in a very irregular way. This pattern (dull red on bright russet) was dove grey on creamy ivory over the exposed timber. For half a minute the chair persisted in this way then suddenly, like an exhausted dancer, slumped in two or three seconds back to its ordinary dull old colours. Had the chair been remembering leaves it had seen in earlier days?

Glancing through the window I noticed a remarkable coincidence. The leaves of the ash tree had the shapes and dancing movements of the pattern which had recently faded from the chair. And I saw another coincidence! Leaves, branches and trunks were flickering, lashing, swaying in the same direction and with the same turbulence as ragged whiteish-grey clouds in the sky beyond, clouds with shifting patches of blue and gleams of unpredictable sunlight between them. Without its underground roots every part of that tree would have flown off with the clouds, which shows the infectious force of a strong example. Had the air between the tree and clouds been visible I might have seen it rushing along too. For a moment I considered working out how the movements within the chair had been caused. People will pay a lot of money for objects that blaze and flicker, as television sets and games machines in public houses show. But I am too old to venture into show business. It is enough for me to passively enjoy the play of natural coincidences and actively enjoy the play of inward speculation. These two plays led to my famous discovery. Of course they did.

Einstein had died without establishing the unified field hypothesis, all the physicists had agreed the thing was impossible when I—a botanist—proved that every part and particle of the universe reflects every other part and particle and every past and eventual possibility inherent in each part and particle. My dissertation proving the identity of sense and motion in water lilies also proved the identity of sense and motion everywhere! And it cleared away all the paradoxes in Newtonian gravitation by showing that Kepler as well as Einstein had been right all along. Look at a star. Astronomers will say it is a distant sun or nebula, but even a moth can see it is a body of light. We know it gives light because we live inside the radiance of the gift—live inside the star. That twinkling little item is the core or central pip of a radiant fruit containing every other star and galaxy. My discovery angered many clever people, for by proving that loneliness is a convenient form of ignorance it left them nowhere to hide. "Nonsense!" roared the hearty pragmatists, "The light, heat, sounds et cetera given out by a body are not parts of the body, they are its excrement. Some bodies fling useful shit at us, some fling the dangerous kind so we need to identify the sources. The source you call a star is a mass of fissile material exuding beams essential to life and useful to navigators." People with this self-centred view cannot be faulted. They want to be nothing but cockroaches in the larder of the universe, so have no interest in the rest of the palace. There was more dignity in the wrath of a great French scientist who was also a practising catholic, and so obsessed by the needless division between mind and body—so certain that only a God *outside* the universe could redeem what he thought was its horrible nature—that he would not see the regenerative side of my discovery. "The silence of these vast spaces appals me," he said, talking about the gaps between the stars. I told him these gaps were spaces between the bodies in a busy market where light was being exchanged so rapidly our eyes could not catch it. "Imbecile!" he cried, "Do you not know that whole blazing star systems are receding from us faster than light can travel, and will collapse into black cinders without a single ray or thought from them ever reaching the frozen cinder which was once our little world?" I pointed out that while answering me his own mind had overtaken these blazing systems, had survived their extinction and returned to our own extinct world, enlivening it with one ray of impossible light, dignifying it with an impossibly gloomy thought. He frowned and said, "You are playing with words. Words are an expression of thought, not a physical force." I pointed out that spoken sounds, though perhaps unable to open a closed mind, were as physical a force as dawn sunbeams that open the petals of daisies. But he so gloried in the faith he needed to face his appalling universe that he muttered, "Solipsist!" and turned his back on me. The Americans did not, or not at first. I expect they used me in propaganda for their space programme, or space race, or whatever the advertisers called it before the Russians made it pointless by stopping pretending to compete.

Having solved the universal problems I now need to exercise my brain with smaller matters like time travel, and where Zoë has been for the last two or three days, and Between Two Toes, or The Case of the Mysterious Pellet.

I cannot now say if I am solving the last of these problems in the present or remembering how I once solved it in the past but the time came (or has come) when I made (or will make) a list of items brought recently into my room from the world outside: food, cleaned clothes and towels, newspapers and letters. Then I made (or will make) another list of items on the floor of the room, items my foot could have pattered across: the linoleum, a fringed rug and things often dropped on these like food, clothes, towels, newspapers and letters. Items common to both lists should then be considered one at a time with great care, for one of these must be item X. And I have just remembered that letters and newspapers should be on neither list. Nobody has written to me for years, and I stopped taking papers during the last great miners' strike in the 1980s when I saw that Britain had again become a financial oligarchy protected by the ancient fraud of a two-party electoral system. But the lists are not needed because I now see the gum MUST have come from inside the sock I wore yesterday, a sock which like all my clothes is washed in a machine outside this room where the clothes of other people (one of whom must be the Unknown Gumchewer) are also washed. UG accidentally attached the P for Pellet to a cardigan or other woollen article. UG's helper (who is probably one of mine too) put it in the drum of a machine whose soapy solutions and hydraulic pressures dissolved most of the dirt but only displaced P for Pellet from the cardigan to the toe of my sock while the sock was inside out: its invariable state after I pull it off at night. Zoë or whoever else looks after me turns the cleaned socks the right way round at night before setting out a cleaned pair for me to put on next day. The fact that all my socks are grey like the Pellet would prevent Zoë or the other one seeing and removing it. Eureka!

I basked in the elegance of this solution for two or three happy and peaceful minutes. Since discovering the Pellet I had been rolling it idly between the ball of my right-hand thumb and forefinger. I was about to flick it into a pail-shaped metal waste-bin near the bed when something in its soft, plastic adhesiveness made me doubt if it was chewing-gum at all. It was very like a more recent invention called Blu-Tack, first marketed in the 1970s (I think) as a means of attaching paper notices and light pictorial reproductions to surfaces without puncturing or staining the notices, reproductions and surfaces. But there are no such things in my room. I don't need them. Zoë's chair in front of the window, the ash tree outside it give me all the entertainment and food for thought I need. Or have I forgotten something? Look suspiciously, carefully, at all nearby surfaces. Yes, there is something I forgot.

Beside my bed is a small metal wardrobe with wheels of a kind I have never before seen outside hospitals and homes for the chronically ill and disabled. On a side of this immediately opposite my face when I lie down is a paper document fastened by blobs of Blu-Tack at the two upper and the right-hand lower corner. This letter has a conventionally regal heading and a signature at the foot scribbled by Charles King number 3. The bit between signature and heading is very prettily printed or exquisitely typed, and congratulates me on attaining my hundredth birthday. Damn. Hell. F, no don't use *fuck* as a curse word. Remember what I wrote in that review of the 1928 edition of *Lady Chatterley's Lover:* "Lawrence has restored to tender uses what should be the tenderest word in any language." The *Glasgow Herald* sacked me for writing that review. I had guts in 1928. Perhaps that was my finest hour. But this letter which I tear down, crumple and fling into the waste-bin proves three unpleasant facts:

1. This is the 21st century.
2. Britain is still a damned and blasted monarchy.
3. I have not seen Zoë lately, or anybody else I know, because she and they died in the decade after Fluffy died, nearly twenty-five years ago.

I'm glad they left me Zoë's chair.
It makes time travel easier.

Alasdair Gray: The Voice of His Prose

Philip Hobsbaum

English is the medium that Alasdair Gray uses, and there is no question but that he uses it with a difference. His prose possesses, to put it mildly, a definite personality. It is very good at conveying intelligence about people, as distinct from ideas, and that intelligence is at one with a characteristic pattern in the selection and combination of words.

> I have had to examine my memory of the events deductively, like an archaeologist investigating a prehistoric midden.

> The inmates of a hospital ward observe their neighbours closely but avoid, at first, contacting them, for each is too engrossed by their own illness to want the burden of sympathizing with someone else.

> I liked her for her kindness, and for being so easy to classify.[1]

Such antecedents as can be produced for this mode of wit do not detract from its individuality. The prose seems plain, but it is not simple. It tends to set up an expectation which it then betrays. The reader is inveigled by the familiar terms in which he or she is addressed, so to speak, onto a rug, sometimes with a prior hint or warning. But the rug is then pulled away, precipitating its victim onto a less than hospitable floor.

The point will become clear if one of the foregoing quotations is repeated, and augmented. The persona is lying ill, in the process of being shifted like a parcel from sea to land, that is, from boat to hospital.

> Sometimes my upward view was irregularly framed by downward-staring faces: the doctor, Ian, customs officers and strangers. Once the lined dry face of a middle-aged lady looked down for a moment, smiled and said, "I say, you hev hed a bit of bed luck, you've come rathah a cropper, heven't you," and some other terse kindly things full of English-hunting-field stoicism. I liked her for her kindness, and for being so easy to classify. (196)

The impression of character is reductive, but guardedly so. We can accept the caricature of Received Pronunciation, proleptic of effects in certain sections of *Something Leather,* but "English-hunting-field stoicism" bears a negative charge. Though the kindness of the hunting field may be genuine, it is undermined by the delight of the lepidopterist—Gray is an admirer of Vladimir Nabokov—in pinning this good lady into his collection of freaks.

The wit of Alasdair Gray is comparable with that of Bernard Shaw or the Samuel Butler of the *Note-Books.* Yet all the extracts so far cited stem from what is a very early work, "A Report to the Trustees of the Bellahouston Travelling Scholarship." The "Report" is an explanation of how the author had failed to fulfill the Travelling Scholarship's terms. But it is nonetheless a short story.

There is, indeed, a gesture towards travelogue.

I decided to visit London for a fortnight, travel from there to Gibraltar by ship, find a cheap place to live in southern Spain, paint there as long as the money would allow, then travel home through Granada, Málaga, Madrid, Toledo, Barcelona and Paris, viewing on the way Moorish mosques, baroque cathedrals, plateresque palaces, the works of El Greco, Velázquez and Goya, with Bosch's *Garden of Earthly Delights,* Brueghel's *Triumph of Death,* and several other grand gaudy things which are supposed to compensate for the crimes of our civilization. (185-86)

But this is a special effect of style, with a euphonious use of names designed to contrast a rococo manner with the plain prose of actuality. We are brought down to earth, however, during the next sentence: "The excellence of this plan, approved by Mr Bliss, is not lessened by the fact that I eventually spent two days in Spain and saw nothing of interest" (186). The Trustees were, according to Bruce Charlton, unappreciative of the Report, and the Travelling Scholarship scheme was subsequently wound up.[2] They would have seen the "Report" as an excuse; they could hardly have seen it as a literary masterpiece. The "Report" is the first of Alasdair Gray's achieved short stories and it is, or purports to be, fact.

Alasdair Gray's master is often identified by his admirers as Robert Louis Stevenson.[3] But even at his most apparently factual, Stevenson has a literary flourish. Such literary flourishing Gray certainly appropriates from time to time but only as a special effect, as in the manner of his hypothetical travelogue, already cited. Rather, Gray's work can be related to that of Daniel Defoe, as analogue if not indeed as antecedent. Defoe has this gift of retailing incidents in so plain a style as to make them seem surrealistic.

One day, being at that part of the town, on some special business, curiosity led me to observe things more than usually; and indeed I walked a great way where I had no business; I went up Holborn, and there the street was full of people; but they walked in the middle of the great street, neither on one side or other, because, as I suppose, they would not mingle with anybody that came out of the houses, or meet with smells and scents from houses that might be infected.[4]

This quiet noting of bizarre circumstances is synergistic: the whole amounts to more than the sum of the parts. But the composite effect is anything but quiet, whatever the incidentals may be. Rather, this composite has something of the insistence of hysteria barely under control. That is what links Alasdair Gray with Daniel Defoe and also with a number of other "realist" writers, such as William Cowper, John Clare, and Jorge Luis Borges.[5] It is a mood that is liable to seize the artist when he sees his world as especially vulnerable and consequently threatened. Such is the vision of Sarah Schulman in her novel *People in Trouble.* This novel characterizes the presence of AIDS as part of the current way of life in California. The very crispness in the writing betrays its author's sorrow.

When Kate and Molly walked up, two men were standing guard duty outside the cellar door entrance, posing nonchalantly, watching for trouble. No one knew how to stand around nonchalantly better than gay men. Almost three hundred people were packed into the windowless space. They lined the walls crammed together on every available inch. Seats were reserved only for the most seriously ill and Kate saw a few young men in various stages of the disease.[6]

The mode of Alasdair Gray is similar to that of Defoe and of Sarah Schulman in that it invokes bizarre experience in a prose that seems ostensibly matter-of-fact, even, for part of the time, low pressure.

His wish to leave this city was powerful and complete and equalled by a certainty that streets and buildings and diseased people stretched infinitely in every direction. He was standing near railings with a bank of snow beyond them which the rain had not dissolved. Some naked trees grew out of it. The trees and snow had such a fresh look that he climbed the railings and waded upward between the trunks. The lamps in the street behind showed a dim hillside laid out as a cemetery. Black gravestones stood on the snowy paleness and he climbed between them, amazed that the ground of this place had once swallowed men in a natural way. He reached a path with a bench on it, brushed snow from the seat with his sleeve, then knelt and banged his brow hard there three times, crying from the centre of his soul, "Let me out! Let me out! Let me out!"[7]

Alasdair Gray has sacrificed much in the course of his prose to achieve that final effect. Some of the description, divorced from context, could seem obvious, if not trite: "a bank of snow," "naked trees." But the rendering of details here is deceptively simple. What is given is due to be taken away, and there are hints relayed during that process of giving. The paratactic relation of "streets and buildings and diseased people" is one such hint. The "dim hillside laid out as a cemetery" is another. That phrase "laid out" shows that the topographical detail is more than mere detail. This is cemetery rather than hillside. The protagonist is "amazed that the ground of this place had once swallowed men in a natural way." "Swallowed" is grim enough, and the implication of "unnatural" swallowing—when we have only just taken in what "natural" swallowing would be—is disturbed and disturbing. Then there is the climax. Any other author would have written "Let me in!" Here, instead, we have the three-times-repeated "Let me out!" This is the agonized soul crying, not for happiness but for escape, escape at any price.

Such proffering and withdrawal, the acceptable description which leads to an unexpected event, is highly characteristic of *Lanark,* the book from which this quotation is culled. No one on a first reading could expect that the flight from the town to the cemetery would culminate in a cry of "Let me out!" Yet, on a second reading, the logic is so palpable as to make us wonder how we could have missed it. After all, the protagonist, Lanark, is seeking to leave Unthank, the huge—and diseased—city. Further, once the logic is apprehended, the effect is even more powerful. It is possible that the true distinction of *Lanark* becomes evident only on a second reading.

At first sight it seems—as some of the early reviewers said—that there are two novels yoked heterogeneously together. One is a science fiction account of "a World lying in its own Rubbish"; the words are those of an earlier visionary, Thomas Burnet.[8] Embedded in Gray's science fiction account is a bildungsroman, a portrait of the artist as a young asthmatic. But the two quasi-novels are one. The diseased city is described as realistically as the account of the fictive Defoe (he was a child and not even in London at the time) walking through the plague-ridden metropolis. And the various downfalls of the diseased artist in the bildungsroman are suffused, despite the plainness of their telling, with a metaphysical extravagance. If there is a yoking together of heterogeneities, it is an effect of texture rather than structure.

The artist's mother has died.

> At the words "Dust to dust and ashes to ashes," there began a lumbering rumbling sound and the red cloth began to sag as the coffin was drawn down under it. For a second it bulged up again with a rush of air from below, then flopped so that a rectangular depression appeared where the coffin had been. Thaw was struck by a poignant sense of loss neutralized at once by a memory of a conjuror who had made a scone disappear from under a handkerchief. (200-01)

That metaphysical quality inheres in the narrator's minute observation of curious detail. Alasdair Gray strips off the generalized outlines, with which most of us rest content, to show the strange effects of which life is composed if we care to take notice. Gray is a master of *ostranenie;* that is to say, defamiliarization. *Ostranenie* entails, among other matters, seeing the likeness between entities that are apparently unlike. Who, other than a metaphysical poet, would see a coffin sinking beneath a crematorium cloth in terms of a scone made to vanish from under a handkerchief?

What is here adduced as local effect is, in fact, the very voice of the prose. The effect is cumulative, though in no simple way. Indeed, the incremental specificity of the writing might have become oppressive, especially as one draws near to the end of the saga. But there are devices that act as releases of tension. They provide "comic distraction at a moment when the narrative sorely needs it" (483). One such device, the protagonist's encounter with his author, occurs in an epilogue that acts as a preparation for the climax that takes place after it, after, that is to say, the epilogue.

A very late but positive scene rejoices in a walk the protagonist takes through the countryside. It is evinced as a kind of fantasy experienced during orgasm: "He was knee-deep in a cold quick little burn gurgling over big rounded stones, some black, some grey, some speckled like oatmeal. He was tugging some of the stones out and carefully flinging them onto the bank a yard or two upstream" (512). The walk is a reprise of one taken 372 pages earlier in a chapter called "Ben Rua": "The glen had taken all the streams of the moor into its gorge where they tumbled and clattered among boulders, leaves and the songs of blackbirds" (140). The difference is that, in the later walk, the protagonist is accompanied by his son. This is one of two unalloyed love passages in a book that condemns the world for being bad at loving. The interplay between father and son includes occasional bickering but in its naturalness and feeling of wonder is, in these surroundings, an intimation of paradise.

> The loch was embanked as a reservoir on one side and on the grass of the embankment a dead seagull lay with outspread wings. Alexander was fascinated and Lanark picked it up. They looked at the yellow beak with the raspberry spot under the tip, the pure grey back and snowy breast which seemed unmarked. Alexander said,
>
> "Should we bury it?"
>
> "That would be difficult without tools. We could build a cairn over it."
>
> They collected stones from the shingle of the lochside and heaped them over the glossy feathers of the unmarked body. (516)

The scene is made poignant by the sense of loss that inevitably—inevitability is a strength of the writing—that inevitably ensues.

> Something cold stung his cheeks. He opened his eyes and saw the sky dark with torn, onrushing clouds. He was alone with nothing at his feet but a scatter of stones with old bones and feathers between them. He said "Sandy?" and looked around. There was nothing human on the moor. The light was fading from two or three sunset streaks in the clouds to the west. The heather was crested with sleet; the wind whipped more of it into his face.
>
> "Sandy!" he screamed, starting to run. "Sandy! Sandy! *Alexander!*"
>
> He plunged across the heather, tripped and fell into darkness.
>
> He wrestled awhile with something entangling, then realized it was blankets and sat up. (517)

It is the breaking of a dream. But the dream has the immediacy of here and now. What follows in the remainder of *Lanark* is a descent into enervating old age. The last prose sentence of the novel reads "He was a slightly worried, ordinary old man but glad to see the light in the sky" (560). And that is the end.

Characteristically, for Alasdair Gray is full of surprises, this final prose is followed by a poem. It is a verse epitaph, and it ends

> I HAVE GROWN UP. MY MAPS ARE OUT OF DATE.
> THE LAND LIES OVER ME NOW.
> I CANNOT MOVE. IT IS TIME TO GO. (560)

On its own, the epitaph seems like something out of Samuel Beckett. But Beckett's writing is essentially, even in his novels, a score for performance. He never has the weight of specificity that characterizes *Lanark.* One cannot help, for example, noticing that the son of Gray's protagonist is called Alexander. This looks back to the title page, which has the dedication "For Andrew Gray," and to the page following the title, which declares "The dedication is to his son."

The other unalloyed love in the novel is that felt by the protagonist for his friend "Aitken Drummond." This figure feels irresistibly part of a roman à clef, occurring, as he does, in various other works of Alasdair Gray.

> He was over six feet tall and usually wore green tram conductor's trousers, a red muffler and an army greatcoat. His dark skin, great arched nose, small glittering eyes, curling black hair and pointed beard were so like the popular notion of the Devil that on first sight everyone felt they had known him intimately for years. (242)

The effect of intimacy is built into the prose. Its detail and precision are a guarantee of authenticity. The past tense here, however, seems more past than in other sections of the book. It is commemoration rather than narrative. The character, though presented colorfully, is already dead. This is a Proustian evocation.

The description of Drummond's appearance is more than graphic. It is haunting: "Drummond and Thaw mounted the steps side by side, Drummond cleaving a path with his great axe-blade-edged nose" (257). And Drummond lives in a place quite different from any that another person would choose to inhabit.

> Thaw entered the queerest house he had ever seen. Parts of it were very like a home but these lay like valleys between piled furniture and objects salvaged from scrap heaps, middens and junk shops. As he edged into the kitchen he felt threatened by empty picture frames, stringless instruments and old wireless sets. (255)

The surrealism is in the careful detailing of peculiar facts. Everything about "Aitken Drummond" glows with passionate reminiscence. And he overflows into other books.

In a fragmented later novel, *1982 Janine,* there is a sustained passage between page 106 and page 117 which is at once love poem and threnody. Here the figure has the same name as Gray's prototype: Alan.

> I can remember none of these things without his great head in its Harpo Marx cloud of curly hair, though black not blonde, and his Groucho Marx face but with a goatee beard improving the slightly weak chin. Nobody who saw him knew if he was strikingly handsome or strikingly ugly. He had a sallow-skinned Arabic-Italian-Jewish look. I think his father was Jewish. His mother was Irish. "Not Catholic Irish but tinker Irish," was how he described her and he certainly dressed like a tinker. On anyone else his clothes would have seemed accidental. On him they looked like the improvisations of a Grand Duke who had lost his fortune and valet in a revolution,

like the casual wear of a more elegant, more easygoing, more practical civilisation. I remember various long woollen scarves, an army tunic with marks on the sleeves where the stripes of a sergeant had been unstitched, slim black evening-dress trousers with a black silk ribbon down the seam on each side. On damp days these trousers were tucked into Wellington boots, and had straps at the bottom which passed under the instep of canvas sandshoes on dry days. We must have been a strange contrast walking side by side, myself rather smaller than he in my conventionally creased trousers, waistcoat, collar, tie and jacket with the white triangle of a folded handkerchief peeping from the breastpocket. I walked with hands clasped behind my back. Alan usually had his arms folded on his chest but he did not strut or swagger. He placed his feet quietly and firmly, as if he only possessed—but possessed completely—the exact ground he trod upon. Sometimes I saw strangers in the distance laughing and pointing at us but if we drew near they grew quiet and respectful. Alan was four or five inches over six feet tall. No doubt this helped.[9]

The prose is, like that describing the walk in the country with Alexander, an evocation of paradise, the paradise of being in the company of the person one truly loves. As with the Alexander walk, these recollections of Alan are withdrawn as suddenly as the breaking of a dream.

Alan has died—we are told that at the beginning of the passage—Alan has died in the past and yet is paradoxically and emphatically present in the text, in the author's prose. The author triumphs over fate, or so the solidity of the narrative seems to assure us. There he is, this figure, with his black cloud of curly hair, his goatee beard, his army tunic carelessly worn over black evening-dress trousers, arms folded on chest, feet treading quietly and firmly the ground he possesses. But this solid description serves only to take us up to the unexpected betrayal, the withdrawal of happiness which is the hallmark of Alasdair Gray. The end of Alan's story is a masterpiece of circumstantial detail, among other things.

It was a sunny summer in Glasgow, the streets quieter than usual. Perhaps it was the start of the fair fortnight. I walked along St George's Road and saw Alan strolling toward me round the curve of Charing Cross Mansions, arms folded on chest, great face surveying the white clouds. I was filled with delighted relief and laughter. I ran to him crying, "You're not dead! You're not dead!"

He smiled and said, "Of course not, that was all just a joke."

And suddenly I got terribly angry with him for making such a cruel joke. And then I awoke, unluckily. (117)

The ironies, four waves of them, successively take away (so to speak) the carpet, the floor, the basement, and all that keeps us from the abyss. It is banal to analyze these ironies, but, for the uninitiated . . .

No. The uninitiated are those who have never lost anything of great value and who therefore cannot empathize with the experience of despair. To feel intensely, yet to discipline one's prose, is surely the sign of a writer. It was certainly a writer, and a very good one, who found that word with its final resonance, *unluckily*.

Alasdair Gray has many themes. But this one, the withdrawal of paradise, is what renders him highly distinctive. It is this that causes the hills and valleys, the variegations of intensity, the quirks and the depressions of his prose. There is something of torment in his effort to establish happiness in action only to use even greater technique for the purpose of taking it away. The loss of Eden becomes more poignant than Eden itself.

No writer can simulate happiness more convincingly than Alasdair Gray. His prose burgeons with joy, with discovery, with—as we have seen—the exhilaration of being with good friends. But this is the fiery surface that is an exhalation over the fathomless depths of despair. A full-length study of this extraordinary writer might well bear the title, after the cry of the anguished soul in Unthank, "Let me out!"

NOTES

[1]Alasdair Gray, "A Report to the Trustees of the Bellahouston Travelling Scholarship" (1959), in *Lean Tales,* by James Kelman, Agnes Owens, and Alasdair Gray (London: Jonathan Cape, 1985), 185, 197, 196; hereafter cited parenthetically.

[2]Bruce Charlton, "The Story So Far," in *The Arts of Alasdair Gray,* ed. Robert Crawford and Thom Nairn (Edinburgh: Edinburgh Univ. Press, 1991), 13.

[3]Robert Crawford, "Introduction," and Marshall Walker, "The Process of Jock McLeish and the Fiction of Alasdair Gray," in *The Arts of Alasdair Gray,* 7, 40.

[4]Daniel Defoe, *Journal of the Plague Year* (1722), ed. Louis Landa (London: Oxford Univ. Press, 1990), 17.

[5]For Borges as realist, see Philip Hobsbaum, "Borges and His Translators," *Lines Review* 50 (1974): 8-21.

[6]Sarah Schulman, *People in Trouble* (Jefferson City: Sheba Feminist Publishers, 1990), 115.

[7]Alasdair Gray, *Lanark* (Edinburgh: Canongate, 1981), 46; hereafter cited parenthetically.

[8]Thomas Burnet, *A Sacred Theory of the Earth* (1684).

[9]Alasdair Gray, *1982 Janine* (London: Jonathan Cape, 1984), 109-10; hereafter cited parenthetically.

Is Eating People Really Wrong? Dining with Alasdair Gray

George Donaldson and Alison Lee

RETURNING TO GLASGOW after a wartime evacuation, Duncan Thaw asks his mother, "How long will it be before we get back to normal?" to which she replies, "What do you mean, normal?" (*Lanark* 146). Although the exchange, in this context, is a purely practical one, it raises what is a persistent question in all of Gray's fiction. Less concerned with validating normality than with examining the lengths to which society will go to preserve its illusion of normalcy, Gray's work comments on the structures of political, institutional, and sexual power that present themselves as "normal." As a postmodern writer, Gray both uses and abuses these structures, just as he does literary conventions and genres. This pattern of use and abuse is mirrored in his novels' forms and often literalized in their content. His fiction is subversive in that it seeks to call into question precisely those literary conventions that seem to reflect reality while they are, in fact, constructing it. In Gray's fiction maintaining what seems to be incontrovertibly normal leads to repression and violence.

This is especially clear in *Something Leather* and *1982 Janine,* two novels in which violent sexuality is used as a metaphor for a whole host of political abuses that the strong foist upon the weak. Bringing ideology into the bedroom and into sexual fantasy is not without its problems. These novels' representations of sexuality are deliberately disturbing in order to raise the issue of power's pervasiveness, in particular its intrusion into intimate thoughts and acts which we like to think have escaped its influence. Much of Gray's writing examines power by making clichés, myths, and metaphors literal: descriptive diseases and credit cards that buy time in *Lanark;* a puppet emperor in "Five Letters from an Eastern Empire"; a split personality in "The Spread of Ian Nicol"; the erratum slip "inserted by mistake" in *Unlikely Stories, Mostly,* to name but a few. This device makes readers aware of the constructedness of language, literary conventions, and power, none of which is innocently normal.

In Gray's fiction there are numerous instances when characters' lives are shaped by politically determined decisions and socially produced normative values. For example, Lanark, Kelvin Walker, and Jock McLeish come to realize that in their public behavior they have been characters in someone else's script. But Gray also points out that publicly and thus politically conceived identities unconsciously form characters' private conceptions and so shape private behavior. This is a much more insidious invasion of the public into the apparently private domain. Indeed, much of Gray's work addresses the illusory distinction between public and private. He examines the ways in which ideologically produced conceptions of such seemingly personal concerns as accent or sexuality shape behavior in private as much as in public. If ideology works to supply assumptions whose power resides in their taken-for-grantedness, then these assumptions must function as cogently in private as in public. In relation to language and sexuality, Gray seeks to emphasize the otherwise elided power relations that form conventional wisdom. And this foregrounding is itself political in that it challenges "nature."

This is certainly the case in both *Something Leather* and *1982 Janine,* novels in which private sexual behavior is shown to be publicly determined. In *1982 Janine* Jock McLeish insists that his fantasies about the bondage and ritual humiliation of women arise from his own feelings of powerlessness and entrapment. By extension, he suggests, his fantasies parallel the political abuse of Scotland.

The presence of overtly sexual scenes is not, of course, necessarily pornographic. In *The Sadeian Woman* Angela Carter argues that most pornography denies the social facts of sexuality: "[t]he sexual act in pornography exists as a metaphor for what people do to one another, often in the cruellest sense; but the present business of the pornographer is to suppress the metaphor as much as he can" (17). Neither in *1982 Janine* nor in *Something Leather* is the metaphor suppressed; in fact, it is foregrounded, as are the ideological assumptions we take into the bedroom.

The social triggers that remain unconscious in private sexuality are less successfully represented in *Something Leather.* Harry's formative experience with a nanny, who taught her to equate abuse with love, does certainly offer the rationale by which she can have an intimate relationship only with a woman who will similarly bruise her. But the status of victim is too vague and perhaps too facile in the cases of Donalda and Senga. All three women victimize June for the purposes of sexually liberating her. June in time concurs. Unless the novel seriously intends to suggest that sadomasochistic lesbian rape leads to liberty, the role of ideology in making victims complicitous with their oppressors needs to be more apparent, since it may be argued that June's final victimization is that she believes her rape helps her.

The politicalization of sexuality is more successful in *1982 Janine.* While Jock admits he is cruel in fantasy, he is terrified when it is suggested to him that such things might indeed exist. Much of the novel is an attempt to come to terms with the realities of his own cruelties, which exist on not quite so spectacular a scale as his sexual dreams but which destroyed his first lover, whom he abandoned because she was the product of a working-class background, far below the class to which he aspires. Although Jock tries to separate sex and politics, he is unsuccessful. Indeed Sontag, one of his more adventurous lovers, suggests to him that his fantasies have "a convincing political structure" (67). Unlike *Something Leather,* the triumph of ideology is clear here in making victims share complicity in, and be grateful for, their own victimization.

At the "crux" of the story, Janine realizes "*it is her inescapable fate to be a character in a story by someone who dictates every one of her movements and emotions, someone she will never meet and cannot appeal to*" (332); here, Janine and Jock occupy a similar ontological space. Author and character alike have been predictable actors in a script written by job, gender, country, and class. Their performances have been measured by their conventionality, by their acceding to subjection by social norms. Jock both does and does not escape this, which points to his liminality as a performer within ideology. Although he redirects his life by quitting his job, coming to terms with his flaws and moving on to other pursuits, his creation, Janine, has a more limited freedom. While her final appearance is marked by her decision to flaunt her sexuality, she is still, in this context, a commodity, and still at the mercy of the audience. Neither convention nor ideology is easy to escape.

The labyrinthine convolutions of ideology are equally constricting in *The Fall of Kelvin Walker,* where they are presented in a Nietzschean context. The death of God confers both liberty and responsibility, as Kelvin seems to understand: "since there was no longer a God to give shape and purpose to life it was necessary for the few who could face this fact to take the responsibility themselves" (29). With such knowledge, Kelvin is in the characteristic position of the Gray hero in challenging the authority of conceived normality. In this novella the union of violence with sexual excitement appears in the secondary, near nursery-rhyme characters, Jake Whittington and Jill. Paradoxically, it is Jake, not Kelvin, who comes to understand the limits of his power in the Godless universe: "Jake had the uncanny sensation of being part of a world he could not control" (101). Kelvin can only cope with the burden imposed by the annihilation of God as authoritarian bully, by becoming an imitation of that figure himself: "most people are so afraid of running their own lives that they feel frightened when there's no-one to bully them" (59). In this novel freedom from the specific creed of institutionalized religion does not bring with it a similar freedom from the structures of "natural" authority inscribed within its hierarchy.

In *Something Leather* the system of authority is wider. Gray's play with linguistic forms makes it clear that sexuality, as well as authoritarian systems like Kelvin's religion, are inscribed in the very language we speak. For a Scottish writer, this is an especially important point. The subjection of Scotland, about which Jock McLeish and others muse, is represented by the mixture of standard English and Scots in many of Gray's texts. In the novels of Walter Scott, James Hogg, Robert Louis Stevenson, and George

Douglas Brown dialect vocabulary is only given to appropriate characters as direct speech and seldom invades the narration itself. In contrast Gray's use of Glasgow patois, as in *Lanark,* is not restricted to the direct speech of a character intended to add local color, nor does it appear exclusively in the realist sections set in Glasgow. This vocabulary does certainly function as part of the novel's setting, but Gray is also concerned with the politics of language, particularly in relation to power. In *Something Leather* the Scots speech of Donalda and Senga and the young Linda's cockney voice are printed phonetically, but so is the Received Pronunciation (R.P.) of Harry, her mother, the headmistress, and all the other pupils at the school. In the acknowledgments Gray describes this speech as "the queen's English dialect" (252), thereby emphasizing that it identifies a class, not a place, and so manifests established authority, not by *what* is said but in its very form. By writing R.P. out phonetically, Gray dislodges it from its position at the top of a hierarchy and places it among, and as equivalent to, other Englishes. As happens elsewhere in his writing, then, a formal change alerts the reader to an assumption so ingrained as to be invisible.

It is in *Lanark* that Gray most successfully explores the ramifications of an authoritarian and diffuse political system and its effect on the personal lives of his characters. Like other more conventional bildungsromans, this novel is a search for normality and order. Usually, in a bildungsroman the hierarchy of discourses is clear: the world is shown as naturally possessing order, and that order is apparent from the outset to both the reader and the narrator. Only to the questing central figure does the world appear confused; the hero's errors educate him or her until his or her personal knowledge of order accords with that of the reader and narrator. The moment of resolution in such a novel is therefore also a guarantee of political order, for the hero's discovery of what the reader and narrator already know at once restores the hero to the knowledgeable community, while substantiating that community's knowledge.

By beginning with book 3, *Lanark* subverts this pattern in two ways: first, genre expectations are both foregrounded and subverted by the antichronological narration; second, Lanark's own estrangement from his world is matched, rather than contrasted, with the reader's, for the novel starts in the fantastic world of Unthank, not in the initially more recognizable order of Glasgow. In Unthank Lanark searches for order when daylight is out of season and when the notion of a day, therefore, is italicized to stress its oddity. In the realist bildungsroman the hierarchy of discourses naturalizes, and so reinforces, both the idea that order exists to be discovered (not created) and also the idea of the authority of existing order. *Lanark*'s opening double subversion of these ingrained expectations directs the reader to question the character of the power that enables this order to appear natural. The question itself is largely political but its expression is formal, for the novel begins not by posing a question about how a hegemony naturalizes itself but rather by inverting some conventions of narrative power and authority. Here, the reader is not discursively superior to Lanark; time is not linear and so experience seems less obviously a journey towards a self-evident, preexisting destination. The power of form to create and maintain authority and the formal means through which that same authority may be undermined are at the paradoxical heart of *Lanark.*

In the bildungsroman the central, questing hero discovers through experience the unified nature of external reality. But examining ways of inventing, rather than discovering Glasgow is one of *Lanark*'s goals: the Glasgow of books 1 and 2 is itself only another version of Glasgow, for there is no single, "real" Glasgow, only the places conceived in each contract between the succession of one's selves and the correlative object, in this case the city. And contracts are made in different ways. Some cities exist vividly and variously through art, cities such as "Florence, Paris, London [and] New York" (243). The Glasgow to which young Duncan Thaw returns after the war has little of that widespread imaginative existence, but nonetheless it has been more transformed by changes in the boy than by Hitler's bombs. The contract has been rewritten: what was once "a tenement block, a school and a stretch of canal," is now "a gloomy huge labyrinth" (146).

Order, external reality, does exist, but it is available to us only as an idea formed from perceptions. Like many heroes of the bildungsroman, Thaw craves certain knowledge about the world and soon learns that the senses, as means to that knowledge, may be deceived: "my idea of a man is never the same as someone else's" (108). Each meeting with a friend involves some rewriting, so that the text of which one is the author, a text whose aim is to describe fully and accurately the outside world, is one that is always being written and that always stands as an imaginative construction predicated upon, but never grasping, external order. As Thaw's schoolboy story, "a blend of realism and fantasy" (155), is a *mise-en-abyme* of *Lanark* itself, so *Lanark*'s own mixture of realism and fantasy represents the negotiations between the countless subjects which form the self and their countless correlative objects. Neither Thaw nor Lanark—nor even *Lanark—discovers* order; each is always in the process of *creating* it, for meaning is conferred by authority rather than recognized: "After considering I asked if he could tell me the name of the city. He said, 'Mr. Lanark, I am a clerk, not a geographer' " (22).

To reveal the constructedness and tentativeness of order is to liberate the subject. Instead of being subjected to an unalterable state of affairs, one is freed into the possibility of otherness. In the bildungsroman the subject is tamed into conformity with constituted authority through education and bruising experience, a process which is wisely overseen by reader and narrator. When the subject rails or rebels or fails to comprehend social order, that act is seen within a defining hierarchy of discourses, so that the form itself conditions the parameters of one's response and indeed fixes both the central character's still imperfect understanding of order and fixes the seemingly objective nature of that order yet more firmly. It follows, then, that to say otherwise one must speak differently. One of the ways in which *Lanark* does this is by representing metaphors literally.

By making metaphors and analogies literal, as one aspect of the mixing of realism and fantasy, Gray revitalizes already familiar comparisons in order to shock the reader into an awareness of what these images really show of political structures. By making the familiar strange, one sees it for the first time. The most pervasive of these literalized metaphors is Thomas Hobbes's picture of the political state as a living body, a leviathan, and this image forms the basis of books 3 and 4 of *Lanark.* In Unthank, "many people are afraid of the cold and try to keep more heat than they give, they stop the heat from leaving through an organ or limb, and the stopped heat forges the surface into hard insulating armour" (68). Emotional, or spiritual, deformity becomes physically manifest in what is called "dragonhide." The political significance is also made explicit: "Like nations losing unjust wars they convert more and more of themselves into armour when they should surrender or retreat" (68).

Within the living political body, it is the private, individual body whose consumption by the state becomes both literal and terrifying. In Unthank the powerful few literally live off the weaker majority through a technologically polite cannibalism. The energies generated at death when patients turn "salamander" (65) fuel Unthank's power system, in more than one sense, and the human remains provide semiedible delicacies such as *Enigma de Filets Congelés.* Like sexuality in *Something Leather* and *1982 Janine,* cannibalism here provides a link between the public and private domains. It is only when Lanark goes to Unthank that he develops dragonhide, and in this sunless city, the cycle of consumption, as it existed less obviously in Glasgow, is made clear. Those subjected to a political system develop diseases propagated by that system, and when they die, they are literally consumed so that the system might continue in the same way. The purpose of the hospital is not to heal the sick but to expand itself, and this is achieved by not striving too vigorously to cure the ailing when they are needed as food. Monsignor Noakes sees ecclesiastical history both as a pandering to and controlling of the prime human problem, which he identifies as cannibalism. His claim that "Man is the pie that bakes and eats himself" (101) is repeated throughout the text as a persistent reminder that the system feasts upon those who nevertheless participate in keeping it going.

Gray's challenge to the illusory distinction between private and public, self and other, may be seen in relation to the larger concern with the dissolution of the Cartesian subject, which begins with Freud's displacement of identity to an anterior unconscious. This has been developed in structuralist and poststructuralist thought by a further displacement of the subject into a language in which the individual speaker does not express himself or herself but is instead *expressed by* language. Within this history of challenges to the transcendent cogito, Gray's particular focus is on the political systems whose power is predicated upon their invisibility, a transparency inscribed in language itself.

WORKS CITED

Carter, Angela. *The Sadeian Woman: An Exercise in Cultural History.* London: Virago, 1979.

Gray, Alasdair. *The Fall of Kelvin Walker.* Edinburgh: Canongate, 1985.

———. *Lanark.* Edinburgh: Canongate, 1981.

———. *1982 Janine.* London: Jonathan Cape, 1984.

———. *Something Leather.* London: Picador, 1991.

———. *Unlikely Stories, Mostly.* Edinburgh: Canongate, 1983.

The Power of Work in the Novels of Alasdair Gray

William M. Harrison

In his 1993 *The Modern British Novel* Malcolm Bradbury calls Alasdair Gray "both a powerful, teasing postmodernist and a writer who has stayed close to Glasgow materials," as if the two authorial qualities are somehow at odds.[1] Perhaps there is an English suspicion that a writer cannot be both Scottish and experimental; however, such a prejudice plays into a larger discourse between northern and southern Britain, one that focuses eventually on the conception of nationalism within a larger "united kingdom." As one of "the Glasgow literary Mafia"[2] that founded in the 1980s the still-contested Scottish Literary Renaissance, Gray positions himself quite clearly as a Scots-Nationalist author whose fiction, plays, poetry, and essays attempt to determine the nature of both Scottish citizenship and nationhood. For example, in his political tract *Why Scots Should Rule Scotland,* Gray envisions a Scotland "where Scots mainly live by making and growing and doing things for each other. It should be possible. We have the room to do it" (64). Implicit here is that with the failure of the 1992 referendum, Scotland presently does not commit itself to making, growing, or doing things for itself, that the nation lacks opportunity and self-sufficiency. Instead, Gray finds the nation a literal (in the far northern highlands) and metaphorical (in its separate and isolated urban centers) "archipelago" subservient to the distant City of London (56). And what the nation lacks, its people do too. Gray himself was on dole in 1964, and as recently as 1977, at forty-three years of age, he painted murals at a chip restaurant for meals. Even after Anthony Burgess's 1984 positive appraisal of *Lanark* in *Ninety-nine Novels,* Gray faced the difficulty of working as an artist and earning enough to eat.[3]

This ironic reality with which Gray is familiar has influenced his and other Scots narratives, for as Beat Witschi has pointed out, the Glasgow literary tradition has often striven for a sense of social realism. Admittedly, Gray breaks somewhat with this aesthetic tradition via an experimental style combining typographical ingenuity with elements of the fantastic, but he shares the Glaswegian focus on the urban center and the individual's existence and placement within the city's socioeconomic construct. In *Lanark* and its sibling novel *1982 Janine,* Scottish urban centers—most often Glasgow or a Glaswegian signifier—function as historical sites of an endangered authentic national culture prizing work, art, and intellect. However, the contemporary early eighties urban arena exists as an abandoned, late-capitalist, postindustrial locus: a city in decay and on the dole. For the novels' protagonists, the journey toward personal and social redemption begins with an understanding of the city's greater past and desire to regain some of the absent cultural dignity and decency. Yet Gray's works call not for a conservative return to past values; clearly postwar socialist Scotland cannot be regained. Instead, the texts call for a regenerative impulse built powerfully upon the Scottish work ethic and capability that can overcome welfare inertia and transnational capitalism.

Where a cooperative Scotland is literally possible according to the political Gray, his fiction's city-as-cultural-source exists either in the past, apparently conceivable only through memory, or as an unreliable future ideal, a utopia perchance unachievable. In *1982 Janine* drunken, vaguely psychotic Jock McLeish, the protagonist and narrator, remembers his now lost youthful idealism. In his flashback McLeish narrates the experience he had as a young man when he climbed a crag and looked down upon the Scottish countryside:

> I realised that Scotland was shaped like a fat messy woman with a surprisingly slender waist. A threestranded belt of road, canal and railway crossed that waist joining Edinburgh and the ports facing Europe to Glasgow and the ports facing Ireland and America. And the woman was rich! She had enough land to feed us all if we used her properly, and sealochs and pure rivers for fish-farming, and hills to grow timber on. Her native iron was exhausted, but we had coalbeds which would last another two centuries, and a skilled industrial population who could make anything in the heavy-engineering line. All we needed were new ideas and the confidence to make them work. . . . I was young, I was learning, I belonged to a splendid country, I was on the edge of an unforseeable future but I knew it would be a great one.[4]

But this vision has not endured for Jock, and, indeed, it cannot. The resolution's simplicity—and the faith in the generation of new ideas, in progress—reconstructs a commonly mythologized Scotland, where the "enterprising Scot" overcomes any number of obstacles.[5] (Gray deconstructs obliquely this high-Victorian concept more fully in *Poor Things.*) Ultimately this conception of Scotland collapses, leaving Jock with the Tory reality he, as a senior consultant in a security corporation, himself labors to create:

> the Clydeside has outlived its usefulness. . . . Glasgow now means nothing to the rest of Britain but unemployment, drunkenness and out-of-date radical militancy. . . . Scotland has been fucked and I am one of the fuckers who fucked her and I REFUSE TO FEEL BITTER OR GUILTY ABOUT THIS. . . . The militarisation and depression of Scotland has been good for the security business. Apart from the breweries my firm has been the only one to expand here in recent years. (136-37)

While this contemporary national depiction reingrains the alternative mythology of Scottish victimization, it does, at least, take history into account with the postindustrial nation's long economic degradation.

As the above quotations demonstrate, *1982 Janine* contrasts Jock McLeish's contemporary, ferocious, and pornographic Tory capitalism to his earlier socialistic engineering aestheticism. Jock's long alcoholic decline corresponds with his employment by and integration into the military-industrial complex, a system free (for there is little economic opportunity apart from the nuclear death industry) to exploit Scotland and endanger Glasgow and Edinburgh, its major urban population centers. This exploitation becomes equally apparent in Denny, McLeish's first love, a sort of Scottish subaltern. Jock meets her while in technical college; his love affair with the seventeen-year-old cafeteria worker provides him with unconditional love and sex. But Denny's roots in the unskilled, unachieving working class fall too near his own self-improving, highly skilled working-to-lower middle-class background, and Jock aims for the upper middle classes.

McLeish convinces Denny to move in with him, for her girls' hostel does not allow its guests to stay out after curfew. She cannot get her own room, for her wages are only "enough to buy food and rent a cheap room if she shared it, but with almost nothing left for entertainment, clothing or transport" (210). Trapped by subsistence wages and Jock's desire, Denny becomes dependent on the eighteen-year-old student just at the time he is attracted to other women; McLeish is motivated by "greed"; he says, "I wanted to discover how much more enjoyment I could have" (219).

Denny's dependency becomes more severe when the summer school holiday puts her out of work for two months. As Jock notes, "She was too young and badly paid to draw national insurance, and if she applied for national assistance she would be visited by an inspector who would ask to see her rent book. If the inspector learned she was living with me he would refuse assistance on the grounds she was *cohabiting*" (241-42). Thus the state welfare system effectively designates Denny a whore, a definition that Jock, in return, reinforces as he starts to take Denny for granted, treating her as "a luxury I could hardly afford" (242). Part of the difficulty lies in that Denny herself lacks decent employment, from which—according to much of Gray's work—identity and self-worth rise. As McLeish commodifies her as whore-luxury, he treats her as a possession, not a person, and leaves her alone in his rented room while he pursues other (sincere and suspect) goals with "the glamorous Anglicised world of the theatre" troupe in Edinburgh.[6] He returns, after sleeping with an actress, to find Denny in his landlord's arms, whereupon—out of selfish pride—Jock abandons her and laments: "I will never discover what you did when you stopped crying my name, Denny" (292).

Later in age, Jock romanticizes Denny, awarding her the sympathy and understanding he could not in youth, partially because he equates her existence with his lost idealism and potential; like the promising Scotland of his vision, Denny too is a chubby, sloppy woman. When middle-aged McLeish drunkenly equates a Glaswegian prostitute ("squat and old with a discolored face") with Denny, he reinscribes, however tragically, the fate of the nation upon a woman's body, one he quite physically desires. But Jock's recognition of the link between his (and southern capital's) exploitation of nation and woman, be it sexual or otherwise, is not enough to relieve him of his guilt and anguish. His memories, no longer repressed and ignored, serve as therapeutic revelations that must instigate action.

Jock understands that his security work, like his misuse of Denny's love, is destructive employment for both self and country; as he says, "We have committed horrible crimes which do no practical good" (310). Yet the cessation of destruction is not enough, for when McLeish "stopped growing, stopped changing," he became complicit in the economic crimes of the south; Jock knows he "will not do nothing" (334).

What he *will do* is as yet unclear; the Edinburgh play's success, for which he was technical inventor and supervisor, reminds Jock of what can be. "We were no accident," the play's director, now also middle-aged, tells him, "we were a co-operative. I suspect all good companies are co-operatives who won't admit it" (329). The slow recognition of the production's dramatic success, combined with his recollection of defending a fellow student against a cruel schoolmaster, leads Jock to resolution: "Before I die I will make folk glad I exist again" (340). Jock overcomes spiritual restrictions by accepting his Glaswegian past (both good and bad), acknowledging his wrongs, and deciding to learn from and participate in life rather than deny it. As he notes by the end, "It is ideas which make people brave, ideas and love of course" (340), ideas that build the ethics of community and culture.

In *Lanark* the dual protagonists, Duncan Thaw and Lanark, each apparently a version of the same character, attempt to determine what ideas and actions can help the city and nation and how to articulate them and make these ideas real. An unemployed Glaswegian artist, Thaw has talent but no market for it (analogously much like post-Second World War Scottish heavy machinists and artisans). Rejecting the possibility of a useless teaching career, Thaw instead desires, somewhat futilely, an art of change—a work ethic providing more for people than mere existence:

> "think of Florence, Paris, London, New York. Nobody visiting them for the first time is a stranger because he's already visited them in paintings, novels, history books and films. But if a city hasn't been used by an artist not even the inhabitants live there imaginatively. . . . And when our imagination needs exercise we use these to visit London, Paris, Rome . . . anywhere but here and now. Imaginatively Glasgow exists as a music-hall song and a few bad novels. That's all we've given to the world outside. It's all we've given to ourselves."[7]

Duncan finds he needs to provide himself and others with that imaginative worth; he says, "I paint because I feel cheap and purposeless when

I don't" (244). And yet despite Thaw's remarkable sense of locale and purpose, Glasgow is still an entropic city, both economically and culturally. In chapter 28, subtitled "Work," Thaw labors over his Genesis mural for a Cowlairs church. The mural becomes an infinite project, however; the three-month job expands to seven, and minor changes in conception force Thaw to repaint entire huge sections, an effort that becomes more quixotic when the demolition of the minor parish church is finally announced. But, as Duncan says aloud to the absent decorator Mr. Rennie, together they "are making [their] own model of the universe" (336):

> "I believe this church will be knocked down, but first the mural must be made perfect. When a thing is perfect it is eternal. It can be destroyed afterward, or slowly decay, but its perfection is safe in the past, which is the only inevitable part of the universe. . . . Let you and I, Mr. Rennie, make eternity a present of a complete, perfect, harmonious, utterly harmless thing; something whose every part is the result of intelligent, loving care; something which isn't a destructive weapon and can't be sold at a profit by public-spirited businessmen." (337)

But while it may be a Platonic realm of perfect forms and, for artists and art, a kind of success, that eternal past is also where existence no longer occurs; more than simply "life-negating," as Cairns Craig points out,[8] this eternity is death itself. The novel reminds us often that the Necropolis, the ornate graveyard filled with tombs of great Victorian industrial magnates, overlooks Glasgow, forming a "tomb-glittering spine" on the ridge above (243). Here the final result of the city's nineteenth-century industrial strength remains a perfect icon of past achievement. But as a symbol of Scotland's labor greatness, the Necropolis restates successful capitalism as the glorification of ownership, *not* work. Gray's urban geographic imagery criticizes implicitly Duncan's conception of labor's value, reminding us that his potentially damaging ideal—the desired perfection of death—must be worked through before Thaw can realize his goal of beneficial, successfully imaginative work. But Duncan cannot fulfill his purpose, and his pursuit of death leads him to murder possibly (the text is vague) and suicide: an "annihilating sweetness" (354). Thus Lanark, Thaw's reborn self, must complete the final movements of the quest for right action and good work.

But Lanark's job is no easier. Where in real Glasgow death is spatially and symbolically contained within the Necropolis boundary, in Unthank (a dystopic, allegorical Glasgow) death runs rampant but without perfection. Thaw's mistakes are revealed more clearly; the sun does not even shine. Lanark, now with wife and son, searches for work and discovers that the hypermodern job center is the city's architectural focus, a great glass and concrete tower "of twenty or thirty floors" (434). Here social welfare consists of "three-in-one," a somatic bread that "nourishes and tranquillizes and stops your feeling cold . . . but after a while it damages the intelligence" (432). There are no jobs in postindustrial Unthank, so the labor exchange's purpose is to defeat the spirit. As the employment administrator Gilchrist explains:

> "A lot of [the unemployed] are still strong and vigorous, and it is a dangerous thing to suddenly deprive a man of hope—he can turn violent. It is important to kill hope *slowly,* so that the loser has time to adjust unconsciously to the loss. We try to keep hope alive till it has burned out the vitality feeding it. Only then is the man allowed to face the truth." (439)

In fact, Lanark accepts employment as a "grade D inquiry clerk" in the job center only because of "the credit card, and . . . home with three or four rooms" (439) promised to him and his family. But Lanark soon abandons his desk, admitting to a client, "It's no use. This place isn't going to help you at all" (442). Lucky Unthank citizens live in "mohomes," graveled lots full of converted subcompact coupes without "clutch or steering column" or toilet, but with a seat that "flatten[s] out to form a bed" and a cluttered cupboard dash. In lieu of a windshield, a wide-screen television numbs the occupants (as many as four to a car) into passivity. Lanark, now aware of urban poverty's scope and his own implication in the system producing it, admits that "We're trying to kill Unthank" (454). But Jimmy McFee, unemployed mohome assembler and occupant, finds Lanark's admission unacceptable: "Let the place die as long as my weans are spared" (455). The same desire that lures Lanark into oppression—to protect and provide for his family—drives McFee to resist, at least in feeble speech.

And it is right action that is key for Gray's work. The ideal cooperative, the community suggested by *Why Scots Should Rule Scotland* and *1982 Janine,* requires work more than thoughtless activity. Laboring over a mural no one will see or enjoy, installing a secure military hell, breaking men's wills at a job exchange, or even constructing shoebox mohomes helps no one but merely defers promise and continues an ethic of suffering. The cooperative, on the other hand, mandates an obligation to others; the combination of love and ideas that may save McLeish is in fact an understanding of one's duty to others. Lanark realizes basically this relationship; as his (ex)wife Rima says to him, "You make life a duty, something to be examined and corrected" (457). And yet this ethic is not without risks, for even though a job provides the promise of nourishing food, good housing, warm clothing, and entertainment (things denied Denny on food service wages, for example), it may not be worth taking. Gray insists on a larger social awareness. Of course, the scale of such duty and the requirements placed on the active subject need to be correctly determined. Lanark finds global council politics as problematic as Jock perceives Scots-National concerns. Still, Gray's potentially simplistic and romantic ethic points to people and not power as the center of value: Jock's "folk" whom he must make glad that he is alive.

At *Lanark*'s close, during what seems the threatened apocalyptic destruction, people flee downtown Unthank for the safer Necropolis heights.

Led to safety by his now-adult son Alexander, the elderly Lanark finds the city of the dead now full of the living: "In the dim cemetery folk crouched on the grass plots or dispersed up the many little paths" (555). Fire, earthquake, and flood do not destroy the city; the sun, to Lanark's delight, finally reappears:

> Drunk with spaciousness he turned every way, gazing with wide-open mouth and eyes as light created colours, clouds, distances and solid, graspable things close at hand. Among all this light the flaming buildings seemed small blazes which would soon burn out. With only mild disappointment he saw the flood ebbing back down the slope of the road. (558).

A new day dawns after the living reclaim the city of the dead for themselves, as the Necropolis (home of Duncan Thaw's eternity) is brought effectively *into* time, and death (manifested as huge, horrific destruction) subsides to its rightful place, part of the life cycle and not existence itself. The severe crisis also demonstrates people's ability to work for one another, and Alexander shows promise as he labors for "Makers, Movers and Menders." Lanark, however, must prepare for his work's end when a "ministry of earth" chamberlain bestows upon Lanark "an extraordinary privilege" and announces he will die within a day (559). (When Lanark complains that "Death is not a privilege," the messenger reminds him that "The privilege is knowing when" [559].)

So the city continues in *Lanark,* despite the efforts of government and institutional powers. Human effort and the need to provide for others overcomes indirectly the machinations of international capital; love and work still have worth and force. Both *1982 Janine* and *Lanark* reinforce this ethic of work's restorative, humane powers. Without such an ideological belief, Gray suggests, spiritual as well as economic defeat is unavoidable. At the novel's end, his death approaching, Lanark surveys a recovering Unthank. The old man, free of remorse or self-pity, is simply "glad to see the light in the sky" (560). While they may be difficult to attain, the hope and promise of community seem finally possible.

NOTES

[1]Malcolm Bradbury, *The Modern British Novel* (London: Secker and Warburg, 1993), 141-45.

[2]Alasdair Gray, *Why Scots Should Rule Scotland* (Edinburgh: Canongate, 1992), 57; hereafter cited parenthetically.

[3]*Lanark,* writes Burgess in this early rave, is a "big and original novel." He continues: "Gray is a fantastic writer (and his own fantastic illustrator) who owes something to Kafka but not much. . . . Scotland produced, in Hugh MacDiarmid, the greatest poet of the century (or so some believe); it was time Scotland produced a shattering work of fiction in the modern idiom. This is it" (*Ninety-nine Novels: The Best in English since 1939* [London: Allison and Busby, 1984], 126). For Gray's

economic troubles see Bruce Charlton, "The Story So Far," in *The Arts of Alasdair Gray,* ed. Robert Crawford and Thom Nairn (Edinburgh: Edinburgh Univ. Press, 1991), 18-21. However, these troubles are not as surprising as they at first appear. In 1981, the year *Lanark* appeared, 32.5 percent of Glasgow's male population and 44.8 percent of its women were either unemployed or "economically inactive," in Edinburgh 20.5 percent of the men and 35.6 percent of the women (John Butt, "The Changing Character of Urban Employment 1901-1981," in *Perspectives of the Scottish City,* ed. George Gordon [Aberdeen: Aberdeen Univ. Press, 1985], 225-26).

[4]Alasdair Gray, *1982 Janine* (New York: Viking, 1984), 281; hereafter cited parenthetically.

[5]Beat Witschi, *Glasgow Urban Writing and Postmodernism,* Scottish Studies 12 (New York: Peter Lang, 1991), 185.

[6]S. J. Boyd, "Black Arts: *1982 Janine* and *Something Leather,*" in *The Arts of Alasdair Gray,* 115.

[7]Alasdair Gray, *Lanark: A Life in Four Books* (New York: George Braziller, 1985), 243; hereafter cited parenthetically.

[8]Cairns Craig, "Going Down to Hell is Easy: *Lanark,* Realism and the Limits of the Imagination," in *The Arts of Alasdair Gray,* 102.

Scottish Enough: The London Novels of Alasdair Gray

Stephen Bernstein

In 1992 British television viewers could watch a commercial that featured an invisibly held bottle filling a glass with carbonated water while a voice-over said, "No kilts. No bagpipes. No Bonnie Prince Charlie. Strathmore Mineral Water—it's Scottish enough." Strikingly posed in this script is the double bind of Anglo-Scottish relations: the English desire for an authentic, thirst-slaking "Scottishness" which nevertheless stops short of sartorial tedium, aesthetic alienation, or political invasion. The project of the Scottish novelist has occasionally—at least since *Humphry Clinker* or *The Heart of Midlothian*—been to record this encounter from the other point of view, to demonstrate what awaits the traveler from the north in metropolitan London. A comparison of Alasdair Gray's novels *McGrotty and Ludmilla* and *The Fall of Kelvin Walker* with Sir Walter Scott's novel suggests how Scottish representations of the Anglo-Scottish encounter have shifted; Gray's fiction offers possibilities quite different from his forebear's. Thus this essay will be concerned with the ways that Gray's novels might be read as variations on the Scot in London theme and with how investigation of Gray in this light helps to demonstrate his dialogic entry into a specifically Scottish novelistic canon.

Viewing Scott's Jeanie Deans as an archetype for the wandering Scot, one can quickly establish a set of key concerns regarding her journey. She travels not for money but for justice, a clemency transcending the worldly law courts. Yet her influence with Queen Caroline is the result more of internecine court squabbles and the intercession of the Duke of Argyle than of Jeanie's own cause. The episode in fact acts as romantic proof of a situation already firmly in place historically. Eighteenth-century British "Scottophobia," as Linda Colley has shown, "was testimony to the fact that the barriers between England and Scotland were coming down, savage proof that Scots were acquiring power and influence within Great Britain to a degree previously unknown."[1] Thus Scott, writing seventy years after the height of Wilkite anti-Scottish sentiment, can use the hazy historicism of his eighteenth-century setting to demonstrate the reality of the nineteenth century. The Queen's mind is changed, and the right-thinking Scottish heroine can live out her days under the patronage of a Scottish aristocrat in a haven of pastoral pleasure, framed between father and husband, pillars of the Scottish church past and present.

Perhaps most striking in Jeanie's interview, however, is the Queen's response to her peroration: "This is eloquence."[2] As Gary Kelly points out, Jeanie "believes speech has a power writing cannot have,"[3] a belief demonstrated in her assertion to Reuben Butler that "a letter canna look, and pray, and beg, and beseech . . . It's word of mouth maun do it, or naething" (267). The Queen's words confirm Jeanie's oral faith and undo the linguistic prejudice so often lying on the other side of the English audition of Scottish dialect, despite the presence in Jeanie's remarks of comments such as "it isna what we hae dune for oursells" (370). Though Caroline initially fears that Jeanie's presence is a manifestation of "the terrible chapter of Scottish genealogy" (365), Jeanie turns out "Scottish enough"—her higher calling helps to situate her romantically outside of a strictly nationalist appraisal.

In the late twentieth century Gray's protagonists will have no such luxury. Going to London to visit the Queen in his novels involves a journey much more speedily accomplished than Jeanie Deans's but in other respects resembling those of the early explorers. Thus Gray assigns McGrotty the Christian name Mungo, aligning him with the Scot Mungo Park, and supplies ironic chapter titles to *Kelvin Walker,* which include "The Discovery of London," "A Meal with a Native," and so on. In the hostile, exotic climate both men are predictably linked with their dialects: though early on McGrotty is treated as "an intruder . . . his accent unintelligible,"[4] he is ultimately lionized at the point when "He had never *sounded* more like an ordinary, down-to-earth, sensible Scotsman," "the kind of Scot folk instinctively trusted" (125, 122; emphasis mine). Walker, "consciously and conscientiously remaking himself," gradually adopts an accent "indistinguishable from BBC English" except when actually on the BBC, "when he reverted to his aboriginal" dialect;[5] his identity cannot, however, sustain such a fundamental schism.

Alan Bold notes that "Fiction haunted by history and constantly aware of linguistic division becomes distinctively Scottish when it admits an element of unsettled psychology."[6] Taken together, these two novels demonstrate the limited but schizoid options of selfhood available to the Londonized Scot. The situation is delineated through a Carlylean emphasis on clothing as well: no kilts, but McGrotty returns to his Harris tweeds after failing to convince in English suits. Walker, however, deciding "there is no reason why my private and public images should correspond" (104), abandons his Scottish clothing after shopping in London. In short, McGrotty's success depends on playing the stereotype, while Walker's failure is linked to his only partial investment in it.

Another element dividing the fates of McGrotty and Walker is the image of the Scottish father. The harsh paternalism of the Scottish church is embodied in *The Heart of Midlothian*'s Douce Davie Deans to the extent that he would rather see his daughter Effie dead than preserved through her sister's perjury. As Kelly notes, Deans "may cling to his Cameronian self-righteousness almost to the ruin of one daughter, the blasted marriage hopes of the other, and the financial ruin of his household."[7] All worldly considerations give way before the dictates of faith. Less than a century after the publication of Scott's novel, George Douglas Brown's *The House with the Green Shutters* would render the monstrous capitalist version of the fearsome Scottish father in the person of John Gourlay, who "would see the town damned" before aiding the progress of a municipal water supply.[8] Not surprisingly, the epilogue to *Lanark* acknowledges the Duncan Thaw narrative's reliance on Brown's novel, where "heavy paternalism forces a weak-minded youth into dread of existence, hallucination, and crime."[9]

Gray's treatment of fathers makes interesting use of this bifurcated tradition. McGrotty's father, long dead, is summoned up in remembrance by Sir Arthur Shots, who tells a World War II story of "a weazened little runt of a fellow, one of those wretched, twisted splinters of humanity which our industrial slums spew forth in such abundance," who saved Shots from being maimed (if not killed) by a land mine only to be blown up himself ("ironically enough," Shots notes) two weeks later (19-20). Shots goes on to assure McGrotty that "The debt I owe your father shall be repaid, with interest, to you" (20). Apocryphal as it is, Shots's tale nevertheless makes the important substitution of the socioeconomic British father for the (satirized) mythic-heroic Scottish one. McGrotty's success will depend on his out-maneuvering Shots in such a way that by the narrative's end he is free of paternal influence altogether; he has become Prime Minister and, to "a million" television viewers, "Christlike!" (125), thus conflating paternalism and filiation in a single divine coup d'état.

Not so with Walker. The young man from Glaik—and here the definition in Brown's "Galt Glossary" of "glaikit" as "useless, silly, foolish (with an implication of wandering from the right path)" seems pointedly relevant[10]—actively seeks to deny his father and the overwhelming religious power with which he is allied. As a Session Clerk, the elder Walker is "elected by the congregation to correct the minister when his preaching wanders from the true doctrine" (26), and he prays as if "talking to somebody in the same room" (27). Thus a different kind of conflation occurs for Kelvin, who feels that God is always "around, watching and judging and condemning," "like having a father with me wherever I went," "a living Hell" (27).

But seeking to evade this scrutinizing presence, Walker moves right back into its gaze. Hector McKellar, the BBC producer who (largely on the basis of Kelvin's dialect) brings him aboard, is a Glaik product who asks about Kelvin's father by name (67). McKellar "believed that the stability of all well-conducted societies depended on bastards like himself" (133) and asserts to Kelvin that "I'm as Scottish as you are" (123). A clear descendant of Stevenson's Mackellar, who had "none of those minds that are in love with the unusual,"[11] he thus becomes as much a surrogate father for Kelvin as Shots does for McGrotty (Shots and McGrotty meet, of course, in the Ministry of Social Stability). But this means that Kelvin still has a Scottish father, even in London, a fact rendering him unable to share McGrotty's ostensibly more positive outcome. In front of the cameras during a pre-employment "screen test" Kelvin feels "a little as he had felt in the days when he had believed in God but it was pleasanter having his words and actions scanned by inhuman machinery than by the headmaster of the universe" (69-70). This pleasant sort of monitoring gives way immediately when Kelvin's father appears on his program. At that point "Only the cameras" pay attention to Kelvin's humiliated speech; his father is busy "destroying" him out of love (130, 132).

Kelvin's crime, according to McKellar, has been to proceed "too fast" for "the British public"; what the BBC desires is a regional gadfly "with no particular standpoint" to "undermine the bigwigs" (122). Such undermining is meant to change nothing: the result is, in McKellar's words, "the British alternative to revolution" (73). Walker's link to the Scottish father produces too great a desire in him for real change, so that even as he works to nullify the father he reproduces a paternal morality. Just as with his dialect, he is living in two worlds, since the English have no wish to see Scottish paternalism imported to their soil. McGrotty's success comes from an outward Scottishness which nevertheless inwardly (and politically) endorses the English status quo of "intelligent hypocrisy" (125). Free of the Scottish father, McGrotty can easily be assimilated.

McGrotty finally meets the Queen; Walker's fall occurs before he has, though invited, a chance to do so. The point that Gray makes, and the change he rings on Scott's model of Scottish/English influence, is that authenticity of eloquence, appearance, ancestry, or anything else has been reduced to its utility on a commodity level, that level where being "Scottish enough" has more to do with a brand name than with anything that can be adequately quantified as personal identity. The exile and cunning that both men engage in, worlds away from Jeanie Deans's determined but ultimately innocent nature, matters far less than does their common susceptibility to measurement and manipulation by English political polls and television ratings. As Gray notes in the characteristic acknowledgments to *McGrotty,* the novel "caricatures nothing but the ability of the British rich to enlist awkward or threatening outsiders" (130).

Even in what might initially be considered some of Gray's slighter work we can observe a self-conscious response to a specifically Scottish literary history. Francis Hart identifies the wandering daughter (in Gibbon's *A Scots Quair*) as "Scotland in archetype, the suffering daughter and wandering orphan, undergoing successive exiles in search of some true Scottish home."[12] Except for her living father, Jeanie Deans could be the subject of the passage. McGrotty and Walker fit a different pattern, finally, one in which a "true Scottish home" is less available than its corrupt simulacrum, either as the stereotypical Scot which McGrotty becomes or as the horrific repatriated reactionary Walker does. Christopher Harvie states that "Kelvin Walker's and Mungo McGrotty's voyages to London might almost be

Lanark's descent (ascent?) to Provan,"[13] and indeed the political themes of *Lanark, 1982 Janine,* or *Poor Things* are fully present in both Gray's London novels. Present as well is Gray's obsessively allusive concern with the text's status as a response to the words and deeds of a controlling, frequently constricting set of nationalist traditions which would dictate what it means to be "Scottish enough."

NOTES

[1]Linda Colley, *Britons: Forging the Nation 1707-1837* (New Haven: Yale Univ. Press, 1992), 121.

[2]Sir Walter Scott, *The Heart of Midlothian* (Oxford: Oxford Univ. Press, 1982), 370; hereafter cited parenthetically.

[3]Gary Kelly, *English Fiction of the Romantic Period: 1789-1830* (London: Longman, 1989), 154.

[4]Alasdair Gray, *McGrotty and Ludmilla, or, The Harbinger Report* (Glasgow: Dog and Bone, 1990), 28; hereafter cited parenthetically.

[5]Alasdair Gray, *The Fall of Kelvin Walker,* rev. ed. (London: Penguin, 1986), 103; hereafter cited parenthetically.

[6]Alan Bold, *Modern Scottish Literature* (London: Longman, 1983), 102.

[7]Kelly, 154.

[8]George Douglas Brown, *The House with the Green Shutters* (Harmondsworth: Penguin, 1985), 70.

[9]Alasdair Gray, *Lanark: A Life in Four Books* (New York: Braziller, 1985), 486.

[10]Brown, 260.

[11]Robert Louis Stevenson, *The Novels and Tales of Robert Louis Stevenson* (New York: Scribner's, 1903), vol. 9, *The Master of Ballantrae: A Winter's Tale,* 255.

[12]Francis Russell Hart, *The Scottish Novel: From Smollett to Spark* (Cambridge: Harvard Univ. Press, 1978), 84.

[13]Christopher Harvie, "Alasdair Gray and the Condition of Scotland Question," in *The Arts of Alasdair Gray,* ed. Robert Crawford and Thom Nairn (Edinburgh: Edinburgh Univ. Press, 1991), 84.

Bell, Book, and Candle: Poor Things *and the Exorcism of Victorian Sentiment*

John C. Hawley

TURNING ONE BLIND EYE on nature and another on nurture, *Poor Things* has been nicely described as "An odd combination of *Pygmalion* and *The Island of Dr. Moreau*" (Henscher 32). With the book's allusions to *Frankenstein,* Hogg's *Confessions of a Justified Sinner,* Rider Haggard's *She,* and various nineteenth-century potboilers, Gray's protagonist is fully justified in asking (most self-reflexively), "*What morbid Victorian fantasy has he* NOT *filched from?*" (Gray 272-73). But the concluding scene, set in 1945, strangely recalls Sue Townsend's recent *The Queen and I* (1992). In Gray's novel the "queen" is Victoria, penniless, surrounded in her basement clinic by lame dogs and stray cats and offering soup to the poor and abortions to the needy. She has become a Miss Havisham cum Beatrice Webb, optimistically devoting her remaining days to the verse decorating the book's cover: "Work as if you live in the early days of a better nation." The irony of *Lanark* is not far away.

Nor are its metaphysical and narrative hijinks. That earlier novel's hero was "a displaced, memory-less, impoverished traveller . . . [who was] trying to grasp where he is, who he is, and where he's come from" (Gifford 230-32). So too with Bella Baxter. The earlier novel's central question, "persistently posed, and ultimately left unanswered . . . has to do with the relationship between its two halves" (Todd 126), and much the same can be said of *Poor Things,* though the division in question has significantly become biological: "Dr. Victoria McCandless was found dead of a cerebral stroke on 3rd December 1945. Reckoning from the birth of her brain in the Humane Society mortuary on Glasgow Green, 18th February 1880, she was exactly sixty-five years, forty weeks and four days old. Reckoning from the birth of her body in a Manchester slum in 1854, she was ninety-one" (Gray 317).

Like *Lanark, Poor Things* combines realistic and nonrealistic narrative in disorienting ways (Murray 220-21) and does so in confrontations "uttered by different voices whose authority cannot be determined, so that they resonate against each other internally, perpetually and inconclusively" (Todd 130). The reader of *Poor Things* puts down the book strangely unsure of how to put the pieces together. Given the ghoulish goings-on in the novel, this clumsiness reverberates uncomfortably, as does the spoof review that accompanies the book: in describing the novel as "another exercise in Victorian pastiche" the "review" implicitly raises questions of how, or why, these moldy bits of nineteenth-century fauna have been resuscitated. When they assume a consciousness of their own in the Victoria McCandless of the early twentieth century, a woman once intent on recovering a past but now intent on denying it, the reader is left pondering the monstrosity of this well-meaning anachronism or of her Creator.

Though she is accused of erotomania, Bella/Victoria claims that the one man she has ever loved is God. This is her nickname for her maker/patron Godwin Baxter and provides a running commentary on such theological questions as the Creator's dubious morality and faltering interest in humanity. But there is the further irony of this constant implied reference to William Godwin (1756-1836) whose wife died in giving birth to Mary Wollstonecraft Shelley. That father gave birth to a form of anarchy, reliant upon reason; that daughter gave birth to *Frankenstein.* In *Poor Things* Godwin gives birth to both. Such "unnatural" engendering continues in his "daughter," who surely becomes the New Woman so feared in late Victorian society, finally exulting that in her husband, McCandless ("without candle"?), she has "a very good wife" who will tend the home while she gives lectures on the Continent (303).

Gray knows his reader as well as he knows his Anatomy: few who follow Bella's development will find *her* unnatural. We follow her progress as we might have once followed Pilgrim's or Candide's. If the world spins madly around her and has schooled itself to ignore the misery it causes, she will tend her garden and help those she can. The one thing she truly regrets (and for which she takes personal responsibility) is the Great War. This is patently absurd and sentimental and invites examination of her entire philosophy. The one message she wishes to impart to British youth is contained in her slim volume *A Loving Economy,* wherein she recommends that families foster enough self-respect in their (one) child that he or she may "*resist that epidemic of self-abasement*" that leads to war (307). She writes, "*the great task of the twentieth century*" is "*to make a Britain where everyone has a good clean home and is well paid for useful work*" (307). Though she feels that "*everything between 1914 and the present day* [1945] *has proved a hideous detour*" (316), she dies happy in her perception that a newly elected Labour government will change all that. Gray lets the years since 1945 speak for themselves. The stories-within-stories, the assertions and denials of what actually happens, the various other metafictional devices of *Poor Things* suggest that Victoria's optimism (the subtitle of *Candide,* after all) is never fully justified, and certainly never the last word.

One suspects Gray's apparent obsession with pastiche has a great deal to do with his theme. Form follows function, and the architecture of the book mirrors the architecture of memory. As outrageous as McCandless's nightmarish version may be, the reader nonetheless suspects Victoria's sanitized account. This story of "a surgical genius [who] used human remains to create a twenty-five-year-old woman" was contained in documents "almost all salvaged from buildings scheduled for demolition" (vii). The papers, almost overlooked as inconsequential, are among those dealing with "families who had helped to shape the city in its earlier days" (viii). The city they have pieced together, one whose old theological college has been replaced with luxury flats, is now wondrously proclaimed the Culture Capital of Europe. But this is, surely, the same city that seems so ominous in *Lanark.*

For all the novel's pyrotechnic allusions to Gothic fiction, there are at least as many to books preoccupied with the social condition of Britain. Among the most prominent are Caryle's *Sartor Resartus* and Samuel Smiles's *Self-Help* in such chapters as "Making Me" and "Making Bella Baxter." The physical appearance of the book, with its intricate cover design, elaborate drawings, and wildly various typography, points in the direction of William Morris, the English poet, artist, craftsman, and socialist. And at the heart of Godwin Baxter's experiments that brought Bella to life was an essentially social concern. "Morbid anatomy," he explains, "is essential to training and research, but leads many doctors into thinking that life is an agitation in something essentially dead. They treat patients' bodies as if the minds, the *lives* were of no account" (17).

What we have in *Poor Things* is a late-twentieth-century nineteenth-century eighteenth century: an endlessly self-referential social experiment that views society as a sick body without a soul. Victoria McCandless, "a skilfully manipulated resurrection" (27), cannot accept her past. In the book's most compelling allusion she has become Faust, a self-creation that has lost its soul. She is, finally, Glasgow itself, tucked away in a basement clinic, content to be eccentric, victimized, and doddering rather than uniquely—if radically—renewed from within.

WORKS CITED

Gifford, Douglas. "Scottish Fiction 1980-81: The Importance of Alasdair Gray's *Lanark.*" *Studies in Scottish Literature* 18 (1983): 210-52.

Gray, Alasdair. *Poor Things.* San Diego: Harcourt Brace, 1992.

Henscher, Philip. "Making a Bad Wife." *Spectator,* 5 September 1992, 32-33.

Murray, Isobel, and Bob Tait. *Ten Modern Scottish Novels.* Aberdeen: Aberdeen Univ. Press, 1984, 219-39.

Todd, Richard. "The Intrusive Author in British Postmodernist Fiction: The Cases of Alasdair Gray and Martin Amis." *Exploring Postmodernism.* Ed. Matei Calinescu and Douwe Fokkema. Amsterdam: John Benjamins, 1987, 123-37.

Gray's Anatomy: *When Words and Images Collide*

Lynne Diamond-Nigh

OUR LIBRARY'S FORTUITOUS and surely unpremeditated placing of the call number and author's name on top of the gray matter (brain) pictured on the dust jacket of *Poor Things* gave me my first clue to this book: *Gray on Gray.* Structured like a cubist work, with no fixed perspective, the novel exposes the underlying pretense of any enterprise that attempts to communicate truth as an objective reality. One would correctly argue that this is not a virgin undertaking, but what Gray has done, quite brilliantly and, I believe, for the first time within a work of literature, is to accomplish this objective by making systematic use of the visual arts.

Recently, I had the good fortune to spend an evening with Ronald Sukenick, the American surfictionist and critic. The conversation turned to a discussion of the reemergence of the importance of the visual arts in contemporary literature: collaborations of French new novelists with artists, paintings that had generated entire novels in France and Latin America, the typographical manipulations of the American surfictionists. He expounded the idea that this focus on the visual was the culmination of the diffusion and decay of the linguistic sign, the natural end point of an evolution manifested in the minimalization (the word is mine) of the word and the metamorphosis of its communicative power from a linguistic to a visual sign. Although I was not at that point acquainted with Alasdair Gray's work, the significance and validity of that thought became apparent to me when I soon after began to study his writing.

Poor Things, Alasdair Gray's most recent novel, suggests the poverty of the real over the imaginary in more than one way. Set in Glasgow over the course of a century, it is a vitriolic satire of urban conditions, social class structure, prejudice against women, the medical and legal establishments, religion and various other institutionalized systems, and, perhaps most important, our continual vain quest for the attainment of truth. This satire plays itself out on the narrative level as well as the level of the media used to create the narrative, words and images, and demolishes their claim to be able to communicate an authoritarian univalent reality.

The novel is a bildungsroman of a decidedly peculiar sort, the heroine being a combination of the body of a twenty-five-year-old and the brain of her baby (at least in one authorized version). Bella, as she is called, matures through the book parallel to her attainment in the end of "proper" language, language that is most authentic early in her growth when it is huge and pictorial, and most inauthentic early in the dry and prosaic "truth-telling" at the end, set against the more fantastic tale of her husband. Early on she writes to her guardian/creator, God(win) Baxter: "*One day you will tell me how to change what I cannot yet describe without my words swelling* HUGE, *vowels vanishing, tears washing ink away*" (164-65). This occurs after a pictorial inset of some six pages, which starts out reproducing her writing with the spelling of perhaps a five-year-old, moves through a stage of page-size letters resembling nothing so much as an automatic graffiti-style painting by Antoni Tapies ("A catastrophic reversion to an earlier phase" [151]), and then returns to what is, for her, normalcy. It is telling, I believe, that this is the only part of Bella's entire "letter" (some 140 pages) that Godwin does not want to read out loud to McCandless, as if it does not have to be linguistically mediated because it is pure experience.

Bella's identity is partially formed through the taking on and trying out of various literary styles and genres. Another recent book, Isabel Allende's *Eva Luna,* has a heroine who does the same; indeed, despite the enormous divergence in tone and cultural context, these two works remind me very much of one another, particularly in their relationships respectively to England and Spain. Eva, a surrogate perhaps of all twentieth-century Spanish-American writers, tries to forge an authentic identity through the creation of a language and literature proper to a Latina (not Spanish) reality; Bella, though maturing by way of an identification with England, finally defines herself as properly "Scottish" in a clear separation from it. Bella says to McCandless: "You grew up on a farm! Was your dad a frugal swain tending his flocks on the Grampian hills or a ploughman homeward plodding his weary way? Tell tell tell your Bell Bell Bell. I am a collector of childhoods since that collision destroyed all memory of my own" (50). Her letters to Baxter, written partially in verse, evoke this response: "My Shakespearean analogy is not far-fetched, McCandless. The close-packed sense within her sentences, her puns, her very cadences are Shakespeare's" (101). A conversation with a Russian in Odessa completes the analogy and makes the vital necessity of storytelling, of fabulation, quite explicit:

To stop him thinking Bell Baxter a total ignoramus I said Burns was a great Scottish poet who lived before Scott, and Shakespeare and Dickens et cetera were all English; but he could not grasp the difference between Scotland and England, though he is wise about other things. I also said most folk thought novels and poetry were idle pastimes—did he not take them too seriously?

"People who care nothing for their country's stories and songs," he said, "are like people without a past—without a memory—they are half people."

Imagine how that made me feel! But perhaps, like Russia, I am making up for lost time. (116)

The opposite of these stories and songs, of course, are the documentary genres which infuse this novel with its pseudo air of truth. Like that Western artifact *Don Quixote,* with which all innovative novels must make peace, *Poor Things* purports to be a found object, rescued from the trash heap by a noble archivist in search of the reality of the city of Glasgow, who then passes it on to an editor who is none other than our real-life author, Alasdair Gray! History, biography, archive, *Gray's Anatomy,* science, medicine, religion, encyclopedia, all purveyors of truth, linguistically encoded, are found to be ultimately subjective. This allusive interplay, across geographies, languages, and centuries, sets up a tissue of resonances that echo back and forth, giving the novel a spatial quality, one which is clearly appropriate to a work focused on the visual.

There is a whole inventory of the visual. Two traditional visual categories are typography and image. A third category, less explicit, is built around spatial intuitions such as those I have just mentioned, the Chinese-boxes structure caused by the stories within the stories and the graphic use of language such as Bella's "*fishy little plants growing babyward*" (134) and "*a wooden-rake-man*" (113). In reading these latter descriptions, which are clearly reminiscent of childhood language, I find it difficult not to make the connection to the surrealists who believed that the only authentic time of human existence was childhood. The fourth category, to which this last is connected, is the incorporation into the novel of qualities related to specific artistic movements, preeminently cubism. And there is a fifth category, from which my title springs and which corroborates Sukenick's thesis: the collision and melding of the word and the image.

Alasdair Gray, a visual artist as well as writer, designs his own books, creating the covers and many of the illustrations, selecting typefaces and designing page layouts. As artifice, artifact, the book becomes a physical object, a three-dimensional sculpture as well as the traditional unobtrusive container of narrative. Conceptually, this links his works to cubism, whereby meaning is apprehended by the fragmentation and recomposition of the plane in the round, and links them in literature to all the innovative twentieth-century works that demand the awareness and participation of the reader in the creation of some armature of meaning(s) through the synthesis of visual or linguistic clues. Cubist multiple perspective reigns through simultaneous contradictory narratives (temporal not spatial simultaneity such as we find in Michel Butor's *Niagara*) forged by the construction and then deconstruction of authoritarian viewpoints. But occult clues and shifting perspective are not all that Gray appropriates from cubism: the dust jacket itself recalls the flatness, the ambiguous multivalent crosscut structuring of cubist space and its integration of fragments of "borrowed" language. The Galatea-like heroine, Bella/Victoria (Beautiful Victory, surely with resonances of ancient Greek statuary and the famous Winged Victory), is herself an artificial construct of disparate elements, two temporal and spatial entities (she and her baby) melding into one, indeed, speaking and maturing her identity through external borrowings or—on the palimpsest of the text—conspicuous pastings of verbiage. It may be licit to suggest that the allusive intertextual nature of this work discussed previously, manipulating and ultimately abolishing a single differential perspective in time and space, follows this cubist principle. Pablo Picasso's *Les Desmoiselles d'Avignon, La Danse,* and *Guernica,* all apogees of this movement, vividly embody in their dislocations of form a propensity for primal cathartic violence that characterizes *Poor Things:* Bella's heightened sexuality, called by her first husband "erotomania," McCandless's description of Godwin Baxter as a Frankenstein figure, and this last's scream, described as follows, suggest the analogy: "Then came the most terrifying experience of my life. The only part of Baxter which moved was his mouth. It slowly and silently opened into a round hole bigger than the original size of his head then grew larger still until his head vanished behind it. His body seemed to support a black, expanding, tooth-fringed cavity in the scarlet sunset behind him. When the scream came the whole sky seemed screaming" (52). Here, perhaps, an interesting circle closes, for no sky was ever more violent and ecstatic than those painted by El Greco and nothing informed the violent protocubist background and fractured ideograms of *Les Desmoiselles d'Avignon* more than El Greco's ambiguously layered draperies of sky. Rather than the more obvious comparison with Edvard Munch's famous painting, the reader encounters here the violence of formal dislocation, overlay, and envelopment disturbing the natural order.

I suggested at the beginning of the last paragraph that Alasdair Gray's books become art objects because of the reader's awareness of their physicality; I would like to argue now that at times in *Poor Things* the primary medium by which these works are constructed, the word, itself becomes abstract form rather than communicative sign, as Sukenick suggested. Several instances present themselves, all of which, I think, function in the same way: when letters do not produce words that are easily identifiable as conveyors of meaning, the reader's awareness moves from the sign itself, that is the black mark on the page, to the negative white space surrounding it, which is usually only a neglected backdrop, then back to the form, not content, of the sign. This emphasis on the interplay of negative and positive space belongs traditionally to visual rather than literary art. Several instances of this expansion come to mind: in Bella's letter to McCandless on page 56 ("*WRDS DNT SM RL 2 M WHN NT SPKN R HRD*"; translation: Words don't seem real to me when not spoken or heard); her very early speech, which fragments words ("Cord dew roy, a *ribbed* fab brick wove ven from cot ton Miss terr Make Candle" [30]); the opposite phenomenon ("detonate vibrate reverberate echo re-echo around this poor empty skull in words words words words wordswordswordswordswordswordswordswordswordswords" [61]). This last unbroken iteration, while suggesting the potency of words as swords, also metamorphoses into the linear image of a sword.

A simple metamorphosis of the same typeface—from plain to italicized text—effects a change in the reader's belief in the credibility of that text. Italics, used sparingly within a nonitalicized block of text, act as a point of emphasis; decontextualized, that is functioning as a block by itself, they lose that power and come close to handwriting, personal and subjective. And so Gray exhibits and works the levels of pseudo authoritarianism by impressionistic hierarchies of typeface. His own INTRODUCTION and CHAPTER NOTES, HISTORICAL AND CRITICAL, the only sections in capitals in his abbreviated contents, are in a bond sans serif type, proclaiming order, lack of gratuitous ornamentation, a no-nonsense attitude, credibility: framing the entire book, they imply the highest degree of authority. The second, below in the hierarchy, is his own "slightly edited" version of the found manuscript, supposedly written by Archie McCandless, Bella's husband, and set in a traditional and plausible serif type, which comes directly after the introduction. Third are the intercalated letters of Wedderburn and Bella, both in the italicized version of the same serif type; sections in these are played off of the more believable nonitalicized exchanges between Godwin and McCandless, who are reading them aloud. Fourth is a return to the found manuscript followed by another italicized section titled "A letter from Victoria McCandless M.D. to her eldest surviving descendant in 1974 correcting what she claims are errors in EPISODES FROM THE EARLY LIFE OF A SCOTTISH PUBLIC HEALTH OFFICER by her late husband Archibald McCandless M.D. b. 1857–d. 1911." Last is the CHAPTER NOTES and then a picture of the Baxter Mausoleum where, we are told, the three principal characters of the novel are buried.

This landscape is the only visual representation of its kind that is not grouped with all the others in a section that is part of CHAPTER NOTES, HISTORICAL AND CRITICAL; there they function as traditional illustration, the only problem, of course, being that many illustrate a fictional reality, which itself is being questioned by another fiction within the entire fictional construct. The placement of the mausoleum image is particularly interesting and ironic: set at the highest vantage point in Glasgow, it should show us the most complete, "truthful" view of that city and, by analogy, the novel. But the image is one of death and enclosure, so once again any hope we have of knowing the truth is subverted by that paradoxical juxtaposition. The visual portraits of the main characters operate in the same way as the layers of authority, reality, and fiction intermingle and collide. They are attributed to a Scottish portraitist, William Strang, but are in their caricaturesque reductions, pastiches of traditional portraits; additionally, there are two of Bella, one a seemingly demonic "belle dame sans merci" within a skull and the other a parody of a Gainsborough lady, both functioning as a commentary on others' perception of her, equally dehumanized, equally unrealistic. And then there are the pictures from *Gray's Anatomy,* as fraught with objectivity and immutability as any visual image could be; indeed, their placement at the end of a chapter that appropriately deals with that specific body part (for example, the skull after a discussion of the crack in Bella's skull) places them in the category of traditional illustration. But they too metamorphose: disembodied body parts become beautiful shapes, often vegetable or flowerlike, soft and supple. Later in the book Bella describes people themselves in the same way as "*soft little cuddlies, tall supple elegants, wild brown exotics*" (180). These same body parts, this time sexual organs, are reprised in the "covers" of the sections framing Bella's and Wedderburn's letters: they look like Victorian decorations and, indeed, are bordered by the same.

So where does all this slippage lead us? Into a fascinating and complex visualizing of text, where the hyperbole of traditional narrative is lifted from its own collusive fabric and given (through various traditional pre-texts of illustration, differentiations of typeface, internal spatial and graphic dimensions, genre subversions) more clearly the formal ambiguities of immediate visual disorganization. This critical visual dimension at once enhances the text with the new densities of artifice and artifact while, in the context of the old animosity between the visual and the linguistic, it signifies the further depletion of language through surrender to the immediate—and now surely more popular—semantics of the visual that since cubism and into the present avalanches of advertising and spitfire collages of MTV have been the dominant of epistemological fragmentation.

WORK CITED

Gray, Alasdair. *Poor Things.* San Diego: Harcourt Brace, 1992.

Language and Its Discontents in Alasdair Gray's "Logopandocy"

Peter G. Christensen

In his interview with Kathy Acker, Alasdair Gray says that not one in twenty readers will take the trouble to read "Logopandocy," the longest and most difficult piece in his collection, *Unlikely Stories, Mostly* (1983).[1] Elsewhere he states that if he came across it, he would not read it from start to finish but rather dip into it bit by bit over a course of a few months.[2] In this story about Sir Thomas Urquhart, the creator of a plan for a universal language, Gray is best seen as the "maker of imagined objects" he cheerfully calls himself in his "Saltire Self-Portrait."[3] "Logopandocy," like the rest of *Unlikely Stories, Mostly,* has so far failed to generate the critical interest that has been granted to *Lanark* and *1982 Janine,* and given the story's difficulty, perhaps this neglect is not surprising.

The fourteen stories (twelve unlikely and two likely) appear to be a catchall collection of short works. They range in length from one to sixty-three pages, and three of the fourteen stories were published as far back as the 1950s.[4] Although five of the longer stories seem to form a unit of three within a two-part frame, they are not set apart as a special section, and they are followed by two one-page likely stories, which prevent the set from being taken as an obvious culmination of the work in the volume. The frame stories, "The Start of the Axletree" and "The End of the Axletree," enclose "Five Letters from an Eastern Empire," "Logopandocy," and "Prometheus." This essay will give a close reading of "Logopandocy" and then briefly relate it to the other stories in the latter part of the collection.

Without some familiarity with the works of Sir Thomas Urquhart of Cromartie (1611-1660?), a rather forgotten courtier and man of letters, readers will not understand "Logopandocy," the title being Urquhart's Latinate name for a universal language. In his acknowledgments Gray writes that a third of the story is "edited from pamphlets Sir Thomas Urquhart published when imprisoned in the Tower of London, with additional phrases from the Earl of Clarendon, John Milton, Edward Philips, John Aubrey and Malcolm Hood" (275). However, Gray does not make any references to any specific passages from their writings.

"Logopandocy" purports to be a lost diary of Urquhart covering some events of 1645, 1651-1653, and 1660-unspecified later date. Gray uses Urquhart's disappearance from the pages of history in 1660 to take him to terra incognita, where he is shown in his later years losing his confidence in the universal language for which he had sketched an outline. In "Logopandocy" Urquhart is presented not as a boisterous charlatan but as an admirable thinker who sincerely looks to improve the human condition with his new invention. Gray stays close to the events in Urquhart's life, his political attitudes, his books, and his style. Thus it may not be apparent that he recontextualizes Urquhart's presentation of the universal language to give it a different emphasis, paying more attention to its potential for human cooperation and less to its abstract completeness as a logical system able to uncover the natural affinity between words and things.

Sir Thomas Urquhart lived a colorful and adventurous life as a consistent supporter of the Royalist cause during the period of the English Civil War and the Commonwealth. In 1638 he went to the Court of Charles I in London and was knighted in 1641. Also in 1641 he published his first work, the *Epigrams: Divine and Moral,* and early in 1645, the *Trissotetras,* a difficult trigonometrical essay. The latter was written in the wildly hyperbolic baroque prose, full of Greek-inspired neologisms, for which he was to become famous in the next decade.

Gray first shows Urquhart in Scotland, having just returned to his estate (and his massive debts) at Cromartie in March 1645, and he uses this occasion to have Urquhart vent his spleen on creditors, Presbyterians, and opponents of the union of Scotland and England. Here Gray does a remarkable job in echoing the sometimes bombastic, sometimes brilliant prose of his model. In the 1645 section of "Logopandocy" we find only one major reference to problems of communication, and it is on the level not of language itself but of social conditions. Urquhart laments that in Scotland, an impoverished country, "many excellent books have perished for want of able and skillful printers, the author happening to dy," whereupon the author's wife uses the manuscripts to "fold perhaps their butter and cheese into" (149). Thus later we are not surprised when "logopandocy" is advocated as an improvement that will promote trade and its economic benefits.

On 3 September 1651 the Royalist army of the future Charles II of England (crowned as King of Scotland at Scone on 1 January 1651) was routed at Worcester by the Parliamentary army led by Cromwell and Charles Fleetwood. Urquhart, who lost the notes for future books (almost 3000 sheets of paper, so he claimed) in the battle, was one of four thousand Scottish prisoners, and he was taken with eighteen others to Windsor Castle. At Windsor he was treated very leniently by Colonel Alsop and soon after was allowed to walk by day through the city of London.

Having made good use of his time in detention, Urquhart published two works in 1652, the *Pantochronochanon; or, a Peculiar Promptuary of Time* and the *Ekskubalauron,* usually known as *The Jewel.*[5] The former is a fanciful genealogical account of his family, in which he traces his ancestry back to Adam and Eve. The latter, a miscellany, includes the sketch for a universal language as well as the famous story of the Admirable James Crichton

(1580-1602), presented as part of a more elaborate defense of the reputation of Scotland. This Scottish material is reworked by Gray into the 1645 diary entry, and in general Gray draws more upon *The Jewel* than on any of Urquhart's other works for his story. Probably coincidentally, a scholarly edition of *The Jewel* was published in Edinburgh by the Scottish Academic Press in 1983, the year that Canongate published *Unlikely Stories, Mostly.*

In late 1652 Urquhart was allowed to make a business trip to Scotland, where he had to take care of creditors who had made him suffer for years. The next year, after his return from Scotland, Urquhart saw printed two books, the *Logopandecteision,* another miscellany (which added a few paragraphs to the sketch for the universal language), and the work for which he is most famous today, his exuberant translation of the first two books of Rabelais's *Gargantua and Pantagruel* (the third book later being found in manuscript). After Urquhart returned to London, he apparently never saw Scotland again, and Gray sees fit to fabricate a spurious meeting between him and John Milton, Protector Cromwell's Latin Secretary, on Midsummer Eve 1653 in the Tower of London for the centerpiece of his story.

In the discussion between the two writers about the universal language Gray adapts a ploy about missing pages already used by Urquhart himself. *The Jewel* is presented as the work of Christianus Presbyteromastix, written for the express sake of getting Urquhart delivered from captivity. Christianus tells how, after the battle, Master Braughton found Urquhart's work on language in the streets of Worcester, whence it had been thrown from his lodgings at Master Spilsbury's. Christianus incorporates the remnants (134 items of about twenty pages) into the early pages of his essay. Thus the battle serves as an excuse for the fact that the numbered items only tell what the new language system does without giving any examples from it. Gray, who numbers the passages of Urquhart's conversation with Milton about the universal language, gives over sections 48-82 and 102-43 to "excisions . . . by the tooth of the editorial rodent" (181) made between 1651 and the recent discovery of the lost diary. Thus Gray's Urquhart does not need to give any examples of actual vocabulary and usage either.

Since, according to its editors, Jack and Lyall, the majority of the critics of *The Jewel* consider it "an entertaining but haphazard muddle" (21), Gray cannot assume that many readers will be familiar with it. Indeed, John Willcock, Urquhart's biographer, describes it as "more like an incoherent dream than anything else," and he reminds us that there is no evidence that Urquhart ever really made a grammar or vocabulary of the new language.[6] On only a few occasions does Gray deliberately recall certain passages of *The Jewel* for the scene in the Tower of London. For example, Milton discusses the opinion of rabbis that at Babel "the first confusion was of accent merely" (168). This view is paralleled by Urquhart's belief that "various and discrepant pronunciation of one and the same language" (*Jewel* 68) caused the separation. In another example Urquhart declares that his new language is so precise that a military general hearing for the first time "the word that represents the name of a soldier" would know what "brigade, regiment, troop, company, squadron or division he is and whether he be of the cavalry or of the foot, a single souldier or an officer, or belonging to the artillery or baggage" (*Jewel* 77). Gray has Urquhart speak of the general's knowing the "soldier's rank, regiment, age, birthplace, ancestry, and character" (177), which is, of course, even more remarkable.

Since much of this episode of "Logopandocy" is given over to Milton's words as well as Urquhart's, very little space is devoted to the universal language in comparison to what we have in *The Jewel.* The only paragraph that mentions any of the specifics of the language reads: "[The language was devised by] grammatical logarithms, said I, for each letter in my alphabet of twenty-five consonants and ten vowels, hath the value of a number linking it to a class of things (in the case of the consonants) or class of actions (in the case of the vowels)" (176). In *The Jewel* similar passages continue for much greater length, so that we know that the language has eleven genders, ten tenses besides the present, seven moods, four voices, twelve parts of speech, ten synonyms per word, etc. Whatever other good features the world's languages have, Urquhart's has more of them. Since every word in it signifies as well backward and forward, we come to the conclusion that this is some type of literary joke. However, this is not the case with Gray's version of the new language, as we never see this hyperbolic elaboration of it, thanks to the rats.

Gray allows Urquhart to develop a line of argument about the virtue of his language that we apparently cannot attribute to the historical Urquhart. In sections 37-42 Gray's hero argues that the defective nature of the current languages aggravates bad personal and political relations. He writes, "It is inexactness of signification which permits false rhetoric to confuse causes with effects, accidents with intentions, abstracts with particulars, thereby provoking (to the corrupt rhetorician's advantage) misled passions in the heart of the malinformed hearer" (175-76). In Urquhart's language even liars, "using it grammatically, will at once contradict themselves or place within the listener's head ample evidence for their own speedy undoing" (176). Similarly, fools cannot help but talk wisely in the new language. If adopted, it will "speed the traffick of human thought as greatly as modern navigation hath speeded traffick in commodities" (173).

Urquhart's desire for truth and free trade is connected to his desire to find a healing for the human alienation symbolized by the linguistic diversity. The Tower of Babel appears here as something more like the original fall than the disobedience of Adam and Eve portrayed in Milton's epic. Milton quotes Genesis 11: 1-9, the story of the Tower, and the two men then discuss whether we should believe that God was the author of the confusion of tongues. Although neither man believes in God as the origin of the disaster, Milton claims that the "*desire for supremacy over their own kind*" (169) on the part of certain men prompted the confusion of tongues, for the building of the Tower stands for the sinful desire to be godlike. The building of

St. Peter's Cathedral in Rome with money raised by the sale of indulgences is for him another example of this hubris.

In contrast, Urquhart does not "concur in the levelling tendency of his remarks" (171-72) and instead offers as a cause the less noxious fact that "Every trade and profession fortifies its power in the state by turning its mastery into a mystery, and cultivating a jargon which is never fully disclosed to the uninitiated" (172). Urquhart's new language will heal people because jargon will be dissipated and lies will be uncovered. The dialogue scene vindicates Urquhart in the sense that he answers Milton's objection that without a feeling for humanity the abstract genius of the universal language is just another example of the attempt to rival God. The question of how to interpret the Tower of Babel story is not answered, despite its obvious relevance to the Axletree in the frame story.

Actually there was much interest in a universal language in the 1600s. Francis Bacon, followed by Francis Lodwick and Cave Beck, hoped to create a Universal Character into which all languages could be transposed. Descartes was interested in the idea of a Universal Language, and his enthusiasm spread to England, where Lodwick published his *Ground-Work for the Framing of a New Perfect Language* in 1652 and George Dalgarno his *Ars Signorum* in 1661 (*Jewel* 23).

Although it was not through any interest on the part of the Commonwealth in his offer to work further on the universal language, Urquhart must have been released in 1653 or shortly thereafter. (In Gray's story Milton actually tells him he will be released soon.) Two surviving letters show him to be in the Dutch town of Zeeland in 1658, and perhaps he was there on 29 May 1660 when Charles II returned to England. Since Urquhart's younger brother Alexander filed a claim in August 1660 as the oldest surviving son of the previous Sir Thomas Urquhart, it is assumed that the author, the younger Thomas, had died during that summer. A rumor circulated that Urquhart expired in a fit of hysterics over the irony of the restoration of Charles II. In Gray's story Urquhart laughs at the occasion but does not die. Gray takes him to Venice, Byzantium, and then eastward into Central Asia, where he loses his bearings and then regains them.

Gray's Urquhart goes temporarily insane in 1660, when he leaves four diary entries that even he cannot account for a year later. It seems that his work on the logopandocy had driven him to linguistic delusions, which we see from the following entry, which he writes when he is lost in some unknown land to the east:

> Can I, in a moment of sublimity (which the Eternal Omniscience may wreak upon whom he listeth) have achieved that logopandochy whose Genesistical root Cromwell's latinist sectary agrees was split at Babelon, and I hold to be the concluding Revelation of the Holy Ghost operant through mankind generally, and myself especially? . . . Did I indeed, when fevered with ague on a foggy island in that wide marsh, write dialects of the tongues of the Cherubim and Seraphim? I doubt. I doubt. (188)

Previously Urquhart had given no indication that he was an agent of Revelation, and, as we have seen, stressed the human rather than the divine cause of the confusion of tongues. His delusions, however, do spring from his humanistic aims.

Douglas Gifford sees Urquhart's goal in "Logopandocy" as basically illusory, leading to his disintegration, although his socially useless choice may ultimately be better than conforming to a stupid world.[7] We should, however, not think of Urquhart as socially useless, and we should remember that Urquhart recovers from his mental disintegration and explores a new world, although he is to be disappointed on a more rational level. He travels to a land whose unclassifiable language shows his new language to have been constructed on a grammar that is not universal. The "speech of the people is so sing-song-sibilant that my ears cannot divide one syllable from another," he claims (189). Their language does not even use verb, adjective, or adverb forms. Similarly, he is confronted by trees, but the names of them defeat him, for, as he asks, "can they be called trees which lack bark, branches, twigs and leaves?" (190). Eventually, he realizes that not only does he fail to communicate to the people in their language but he also cannot get them to understand the blueprint for a palace that he has drawn.

The story ends on a surprisingly happy note as Urquhart finds a female guide who is able to communicate with him through human gestures:

> The guide says we will arrive in an hour. She conveys her meaning by smiles and stroaks of the hand which I comprehend perfectly (there are waterfalls all round whose liquid cluckings, gurglings and yellings drown all words) and it occurs to me that the first pure language my ancestors shared before Babylon was not of voice but of exactly these smiles and stroaks of the hand. (194)

Below this passage about what Urquhart categorizes as the greatest and happiest discovery of his life we find a pencil sketch of a man and woman's hands clasped. However, the possibility of unambiguous gestures is undercut by the two "likely stories" that close the collection directly after the second part of the Axletree frame story.

"A Likely Story in a Nonmarital Setting" (272) and "A Likely Story in a Domestic Setting" (273) share with each other the same illustration of a standing man and woman touching. However, the position of the man and woman is reversed in the two drawings, and the captions under the pictures are different. These captions indicate that one gesture can have more than one meaning, thus leaving us with the feeling that Urquhart's last diary entry describes a happy fantasy. The first interchange between the couple reads:

> "Listen, you owe me an explanation. We've had such great times together—you're beautiful—you know I love you—and now you don't want to see me again. Why? Why?"
>
> "Jings, you take everything very seriously." (272)

When we transpose the drawing to the domestic setting, the gestures accompany the following dialogue:

"Fuck who you like but the rent is overdue and the electricity is going to be cut off and we've no food and the baby is hungry."

"Our love once meant much more to me than money so I'm not giving you any." (273)

Gray is showing that the context of the captions cues us to interpret the gestures differently in each case. The domestic setting locks the characters in gestures that were not previously imprisoning. Urquhart never sees these drawings, and so they cannot disturb him.

The story of the Tower of Babel, which so moved Urquhart and Milton, is reworked before the likely stories in the frame story of the race to reach heaven with the Axletree. Gray says that the Axletree story is an analogy for the greed, waste, and stupidity of the arms race, which corrupts both the public and private sectors of the economy.[8] The empires and corporations try to reach heaven by working on this two-thousand-year-long project that "gave employment to mankind and a purpose to history" (83) but prevented any realistic attempt to improve social ills. The Axletree would have been called a tower had not towers (and here we can include Babel) been "notorious for falling down" (82). At the end of the second part of the Axletree story, the construction workers break into the sky, causing the tower to fall, bringing massive death and destruction with it. The nameless narrator of this story leaves behind him an account of the Axletree, written on a sheepskin. Unless there is an intervening earthquake, it will not be found until the next world empire is established on the accumulation of sufficient capital. Just as Urquhart's belief in the readability of gestures is undercut by the likely stories, so too is his belief that Milton had gone too far in attributing hubris and greed to the makers of the Tower of Babel. Urquhart is wrong in thinking that he can restore language to its pristine state. Nevertheless, this is only an intellectual error leading to a temporary madness, and his great plan comes without the pride and arrogance characteristic of the empire builders.

Despite his temporary insanity, Urquhart is more admirable than the men of letters who are the heroes of either "Five Letters from an Eastern Empire" or "Prometheus," who each fall victim to worse illusions.[9] The letters from the Eastern Empire are written home by the poet, Bohu, who is a castrated functionary at the court of an emperor ruling from beyond the grave through the petrified forms of a bureaucratic police state. Bohu finally gains the courage to write a short poem denouncing the empire. Although he fears that no one will read his words, he dies "in perfect satisfaction" (128). He does not realize that officials will co-opt the poem, getting it to read as a memorial to the justice of the empire. Bohu's ineffectual idealism is not shared by Urquhart, who notes that the wicked know how to adapt language to their own evil ends.

In "Prometheus" Pollard is even less heroic than Bohu. A French writer of Sartre's generation, he attempts to seduce a younger woman of revolutionary inclinations by convincing her of his power to rewrite Genesis with his version of *Prometheus Unbound.* Zeus' chaining of Prometheus serves as a parallel to God's furious retaliation on the people building the Tower of Babel on the plain of Shinar. Near the end of the story Pollard confesses that he is not what he seems: "This story is a poem, a wordgame. I am not a highly literate French dwarf, my lost woman is not a revolutionary writer manque, my details are fictions, only my meaning is true and I must make that meaning clear by playing the wordgame to the bitter end" (231). Pollard has apparently used the story's language to confuse his readers about his identity, himself about his sense of worth, and his potential lover about his talents. He ends by lamenting that his desire to be Prometheus has led him to a type of uncontrollable loneliness.

In the final evaluation Urquhart, often dismissed as an insignificant writer save as a translator of Rabelais, is turned by his fellow Scotsman, Gray, into a hero. When we cut through his self-promotions, Urquhart looks like a commonsensical Constitutional Episcopalian Royalist whose utopian linguistic hopes are far more reasonable than Cromwell's dictatorship or the dreams of emperors. Urquhart's acceptance of the fallen world, as symbolized by human language in all its imperfections and misuses, conserves his humanity, despite the failure of his plan. Gray reminds us that the creation of a better future will require our understanding the limits of human existence rather than the spinning out of utopian dreams.[10]

NOTES

[1]Kathy Acker, "Alasdair Gray Interviewed," *Edinburgh Review* 74 (1986): 89; Alasdair Gray, *Unlikely Stories, Mostly* (Harmondsworth: Penguin, 1984); hereafter cited parenthetically.

[2]Carol Anderson and Glenda Norquay, "Interview with Alasdair Gray," *Cencrastus* 13 (1983): 8.

[3]Alasdair Gray, *Saltire Self-Portrait 4* (Edinburgh: Saltire Society, 1988), 4.

[4]Of the thirteen stories in Gray's third of *Lean Tales,* "The Story of a Recluse" is closest to the unlikely stories; see *Lean Tales,* by James Kelman, Agnes Owens, and Alasdair Gray (London: Jonathan Cape, 1985), 222-46.

[5]All references to *The Jewel* can be found in Sir Thomas Urquhart of Cromarty, *The Jewel,* ed. R. D. S. Jack and R. J. Lyall (Edinburgh: Scottish Academic Press, 1983); hereafter cited parenthetically. *The Jewel* can also be found in Thomas Urquhart, *Works* (1834; rpt. New York: AMS Press, 1971).

[6]John Willcock, *Sir Thomas Urquhart of Cromartie* (Edinburgh: Anderson and Ferrier, 1899), 178. For more on Urquhart and the universal language, see the following: Henrietta Taylor, *History of the Family of Urquhart* (Aberdeen, 1946); James Knowlson, *Universal Language Schemes in England and France, 1600-1800* (Toronto, 1975); Charles Wimbley, *Studies in Frankness* (London, 1926); Frederick Charles Roe, *Sir Thomas Urquhart and Rabelais* (Oxford, 1957); J. D. McClure,

"The 'Universal Languages' of Thomas Urquhart and George Dalgarno," in *Actes du 2ᵉ Colloque de Langue et de Littérature Ecossaises (Moyen Age et Renaissance),* ed. J.-J. Blanchot and C. Graf (Strasbourg, 1979), 133-47.

[7]Douglas Gifford, "Private Confessions and Public Satire in the Fiction of Alasdair Gray," *Chapman* 50-51 (Summer 1987): 108.

[8]Anderson and Norquay, 10.

[9]For Gray the three stories within the frame treat the poet as bureaucrat, aristocrat, and democrat. See Sean Figgis and Andrew McAllister, "Alasdair Gray: An Interview with Sean Figgis and Andrew McAllister, 6th February 1988," *Bête Noire* 5 (Spring 1988): 17-44.

[10]Some of the same message is visible in *Lanark* in the contrast between the small personal things that Lanark learns and the claims of the life-denying but supposedly improvement-oriented public sphere. For various views of the message of this complex novel, see Douglas Gifford, "Scottish Fiction 1980-81: The Importance of Alasdair Gray's *Lanark,*" *Studies in Scottish Literature* 18 (1983): 210-52; Isobel Murray, "Alasdair Gray: *Lanark,*" in *Ten Modern Scottish Novels,* by Isobel Murray and Bob Tait (Aberdeen: Aberdeen Univ. Press, 1984), 219-39; Richard Todd, "The Intrusive Author in British Postmodernist Fiction: The Cases of Alasdair Gray and Martin Amis," in *Exploring Postmodernism,* ed. Matei Calinescu and Douwe Fokkema (Amsterdam: John Benjamin, 1987), 123-38; Rudiger Imhof, "Chinese Boxes: Flann O'Brien in the Metafiction of Alasdair Gray, John Fowles, and Robert Coover," *Eire-Ireland* 25.1 (Spring 1990): 64-79; Dominique Costa, "In the Scottish Tradition: Alasdair Gray's *Lanark* and *1982 Janine,*" *Literature of Region and Nation* 2.3 (November 1990): 2-7.

Different Oracles: Me and Alasdair Gray

Janice Galloway

He said, "That was very unsatisfying. . . . Why did the oracle not make clear which of these happened?"

Rima said, "What are you talking about?"

"The oracle's account of my life before Unthank. He's just finished it."

Rima said firmly, "In the first place that oracle was a woman, not a man. In the second place her story was about me. You were so bored you fell asleep and obviously dreamed something else."

—*Lanark* (357)

I FIRST ENCOUNTERED Alasdair Gray's work at a friend's house. It was the middle of a not good time for me. Suffering from a tenacious depression that made most attempts at talking, getting out of bed, everything really, seem nothing more than variations on a theme of wasting time, I nonetheless persisted with reading because (1) it reminded me there had been things I enjoyed previously and (2) I hoped reading might, sooner or later, turn up something that might help. I wasn't sure how it was going to do this exactly but the hope lingered nonetheless. Off and on, without enthusiasm, I visited people. On one such visit, I fell over *Lanark.* Literally. It was on the floor where my friend had dropped it and I tripped on the open cover as I crossed to the fire. "Borrow that if you like," she said. "I'll be interested to know what you think."

She didn't hear for a while. I deliberately didn't mention it again in case she asked for it back and I had fallen in love—or something—with it. The mixture of clarity, exactness, and near-childlike sincerity; its high expectations of me as a reader, that I was somehow a partner in the enterprise, capable of creative insights and interaction with an author who was prepared to share his power had a profound effect. Remember I hadn't read prose like that before, not Machado de Assis or Marguerite Duras or Jorge Luis Borges—not yet—so this was mind-expanding stuff, all the more so for its syntax and references being close to home. I'd always assumed what my education had taught me was true: that my country was a toty wee place with no political clout, a joke heritage, dour people, and writers who were all male and all dead. Not so, the book said: on a number of levels, not so.

I was so grateful I carried the thing around with me, even when I went out. I forgot meals, went by my stops on buses and had to walk, didn't care I couldn't sleep reading that book. It mattered more than remembering to take the Valium my doctor was so keen to have me get addicted to and certainly did me more good.

Why was a question I asked only much later.

I'm asking it again now for the purposes of this piece and find answers shift—of course they do. They redistribute their weight, sometimes change aspect altogether, and I am reluctant to pin them down as though they don't. The important part, however, the gratitude, stays pretty much a constant. Through all the self-referential twaddle I've read about Alasdair's "post-modern postmodernity," the irritable textbook analyses of his techniques and evasions (few of which ever have the grace to acknowledge the irritability of their authors is often Alasdair's work simply doing what it's supposed to do, i.e., confounding pigeonholing as much as possible); through all the twaddle, indeed, I've read about all sorts of current writers' work, I've held that gratitude tight to remind me of something obvious. IT'S NOT CRITICISM THAT MATTERS, IT'S THE WORK ITSELF. IT'S NOT CRITICS THAT MATTER BUT READERS. Remembering that helps me cope with the frustrating reality that establishment analysis fails to respond intelligently to some kinds of writing as a given: politically, after all, that's what it's for. Work by women, for example, if it's noticed at all, is usually noticed reductively. Sidelined or misunderstood as a rather recalcitrant part of objective (i.e., masculinist) discourse, the things in it which simply have nothing to do with established notions of "significance" or "importance" are rendered invisible. It's only through reading feminist analysis, analysis more properly designed to read in ways more inclusive of what may well be non- or antiestablishment priorities, I've realized how awkward mainstream literary techniques make it to discuss the bravery, passion, or hope that exists in an author's work—and how awkward, then, it must be for mainstream literary techniques to deal with Gray.

Even within Scotland, a country you'd think would be keen to develop more democratic analytic discourse on account of its own marginalization within the British literary establishment, this persists. Due to the extent of internalized second-class nationhood in Scotland which presupposes Scottish artistic status and priorities as naturally lesser (as opposed to different) to those of the English canon, it can actually be worse. Now I'm not saying Alasdair's work suffers mortally or most from this kind of thing, not by a long chalk (the work of James Kelman, Tom Leonard, and of course, a whole brace of Scottish women including me raise their own "difficulties" too), but it is, in general, not well served. This then is a nonacademic piece, another writer's piece, a personal piece. It hopes to offer something that conventional techniques can't.

Alasdair Gray's was a voice that offered me something freeing. It wasn't distant or assumptive. It knew words, syntax, and places I also knew yet used them without any tang of apology: it took its own experience and culture as valid and central, not ancient or rural, tourist-trade quaint or rude-mechanical humorous. It spoke to the intellect directly and simply, didn't proscribe what I was meant to see or think, and was not afraid of fun or admissions of emotion. It was aware too of the kinds of self-consciousness and repressions I knew, the tangle of guilts that so often inform the Scottish psyche and bedevil its written expression, yet, by using ingenious technical devices like the asides and list of plagiarisms, could contain them enough to let the story not only emerge but be even truer for their inclusion. Even more, however, it was a voice that took for granted it wasn't the only voice. From its own experience of marginalization (and they are multiple), it knew the whole truth didn't belong to one sex either. In short, *it was a man's voice that knew that's all it was—a man's.*

It seems uncontentious to say that Scotland, a country still weighed down psychologically by its own political impotence and perceived secondary status, seems to consider gender and sex questions as relatively unimportant. Ironic, I know, but there it is. The bulk of our democratic writers and thinkers still, by and large, seem as secure in their ignorance of feminist issues as the Scottish press and our homegrown literary critical elite. Gray's writing, however, is informed by a democratic urge that does not sell women short: he knows our version of the story is different, possibly even opposed, yet of equal force.

I felt this knowing before I traced it: the tracing found it on a number of levels. First, outright. Rima's shrugged "We must have been listening to different oracles, I'm sure you imagined all that," is plain enough. But also, with Gray, there is a feeling of Woman as somehow inescapable, a sometimes paranoid, sometimes warm perception of her suffusing or permeating the narrative and its menfolk even in her absence. Kelman, for all his innovation and subversion of traditional narrative, is very much informed by what Anthony Burgess calls "male thrust": women surface in the writing as outside the main action. This is, of course, as it should be: it's daft to expect writers to do things they don't feel in the interests of some political notion and Kelman's writing seems the more honest for its candid revelation of wariness, its tender suspicion of the female. Gray's narrative, however, seems intensely aware of a kind of incompleteness. His men long for (or obsess about) women and what they offer or do not offer their lives in a way Kelman's do not. That longing, further, is colored by a wish to be valued by women and what they know, to learn from or join with them. This is especially keen in *Lanark* and *1982 Janine* where the sense of loss and distance from the female is something that seems to be endured only with difficulty, with an almost overpowering sadness. Gray's writing not only knows that women experience, feel, and often think differently, it seems to be filled with a regret for that fact, and in this way, Woman—the female principal—exists in Gray's writing the way she exists in no other current male writer's work. Whereas Tom Leonard seems to wish women would make more of an effort to understand his dilemma and Kelman seems to perceive women as very much separate (though definitely sexual) beings, Gray *yearns.* This yearning, this blighted need to bond or communicate more fully with the unknowable experience of the other sex, seems to me one of the most interesting aspects of his work, an aspect I suggest powers much of his creative vision.

Simultaneously, of course, men and male roles, the anguish of sensitive men forced into the tight sausage skin of what passes for normal masculine behavior, recurs again and again and the effects of such restriction on his men's sometimes cruel, sometimes selfish, sometimes simply bewildered attitudes to women are keenly detailed. Such generosity helps honest dialogue, yet repeatedly I've found criticism unable or unwilling, perhaps because of his sex (maybe they think men have more important things to do than examine gender?), to even acknowledge it. I can though. I do.

As a writer, Alasdair Gray's writing makes me feel braver. As a woman, it makes me feel acknowledged, spoken to. Sometimes, even listened for. As a woman writer in Scotland, those gifts are still rare enough to make me very grateful indeed.

An Alasdair Gray Checklist

Mark Axelrod

Prose and Poetry

Lanark: A Life in Four Books. Edinburgh: Canongate, 1981; London: Granada, 1982; New York: Braziller, 1985.

Unlikely Stories, Mostly. Edinburgh: Canongate, 1983; Harmondsworth and New York: Penguin, 1984.

1982 Janine. London: Jonathan Cape, 1984; New York: Viking, 1984.

The Fall of Kelvin Walker: A Fable of the Sixties. Edinburgh: Canongate, 1985; New York: Braziller, 1986.

Lean Tales (with James Kelman and Agnes Owen). London: Jonathan Cape, 1985.

Saltire Self-Portrait 4. Edinburgh: Saltire Society, 1988.

Old Negatives. London: Jonathan Cape, 1989.

McGrotty and Ludmilla; or, The Harbinger Report: A Romance of the Eighties. White Leaf, 1989; Glasgow: Dog and Bone, 1990.

Something Leather. London: Jonathan Cape, 1990; New York: Random House, 1990; London: Picador, 1991.

Poor Things. London: Bloomsbury, 1992; San Diego: Harcourt Brace, 1992.

Ten Tales Tree and Tall. London: Bloomsbury, 1993; San Diego: Harcourt Brace, 1994.

A History Maker. Edinburgh: Canongate, 1994.

Stage Plays

Dialogue (one act), 1971.

The Fall of Kelvin Walker (two act), 1972.

The Loss of the Golden Silence (one act), 1973.

Homeward Bound (one act), 1973.

Tickly Mince, with Tom Leonard and Liz Lochhead (two act), 1982.

The Pie of Damocles, with Tom Leonard and Liz Lochhead (two act), 1983.

Radio Plays

Quiet People, 1968.
The Night Off, 1969.
Thomas Muir of Huntershill, 1970.
The Loss of the Golden Silence, 1974.
McGrotty and Ludmilla, 1976.
The Vital Witness, 1979.
Near the Driver, 1988.

Television Plays

The Fall of Kelvin Walker, 1968.
Dialogue, 1972.
Triangles, 1972.
The Man Who Knew about Electricity, 1973.
Honesty, 1974.
Today and Yesterday, 1975.
Beloved, 1976.
The Gadfly, 1977.
The Story of a Recluse, 1987.

Book Reviews

James Kelman. *How Late It Was, How Late.* Norton, 1995. 374 pp. $21.00.

Although James Kelman's fifth novel seems to spit in the face of the British literary establishment and to relentlessly molest the Queen's own English, *How Late It Was, How Late* won the very well-established, institutionalized Booker Prize last year. While this irony alone was enough to spur many a volatile review and many heated discussions concerning linguistic oppression and the value of a native language, *How Late It Was, How Late* warrants its own attention as a brilliant novel apart from the battling literary politicians. In fact, within the very narrow confines of this novel, namely the blind and battered Sammy's head, the Glaswegian dialect stands up for its own legitimacy and artistic value as it eloquently elucidates a vital part of Scottish culture. The dialect, the language of the pathetic and lovable ex-con Sammy, serves its literary and political purposes with skill and compassion aplenty.

As a narrative, *How Late It Was, How Late* is a hapless meander through a small part of Glasgow, after Sammy wakes up from a drunken weekend in a vacant lot wearing a pair of too-small sneakers and feeling "clatty as fuck." He takes a poorly conceived swing at a "sodjer" and ends up blind and beaten in prison—again. He gropes home, feeling fuckt and fuckt indeed, to find his girlfriend gone and no way to know if she even left a note. The situation never improves for Sammy as he gets hauled in for questioning and attempts to get some medical assistance. From the police who beat him, the medical authorities who won't even commit to a statement of his condition, and the disability bureaucrats who trap him in a forbidding, formal questionnaire, he doesn't seem to expect a thing, doesn't even seem to think he should. He's an ancient innocent, fated to a hell of a life but smiling now and then at the pleasure of a smoke or the lyrics of some sorrowful country music. Appropriately enough, Sammy's sordid past remains muffled and blurred, surfacing only in broken bits of recollection.

Sammy's optimism and humor allow for some much needed relief from the breathless, blind confinement of 374 pages in his head, and begin to feel like survival mechanisms more essential than the tins of beans he finds left in the kitchen cupboard. He chuckles at himself and his predicament, as if he can't believe he's really blind. What a kick, what'll his friends say? He imagines signing on for a guide dog and a stick, or going to the Blind Asylum, "but what a hell-hole that sounded, straight out of some victorian fucking nightmare in the name of christ ye could picture them all, the poor bastards, moping and groping their way about these whitewashed stone rooms . . . the gentry coming in to check their shareholdings . . . on their way to the fucking ballet or something, a private box at Ibrox Park for champagne and fucking french kippers or whatever the fuck they get." Even as Kelman switches between a narrator and Sammy himself, he never misses a beat, never loses the intensity of the world from inside Sammy's head. Vivid and even poetic at times, *How Late It Was, How Late* has a profound pathos and a rich story in addition to being a bold statement against literary elitism. [Carolyn Kuebler]

*

Georges Perec. *A Void.* Trans. Gilbert Adair. HarperCollins, 1994. 285 pp. $24.00.

It is impossible to convey the oddities and beauties of this text. There are plots within plots, mysteries within mysteries, times within times, shadows within shadows. The text is, in a sense, a whirlpool. Perec, in effect, wants to suggest that language (is there a world *within* a word?) is an attempt to convey consciousness; it is the "bond" that connects us (even though we take words for granted). By compelling us to understand that our very existence as social creatures depends on language, he forces us to hear and say and write with concentrated (consecrated?) understanding. As one "character" puts it: "dumbstruck, as I say you and I, although not totally grasping at this point what its [inscription] is saying to us, call at last boast of proving its validity as a signal, as a communication." But Perec also understands that we often deliberately *deform* communication. We use words as white lies, as political slogans. We construct to deconstruct crimes.

I assume that readers of this review know that Perec's text does not contain the vowel *e*. Why should he even attempt to make it *disappear*? Why is he so *obsessive* about absence, loss, rupture? By stressing absence, he suggests that it ultimately refers to the lives of *those we once knew*, to the *times we once treasured.* And, of course, he knows that in a paradoxical way, we often grant greater presence to absence than to presence. We don't take into account present life; we yearn for a "golden past."

Perec is, of course, using the "formula" to mourn the missing relatives who were sent to the death camps. Thus it would be foolish to consider this text as a *mere puzzle*. It is a moral statement that masks itself; it makes us *participate* in the search for meaning (linguistic, political, religious).

The novel concerns Anton *Vowl*, an incurable insomniac who cannot understand his surroundings. "Far off, a church clock starts chiming—a chiming as mournful as a last post, as an air-raid alarm, as an SOS signal from a sinking ship." Time is described metaphorically as an SOS of loss, alarm, sinking—perhaps of death itself. Vowl cannot sleep because he is afraid of "the big sleep." His companions, with their absurd names, occupations, grotesque and amusing words, are perhaps his "occult shadows," his "secret sharers."

Although there is a "last" chapter, there is another "last" (lost?) chapter after that. It appears that the author—or the book itself—doesn't *want closure*. Finally, we are given passages that appear as "metagraphs." A quotation from "E. Baron": "The language of the Papuans is very impoverished; each tribe has its own language and its vocabulary is ceaselessly diminishing because, after every death, a few words are eliminated as a sign of mourning." Perec's text "ceaselessly diminishes." We readers *diminish* as we move—or are moved? —through its labyrinthine trails (trials?). But we don't mourn because we perceive an oddity there, an amulet here. We are, in fact, laughing as we are crying. [Irving Malin]

*

Luisa Valenzuela. *Bedside Manners*. Trans. Margaret Jull Costa. High Risk Books, 1995. 121 pp. Paper: $12.99.

Luisa Valenzuela's short novel *Bedside Manners* offers a fresh perspective on the difficulties of facing reality, specifically the reality of economic and political instability in an unnamed Latin American country. Valenzuela somehow manages to communicate this theme while creating a landscape that evades realism at every turn. The result is a playful account of one woman's quest to come to terms with her changing homeland and her fractured identity.

The protagonist, referred to only as the Señora, returns from New York to the country of her birth "in search of refuge" from the spiritually destructive world she inhabits. She takes up residence in a country club, where she is to rest and recuperate, but finds that her bed becomes "a boat adrift on troubled waters." The country club is supposed to be sheltered from the world surrounding it, but the changed landscape of her country penetrates her room relentlessly. The invasion of the Señora's world, specifically by her chambermaid María, a psychologist/cab driver named Alfredi, and Lucho, one of a number of soldiers on military maneuvers outside the country club, comprises the primary action of the novel.

The world that cannot be kept out is characterized by hyperinflation; María charges the Señora more for services rendered even as they haggle over prices, since the currency is devalued so often. The government has created a cheery version of present conditions on television to placate its citizens, and María does her best to isolate the Señora from the world outside by refusing to bring her a newspaper and drawing her curtains against her will. Yet the intrusion of reality is inevitable, and it affects the Señora's quest to make sense of her life, which begins to overlap with the military's struggle for governmental control: "She's learned counterinsurgency and non-conventional warfare techniques." Defense mechanisms become literal as well as figurative, as the Señora takes part in a military offensive called Operation Identity, which parallels her own struggle to recover her ability to think and to remember.

This overlapping of military and personal struggles is what makes *Bedside Manners* so appealing. The reader may be like the protagonist, who is initially described as "suspecting nothing of the superimposition of different planes of reality," yet once we have accepted the way the author is superimposing these planes, we can begin to share her vision of the Señora's all-too-familiar world. [D. Quentin Miller]

*

Lance Olsen. *Scherzi, I Believe.* Wordcraft/Jazz Police Books (P.O. Box 3235, La Grande, OR 97850), 1994. 130 pp. Paper: $9.95; *Tonguing the Zeitgeist.* Permeable Press (47 Noe St., #4, San Francisco, CA 94114), 1994. 192 pp. Paper: $11.95.

Lance Olsen is a prolific writer of fiction, essays, and reviews. He also teaches creative writing and contemporary literature at the University of Idaho. The twenty-two short fictions collected in *Scherzi, I Believe* display his talent and his range. Think of it as Olsen's *ficciones,* or "my postmodern world and welcome to it"—a multimedia presentation in black and white on paper. Highlights include "Family," a strange ghost story set in rural Kentucky; "Madman Agonistes," a non sequitur love story with a *National Enquirer* interlude; "Egyptian Hyperspace, Although," postmodern fantasy; "I Was a Teenage Werewolf," Lon Chaney, Jr., as the first postmodernist; "Live Sex, Microwaves, London," a couple from Spokane vacations in London: Allison wants to see a live bed show; "Plasma Blizzard," story, explication, demonstration ("One understands the text will never be fully comprehensible, yet one no longer feels radically unsettled in one's thought processes. CONCLUSION: *The more one experiences a postmodern text, the less postmodern it becomes.*"); "My Dates with Franz," a receptionist's journal chronicles her relationship with a writer: Kafkaesque; "The Death of Hieronymus Bosch," cyberpunk juxtapositions; "Two Children Are Menaced by a Nightingale," the story behind the story of a collage by Max Ernst perhaps; "Thirty Messages," lessons from Barthelme, Wittgenstein: question reality; absurdity is interested in YOU; and "Final," a multiple-choice essay test. There is some narrative in these fictions but it is used primarily as centerpost of maypole reality. Like his more obvious influences—Barth, Barthelme, Borges—Olsen is concerned with the translation of nonlinear reality to linear medium. We *are* postmodern (or post-postmodern), he seems to say, so we might as well get good at it.

Olsen's novels explore territory discovered in the short fictions. His first, *Live from Earth* (1991), is a relatively gentle postmodern fantasy. *Tonguing the Zeitgeist,* Olsen's second novel and a finalist for the Philip K. Dick Award, is full-contact cyberpunk. An image suggests itself of the author at work. He rides an exercycle that powers a computer, a CD player, and a bank of video screens. He uses his keyboard to simultaneously access information, select cuts, zap channels, and write this novel. The result is a plausible near-future reality influenced by the works of Gibson and Burroughs but put together from a fresh perspective informed by popular culture, computer technology, and the gamut of literary genres. With humor and awareness Olsen takes advantage of the contemporary complex-to-the-point-of-chaos situation by styling creatively as he surfs the waves churned up by data storm.

Ben Tendo is a guitarist with the band Lithium Breed in the city of Spocoeur in the fifty-first state, Columbia. He works a day job at Beautiful Mutants, Ltd., a holoporn mail-order business. But he is destined for a much stranger trip. For unknown reasons he is kidnapped and taken to a plush Seattle penthouse occupied by two porn goddesses. From there he is transported to London and the coast of Scotland where he learns who had him kidnapped and what stakes they are playing for.

I don't want to give away too much, because for all its inventiveness, satire, and playful recombination of cyberpunk motifs, a large part of the joy of this novel is in the page-turning "what will happen?" factor. The conclusion is satisfying and leaves the reader with some certainties: that Fame is a fool's game; that the world (everywhere and everywhen) is absurd and funny and sad. But what predominates, what walks off the last page and follows the reader around, is a head-shaking sense of wonder at a too-crowded, all-too-possible, not-so-distant future; and one haunting question: Will there be room in it for love and compassion? [Daniel Barth]

*

Silviano Santiago. *Stella Manhattan.* Trans. George Yúdice. Duke Univ. Press, 1994. 212 pp. Paper: $14.95.

Stella Manhattan is a multiple novel that transcends the "gay novel" label as well as the purely literary to enter the larger realm of culture. By virtue of his "deviance" the protagonist, Eduardo, aka Stella Manhattan, exposes the cracks and inconsistencies in a sociopolitical system (be it the Brazilian military regime, a society based on order and productivity, or a rigidly white/heterosexual/Christian culture) that presents itself as unitary. The novel's challenge to this hegemonic and monolithic power is conducted on multiple fronts, under the postmodern aegis of the freedom of coexistence of many realities, masks, sexual orientations, styles, and narrative voices. As Santiago himself notes (in a sort of postscript inexplicably omitted in the English edition), the structure of the book is flexible and double. It hinges upon a series of antithetical pairs ranging from the central opposition of (official) history and (personal) history to the split narrator of "Beginning: The Narrator," to a series of characters with double identities—such as Eduardo, who cruises the gay bars of New York as Stella, and the sadomasochistic Black Widow, alter ego of Colonel Vianna.

The theme of potential disruption brewing within the apparently unified structure of power is reflected in the novel's fragmentation of the narrative and changes of rhythm, highlighted by the frequent use of blank spaces to separate fragments, a choice this edition doesn't always respect (as with chapter 8), significantly altering the reading experience. The multiple linguistic registers, incorporating colloquial elements with scholarly ones and playfully mingling English, Portuguese, and Spanish, as well as the postmodern mixture of high and popular culture contribute to the polyphonic quality of this work and reflect the idea of diversity and dissidence implicit in the theme of transvestism, which in turn functions as a central metaphor in the book.

All these elements comprise the composite yet apparently orderly reconstruction of Eduardo's last two days at his apartment (October 18 and 19, 1969). The story culminates in the extreme fragmentation of the final pages which, rather than restoring order by solving the mystery in the fashion of traditional detective stories, present a kaleidoscope of impressions, reactions, and versions of Eduardo's disappearance through many different narrators, thus leaving the story open and the reader to his own critical and creative devices.

George Yúdice's translation competently conveys the multiple levels of this work. There is, however, a problematic feature inherent in the linguistic interplay of English and Portuguese and the cultural implications that go with it: it's a relationship that can't always be made visible or reversed as successfully due to the hegemonic status of the American language and culture—Portuguese, for the average English speaker, lacks the familiarity and cultural resonances English has acquired in most of the Western world. Nevertheless, this remains a compelling novel, and an important addition to the slowly growing number of Brazilian books available to American readers. [Adria Frizzi]

*

Joanna Scott. *Various Antidotes.* Holt, 1994. 240 pp. $20.00.

Reading this collection of Joanna Scott's short fiction, one is at first struck by the wealth of historical detail. Beginning in seventeenth-century Holland, and marching up through the years against a backdrop of various European and American settings, Scott's collection gives the reader a sense of the important role history plays in communicating human experience, emotion, and understanding. By the time we reach present-day United States in the final story, we are conscious of the fact that the world around us falls into a pattern of history, and that our lives make sense only when we take into account the times that surround them.

As the title indicates, though, the stories in *Various Antidotes* are not anecdotes, or mere glimpses of characters' lives viewed through the lens of history. In nearly every story, Scott begins by setting historical scenes, and then concerns herself with scientific trends that define the times—the use of chloroform in childbirth, for instance, or early experiments with X rays. But the focus eventually shifts to characters who exist on the fringes of society, characters who can be seen as yardsticks for the world they inhabit. Through the lives of these characters, Scott reveals the pain of human experience; the "various antidotes" of the title serve either to assuage this pain or to have little effect upon it.

Like Francis Huber in "Bees Bees Bees," the second story in the collection, the central character of each story is "eccentric, perhaps, but famous." This fame, usually local fame tempered by its concurrent eccentricity, is frequently the chief reason for the pain these characters experience or cause in others. The mad lens-grinder of Delft, the main character in "Concerning Mold upon the Skin, Etc.," is obsessed with perfecting a microscope to the point that he becomes "deliciously alone in his invisible world." After causing his daughter Marie to cry, he is unwilling to comfort her, so great is his obsession with scientific understanding: "He caught the tear on the knuckle of his thumb and transferred it to a specimen slide." Such frustrated attempts to connect with others typify Scott's stories, and give them a dimension that transcends history and science. One comes away from the book having glimpsed a vision of genuine human frailty; despite our great achievements, we are a timid race, plagued by the need to understand completely the world around us and the realization that we never can. Scott's ability to render this theme in prose that is at times scientific and at times figurative makes this collection appealing to both sides of the reader's brain. [D. Quentin Miller]

*

Samuel Delany. *Hogg*. Black Ice, 1995. 219 pp. $24.95.

The dateline for this novel's composition is 1969–1973 although it has only now been published. *Hogg* can be read as a companion piece to Delany's other non-science fiction novel *Tides of Lust* which, for all its thematic similarities, possesses a more complex narrative structure and which draws on the figure of Faust to underpin its accounts of sexual transgression. *Hogg* too focuses on the breaking of taboos, especially the limits of literary expression. Narrated by a teenage white boy, it describes his association with a trucker nicknamed Hogg because he "lives dirty." It scarcely matters that the boy has no name because like Pauline Réage's O he reduces himself to a sexual function, either performing fellatio or submitting to pederasty. The novel is set in an unspecified American city and does not even structure itself as an extended struggle against time like John Rechy's *Numbers*. Instead it repeats in greater and greater detail cases of buggery and sexual assault where the female figures are reified as "meat" or fair game for male sexual predators. Hogg and his cronies eke out a living raping and assaulting women for money. In a sense they are the sexual gangsters of the novel with the narrator alternating between the roles of witness and realizer of others' sexual fantasies. In the course of a "job" a husband is half killed and his son and wife raped before his eyes. Violence proves to be sexually addictive because Denny, a member of Hogg's group, embarks on an orgy of slaughter, disemboweling a pregnant woman. Again and again Delany suggests that the sexual impulse can be turned into a drive for self-mutilation. Denny, for instance, hammers a nail into his own penis as a prelude to the sequence of murders. And sexuality is repeatedly shading over into bodily waste. It is no coincidence that Delany should juxtapose the soiled Hogg, a murdered fetus, and a waste barge towards the end of the novel because there is a steady process at work whereby humans are reduced to dead matter. The major variation from the main first-person narrative is a local radio station that constantly recycles reports of the serial killings. Delany here writes into the novel the reader's vicarious involvement with the violence running through the novel. Hogg and his group become their own audience briefly and, more significantly, Delany denies us the relief of the murderers getting their just desserts. They escape capture and by implication the round of sexual violence will continue. *Hogg* is an unusually austere report then on the perpetrators of this violence, not the victims, and forces the reader to confront scenes without the mitigation of moral comment. [David Seed]

*

Marie Redonnet. *Hôtel Splendid. Forever Valley. Rose Mellie Rose.* All trans. Jordan Stump. Univ. of Nebraska Press, 1994. 113, 113, 120 pp. Paper: $10.00 each.

Marie Redonnet is one of the most talented new writers in France today. *Hôtel Splendid, Forever Valley,* and *Rose Mellie Rose,* published in 1986 and 1987 by the prestigious Editions de Minuit, are the first of her works to be translated into English. The three novels form a trilogy—a triptych, as Redonnet puts it. While each novel tells a different story, all contain similar events, characters, themes, and images, which create a sense of continuity from one novel to the next, somewhat in the manner of a fugue. The seemingly interchangeable characters with simple, rhyming names—Bob, Cob, Yem, Nem, Ted, Fred, Ada, Adel—live lives that are at once banal and surreal. In *Hôtel Splendid,* the youngest of three sisters cares for her two ailing siblings and fights to save the decrepit family hotel from total decay as it sinks slowly into a swamp; the adolescent narrator of *Forever Valley,* who works in a sleazy dancehall, spends the rest of her time looking after an aging priest and digging pits in the rectory garden in search of old graves she believes are buried there; at the beginning of *Rose Mellie Rose,* Rose finds the baby Mellie in a grotto, and at the end of the novel Mellie goes back to the same grotto to give birth to her own daughter—also called Rose—and abandons her there before returning to the town of Oât to die on the back seat of an old Buick that is half buried in sand next to a lagoon.

In this strange world, death and decay of every kind assail the characters from all sides—epidemics, rust, leaks, blocked toilets, and rotting wood caused by the waters of the encroaching swamp in *Hôtel Splendid;* death, paralysis, liver disease, prostitution, flooding, and failed businesses in *Forever Valley;* the declining population, closed shops, and flooded neighborhoods of Oât in *Rose Mellie Rose.* The narrators, however, display remarkable persistence. In a small yet heroic way, each affirms the survival of the human spirit in the face of adversity and struggles to pass on a legacy—however small—to those who come after her. Mellie, for example, bequeaths to her daughter the book of legends she herself received from Rose and to which she has added twelve Polaroid photos that record the events of her own life.

The novels are difficult to anchor in any particular time or place. The present tense in which they are narrated gives them the timeless quality of myths and legends, and the characters come face to face with the elemental forces of life and death in places that recall the world of fairy tales: Fairy Grotto, Charms neighborhood, the impenetrable forest where woodcutters work, the Hôtel Splendid rising out of the middle of the marsh, the boat called *The Queen of Fairies* that sets sail for a legendary shipping channel. Echoes of familiar tales recur throughout the novels, and events are governed by atemporal cyclical rhythms. The characters—like Redonnet herself in her search for a new style of writing—strive to break out of these repetitive cycles, to bury the dead in their family, and to move on. In this sense, the novels convey a quiet optimism, a belief in the possibility of renewal after decay.

Jordan Stump's excellent translation successfully captures the haunting, impressionistic nature of Redonnet's prose. Her deceptively simple style, with its short sentences and minimalist vocabulary, evokes fleeting moods and situations and gives the novels a poetic, musical quality. Strangely moving in its simplicity, her work is to be highly recommended to all those who appreciate the soothing effects of fairy tales and legends. [Susan Ireland]

*

Trudy Lewis. *Private Correspondences.* TriQuarterly Books, 1994. 198 pp. $19.95.

This first novel is written like a love letter to a killer. It begins: "When I first got your letter, I was only fifteen." The narrator, daughter of a charming drunkard senator and his bitter political widow wife, has received an anonymous letter detailing intent to rape and mutilate. From the start, Libby is not disgusted or afraid but entranced, "called," and wants to keep this experience to herself. She dutifully tells her parents, but when her father confronts a political rival whom he suspects could be the culprit, Libby "didn't want to hear the tape. . . . I didn't want to meet you that way, with four or five other people between us." Capable of acute observations (a grandfather's bed smells of "raw piecrust," a woman's breasts are "loose and jiggy as nervous gerbils"), Libby is nonetheless detached from evidence of run-of-the-mill tragedy in her family: an angry mother dropping her husband's golf shoes in the bathwater, a drunk father asleep in the driveway. She's got the concentration of a horseback rider coaxing her mount through a jump course: balanced between fear and longing. The letter rips open her complacent life and makes her see deceit and cruelty everywhere. She wants to face it.

On a road trip with her father and his minions, Libby begins her accelerated encounter-sessions with male aggression. The crew stays at the house of another senator, apparently Daddy's lover, and her two young sons. Libby "kidnaps" the good-for-less son, driving him to some remote location where, powerplay flipped, he accosts her physically and sexually. Here our innocent-enough fifteen-year-old cuts her losses: she submits to gropes, and the unpleasant boy supplies info on her dad's infidelity. Then Libby and her dubious partner journey to an arc built in preparation for the apocalypse by a local millionaire lunatic who is in cahoots with her father's secretary, for one, and who uses lots of language about Babylonian whores and Pharisees and Jezebel. Abandoned here by guy and secretary, Libby mistakenly pegs the nut as the man who wrote the letter (of course, he and the teenage defiler are both easy stand-ins, sentimentally speaking). Horrors and ugly physical things occur.

The narrator's relationship with the letter writer—mused about, questioned, and spoken to in terms intimate and fearful—is a curious complicity with evil that will, eventually, culminate in revenge. "In the end, you always have to rape yourself, is what I learned from you," she says. Is this a rape fantasy? The book presents it more as baptism-through-fire. Libby is not brought down by her attraction—she is seemingly saved by it. This is a bold premise, bespeaking courage or delusion, but in any case redemption. [Aurelie Sheehan]

Grace Andreacchi. *Music for Glass Orchestra.* Serpent's Tail, 1993. 199 pp. Paper: $12.99.

The narrator—or better said, instrumentalist—of *Music for Glass Orchestra* flees the suburbs of Boston, its poisonous air and hugely indifferent denizens, to come to Paris, "a vast bright place, teeming with the living and the dead." She takes a lover, Stéphane, a famous violinist, alcoholic, and battered by his wife, and when the novel opens, Paris is in the throes of preparing for the Bicentennial celebrations of 1989. There's a wealthy husband who shows up from America, and Stéphane's monstrous wife, and Willy, a little bald Russian boy who takes violin lessons from Stéphane, but the great success of this novel is not so much the characters but the wild, often beautifully surreal, linguistic music that orchestrates our narrator's telling of their lives. All of the twenty-one chapters and certainly the "Coda" in *Music for Glass Orchestra* are scored, sometimes by Gustav Mahler, sometimes by Jim Morrison, often by Bach. Music is a way of marking time, of capturing manifold histories, and more importantly, of capturing psychological history in all its various fantastical soundings within the mind.

The amazing sonority of Grace Andreacchi's prose is achieved in part by several stories within the greater story of the novel listening to themselves, and returning and sounding variations, often ones that suggest the story which happens in America is very different from the one which happens in Europe. When an American father taking his son to Disneyworld for the weekend douses the son with kerosene and sets him afire, this story sounds against the story of Antonio Stradivari torturing a child repeatedly with a candle flame. "When the flesh began to burn, Stradivari would collect the sweat and tears with the oil-soaked rags, in which he would later wrap the nascent violin. Only thus could dumb wood be taught to cry." As readers we ask similar questions of each story: Did Stradiveri really torture a boy soprano from the cathedral choir in Cremona in order to teach his violins to cry? We do not wonder long at all about the story of the American father immolating his son. If it didn't happen, it will soon, or something like it. The American story hardly resonates for us. *Music for Glass Orchestra* is in some ways about the vitrifications of our minds, how these glass harmonicas should be played, should perhaps be shattered and used to cut ourselves open again. This is Grace Andreacchi's second novel and it's as fine as the first. [Michelle Latiolais]

*

Anna Maria Ortese. *A Music behind the Wall: Selected Stories, Volume One.* Trans. Henry Martin. McPherson, 1994. 160 pp. $20.00. Ursule Molinaro. *Power Dreamers: The Jocasta Complex.* McPherson, 1995. 128 pp. $16.00.

Ortese stands out in high relief as one of the main figures of Italian literature in the twentieth century along with Calvino and Pasolini. Although she has published numerous novels in Italy, Ortese is known here mainly for her 1987 novel, *The Iguana.* In this important new volume, Ortese explores the themes of memory and time, refracted through her eccentric style and intellectual narratives in which linearity becomes blended into a tone both dream- and fable-like.

These wonderful stories make "magic realism" seem like a pulp genre for those idiots who think that Franz Kafka and Isabel Allende breathe the same air. In stories as strangely diverse as "The Submerged Continent" and "Torture" one can perceive an interior voice so complex and immaculately haunting that a family's mundane experience can aspire to the level of myth. Any attempt to categorize something as sublime and mysteriously deep as Ortese's work is ultimately impossible, and those who cannot appreciate the enigma of such an imaginative vision should go back to the palpable excrement of shallow mediocrity. We should all ask ourselves, in the spirit of this book, those unanswerable questions such as "What is the past?" or "What is memory?"

Molinaro has often intelligently worked in retelling Greek stories, as in *The Autobiography of Cassandra,* and her renderings are always unique and the stuff of interesting reading. In *Power Dreamers,* Molinaro tells the story of Oedipus and Jocasta, and in her version covers most of the territory of the Sophocles plays. But in *Power Dreamers,* the story is told from the point of view of Jocasta. This view is influenced by gossip, the opinions of seers, and the letters of Oedipus. Jocasta's spin on things is flowing, speculative, and dreamlike. It presents a counterbalance to Oedipus' rational detective outlook. Things become humorous when they argue about having more children: "Not everything a woman thinks & says & does is dictated by her menstrual cycle. My brain isn't located between my legs." Her interests include their sexual life, rejecting motherhood, and consultation of the gods. Under the influence of Tiresias, who changes sex every seven years, Jocasta has an awareness of Oedipus' identity early on. She has consulted the gods, and remembers the prophecy of King Laius being killed by his own son.

Molinaro's style is playful, and her elastic attitude toward history is effective. This is a great story that includes murder, incest, plague—all that good stuff—and is supplemented by Molinaro's inclusion of a weird sexuality and other important details, which are often done offstage. [Alexander Laurence]

*

Evelin Sullivan. *Four of Fools.* Fromm, 1995. 192 pp. $19.95.

In many ways, Evelin Sullivan's novel is old-fashioned: a narrator reflects on the events of a recent trip to Italy, disclosing how little he knew of either the wife or friend who accompanied him. The events are disclosed to us per a logic of association, the narrator now knowing where the events of his life were leading. Ignorance may be bliss but it's a dangerous bliss when surrounded by plotters. John Anders, the narrator, then is brought to face the necessity of knowing what he has hitherto preferred not to know.

On the surface, Anders's story concerns a trip to Italy. The impetus for the trip was a grant for Anders's wife Vida Morse to study the famous scientist Geoffrey Fry. Accompanying Anders and his wife is their friend Jim Quarrel.

Neither Anders nor Quarrel have a compelling reason to go to Italy, so while Vida works they occupy themselves the best they can. But things are not just what they appear. Vida's reasons for studying Fry go deeper than a projected book. And the tensions among the group don't take long to surface.

Fry's research interest is coincidence theory. This becomes a way of thematizing the ingredients of plot. We could read coincidence as an updating of the old deus ex machina. For there is more to Vida and Jim's relationship, more to Vida and Fry's relationship (one could add, more to Jim and Fry's relationship) than is first apparent. Past events that have been unresolved spur these people to a current resolution.

Yet we will never be able to be sure how much coincidence explains or recuperates. Indeed, it is possible to see Fry's interest in coincidence as the desire to control outcomes. (Thus, Signor Valga, reader of tarot cards, criticizes Fry on this score: one should, according to Valga, have a more disinterested, more spiritual view of coincidence.) If there is an underlying coincidence (along the lines of "life itself's a plot"), lying atop that is a competition among plotters. Indeed, one of the most telling events of the novel concerns an experiment in which Anders and Fry each try by their powers of concentration to move a light on a circle. Here one is set against the other. Plots, after all, lead to conflict. The possibility of seeing the conflict resolve itself depends upon perspective, most clearly (and, perhaps, most simply), upon being left to see the resolution. So we are left with the tension between the personal limits and the impersonal vista, a tension that coincidence theory cannot relieve. [Bruce Campbell]

*

Richard Kadrey. *Kamikaze L'Amour.* St. Martin's, 1995. 228 pp. $20.95.

Ryder, an embittered, heavy-drinking, manic-depressive, one-eyed thirty-four-year-old rock superstar and synesthete, can't stand the idea of the twenty-first century and tries to snuff himself with pills and vodka just a few hours after its debut. His suicide bid fails, however, and he wakes to find himself recovering in a sanitarium for celebrities. Realizing he's stuck with his life, if not necessarily his fame, he decides to let the media believe he's been luckier than he in fact has been, collects himself, and, reborn Odysseus-fashion by the sea, walks away from his previous existence. He embarks on a mythic night-sea journey that begins in a damp, decrepit, phantasmagoric San Francisco of abandoned cars and refugees from what used to be LA, and he enters the green world of (despite our government's best attempts at defoliation) a creeping rain forest to the east of the city, chaos music with a wealthy undercurrent of Ilya Prigogine's thought in it, and a spirited spiritual composer almost as delusional as Ryder himself named Frida.

Thus we navigate the deranged waters of Richard Kadrey's impressive follow-up to his first hard-edged novel, *Metrophage,* which involved another post-apocalyptic narrative set in another worn-out, jerry-rigged, disease-ridden, rocked and rolled southern California, and another sadly believable streetwise hustler as lead man—and which proved to be one of the very best science fictions of 1988. *Kamikaze L'Amour* turns out to be less SF, though, than what Bruce Sterling in 1989 labeled *slipstream.* It is, in other words, less preoccupied with gadgets and distant futures, say, than with being the kind of writing that aims to provoke a sense of wonder in you the same way a book like García Márquez's *One Hundred Years of Solitude* does; aims to make you feel, simply, very strange . . . like, as Sterling suggests, living at the turn of the millennium makes you feel. In Kadrey's universe sleepwalkers roam the night streets reliving the lives they drifted through during the day in a kind of mindless ghost dance. Suicides—whole families of them—buy tickets for access to the top floors of skyscrapers. Ecoterrorists spread seeds of fast-developing foliage that takes over everything in its path, extending Amazonia north from the equator, turning most of California into a dark and tangled jungle as overgrown and fissured as Ryder's fragile mind.

Behind this key metaphor of a jungle and mind out of control echoes the brilliant Borneo section of Stephen Wright's gorgeous *Going Native,* and, behind that, the Ur night-sea journey of our century, Conrad's *Heart of Darkness,* with its richly metaphoric, resonantly mythic, and blackly psychological quest for identity during whose itinerary we come to understand that there's a wicked strain of Kurtz within us all. But *Kamikaze L'Amour,* ostensibly a reference to the album Ryder abandons to begin his passage into the woods, into himself, and into what California has become, also echoes the title of André Breton's *L'Amour fou,* or *Mad Love,* signaling perhaps the most important early-century antecedent to Kadrey's project—surrealism. Kadrey borrows not only that movement's use of startling juxtaposition and its obsession with unreason but also its hallucinogenic imagery. His fiery prose is tactile, painterly, synesthetic as Ryder himself, shocking as a pissed-off Dali on crack: "Mahler is a boiling red fog," Ryder writes, "and the Velvet Underground's first album is black wax floating in a pool of mercury."

Visionary as Jim Morrison at his most electric, desperate, and bizarre, paced like a runaway jet-ski, crafted with the deliberateness of the insides of a cruise missile's nose cone, *Kamikaze L'Amour* is an extraordinarily successful novel about the instability of selfhood and sanity, the distance between who we want to be and who we have become, how much of its soul our art has had to sell for fame at this late date in our commodified century, and how many dreams California—and, by extension, of course, the rest of America—has forgotten in the course of its slow unfurling. [Lance Olsen]

*

Mark Axelrod. *Bombay California.* Pacific Writers Press, 1994. 382 pp. Paper: no price given.

When O. Henry called New York Baghdad-on-the-Subway (and someone else Baghdad-on-the-Hudson!), it wasn't long after that we heard about Hollywood and environs as Baghdad-by-the-Sea and Sodom-by-the-Sea. Also Babylon. The De Mille syndrome. Now we have Mark Axelrod's witty, up-to-date "feature" novel about the writer's trade in the "dream factory" not too far from the Emerald City. Now it is Bombay, California, or Somewhere West of Vine, where our hero, Oliveira Katz, lives with his wife and daughter, "an enchanting village dotted with gingerbread cottages and outdoor cafés, a place where one can breathe in the salt air coming full off the ocean." Presented as a comic defense of Raymond Chandler's dictum that "the basic art of motion pictures is the screenplay; it is fundamental, without it there is nothing," Axelrod gives us a novel with a screenplay and a teleplay and a "treatment." It is the treatment that he has the most fun with, given the experience most talented writers have had with moguls, producers, directors, actors, and the technical entourages. So that when Irving Thalberg said that the writer is a necessary evil, he was probably anticipating the ultimate importance of the treatment, usually the brief presentation (like a short short story) of a yet-to-be-written screenplay. Sometimes it is as short as the synopsis of a "concept," written on a cocktail napkin from one of the sacred "eateries." Sometimes it is expanded, as in the case of Katz's "Paul Bunyan and the Adventures of the Apple Pie Gang—A Tall Tale for Youthful Adults—A Film Treatment." In any case the treatment is the common currency of script acceptance, even though the typical length belies the arduous task of acceptance. After four years, 1989-93, and nearly a dozen memos from Cristiyah Productions, during which time Katz is jollied into believing his treatment is being considered, he is told in a rejection memo, "Had you submitted this idea several years ago, say in 1989 [!], I think it might have had a chance of being produced. Sorry to give you such bad news, but we thank you for thinking of Cristiyah Productions and wish you success in your future endeavors." Shades of Waugh. Nothing missing except "Have a nice day!" The subject of *Bombay, California* is the intricate maze through which the screenwriter must struggle in order to become a part of the necessary evil that creates great screenplays. Axelrod's treatment of the screenwriter's treatment by the industry is not a novel; it is closer to Graham Greene's "entertainments." [Jack Byrne]

*

Derek Pell. *X-Texts.* Autonomedia, 1995. 158 pp. Paper: $7.00.

Don't read this book in public, you'll start giggling uncontrollably and people will give you funny looks; I found this out today as I was reading Derek Pell's long-awaited collection, *X-Texts.* Comprised of thirty short pieces written over the past twenty years, having first appeared in places from underground zines all the way to the top, in *Playboy,* this book again proves (as he did with his Semiotext(e) title, *Assassination Rhapsody*) that Pell is the pomo master of parody. All the pieces here pantomime some classic of erotic literature, even up to the present, as in "Sox," Pell's take on Baker's infamous phone-sex novel, *Vox.* Pell weaves his way into "Lady Chatterly's Loafer," "Naked Lunch at Tiffany's," and "Madame Bovary's Training Bra" like a literary stand-up comic, informing us that these classical texts are not givens, are not sacred, but available to be played with and made anew. In "Tropic of Crater,"

Pell uses the form of a hard-boiled detective story as told by one Henry Miller as he searches for a man wanted for crushing the skull of a woman with a Tibetan dildo. "Madeline's Answer" is a hilarious romp about a beautiful virgin being chased by all the men in the world; she only wishes to be immaculate, and believes she has been made beautiful as punishment because she can't seem to ever spell or say the name "Jesus" correctly. Pell's most striking parody (or even "rewrite" in an Ackeresque way) is "The Short Story of O," a one-page piece where O says . . . no.

The introduction by Larry McCaffery is almost worth the price of admission alone, a very unusual and iconoclastic introduction written in a way only McCaffery can. But forget the intro, get on to the stories, or x-texts, and you'll find that Derek Pell is the best there is at this sort of (to appropriate from Raymond Federman) literary pla(y)gerism. [Michael Hemmingson]

*

Nina Zivancevic. *Inside & Out of Byzantium.* Trans. Nina Zivancevic, Ken Jordan, and Dawn Michelle Baude. Semiotext(e), 1994. 151 pp. Paper: $9.00.

The twenty-one stories comprising this often autobiographical collection seem driven by the conviction that "an awkward, poetic truth in terrible English will always mean more than the polished lie that comes straight from the PR man's press release or the politician's office." Not that "terrible English" (i.e., bad writing) is necessarily any more accurate a self-assessment than is Zivancevic's claim in another story to "write about the insignificant." But her embrace of the awkward and terrible (i.e., the difficult and fearful) and her rejection of polished lies do alert us to her agenda, which is less to entertain or to refine aesthetic/rhetorical objects than to witness to the sometimes amusing, sometimes appalling imperfections of life as we live it now. Toward this end, Zivancevic brings an array of narrative strategies to bear upon a variety of subject matter—from a realistic account of almost buying a bracelet to a metafictional reworking of the Lamia myth in which Philippe Sollers appears as antagonist, from surreal Gothic dreams of "endless corridors" and "thick, muddy marsh" to an intertextual parody of outlaw fantasies. But throughout, whether visiting the temples of Luxor or getting her phone reconnected or offering a Serb's perspective on "the Yugoslav situation," Zivancevic's strongest offerings conjure a life of expatriation, of being a stranger in a strange land (Bosnia, America, wherever) and an artist who must imagine an identity and a vocation and write both into existence.

In Zivancevic's final story, one character says to another, "I've been out of the country for so long. Please excuse my ignorance, but would you explain to me, slowly, what has been happening here?" In whatever country we are living, we have Zivancevic to remind us that this question is one we all need periodically to ask. She reminds us as well that the sound of an honest voice attempting a serious reply may be all the answer we can reasonably expect. [Brooke Horvath]

Friederike Mayrocker. *Heiligenanstalt.* Trans. Rosmarie Waldrop. Burning Deck, 1994. 96 pp. Paper: $8.00.

The four poetic fictions by Austrian writer Mayrocker that comprise this short volume, originally published in 1978, have been ably translated by Rosmarie Waldrop. Readers of challenging new creative work owe much to Waldrop for her many fine translations, most notably those of Jabès and Roubaud.

Heiligenanstalt, which literally means "Saints' Asylum," opens with a series of "lost" letters by Chopin. Here the prose dances like fingerwork on keys: "the raging sky-machine was coming to rest, the bleeding of mimetic music stanched, the thinly brushed blue waters / of her net of pulsing arteries had seeped away and a lucky star finally risen for us." The body of each of these pseudo letters has been prefaced by a statement, a question, a command, an exclamation, a fragment, etc. Each of the four writings sprung from composers' lives finds its own form of telling yet all share an elegiac tone concerned with "the last time" and the time before that: not the next time.

The nineteen quarter pages of the title piece move back and forth from Brahms to Clara Schumann, from Clara Schumann to Brahms. (This work reminds one of Waldrop's own Schumann-inspired writing, *Differences for Four Hands.*) Pain and consolation—"whether it made sense to buy the newspaper when it remained unread for days, to unfold the towel before drying your hands, to shake the leaves of the calendar"—is the theme of the Bruckner-centered piece that precedes a Schubert-centered one. The latter provides a formalistic balance to this brief book of saints' lives whose own angels made them "suffer most horribly." [Dennis Barone]

*

R. H. W. Dillard. *Omniphobia.* Louisiana State Univ. Press, 1994. 186 pp. $22.95.

Dillard has written wonderful essays on *Pale Fire* and Fellini's *Satyricon* as horror film. He has written poems "after Borges" (reflections of the Master) which are, at times, better than the Master's own poems. I mention these few facts to demonstrate that he is a daring, duplicitous writer. His first collection of stories is terrifying.

Dillard recognizes that the world is "mindless"; that it is a "bug": "a mass of *snarled* being, of life and death woven like a tangle of vines, the sweet white blossoms *almost lost* in the *choking* leaves" (my italics). His phobic, philosophical characters want to "order" it by any means possible, but they also want to surrender to its Gothic entanglements. They seek obscure meaning, a "web of sense" (Nabokov).

Dillard's narrators are, for the most part, solitaries. They assume that death is close. The body is decaying. In one story a honeymooner "splits his right front tooth off practically at the root" and he is aroused! In another story a mad cook—ironically characterized as a "truly beautiful soul" (Dostoevski)—thinks: "How can you love anybody that eats? Death on the lips, death on the teeth, death on the tongue—the furry red tongue that comes out and licks the greasy lips." And the title story, surely one of the strangest I've read in recent years, "dissolves" so that four narratives seem to fade and die (metafictional death or deathly metafiction?).

I "count chapter and verse," forbidden, occult metaphors, hoping that Dillard will not consume me. But he is frighteningly close—and he is my "double." [Irving Malin]

*

Annie Ernaux. *A Frozen Woman.* Trans. Linda Coverdale. Four Walls Eight Windows, 1995. 160 pp. $17.00.

Annie Ernaux's unflinching, unabashed prose flows with such seeming spontaneity and such unguarded honesty that language seems a natural extension of her fierce mind. Even in translation (which is the only way I know it) the words seem unstoppable as they pile upon each other, forming an always clearer, always deeper path into the psyche of the central character of the story. Similar to her other books (*Cleaned Out, A Woman's Story*), *A Frozen Woman* is the interior monologue of a woman who grew up in a small town in France, the daughter of two shopkeepers, a girl who moves away from her parents to an elite, more educated society. The narrator of *A Frozen Woman* presents the same glorious, chaotic childhood in the café, and the same fearless sexual and intellectual discoveries of her other novels but with a different, even more autobiographical emphasis. The despair of *A Frozen Woman* is more complete, more shattering, because now its presence seems inescapable, both the result of fate and of the author's own actions.

Here is a woman trapped in the exhausting routine of mothering, teaching, and a traditional marriage, despite the commitment she and her husband had made to equality and intellectual freedom. Despite their efforts to avoid the compromises men and women often make when they accept the responsibility of a family, the woman's aspirations are always sacrificed first. Similar to when she was a teenager discovering her sexuality, Ernaux realizes in adulthood that men enjoy more freedom than women do. As a teenager, sex soon became the "defensive gamc of dividing my body into territories from head to toe: permitted area; the uncertain field of current maneuvers; the forbidden zone. Cede territory only inch by inch. Each pleasure is labeled defeat for me, victory for him. I had not anticipated experiencing the discovery of the Other in terms of loss, and it isn't amusing."

In flawless detail Ernaux evokes from her own experience the common struggle of any person to remain creatively engaged with the world. Ernaux's passion for living, her intellectual capability, and her perspicuity remove layers of social and literary taboo and take language to a level of expression that supersedes jargon or literary affectation. *A Frozen Woman,* first published in France by Gallimard in 1981, is devastating and exhilarating at the same time. There are no answers but there is passion, linguistic power, and a vibrant voice coming through the pain and disappointment. [Carolyn Kuebler]

Jesús Urzagasti. *In the Land of Silence.* Trans. Kay Pritchett. Univ. of Arkansas Press, 1994. 366 pp. $32.00; paper: $20.00.

Bolivian writer Jesús Urzagasti's novel *In the Land of Silence* consists of a meditation on the nature of identity, of the way in which identity is shaped by the interaction of cultures. Philosophical and practical by turns, *In the Land of Silence* serves as fictionalized autobiography, as an elucidation of the always multiple qualities of the self.

The story is told by three narrators, all of whom speak extensively about one another, all of whom are three sides of the same individual. The interrelationships of the three become more complex and concrete as the book, arranged into five notebooks, moves forward. It is only in the fourth notebook (which is almost half the book and in which each narrator comments on the other two in turn) that Urzagasti's writing becomes consistently and inescapably intriguing.

The main narrator, Jursafú, seems to contain the other two narrators within himself. Touched by European thought and participating in the life of the city, he seems to have shunted his heritage to one side. The Other represents Jursafú's native culture, his non-European side attached to the natural and irrational world. The Dead Man—perhaps the most interesting narrator but also the most difficult to pin down—seems to represent Jursafú's relationship with death and his consciousness of death.

In its meditation on the nature of selfhood, *In the Land of Silence* recalls Clarice Lispector's *Passion according to G. H.* and Fernando Pessoa's *Book of Disquiet,* though the movement between selves presented seems much more distinct and less spontaneous than in the latter book. Low on plot, the book operates according to a poetic logic that makes connections between sections oblique and intriguing. The central events of the story are revealed in steps, gradually, naturally, with the narrative moving in circles. As with Pessoa's poetic heteronyms, each of the narrators has different qualities, the Dead Man being the most compelling in terms both of the consistency of his style and the tension established through the interrelations of the events he describes. Though the translation is strong, it runs into the problem that translations of lyrical and language-oriented work often run into: when you lose a little, you lose a lot. Yet here less is lost than most: taken as a whole, *In the Land of Silence* is an impressive and intriguing work that shows that powerful experiments in Latin American fiction are still taking place. [Brian Evenson]

*

Will Self. *The Quantity Theory of Insanity.* Grove/Atlantic, 1995. 211 pp. $21.00. Stewart Home. *Red London.* AK Press, 1994. 158 pp. Paper: $12.95.

Will Self has been well known in England for quite a while, but now is being endlessly introduced to American readers. This book is chronologically his first, but not at all an immature early work. This work lays down Self's literary theme in its most basic form, then again employs literary influences such as

Georges Perec and Jorge Luis Borges, which are oddly absent from his succeeding works of satire, *Cock and Bull* and *My Idea of Fun.* The basic theme that Self is so good at is encountering the ordinary and discovering the extraordinary, as in the story "The North London Book of the Dead," where the main character finds his dead mother in Crouch End. He learns that people do not die but are relocated. In "Understanding the Ur-Bororo" two anthropologists recall a tribe that has no semiological systems and whose language has several different inflections to indicate levels of boredom.

Self is able to twist around our conceptions and expectations to keep the reader on the ball. Although not a member of the OuLiPo, Self creates a truly Oulipian story with "The Quantity Theory of Insanity." In a series of literary and mathematical games, Harold, a student, begins to read coded messages in the bathroom, then tries to make sense of them. Having failed, Harold becomes involved with research centered on the "Quantity Theory" that deals with the collective psyche; for instance "if you decrease the number of social class 2 anorexics you necessarily increase the number of valium abusers." Paranoia is another of Self's favorite subjects, as in "Ward 9" and "Mono-Cellular." The latter story becomes claustrophobic and Célinesque as the narrator encounters the objective world through a drugged-out haze. One feels premonitions of *My Idea of Fun,* and the humor of Monty Python where it's both funny and sad. Self often sticks to one conceptual idea at a time and takes it as far as he can. He mixes literary games with the mundane world, through a very stylized and adept use of language, like no other contemporary British writer. His only shortcoming is that he has something of a tin ear, and sometimes one feels that his knack for controversy is very studied.

A little less pretentious, and much more fun, is the writing of Stewart Home. He is the most interesting writer to come out of England for quite a while, even though he has not and never will win the Booker prize. Home brings together stuff from pulp fiction, boot boy novels of Richard Allen, and theoretical manifestos, and surprises the reader with his insane, plagiarized worlds. In *Red London,* probably Home's most solid work to date, he focuses on a group of anarchist skinheads who are terrorizing a neighborhood in London. The main character, Fellatio Jones, is fueled by his Charles Manson identity and by a book called *Christ and Satan United in Struggle,* a book about total revolution which causes its readers to go mad. Fellatio also works on *Hookers Magazine* in his spare time, a subversive publication with interviews with prostitutes. The skinheads live in a Buddhist temple where they have sex with priests.

The main concern of this book is the impact ideologies have on certain people. All segments of society are involved: prostitutes, workers, anarchists, punks, the rich. The relationships between the characters are both sadistic and sexual, and demonstrate the cynical society that Home wants to describe. That along with the repetition of similar sex scenes every other page where the characters become robotic; all of which is a parody of British porn. Yet, readers should be warned that there is much brutality and unfelt, sadistic sex.

How *Red London* differs from and might mean more than *American Psycho* is that the whole aspect of class distinction is still intact. Home's novel is disturbing but necessary, very artfully collaged and revealing, and also a breath of fresh air from such a stuffy puritanical place. Home is also the author of many books about art movements, the most important being *The Assault on Culture* (also AK Press). In these books, Home has written widely on neoism, situationism, and plagiarism. His books are finding their audience in the American underground. [Alexander Laurence]

*

Michael H. Cooper. *Dues: A Novel of War and After.* Curbstone, 1994. 298 pp. Paper: $11.95.

At the end of *Dues,* David Thorne decides he and his fellow Vietnam vets "were just late bloomers and they got nailed for it. He guessed the lesson was if you hesitate to jump on the band wagon to a successful career you lose. And if history was right the price could be very high." Michael Cooper offers few such direct summations in this fine first novel, a story of those whom the war destroyed.

Under a different set of circumstances Thorne would have had every chance to outgrow the adolescent confusion and indecisiveness that trigger his dropping out of college and winding up in the mucky currents of the rice paddies, rivers, and marshes of the Mekong Delta. There he becomes very good at killing people. I know of no other serious Vietnam novel whose author so fearlessly depicts his protagonist in the act of shooting the enemy as if they were so many ducks on a pond.

Thorne's generalized feelings of guilt and betrayal become concretized one afternoon when he beats his way through vision-obscuring elephant grass only to stumble upon three American soldiers raping a Vietnamese girl. Before leaving, the incipient psychopath Doran wheels around and shoots the girl. Thorne's conscience is plagued ever after because he does nothing to stop the rape and because he is forced to put a bullet through the dying girl's head in order to curtail her misery.

If there is badness in the book's universe, it is an accidental sort of thing and arises not from the characters' actions but rather from their inaction. The degrading world of dope and drink is entered and reentered swiftly—with a measure of regret, yes, but with little resistance.

Cooper's style is demotic, his prose deceptively simple. The book is a vortex of grimness and suicide, frothed with the easy adolescent sarcasms of his characters and a propensity for Vonnegut-like meioses on the part of the narrator. Vietnam's terrain, on the verge of becoming a clichéd symbolic landscape in books on the subject, is rendered here with a dreadful freshness at once concrete and alive as metaphor.

Part three of the novel could have benefited from some trimming and tightening, and the hopefulness of the epilogue runs counter to the entire novel. But despite these weaknesses, this is a memorable, compelling novel. The Vietnam War novel is a genre that may yet play itself out, but this novel shows that it still has life. [Matthew C. Stewart]

JoAllen Bradham. *Some Personal Papers.* Texas Review Press, 1994. 137 pp. Paper: $11.95.

This disturbing first novel will probably not reach a wide audience (despite the blurbs by George Garrett and Madison Smartt Bell). It deals with such problems as euthanasia, child abuse, and the underclass; but it resists propaganda and comfortable clichés. It is an accomplished, daring work of art.

The narrator speaks "simply" about child care and governmental services. She tells us at the first that "my training was clinical." We accept her rational thoughts, her desire to benefit the children under her care. But we soon discover that she cares "too much" for her charges: she wants to put them out of their misery. She regards herself as a savior; her language moves into grandiose, biblical tones. And we recognize that her voices are at war; that, indeed, they control her, driving her into strange, violent moods. She is a twisted voiceprint. The novel suggests that the narrator's voices—including the one she hears—confuse her. She becomes a mere vessel. She is victimized by the voices to the extent that her personal identity dissolves. She, finally, has no self; she is merely the product of a "strange debate."

Bradham's novel is haunted, skewed, deformed (despite its apparent clarity). It speaks to us in indeterminate, secretive tongues. [Irving Malin]

*

Matthew Stadler. *The Sex Offender.* HarperCollins, 1994. 206 pp. $22.00.
Bruce Benderson. *User.* Dutton, 1994. 227 pp. $19.95.

These two books are among the most interesting to be written out of the gay experience, although two different and distinct approaches to separate milieus of society. First the psychiatric approach of Matthew Stadler's *The Sex Offender,* and second, the hard edge of Bruce Benderson's *User,* which is a portrayal of the Times Square crowd.

The nameless narrator of *The Sex Offender* recalls very directly the events that happened to him while in recuperation at a medical facility for his love for children. But this book is not really about child love and molestation as much as it's about the offender's relationship to the Doctor General and his interest in drag queens. This tale focuses on the rehabilitation of a lapsed teacher, and most of the novel takes the form of a dialogue. The Doctor General Nicholas Nicholas evokes both Nabokov and Gogol in a flash. The doctor is assisted by some weird scientists, Ponz and Flessinger, who act as a single entity. One often expects a bad doctor/good patient situation, but most of the narrator's journal imagines his inner life. This inner world includes his fascination with opera and drag queens, especially one named Lucrezia.

All this calls into question the distinction between the surface expressiveness of drag queens as opposed to the interiority, the subject of the patient, which the doctors are trying to discover. The book centers on the relationship between the doctor and patient, and the reader accepting the idea of the doctor's empathy, which is eventually an uncomfortable position. Yet this is Stadler's big risk in writing the book. As a reader, you must believe that empathy is possible in a very unemotional and often cynical world. Stadler's style is often dry and without music.

Bruce Benderson evokes an interesting world with his new novel, which reeks of the experiential sort. From the center of transvestite bars, Times Square, the male hustlers, the heroin-addicted, the crack smokers, *User* rises out of the ashes and depicts an ugly world in a beautiful way. Benderson tells the story of Apollo, heroin user and hustler, and his descent into his private hell. Apollo's story is both tragic and tender.

The fragmented narrative switches from character to character—from third person to first and to stream of consciousness—forming a mosaic that outlines both drugged consciousness and urban realism. Nothing in this novel is sentimental. It deals with poverty culture without slumming. Apollo is on the run, spiraling down deeper into the bowels of Times Square and Port Authority. Such subject matter has been avoided since the days of the Beats and Hubert Selby.

Benderson himself has often indulged in literary excesses and has flirted with the nouveau roman, but this time he writes like a sociologist. This book is strong and rich in detail, written directly, with heart, recalling the better days of that other underworld figure, Jean Genet. The mainstream media lives nowhere near these places. Benderson definitely shows us the frontiers in a world where people are only pretending to be hard. [Alexander Laurence]

*

Rosina Conde. *Women on the Road.* San Diego State Univ. Press, 1994. 146 pp. Paper: $12.95.

In the introduction to this collection of eleven poignant short fictions, Gustavo V. Segade cites André Lefevere that there is no "original" until there is a translation. There are several translators at work in this book and this collection might not be what it is had there been a biased translation by one person. Conde is not shy about her feminist objectives; she has wounds to reveal, personal and cultural. One is the submissive role of the young woman in Mexican culture and what that eventually does to many (often uneducated) women. The first piece, "Rice and Chains," is the monologue of a teenage girl who has become pregnant by her first boyfriend, confused about the attitude of her parents. At first, her mother wanted her to "catch" the boyfriend as a husband, even if he was poor and a "dreamer." Now that she's pregnant and the boyfriend has left, her parents make her feel useless, telling her she's ruined her life, and they wish they had "pushed" her onto one of the older, rich men in the village to be a mistress. In fact, her mother wishes that she had become a mistress herself, so she would never have to deal with a husband. "Do You Work or Go to School?" is about a young woman lured into a modeling scam and becoming a sex object to a sleazy businessman, not realizing what she's done to her life until it's too late. "The Little Boy and His Mother" is a one-page fiction that says more in forty-eight words than many writers can say in four thousand. Finally, the book ends with a novella, "Señora Nina," that presents dialogue between characters only, no exposition, no setting; a challenging piece, and a further example of the theater's influence on Conde. [Michael Hemmingson]

*

Cyrus Colter. *The Hippodrome.* TriQuarterly Books, 1994. 213 pp. Paper: $13.95.

First published in 1973, *The Hippodrome* begins with a drunk, mentally tormented Willie Yeager on the run, having just murdered his wife and her white lover. Stumbling into a cafeteria for a meal, Yeager reveals his crime to Bea, the manager of a sex show, and Darlene, one of the show's performers, and ironically ends up a prisoner—and the new attraction at the Hippodrome, the ghetto house where Bea's black troupe performs for white audiences (the content of these shows is never made explicit). As Bea repeatedly reminds Yeager of his debt to her for providing him with a refuge and how easily she could turn him over to the cops, Yeager turns to Darlene for support. Darlene becomes Yeager's confessor, listening to him talk about his marriage, his job as a religion writer for a black newspaper, and his plotting the murder; she exhorts him to escape the house and offers to help—advice he disregards. When Yeager finally performs, after promising Bea an unforgettable show, he attempts to commit suicide on stage but loses his nerve in the process, nevertheless sparking a startling performance that exceeds the expectations of all involved. In a final climactic scene the following day, Yeager strangles Bea and then bolts from the house with Darlene, wanted now not only by the police but by Kalandyk, the gangster who owns the Hippodrome.

This ultimately psychological story about a man's spiritual, mental, and physical debasement—alongside his recognition of his capacity to do evil in a society that demeans him in alternating fits of terror and fascination—suffers from the overlong, forced quality of Yeager's revelations to Darlene and from Bea's insistent threats to put Yeager on the streets, which raise more questions about why Yeager does not run from the house than explaining why he stays. The themes Colter raises of power, exploitation, sexuality, obsession, and spectacles, all at the intersection of race, however, are intriguing. The force of these questions, and the often thrilling narrative, make this a provocative book. [Frank Marquardt]

*

Julio Ortega. *Ayacucho, Goodbye* and *Moscow's Gold: Two Novellas on Peruvian Politics and Violence.* Trans. Edith Grossman and Alita Kelley. Latin American Literary Review Press, 1994. 103 pp. Paper: $13.95.

Moscow's Gold is a sharp and sensitive evocation of a young man's teenage years in Peru. Expectable teenage themes—sexual insecurities, favorite books and movies, budding loves, friendships, school life—are played out against the extra burden of Cold War politics entering the lives of Third World adolescents. The first-person narrator is appealing; the story (which is really a short story and not a novella, as the publisher has billed it) lives vividly and convincingly.

Alfonso Cánepa is murdered by the Peruvian police on the first page of *Ayacucho, Goodbye,* and for its remaining pages his mutilated corpse takes a strange and allegorical tour of contemporary Peru. The Peruvian sociopolitical landscape contains the usual dreary Latin American features: repressive leaders spouting empty political rhetoric; brutal and stupid police; slash-and-burn terrorists; bought-and-paid-for journalists; ruthless, self-aggrandizing narcotics traffickers; the American ambassador who is said to be the true power in the country; shoe-shine boys; beggars; prostitutes. Singled out for a particularly heavy dose of scorn is the anthropologist, a sort of Judas figure who cares nothing for the people he purports to study.

Ortega chooses two methods of defamiliarizing this all too horribly familiar terrain. One is his mutilated, dead narrator, who makes his journey as if alive. The other is the language itself, which is a mixture of baldly stated truths, grisly comedy, sarcastic conversation, and mocking commentary on the foibles and sins of Peru. This mixed bag has been staged as a play, and I cannot help supposing that much that falls flat here could be brought to life in an imaginative dramatic production.

The reader with a special interest in contemporary Peruvian letters will be able to appreciate the more subtle cultural references in *Ayacucho Gold* and may find its experimental nature of interest. The general reader looking for an undiscovered masterpiece of contemporary Latin American fiction will not find it in this volume, but he or she will encounter a fine short story of adolescence written by an underappreciated writer. [Matthew C. Stewart]

*

Graham Purchase. *My Journey with Aristotle to the Anarchist Utopia.* III Publishing, 1994. 125 pp. Paper: $7.00.

This odd little book opens up during a riot between the oppressed mine workers and the police in some dystopic near-future Australia. Tom, the narrator, gets beaten badly by two troopers (one named Adolf) and left for dead in a mine. Tom recovers, leaves the mine, and encounters Aristotle. He finds he has been transported a thousand years into the future, or to some alternate universe. Yes, this is the same Aristotle we all know and love, and who reminisces on the good and bad points of his old pal Plato. Aristotle takes Tom back to Bear City, where he has kids and grandchildren. Bear City is a non-government society with organic clothing and cars (basing the car on Henry Ford's design on the organic vehicle). People smoke pot legally and there is even a sex scene in here (lots of free love going on) where the woman Tom couples with tells him her underwear is organic and he can eat them off. (Fear not, they still use condoms a thousand years into this future.) I don't know if this book is supposed to be humorous or serious, but a lot of anarchist/libertarian ideals are put forth, much appropriation of ideas from such notables as Noam Chomsky and Emma Goldman. In the true Aristotelian manner, much of the text consists of dialogues between Tom and Aristotle. Purchase's use of a fictional form left me wanting; this may have worked better if he'd put his ideas into an essay. [Michael Hemmingson]

*

Alain Ferry. *La Mer des mamelles.* Editions du Seuil, 1995. 596 pp.

With *La Mer des mamelles* (Sea of Mammaries) Alain Ferry has written one of the most original works of French fiction in a generation. Ferry calls his work "a love novel in letters." Actually, it is a novel about the love of letters, belles and otherwise. The narrative frame is a madly spiraling series of novella-length letters in which a "real" author attempts to court his maid. Each writer begins by expatiating on a painting. Soon, the subjects of these letters, namely Rembrandt's Bethshabee and Watteau's Gilles, join the circle of letter writers. The circle expands in ever widening rings to include the likes of Marilyn Monroe, André Malraux, and (my personal favorite) Pauline Littré, wife of the famous nineteenth-century lexographer, who yearns that her husband's passion for words might one day be transferred to her.

Ferry writes a postmodern libertine prose, learned and lascivious. The amount of sheer erudition in these pages is prodigious. As the maid Marianne (who shares her name with the icon for the French Republic) writes to her professor suitor: "You make no secret of your learning. Your erudition is on the flashy side. People will hold it against you as they did with Musil. But one surmises that, just as in *The Man without Qualities,* it does not serve an ornamental purpose: it functions as a testimony to the author's sincerity." No ordinary maid, as one can see.

Ferry's vast intellectual stage allows him to set into motion a wonderfully playful panorama of our culture, both high and low. Inevitably in a work of this length, there are passages where inspiration appears to flag, and you feel that you're trapped at some madcap Left Bank costume party, forced to listen to dry monologues compiled from research cards. However, the greater part of this novel does work because of the author's ability to ferry (his pun) such a broad range of knowledge with self-mocking charm and unfailing humor. Ferry has the cultural breadth of a Montaigne coupled with the sensibility of a Monty Python skit writer. In the breadth of two pages (I choose one among countless examples) he accommodates Katharine Hepburn, Marilyn Monroe, Thomas Berhard, Yves Bonnefoy, and Brigitte Bardot. And, most amazingly, they and the reader all feel right at home! If Roland Barthes had a sense of humor and had taken the plunge into novel writing, he might well have written such a book. [Dominic Di Bernardi]

*

Tim Lucas. *Throat Sprockets.* Delta/Cutting Edge, 1994. 232 pp. Paper: $9.95.

The second book from this new imprint shows wonderful promise. However, I almost didn't read it when I saw a blurb from Bret Easton Ellis, perhaps the most promising of the failed young writers of the 1980s. But what's in a blurb? I'm glad I opened these pages, which were hard to pull my teeth from. Lucas's style is vigorous and assured; I don't think I've read a book quite like this—strange, perverse, and sad: a fiction about what happens when one becomes obsessed over a film.

Throat Sprockets is narrated by a young and successful ad man, now turned thirty, married since his teens, looking for visual and mental excitement by wandering into a porno theater. One of the films he sees, though, isn't quite porno—not the usual connections of genitalia and observable orgasms; the film he sees, *Throat Sprockets,* is erotic, yes, and has to do with women's necks. Various women are followed, and their necks portrayed, around the world, which leads toward a vampiric end. The narrator is moved by this film, goes back to see it, and becomes obsessed with the images, and the necks of women. His obsession has both a positive and a negative effect on his life: his wife leaves him, but he gets such great amatory ideas in his advertising campaigns that he skyrockets to an executive position. Money and power, now he has it; all he needs is the perfect female neck.

The ad man seeks others like himself, and he finds them. When at first he believes he is alone in his obsession with necks and the "sprockets" teeth make on them, he discovers a subterranean movement of like-minded people, all of whom have been infected by the images of this cult film. After some time, the film gains popular status, where "sprocketing" and social groups of "chokers" spread nationally, then globally: true vampires, without the supernatural. Still, no one knows who made this film. The narrator goes on an investigation to find out who the filmmaker is—asking the questions: *who did this to me? who is the artist? who is the artist who did this to me?*

The payoff is a beautifully rendered exploration into both human desire and the human heart, for at the heart of *Throat Sprockets* is a love story, where the lovers go beyond the norm to show each other their feelings, even if it means death. Weaving in and out of reality, dreams, and hallucinogenic encounters, Tim Lucas kicks ass. [Michael Hemmingson]

*

Verena Stefan. *Shedding* and *Literally Dreaming.* Trans. Johanna Seiglander Moore, et al. Feminist Press, 1994. 176 pp. Paper: $14.95.

Following its appearance in 1975, *Shedding* quickly became the unofficial herald of the German women's movement. In *Shedding* the Swiss-born Stefan traces her own search for identity in a mixed genre of autobiographical sketches, poems, and dreams, plotting the female body and women's sexuality as the pivot of her own unfolding. As she describes her intimate relations with an Afro-American and then moves on to her longer affair with a leftist German activist, Stefan locates and reiterates women's sexuality as the locus of her oppression. Gradually shedding layers of social expectations, the narrator haltingly takes the path to a "companion female lover," as she prefers to term the lesbian relationship that ultimately affords her recognition, self-acceptance and community. Stefan not only narrates a personal journey of self-discovery but also discusses those delicate aspects of human sexuality and love that are traditionally left "untouched."

Shedding is accompanied by a more recent collection of eight short stories entitled *Literally Dreaming* (1987). These introspective tales, obviously influenced by ecofeminism and the women's health movement, focus on the uniqueness of women's culture and communities. Stefan takes up the themes of stripping and shedding anew when describing the renovation of a house or the changing of the seasons. These finely tuned and moody prose pieces portray a different life, one without men; in *Literally Dreaming* Stefan avoids prescriptive preachiness through her honesty in depicting the strength of women's communities as well as the interpersonal conflict and personal self-doubt to which its members are subject.

The volume is rounded off by two essays by the author. In one she discusses the genesis of *Shedding,* its reception, and backlash. The other contains Stefan's reflections on the German and international women's movements, marks *Shedding*'s place within these movements, and offers insights into her own development as a writer. *Shedding* and *Literally Dreaming* should be required reading for *anyone* who has dared to love a woman. [Lynda Hoffman-Jeep]

*

Richard Peabody and Lucinda Ebersole, eds. *Mondo Marilyn: An Anthology of Fiction and Poetry.* St. Martin's, 1995. 224 pp. Paper: $13.95.

After the very successful Elvis and Barbie anthologies, we now have a Marilyn Monroe tribute, brought to us by those American icon collectors Peabody and Ebersole. MM is a favorite subject of many writers, from that Grove Press man John Rechy (included here) to obsessed Norman Mailer (not included). Good Marilyn stories tend to take as their point of departure "What if she lived?" Leslie Pietrzyk's "Marilyn Monroe Comes to Rock Falls" tells about a funny encounter with MM in a diner. Lynne Tillman's "Dead Talk" is a voracious rant as if MM returned as a zombie to haunt us all. Michael Hemmingson's "26 Marilyns" is a comedic romp with Oulipian alphabetical delights. Some of the poetry just sits there on the page, waiting to be read by some Nuyorican on MTV, but the most impressive poetry is David Trinidad and Robert Peters's pop culture glut, which is both encyclopedic and Whitmanesque. J. G. Ballard's "You: Coma: Marilyn Monroe" steals the show and may be the nexus of this tome: a good reason to read it, if we need one. Ballard's surgical style is still amazing and great. [Alexander Laurence]

*

Brooke Bergan. *Storyville: A Hidden Mirror.* Asphodel Press, 1994. 135 pp. Paper: $12.95.

Those who squirmed with guilt at viewing the pubescent Brooke Shields in *Pretty Baby* some years back can read with a clearer conscience the mature Brooke Bergan's treatment of the same material in *Storyville.* Like Louis Malle before her, she uses Ernest J. Belloq's photographs of the turn-of-the-century red-light district of New Orleans as her point of departure. Accompanying several of his striking photographs are her no less striking "plates"—poems that interpret the photos—along with other sections mixing prose and poetry called "voices," "arguments," "discourses," and "extrapolations," concluding with source notes. The result is a fascinating multimedia meditation on the place of prostitution in American culture and the politics of eroticism.

Bergan's extensive background reading gives the material a firm historical base, preventing any romanticization of what was a squalid life for most of the prostitutes, but at the same time allowing her to capture with precision the faded charm and desperate beauty of Storyville and its inhabitants. It also allows her to explore the complex sociology of the time, with middle-class tricks falling in love with "fallen" higher class women, the relations between blacks and whites, the familiar economics whereby prostitution offered some women the only means to achieve financial independence, Old World French mores clashing with American Puritanism, and much more. Bergan's grasp of the subject embraces everything from ancient myths of sacred prostitution to the latest theories of photography's ambivalent relation to its subject.

Reminiscent in form and texture of Pound's *Cantos,* Olson's *Maximus Poems,* and Metcalf's historical collages, *Storyville* is a richly complex and sensuously beguiling work of art. [Steven Moore]

*

Bob Arnold. *American Train Letters.* Coyote Books, 1995. 238 pp. Paper: $10.00.

From the title, and the cover photograph—the author and his son standing by the tracks in what would seem to be somewhere in the southwest—one would have the impression that this is a book about rail travel in the U.S. It is, in fact, an odd olio of a book: part rail travel, part generalized travel—descriptions of places visited, etc.—and part literary tour, visits to sites associated with American authors. Rambling and discursive, it works itself at times into an eccentric syntax, sometimes intriguing, sometimes irritating. Perhaps this has something to do with the nature, the rhythms, of rail travel: "But then trains are not for the hurried, nor are they for the slower, they should be for the traveler, that type who likes their train station, milling people, the anticipation for something spacious moving on the ground . . . it's a human speed with much more leg room than a bus, and unlike a bus or a car, the train seems to have the priority to pass through more backyards and dumps and factory sights than any highway. From Pensacola, Florida to New Orleans is quite an invigorating sight of bayou and Gulf breeze one room shack big porch waves." As a general travel book, it is not exceptional; descriptions of the places visited are undistinguished. But some of the literary excursions are small gems, worthy digressions. The best of these deal with Jack London, Jaime de Angulo, and Neal Cassady. There is another element, an element common to so many books: the injection of the self, the author's suspicion that the material itself isn't "interesting" enough, that it must be larded with "opinions" and "responses." Fortunately, this doesn't happen too often.

In any event, it is in the experiences rooted in rails and cars that the strength of the book lies: Arnold claims he has never set foot on an airplane. As a contemporary American, traveling widely around the country, this, it seems, would certify him as a crank. On one of his journeys, one segment was planned for a flight, but at the last moment the travel bureau was able to transfer him to Amtrak. Saved!

It is precisely on this level that the book, as the work of an Amtrak crank, has its vitality. [Paul Metcalf]

*

William S. Burroughs. *My Education: A Book of Dreams.* Viking, 1995. 193 pp. $21.95.

As Burroughs himself has admitted in the past, dreams have long provided him with various characters and scenarios in his fiction. Here, uncut with any fiction, are transcriptions of various dreams he's had over the years, along with waking thoughts on matters arising from the dreams: his inability to feel part of any group, Genet's *Prisoner of Love,* a recipe for botulism from Pancho Villa, and occult speculations, among other things. Burroughs's dreamworld, the Land of the Dead as he calls it (the Western Lands of his fiction), is a desolate and rather seedy place where breakfast is never served. But important figures from his life like Brion Gysin and Ian Sommerville are here, as are his ubiquitous purple-assed baboons and his beloved cats. Like Kerouac's *Book of Dreams,* this is a useful companion to the Beat writer's work. [Steven Moore]

*

Brad Leithauser. *Penchants and Places: Essays and Criticism.* Knopf, 1995. 291 pp. $25.00.

Leithauser is one of our most provocative, wide-ranging, accomplished writers. Although he is under forty-five, he has written three fascinating novels, three acclaimed collections of poetry, and the "essays and criticism" in this volume. *Equal Distance* (1985), his first novel, is set in Japan; it is, among other things, a study of linguistic and cultural differences. *Hence* (1989) is a meditation on chess, chance, and artificial intelligence. *Seaward* (1993) is an exploration of "the other side," an encounter with a ghost. All three novels are linked by an interrogation into alternative worlds, into the nature of perception and (as) performance—and thus, reflexively, about the creation of art. The novels, apparently conventional, question their own conventions, their "peopled worlds" (to use the title of one of his poetic sections in *The Mail from Anywhere* [1990]).

Leithauser's criticism often deals with writers who have seen what he describes in one of his poems as "a rip in some / Canvas whose scene must also show the seam." In a brilliant essay on Calvino's *Mr. Palomar* he notes the mixture of certainty and uncertainty; he is fond of the "tiered intricacy" (what a wonderful phrase!). He speculates on the relation between gays and ghost-story writers; he decodes the "divine" codes of James's "The Jolly Corner" and "The Beast in the Jungle," linking them to the Swedenborgism of Henry Senior. He writes that in contrast to the Pynchon of *Vineland* "J. D. Salinger and Flannery O'Connor owe many of their most winning effects to an ear attuned to the preposterous ways in which words get mangled around them and a tongue prepared to go the manglers one better." He reads *The Satanic Verses* in a unique way, noticing the unsettling effects achieved by "tossing out the spaces between words." He links Rushdie to Lewis Carroll, Coleridge, and Kafka—creators of a "nonesuch style" that creates a nonesuch world. He is able to see "the missing person" motif in all of Abe Kobo's fiction. And he notes that Endo, like Graham Greene, is obsessed by the "ways in which the body—that mere envelope of the everlasting soul—can distort or canker our spiritual convictions."

It should be obvious that Leithauser's essays are, in effect, poetic meditations on occlusion, obsession, absence, "fearful symmetry." They are, at times, more remarkable than the writers they discuss. They are surely wonderful creations; they demonstrate that he is always surprising; he is, indeed, a special case. He has—do I dare say it?—wise blood. [Irving Malin]

*

Raymond Federman. *Critifiction: Postmodern Essays.* State Univ. of New York Press, 1993. 133 pp. $14.95.

"Postmodernism" is an elusive notion, which is perhaps why Raymond Federman prefers other terms—"surfiction," "critifiction"—whose meaning he can better delimit. "Critifiction," for instance, refers to a text that "contains its own theory and even its own criticism" and/or collapses the distinction between criticism and fiction. The eight essays collected in *Critifiction* are critifictional insofar as they are both self-conscious and self-reflexive (see the second essay for the difference) as well as fictitious insofar as Federman considers all texts fictions (i.e., lies). The essays are "postmodern" both because of how they sometimes build their arguments (via ludic digressions, collage, juxtaposed fragments, "verbal doodles") and because of the topics treated: postmodernism's origins and demise, its pla(y)giaristic imagination and "pursuit of non-knowledge," the reasons for its unreadability and for its rejection of memory and representation (i.e., realism) in favor of invented presentations (i.e., self-reflexive enactments).

From the earliest essay offered here—a revised version of Federman's 1973 manifesto "Surfiction: A Position"—through two more-or-less autobiographical pieces (one on bilingualism, the other on "fiction as autobiography/autobiography as fiction") to a recent two-part valedictory that praises postmodernism as a doomed movement dedicated to radical doubt and disorientation, *Critifiction* fascinates. Not only is Federman's smart, mock-humble persona engaging, but he has a gift for articulating postmodern doctrine both clearly and memorably (e.g., "all modern discourses can be pre-texts—pre-texts in the sense that they precede their eventual meaning"). Much that Federman says will doubtless bemuse and/or annoy some readers (for instance, his conviction that those opposed to postmodernism are motivated by a cowardly need to preserve the comfortably familiar), and others will possibly be vexed by his cavalier indifference to factual details (Norman Mailer was not the author of *The Day Kennedy Was Shot; Willie Masters' Lonesome Wife* was not first published in 1971). Because Federman himself argues that all writers are plagiarists, I trust he won't mind if I close by describing *Critifiction* as a compendium of pomo/poststructuralist concerns (from indeterminacy to intertextuality) that succinctly synthesizes the thoughts of many—from Stéphane Mallarmé and Samuel Beckett to William Gass and Ronald Sukenick. It is also a splendid introduction to postmodern fiction from one of its most committed advocates and ablest practitioners. [Brooke Horvath]

*

Robert Phillips, ed. *William Goyen: Selected Letters from a Writer's Life.* Univ. of Texas Press, 1995. 427 pp. $35.00.

I am pleased that this collection of Goyen's letters—edited by his friend and admirable critic—appears now. It adds to the growing interest in this neglected writer, joining the novels being reprinted by *TriQuarterly*/Northwestern and the forthcoming collection of essays on Goyen I have recently coedited for the *Texas Review*. These letters clearly demonstrate the problems facing a visionary writer who cannot even now fight the trash-filled marketplace. Perhaps those heart-breaking letters detailing the destruction of leftover copies (by Doubleday) best demonstrates the neglect. Goyen's letters are not only worth reading for the sake of a writer's fate in our commercial world; they demonstrate his unmistakable voice, his metaphorical intensity. At age thirty-two he writes: "There is always something lacking, something, half-finished, not all done, wanting and begging and yearning to be whole, but never that. No circles are complete. Oh Jesus Christ it gets so tortured, this trying to make one's way through doubt and catechism." The passage clearly captures the sense Goyen always had—he was driven by his wounded muse to create some work that would capture the wholeness (holiness) he sought. He was a religious writer; he knew his *vocation*. But he had to face the fact that the "others" could never appreciate his artistic *vocation*, his special calling. At age thirty-four Goyen writes to Dorothy Brett: "How much preparation one has had to go through, *inside* for this miraculous moment, one can never know. The point is to believe that everything one does or says or feels or thinks is *preparation* for some marvelous moment of execution and illumination that is surely coming if he will be patient and suffer in a kind of spiritual endurance." Goyen's "creative faith" sustained him despite the barbarians—the stupid reviewers and crass businessmen who still demean publishing. Although I am not sure that he was a "major" writer—whatever the adjective means—he wrote several remarkable stories and novels that transformed me. I owe a debt to Goyen; he made me understand my little calling, my faith in words (despite my questions about their ultimate "meaning"). I hope that Goyen's voice will reach younger readers who will appreciate his noble qualities. [Irving Malin]

*

Anne Waldman and Andrew Schelling, eds. *Disembodied Poetics: Annals of the Jack Kerouac School.* Univ. of New Mexico Press, 1995. 501 pp. $50.00; paper: $29.95.

Creative writing programs have an ambivalent status, many finding them too narrow in their approach to writing and literature, which (detractors say) accounts for the sameness and bloodlessness of so much of the writing that emerges from them. The Naropa Institute in Boulder, Colorado, on the other hand, home to the Jack Kerouac School of Disembodied Poetics, encourages a wild eclecticism, convinced that the true artist needs to be as acquainted with ecology as with metrics, with spiritual traditions as with aesthetics, with economics as with mythology. This is of course what Pound recommended, and such schools are not new, as the editors point out in their introduction; India, China, Sappho's Lesbos, medieval Ireland—all had what today would be called an interdisciplinary approach to the arts, and as a result the art that emerges from the Naropa Institute is anything but narrow or bloodless. This collection of essays, many of them transcribed from lectures, embraces a wide range of topics, everything from Amiri Baraka on cultural activism to William Burroughs on filmmaking to Rikki Ducornet on the cabala. Other highlights are Peter Warshall on "ecopoetics," Peter Lamborn Wilson on Fourier, and two excellent talks (by Allen Ginsberg and Clark Coolidge) on Kerouac. There are interviews (with Waldman, Philip Whalen), creative essays on creativity (Ed Sanders's is especially good), aesthetic manifestos, and much else. The price is rather steep, but if you can't attend one of the school's invigorating summer sessions, this anthology is the next best thing. [Steven Moore]

*

Andrew Schelling. *The India Book.* O Books, 1993; *For Love of the Dark One: Songs of Mirabai.* Shambhala, 1993; *Dropping the Bow: Poems from Ancient India.* Broken Moon, 1992.

The terrible beauty of India animates the brief essays of *The India Book,* in which time erodes surfaces "with a leper's rot," a day's signature is sealed with a leaden ball of opium, "a pariah wipes down [a] toilet with a rag," and harlots in stacked cages spit scarlet betel juice into the street. Spare and evocative, these are reveries in the best tradition of travel-writing: resonant and resonating like the percussion-driven ragas (and the word means "desire") Schelling so admires.

Schelling writes in a vivid, transforming ink. His black is opium: "In a moment the smoke enters your throat. You become overwhelmed by the deadness of it. . . . It enters your lungs like a dead fog"; his grey is the color of raw chappatis; his red Kali flowering with menses; his blue the ash-smeared genitals of a holy man. His white is the white of milk and bone, his yellow gold:

> The goddess Lakshmi has a temple down one of these twisting Bombay streets. It is a large sumptuous gold-enameled compound with a spacious portico, where people drive small coins into the wall with a nail. Or they buy coconuts from a cart in the courtyard and crack the soft shells over the head of a life-size brass lion in the balcony, letting thin milk flood over the lion's mane.

"Some mornings," Schelling writes at the opening of *The India Book,* "I waken and realize that were it not for those gestures called poetry, gestures that somehow survive the turbulence of history, we might none of us have found birth."

I first met Andrew Schelling in a Nepalese tea room in Boulder, Colorado. Delighted by his erudite and passionate descriptions of India, I returned to Denver with a few of his elegant translations—all of which have since been brought together by Broken Moon Press. The book is called *Dropping the Bow.* Sanskrit, that most ancient of Indo-European languages, is (according to Schelling) also one of the most complex, so complex that the grammarians of ancient India compared its alphabet to "a city of gods." And it is Schelling's intimate knowledge of this alphabet and its complexities that enables him to capture the essence of a world both distant and subtle, a world civilized in a manner nearly unfathomable at a time when the unstoppable machine of capital has, in every corner of the globe, laid waste landscape, cultural inheritance, and spirit. In this epoch of chronic turbulence punctuated by genocide and ecological disaster, Schelling proposes answers in the form of poems and essays exploring those potent spaces wherein the sacred and the secular embrace. His profoundly ethical, aesthetic, and compassionate sensibility has led him to India time and time again—that nightmare, that enchantment, that "weave of images" wherein the worldly and divine join together to form a species of lucent grammar. Some of Schelling's most inspired translations are love poems. This one I had the luck to hear him read with a tender and a gentle irony: "This time let me / be the lady / you play the lover— // to which the girl / protests / shaking her head // but eyes / wide like a / deer's eyes she threads / a bracelet onto / his wrist."

Back to *The India Book.* A small book filled with pleasures: "Some Notes on Drinking a Pipe," "Thighbone Trumpets and Attendant Spirits," "Poems of Renunciation and Romance"—it contains a gorgeous essay titled "Jataka Mind" that opens with a retelling of the legend in which the Buddha, seeing that a starving tigress is about to devour her cubs, offers her his own body to eat. By this act of compassion, he hopes to release all creatures from suffering. Schelling writes: "The Jataka tales register the first instance in written literature of what I'd call cross-species compassion. . . . Perhaps the tales retain traces of a universal contract between living creatures, so long ago vanished that no one remembers its ancient imperatives." And: "What we have begun to witness in our day among eco-activists, among radical animal rights workers, among those who draw any line against thoughtless, mechanized, greed-inspired destruction of wild lands, is a resurgence of the old spirit of the Jataka Tales. . . . It also suggests a new wakening, perhaps a widening of what I earlier called Jataka mind." And, in his introduction to his translations of the great Mirabai, *For Love of the Dark One,* Schelling writes:

> There exists in poetry a tradition of outriders or night cadres, of nomads, exiles and rebels of song. Throughout history, within every literate culture, poets belonging to this lineage have emerged to articulate a brave and defiant opposition to unjust distributions of wealth, religious persecution, oppression of women, racial discord, and aggressive military exploits. Marauding armies, abusive governments, exploitative churches—these come and go across the planet like storm clouds, and in their passage cause grievous suffering. Somehow the poets who sign within this outrider tradition stay with us.

If these fearless voices "salted with poetic fire" survive, these voices that evoke our transcendent capacities and remind us that compassion burns at the heart of truly great human cultures—not rage, not greed—it is thanks to the generosity of spirit of poets like Schelling who, with rigor and affection, bring the ancient, the essential texts back to life. [Rikki Ducornet]

*

Steven Weisenburger. *Fables of Subversion: Satire and the American Novel, 1930-1980.* Univ. of Georgia Press, 1995. 320 pp. $45.00.

Weisenburger argues elegantly that the decades between 1930 and 1980 introduced a radically subversive and degenerative mode of satire into American fiction, the main practitioners of which included Nathanael West, Flannery O'Connor, and James Purdy. This new discourse of violence dismantled the formalism and humanism associated with traditional satire; John Hawkes, for example, rid his work of the conventions of character and plot together with any attempt to be therapeutic, normative, and corrective. Mixing humor and horror, he and his ilk prefer parody, carnival, and the grotesque to depict a world encroaching upon violence and mob rule. Tropes like Brigadier General Pudding's eating of the freshly passed turds of a dominatrix called Domina Nocturna in Pynchon's *Gravity's Rainbow* and Richard Nixon's sodomizing by Uncle Sam in Coover's *The Public Burning* describe a culture both displaced and degraded. As his noting of these tropes suggests, Weisenburger is a careful, selective reader who also knows how to clinch an argument. His rare miscues occur in the area of rhetoric. How telling, for instance, is his contrast between deconstrictive and deconstructive agendas? Also, his practice of enclosing words like *syntax, precision,* and *principles* in inverted commas suggests a lack of self-confidence. This impression holds. A paragraph on page 196 gains little by including the words *extradiegetic, hypodiegetic,* and *hyperdiegetic.* In fact, such inclusions make us think that Weisenburger wrote *Fables* to gain the approval of those semioticians and deconstructionists in whose elite club he seeks membership.

Actually, these critics should aspire to join *him.* Weisenburger prevails in spite of himself. Playing it straight with his materials, he makes some excellent points about *Lolita* and Donald Barthelme's *Snow White.* He's also sharp on the novels of William Gaddis. He describes the issues raised by the main character's attempts to reconcile the demands of his maternal and paternal legacies in *The Recognitions,* and he shows how Wagner's *Ring* cycle served as Gaddis's template in *J R.* But such rehearsals, forceful and groundbreaking as they are, run the shoals of editorial carelessness: Sinclair Lewis's *Main Street* first appeared in 1920, not 1926; the words *disinterested* (76) and *notoriety* (95) are misused; the phrase "reversing the dispersal" (71) betrays a bad ear; the character who castrates (or emasculates) himself in *The Recognitions* is Anselm, not Stanley. But *Fables* has enough solid learning, wit, and sensitivity to transcend such flubs. [Peter Wolfe]

*

Julius Rowan Raper, Melody L. Enscore, and Paige Matthey Bynum, eds. *Lawrence Durrell: Comprehending the Whole.* Univ. of Missouri, 1995. 193 pp. $39.95.

Thirty years ago Lawrence Durrell was universally considered one of the most important British novelists of our time, but since his death in 1990 he seems to have dropped off the map a bit. His U.S. publisher declined his U.K. publisher's offer to publish the one-volume *The Avignon Quintet* published there in 1992, and except for *The Alexandria Quartet* all of his novels are now out of print (as is much of the poetry and nonfiction). Until his work comes into favor again, it may be up to academics to keep the fires burning (as they did with William Gaddis during his dark decades of neglect), and this new book demonstrates that Durrell's contribution to modern literature is significant enough to warrant continued attention.

The subtitle, *Comprehending the Whole,* is exactly what the book sets out to achieve. There are essays here on the two novels Durrell published before *The Black Book* (of whose existence I wasn't aware), as well as that breakthrough novel and all that followed, up to the concluding volumes of the *Quintet.* There are also essays on his Antrobus stories, his poetry, his relationship to Greece, a comparison between his underrated *Revolt of Aphrodite* and Pynchon's *V.,* and a description of the large Durrell collection at Southern Illinois University. As such, the book serves as an excellent introduction to Durrell's corpus as well as a fresh re-evaluation of the work. [Steven Moore]

Mark Rudman. *Realm of Unknowing: Meditations on Art, Suicide, and Other Transformations*. Wesleyan, 1995. 192 pp. $35.00.

Mark Rudman is one of our most interesting essayists and poets. He is a master of the "crossover" text. He informs us in his preface that he writes a "mosaic form," which "mirrors what the essays struggle to convey; the sentence, paragraphs, or section as a unit—parallel perhaps to the stanza in a poem or the triadic structure of a sonnet—allows me to touch only on what compels me, on what is necessary, and to explore how the margin informs the center without having to, in the Balzacian sense, spend pages describing the furniture in the room." Rudman is aware of the *margins* of meditation, of the *indeterminate* folding of content and texture.

I turn to Rudman's wonderful essay on *Catastrophe Practice*. He writes that in the series "Mosley fights against his father's central flaw—his willingness to embrace fixed ideas while managing to miss the point." He applauds *Hopeful Monsters*' "bold mixture of synapses and adventure"; he writes that "Mosley's compressed leaps are always emotionally impelled." The sentences —and the entire essay, or "meditation"—renders not only Mosley's perception of "the imagination of disaster" (James's famous beautiful phrase) but also reflect Rudman's leaping mind. He is one of the best critics of Mosley because he is his "secret sharer."

I also want to commend Rudman's essay on William Arrowsmith. He admires Arrowsmith's erudition, his daring insights. Arrowsmith once wrote: "If the hero had self-knowledge, he would never have become a hero." This apparently paradoxical sentence—it is of course about knowing and unknowing—can perhaps represent this brilliant collection, this tentative interpretation of interpretation. [Irving Malin]

*

J. Kerry Grant. *A Companion to "The Crying of Lot 49."* Univ. of Georgia, 1994. 154 pp. $25.00; paper, $12.95.

Although modeled on Steven Weisenburger's *A "Gravity's Rainbow" Companion* (also published by Georgia), Grant's book is less a compilation of annotations than a variorum gathering of critical comments on various lines in Pynchon's enigmatic novel, along with Grant's own line-by-line analysis. Most annotatable items in *Lot 49* are indeed explained (it might have been pointed out that the book dealer Zapf is probably named after that typeface) and there are long discussions of central concerns like entropy and the Tristero. Page numbers are keyed to both the Harper Perennial edition (offset from the original Lippincott edition, though Grant doesn't say so) and Bantam's mass-market edition. As Grant points out in his introduction, *Lot 49* is the Pynchon text most often taught, so anyone who teaches the novel or writes about it in the future will want to take along this useful companion. [Steven Moore]

Back in Print

• Gertrude Stein's *Stanzas in Meditation* was written in 1932 but not published until 1956 as part of Yale University Press's eight-volume edition of her unpublished writings, which has been o.p. for decades. Sun & Moon has reissued it in paperback ($11.95), reset but based on that edition and containing a preface and textual note by Sun & Moon's indefatigable publisher Douglas Messerli.

• Sun & Moon has also reissued Ronald Firbank's fifth and shortest novel, *Santal* (paper, $7.95), first published in 1921. New Directions has kept his other novels in print in two omnibuses, but this one—set in North Africa and concerning a young boy's spiritual quest—has not been available in this country since the 1960s. Less outrageous than his other novels but as beautifully written, *Santal* was the most favorably reviewed of his works and for those new to his fictional world is a good port of entry.

• Lance Olsen edited a special issue of *American Notes & Queries* a few years back on the future of American fiction, which has now been published in book form (with three additional essays) as *Surfing Tomorrow: Essays on the Future of American Fiction* (paper, $9.95, available from Potpourri Publications, P.O. Box 8278, Prairie Village, KS 66208).

Books Received

Achberger, Karen R. *Understanding Ingeborg Bachmann.* South Carolina, 1995. $34.95. (NF)

Adell, Sandra. *Double-Consciousness/Double Bind: Theoretical Issues in Twentieth-Century Black Literature.* Illinois, 1995. $25.95. (NF)

Al-Amir, Daisy. *The Waiting List: An Iraqi Woman's Tales of Alienation.* Trans. Barbara McKean Parmenter. Texas, 1995. (F)

Alcott, Louisa May. *The Lost Stories.* Citadel, 1995. Paper: $10.95. (F)

Amerika, Mark. *Sexual Blood.* Black Ice, 1995. Paper: $9.00. (F)

Ammons, A. R. *The North Carolina Poems.* North Carolina Wesleyan, 1994. Paper: $ 10.00. (Poetry)

Antin, Eleanor. *Eleanora Antinova Plays.* Sun & Moon, 1995. Paper: $12.95. (Drama)

Arthur, Elizabeth. *Antarctic Navigation.* Knopf, 1995. $25.00. (F)

Bair, Deirdre. *Anaïs Nin: A Biography.* Putnam, 1995. $39.95. (NF)

Baker, Lori. *Scraps.* Paradigm, 1995. Paper: $10.00. (Poetry)

Ballard, J. G. *Rushing to Paradise.* Picador, 1995. $21.00. (F)

Banti, Anna. *Artemisia.* Trans. Shirley D'Ardia Caracciolo. Nebraska, 1995. Paper: $10.00. (F)

Bao Ninh. *The Sorrow of War.* Pantheon, 1993. $21 (F)

Barone, Dennis. *A Matter of Habit.* Generator Press, 1995. Paper: $5. (Poetry)

Beidler, Phillip D. *Scriptures for a Generation: What We Were Reading in the '60s.* Georgia, 1994. No Price Given. (NF)

Belamri, Rabah. *Shattered Vision.* Trans. Hugh A. Harter. Holmes & Meier, 1995. $19.95. (F)

Black, Martha Fodaski. *Shaw and Joyce: "The Last Word in Stolentelling."* Florida, 1995. $49.95. (NF)

Boland, Eavan. *Object Lessons: The Life of the Woman and the Poet in Our Time.* Norton, 1995. $23.00. (NF)

Bowen, Zack. *Bloom's Old Sweet Song: Essays on Joyce and Music.* Florida, 1995. $24.95. (NF)

Brown, John Gregory. *Decoration in a Ruined Cemetery.* Avon, 1995. Paper: $10.00. (F)

Carr, A. A. *Eye Killers.* Oklahoma, 1995. $19.95. (F)

Chong, Denise. *The Concubine's Children.* Viking, 1995. $21.95. (NF)

Conley, Robert J. *Mountain Windsong: A Novel of the Trail of Tears.* Oklahoma, 1995. Paper: $10.95. (F)

Cooper, Fiona. *Skyhook in the Midnight Sun.* Serpent's Tail, 1995. Paper: $14.95. (F)

Daeninckx, Didier. *A Very Profitable War.* Trans. Sarah Martin. Serpent's Tail, 1995. Paper: $11.99. (F)

Danticat, Edwidge. *Krik? Krak!* Soho, 1995. $20.00. (F)

Dawson, Fielding. *The Orange in the Orange: A Novella and Two Stories.* Black Sparrow, 1995. $25.00. (F)

Dennett, Nolan. *Place of Shelter.* Sun & Moon, 1994. $19.95. (F)

Di Filippo, Paul. *The Steampunk Trilogy.* Four Walls Eight Windows, 1995. $20.00. (F)

Domanski, Don. *Stations of the Left Hand.* Coach House, 1995. Paper: $11.95. (Poetry)

Donoghue, Denis. *Warrenpoint.* Syracuse, 1995. Paper: $14.95. (NF)

Endo, Shusaku. *Deep River.* Trans. Van C. Gessel. New Directions, 1995. $19.95. (F)

El-Ramly, Lenin. *In Plain Arabic.* Columbia, 1995. $25.00. (Drama)

Escudero Rodríguez, Javier. *Eros, Mística y Muerte en Juan Goytisolo (1982-1992).* Instituto de Estudios Almerienses, 1994. Paper: no price given. (NF)

Exact Change Yearbook 1995, no. 1. Exact Change, 1995. $35.00. (Anthology with CD)

Federman, Raymond. *Smiles on Washington Square.* Sun & Moon, 1995. Paper: $10.95. (F)

Fernández Olmos, Margarite, and Lizabeth Paravisini-Gebert, eds. *Pleasure in the Word: Erotic Writing by Latin American Women.* Plume, 1994. Paper: $10.95. (F)

Flanagan, Mary. *The Blue Woman.* Norton, 1995. $21.00. (F)

Foos, Laurie. *Ex Utero.* Coffee House, 1995. $16.95. (F)

Forbes, Jack D. *Only Approved Indians.* Oklahoma, 1995. $22.95. (F)

Foster, Edward Halsey. *Understanding the Black Mountain Poets.* Univ. of South Carolina Press, 1995. $34.95. (NF)

Frey, Rodney, ed. *Stories That Make the World: Oral Literature of the Indian Peoples of the Inland Northwest.* Oklahoma, 1995. $24.95. (F)

Fried, Erich. *Children and Fools.* Trans. Martin Chalmers. Serpent's Tail, 1995. Paper: $14.99. (F)

Gagnon, Madelaine. *Song for a Far Quebec.* Coach House, 1995. Paper: $10.95. (Poetry)

Gardner, Mary. *Bôàt Peôplê.* Norton, 1995. $21.00. (F)

Ghanem, Fathy. *The Man Who Lost His Shadow.* Trans. Desmond Stewart. Columbia, 1995. $40.00. (F)

Giraudon, Liliane. *Fur.* Trans. Guy Bennett. Sun & Moon, 1995. Paper: $12.95. (F)

Gizzi, Peter. *Music for Films.* Paradigm, 1992. Paper: $5.00 (Poetry)

Glancy, Diane. *Monkey Secret.* Northwestern, 1995. $19.95. (F)

Good Country People: An Irregular Journal of the Cultures of Eastern North Carolina. North Carolina Wesleyan, 1995. Paper: $11.95. (NF)

Greer, Bonnie. *Hanging by Her Teeth.* Serpent's Tail, 1995. Paper: $11.99. (F).

Gunn, Kirsty. *Rain.* Atlantic Monthly, 1994. $15.00. (F)

Harrison, Russell. *Against the American Dream: Essays on Charles Bukowski.* Black Sparrow, 1994. $30.00. Paper: $15.00. (NF)

Hastings, Selina. *Evelyn Waugh: A Biography.* Houghton Mifflin, 1994. $40. (NF)

Hawkes, G.W. *Playing Out of the Deep Woods*. Missouri, 1995. Paper: No price given.

Hayman, Ronald. *Thomas Mann: A Biography*. Scribner, 1995. $35. (NF)

Henry, Gordon, Jr. *The Light People*. Oklahoma, 1995. Paper: $11.95. (F)

Huelle, Pawel. *Moving House: Stories*. Trans. Michael Kandel. Harcourt, Brace, 1995. $18.95. (F)

Hussein, Taha. *A Man of Letters*. Trans. Mona El-Zayyat. Columbia, 1995. $25.00. (F)

Izquierdo, Agustina. *An Indecent Recollection*. Trans. Paul Weidmann. Marlboro, 1994. $17.95. (F)

Jacobson, Howard. *The Very Model of a Man*. Overlook, 1994. $22.95. (F)

Jaffe, Harold. *Straight Razor*. Illus. Norman Conquest. Black Ice, 1995. Paper: $7.00. (F)

Jakubowski, Maxim, ed. *London Noir*. Serpent's Tail, 1995. Paper: $11.99. (F)

Jeffares, Norman A., and Anna McBride White, eds. *The Gonne-Yeats Letters, 1893-1938*. Syracuse, 1995. Paper: $19.95. (NF)

Kali for Women, eds. *The Slate of Life: More Contemporary Stories by Women Writers of India*. Feminist, 1994. Paper: $12.95. (F)

Kaplan, Steve. *Understanding Tim O'Brien*. South Carolina, 1995. $34.95. (NF)

Kasper, M. *The Shapes and Spacing of Letters*. Weighted Anchor, 1994. Paper: $10.00. (NF)

Kilpatrick, Jack F., and Anna G. Kilpatrick. *Friends of Thunder: Folktales of the Oklahoma Cherokees*. Oklahoma, 1995. Paper: $11.95.

Kirshenbaum, Binnie. *History on a Personal Note*. Fromm, 1995. Paper: $10.00. (F)

Klima, Ivan. *Waiting for the Dark, Waiting for the Light*. Grove, 1995. $21.00. (F)

Knox, Ann B. *Late Summer Break*. Papier-Mache, 1995. $14.00; paper: $9.00. (F)

Koch, Kenneth. *On the Great Atlantic Rainway: Selected Poems 1950-1988*. Knopf, 1994. $25.00. (Poetry)

———. *One Train*. Knopf, 1994. $20.00. (Poetry)

Kristeva, Julia. *The Old Man and the Wolves*. Trans. Barbara Bray. Columbia, 1994. $25.00. (F)

La Farge, Tom. *The Crimson Bears*. Sun & Moon, 1993. Paper: No price given. (F)

———. *A Hundred Doors: The Crimson Bears, Part 2*. Sun & Moon, 1995. Paper: $12.95. (F)

Langford, Diane. *Shame about the Street*. Serpent's Tail, 1995. Paper: $11.99. (F)

Lau, Evelyn. *Fresh Girls and Other Stories*. Hyperion, 1995. $17.95. (F)

Lawler, Justus George. *Celestial Pantomime: Poetic Structures of Transcendence*. Continuum, 1995. Paper: $19.95. (NF)

Lipkin, Randie. *Untitled (A Skier)*. Fugue State, 1995. Paper: $8.00. (F)

Locklin, Gerald. *The Old Mongoose and Other Poems*. Pearl Editions, 1994. Paper: $6.00. (Poetry)

Long, David. *Blue Spruce*. Scribner, 1995. $20.00. (F)

Lowe, John. *Jump at the Sun: Zora Neal Hurston's Cosmic Comedy*. Illinois, 1995. $19.95. (NF)

MacLaverty, Bernard. *Walking the Dog and Other Stories*. Norton, 1995. $20.00. (F)

MacLeod, Joan. *The Hope Slide/Little Sister*. Coach House, 1995. Paper: $11.95. (Plays)

Mac Lochlainn, Alf, and Andrée Sheehy Skeffington. *Writers, Raconteurs and Notable Feminists*. Nation Library of Ireland Society, 1993. No price given. (NF)

Mahaffey, Vicki. *Reauthorizing Joyce*. Univ. Press of Florida, 1995. Paper: $19.95. (NF)

Martínez, Dionisio D. *Bad Alchemy*. Norton, 1995. $17.95. (Poetry)

Mattison, Alice. *Hilda and Pearl*. Morrow, 1995. $22.00. (F)

Maxwell, William. *All the Days and Nights: The Collected Stories*. Knopf, 1995. $25.00. (F)

McMorris, Mark. *Palinurus Suite*. Paradigm, 1992. Paper: $5.00. (Poetry)

Mencken, H.L. *A Second Mencken Chrestomathy: A New Selection from the Writings of America's Legendary Editor, Critic, and Wit*. Ed. Terry Teachout. Knopf, 1995. $30.00. (NF)

Metcalf, Paul. *". . . and nobody objected."* Paradigm, 1992. Paper: $5.00. (F)

Meyers, Jessica. *Fall's Gems*. Paradigm, 1992. Paper: $3.00. (Poetry)

Moorhead, Andrea. *Winter Light*. Oasis, 1994. Paper: $9.00. (Poetry)

Moosa, Matti. *The Early Novels of Naguib Mahfouz: Images of Modern Egypt*. Florida, 1994. $39.95. (NF)

Morris, Wright. *Two for the Road*. Black Sparrow, 1995. Paper: $15.00. (F)

Murphy, William M. *Family Secrets: William Butler Yeats and His Relatives*. Syracuse, 1995. $39.95. (NF)

Nash, Susan Smith. *The Airport Is My Étude*. Paradigm, 1993. Paper: $5.00. (Poetry)

Nayman, Michèle. *Jetlag*. Serpent's Tail, 1995. Paper: $11.99. (F)

Nicholson, Geoff. *Hunters and Gatherers*. Overlook, 1995. $21.95. (F)

Nimier, Marie. *The Giraffe*. Trans. Mary Feeney. Four Walls Eight Windows, 1995. $18.00. (F)

O'Brian, Patrick. *The Commodore*. Norton, 1995. $22.50. (F)

Oe, Kenzaburo. *Nip the Buds, Shoot the Kids*. Trans. Paul St. John Mackintosh and Maki Sugiyama. Marion Boyars, 1995. $22.95. (F)

O'Hara, Daniel T. *Radical Parody: American Culture and Critical Agency after Foucault*. Columbia, 1995. Paper: $19.50. (NF)

Owens, Louis. *Wolfsong*. Oklahoma, 1995. Paper: $12.95. (F)

Pastan, Linda. *An Early Afterlife*. Norton, 1995. $17.95. (Poetry)

Paulhan, Jean. *Progress in Love on the Slow Side*. Trans. Christine Moneera Laennec and Michael Syrotinski. Nebraska, 1995. $25.00. (F)

Peacock, Molly. *Original Love*. Norton, 1995. $17.95. (F)

Peake, Tony, ed. *Seduction: A Book of Stories*. Serpent's Tail, 1995. Paper: $11.99. (F)

Penn, W.S. *The Absence of Angels*. Oklahoma, 1995. Paper: $13.95. (F)

Phillips, Robert, ed. *William Goyen: Selected Letters from a Writer's Life*. Texas, 1995. $34.95. (NF)

Price, Reynolds. *The Honest Account of a Memorable Life*. North Carolina Wesleyan College, 1994. $25.00. (F)

Ragosta, Ray. *From the Varieties of Religious Experience Book 2*. Paradigm, 1991. Paper: $4.00. (Poetry)

Reynolds, David S. *Walt Whitman's America: A Cultural Biography*. Knopf, 1995. $35.00. (F)

Riding Jackson, Laura. *Lives of Wives*. Sun & Moon, 1995. Paper: $12.95. (NF)

Robbe-Grillet, Alain. *La Belle Captive*. Trans. Ben Stoltzfus. Illus. René Magritte. California, 1995. $35.00. (F)

Rosenberg, David. *The Lost Book of Paradise: Adam and Eve in the Garden of Eden*. Hyperion, 1995. Paper: $12.95. (F)

Schneider, Robert. *Brother of Sleep*. Overlook, 1995. $21.95. (F)

Skloot, Floyd. *Summer Blue*. Story Line, 1994. $18.95. (F)

Soto, Francisco. *Reinaldo Arenas: The Pentagonia*. Florida, 1994. $24.95. (NF)

Spencer, Brent. *The Lost Son*. Arcade, 1995. $19.95. (F)

Stendahl, Renate, ed. *Gertrude Stein in Pictures*. Algonquin, 1994. Paper: $19.95. (NF)

Sutton, Walter, ed. *Pound, Thayer, Watson, and "The Dial": A Story in Letters*. Florida, 1994. $49.95. (NF)

Svoboda, Terese. *Cannibal*. NYU, 1995. $19.95. (F)

Thomas, Sue, ed. *Wild Women: Contemporary Short Stories by Women Celebrating Women*. Overlook, 1994. Paper: $14.95. (F)

Tytell, John. *The Living Theatre: Art, Exile, and Outrage*. Grove, 1995. $23.00. (NF)

Val Moore, Rod. *Igloo among Palms*. Iowa, 1994. $22.95. (F)

Waldrop, Keith. *Potential Random*. Paradigm, 1992. Paper: $5.00. (Poetry)

Watson, Larry. *Justice*. Milkweed, 1995. $17.95. (F)

Weldon, Fay. *Splitting*. Grove, 1995. $21.00. (F)

Werner, Craig Hansen. *Playing the Changes: From Afro-Modernism to the Jazz Impulse*. Univ. of Illinois, 1995. $39.95. (NF)

Wioebe, Dallas. *Skyblue's Essays*. Burning Deck, 1995. $8.95. (F)

Wilson, Paul, ed. *Prague: A Traveler's Literary Companion*. Whereabouts, 1995. Paper: $12.95. (F)

Xue Di. *Flames*. Trans. Wang Ping, Iona Crook, and Keith Waldrop. Paradigm, 1995. Paper: $5.00. (Poetry)

Yau, John. *Hawaiian Cowboys*. Black Sparrow, 1995. $25.00. (F)

Contributors

MARK AXELROD is Assistant Professor of Comparative Literature at Chapman University, Orange, California. His most recent critical study is *The Politics of Style in the Fiction of Balzac, Beckett and Cortázar,* and he is working on a book entitled *The Poetics of Novels.* His latest novel is *Bombay California* (reviewed on pp. 211-12) and he is currently editing *Malato,* a collection of essays and fiction devoted to world hunger.

PETER J. BAILEY teaches fiction writing and American literature at St. Lawrence University. He is the author of *Reading Stanley Elkin.*

STEPHEN BERNSTEIN is Assistant Professor of English at the University of Michigan, Flint. He has published articles on Beckett, Dickens, Wilkie Collins, and Paul Auster, and is currently coediting an issue of *Postmodern Culture* devoted to Don DeLillo.

JEROME CHARYN is the author of more than two dozen novels, most recently *Little Angel Street.* Dalkey Archive has just reissued his 1973 novel *The Tar Baby.*

PETER G. CHRISTENSEN teaches at Marquette University and has published numerous articles on modern writers in a variety of journals. He has an essay in *Lawrence Durrell: Comprehending the Whole* (reviewed on p. 233).

LYNNE DIAMOND-NIGH is Assistant Professor of Romance Languages at Elmira College. She is the founder and editor of the *New Novel Review* and has published articles in *Hispanofila, Romance Quarterly,* and *Romance Notes.* She is currently editing a book entitled *The New Novel: An Interdisciplinary Perspective.*

GEORGE DONALDSON teaches at Huron College in Ontario, and has a particular interest in Victorian fiction. His "Art and Propaganda" appeared in *RACAR.*

DAVID C. DOUGHERTY teaches at Loyola College in Maryland. He is the author of the Twayne book on Stanley Elkin.

JANICE GALLOWAY is one of Scotland's leading younger writers. In this country, Random House published her story collection *Blood* in 1991, and Dalkey Archive is the publisher of her two novels: *The Trick Is to Keep Breathing* last year, and *Foreign Parts* this fall.

WILLIAM H. GASS is the David May Distinguished Professor in the Humanities and Director of the International Writers' Center at Washington University. His monumental novel *The Tunnel* appeared last spring.

WILLIAM M. HARRISON is completing a dissertation for the University of Delaware on the writers published by the Hogarth Press. His essays have appeared in the *D. H. Lawrence Review* and the *Journal of Irish Literature.*

JOHN C. HAWLEY teaches at Santa Clara University. He has contributed to *Victorian Literature and Culture, ARIEL,* and *Nineteenth-Century Prose.*

PHILIP HOBSBAUM, Professor of English Literature at the University of Glasgow, is the author of *Essentials of Literary Criticism* and *A Reader's Guide to Charles Dickens,* as well as *In Retreat and Other Poems.*

JEROME KLINKOWITZ teaches at the University of Northern Iowa. He is the author of nearly two dozen books of literary criticism as well as *Short Season,* a collection of baseball stories.

ALISON LEE teaches at the University of Western Ontario. She is the author of *Realism and Power: Postmodern British Fiction* and is coediting a collection of essays entitled *Postmodern Life.*

CHARLES MOLESWORTH teaches at Queens College, CUNY. His publications include a book on Donald Barthelme's fiction and a biography of Marianne Moore.

PATRICK O'DONNELL teaches at Purdue, where he edits *Modern Fiction Studies.* His books include *Passionate Doubts: Designs of Interpretation in Contemporary American Fiction* and *Echo Chambers: Figuring Voice in Modern Narrative.*

ARTHUR M. SALTZMAN teaches at Missouri Southern State College. His two most recent books are *Designs of Darkness in Contemporary American Fiction* and *The Novel in the Balance.* He edited the special half issue of the *Review of Contemporary Fiction* on William H. Gass (fall 1991).

ALAN WILDE teaches at Temple University. He is the author of two highly regarded studies of contemporary fiction, *Horizons of Assent* and *Middle Grounds.* His next book, *Among Friends,* will, like his essay in this issue, take the form of E-mail letters.

NOVEL A FORUM ON FICTION

VOLUME 28 NUMBER 1 FALL 1994

PUBLISHED IN THE FALL, WINTER, AND SPRING OF EACH YEAR

VQR

The Virginia
Quarterly Review

*A National Journal of
Literature and Discussion*

SPRING 1995
Volume 71, Number 2
The Virginia Quarterly Review
One West Range
Charlottesville, VA 22903